TRUE CRIME CASES

Ron Rupert

TRUE CRIME CASES

Stratton Press Publishing
831 N Tatnall Street Suite M #188,
Wilmington, DE 19801
www.stratton-press.com
1-888-323-7009

ISBN (Paperback): 978-1-64345-632-4
ISBN (Ebook): 978-1-64345-786-4

Printed in the United States of America

INTRODUCTION

I, Ron Rupert, joined the Ontario Police in 1951. My first posting was in the Anti-Gambling Branch doing undercover work throughout the province. After eighteen months and as the result of an accident, I was on sick leave for the next eleven months. Coming back to work, I was placed on light duties at the Accident Recording Section at general headquarters.

When I was finally in uniform, I worked on the switchboard in the main GHQ office. I worked on the afternoon and midnight shifts and on the weekends. From Monday to Friday, the day shift was security duties, working around the Parliament buildings, which included the Canada Savings Bank.

From GHQ, I was transferred to no. 3 DHQ (district headquarters) Alcantara, working highway patrol and general law enforcement. From there, I was transferred to Milton Municipal Detachment in 1955, and after five and a half years there, Milton started their own police department, and I was transferred to the Acton Municipal Detachment for four years.

The final twenty-two years of my career were spent at no. 2 DHQ London, working in the Identification Unit.

The Identification Unit is the unit that does CSI (crime scene investigation). From here the identification officers are dispatched to traffic accidents, deaths of all kinds, and different types of crime scenes. They search for fingerprints where needed and match the found prints to the good guys, the bad guys, or the victims. They photograph the complete crime scene, showing the location where the crime took place, the victim, and whether that person was injured, dead, or alive.

When finding fingerprints at a crime scene, the prints that were found were compared with the fingerprints of the suspect when he or she was arrested or looked for matches in their criminal fingerprint files, which they maintained in their office. If the fingerprints were not identified in the office fingerprint files, they were sent to the RCMP data base in Ottawa, which contained the prints of all persons in Canada charged with a criminal offense. In a few cases they would also send our unidentified fingerprints to the FBI in Washington for a search of their fingerprint files.

At some crime scenes and hit-and-run traffic accidents, they sometimes found parts or articles left at the scene by the vehicle or person causing the accident. These artifacts would be tagged and bagged, and in several cases, they would match the found item to the victim or the culprit, or to a matching piece in their possession, or matched to their vehicle. If a comparison was made, a chart would be prepared for court showing the matching items.

Physical comparisons were made on many different items found at many different crime scenes. For example, photographs of footprints left at a crime scene were compared to the footwear of the arrested culprit that he or she was wearing when allegedly committing the crime.

If a victim or witness had seen the person that committed the crime, they interviewed the victim or witness, and with their description, they could use the Identi-Kit to make an image of a person, coming up with a very good likeness of the culprit.

Taking measurements at a crime scene allowed them to make a detailed scale drawing of the crime scene, whether it was inside or outside a building. They could make the drawing complete with furniture or other items where needed. At traffic accidents, measurements were also taken at the scene, allowing them to make scale drawings of the road area there as well. All these drawing were made for the trial in court.

They were also trained and called out for bomb disposal. If a person found old dynamite on their property or place of business, they went there to remove and dispose of it. They were also called to bomb threats. Some were false alarms, such as a briefcase left in a vulnerable area where it should not be. In cases where they found an explosive device in an area where it should not be, they seized the device, and then they would dispose of it in a safe place, often using an abandoned quarry for that purpose.

After retiring from the police, I worked another ten years for the Woodstock Department at the request of the chief of police, as he did not have anyone in his department qualified to do CSI.

PART ONE

THE BEGINNING:

Undercover for Illegal Gambling, Highway Patrol, General Law Enforcement, and Then Municipal Town Police

CHAPTER ONE

Beginning a Rewarding Career

I had been working in the grocery store in Ontario for seven or eight months, earning $43 a week, after being transferred from the Fort Erie store. One day while I was working in the grocery department, a police officer in uniform came down the aisle with his wife. I didn't pay much attention as I was busy stocking the shelves.

The police officer stopped beside me and said, "How are you, Ron? I haven't seen you for a long time."

It was a police officer I knew, Ted Smith. I was completely surprised to see him as I did not know he was stationed in Welland. When I first met Ted, he lived in Fort Erie, where we both grew up.

After we chatted for a few minutes, Ted said, "Why don't you come over to our place tomorrow evening, and we can shoot the breeze for a while and get caught up on what's going on in our lives."

"Okay, that sounds good to me. I'll do that. See you tomorrow evening."

The next night, I went over to Ted's place. Ted told me he had been in Welland now for almost three years and enjoyed working in this area. He also told me about a few occurrences that he had to deal with. It all sounded very interesting and exciting.

Sometime during the evening, Ted asked, "Have you ever thought of becoming a policeman?"

"No, not really. I never thought about it before seeing and talking to you again. It sounds like it might be a good idea to try. What would I have to do to get a job with the police?"

"I'll get an application form for you if you're interested. Just fill it out. Get some good references. Mail the paperwork to the address on the form. Then sit and wait."

Not long after that, he brought me the application form. I filled it out, got a few good character references, and with the other required documents, I sent it to the Queens Park address.

A week or so later, I received a letter from the police, and as requested, I went to Toronto for the required medical examination and other verbal and written tests. I was advised that I would receive a letter indicating whether I had been accepted or not.

In the middle of May 1951, I received a letter from the Ontario Provincial Police General Headquarters requesting me to attend the Canada Police College in Toronto starting June 4, 1951. The course of instruction, I was told, would last approximately six weeks.

The college consisted of two buildings situated at 291 and 295 Sherburne Street. The main floor of the building at 291 consisted of the administration office for the college and the dining room where the students were fed, and the classroom was located in the back part of the building. The second floor in each building was the living quarters for the recruits attending the college. Later (and to my surprise), I found out that the main floor at 295 was the office where the police Anti-Gambling Squad was located.

I reported as requested. At the time, I was twenty-two, weighed 149 pounds, and at just less than six feet tall, I looked about fifteen years old.

On the morning of the last day at the police college, the inspector in charge came into the classroom with a list from which he assigned each recruit to the district headquarters (DHQ) where he would work. From that headquarters, he would be assigned to the detachment where he was needed and where he would work. There were seventeen DHQs in the province.

I was assigned, along with George Brown, to the Anti-Gambling Branch right next door to the police college.

After lunch that day, we were permitted to go home for the weekend. We were then to report for duty to our assigned location on Monday morning.

Arriving at the Anti-Gambling Branch office on Monday morning, George and I were interviewed by Staff Inspector Jacobs, the officer in charge. He gave us an outline of the duties that the members of this unit did throughout the province, mainly working undercover. He told us that we should do pretty well in the unit, adding that even though I was twenty-two and didn't look old enough to be a policeman, Jacobs thought that would be to my advantage.

Jacobs then took us into the general office and introduced us to other members of the unit. Sergeant Charles Baker talked to us about the work done by the officers in the unit and questioned us about playing poker and dice games. He asked us whether they knew anything about betting on horse races, particularly if we knew how to read a racing form.

The rest of the morning, we played poker. They found that I knew how to play the game and knew the winning combinations and the order of cards to make winning hands. I was also able to satisfy questions about horse racing as I had lived two blocks from the Fort Erie racetrack and had worked there during the racing seasons for a few years. I also knew a couple of horse trainers whose horses were stabled there during the racing season. I had helped out the trainers a few times, walking and feeding the horses in the paddock area. I had also made bets on races using the racing form to pick the horses, winning more times than losing, which was great fun.

Sergeant Baker said, "I see you know your way around the horse racing tracks, poker games, and also the gambling machines that are out there. Next Monday you will be going out on an undercover assignment, which may last a month or more, so go home relax and enjoy the rest of the week."

"Yes, sir, I can handle that," I responded. I then talked to some of the other members of the team, Sergeant Pete Ramsay, Corporal Jim Bailey, and Constable Don Grimshaw, who were the only ones in the office at the time. They told me about some cases they had worked on, which I found very interesting.

My only means of travel at the time was a 1951 Triumph Thunderbird motorcycle. On the way home, I stopped in Hamilton at the motorcycle dealer to get some work done and took the train back to Fort Erie. The next day I visited a friend, Barney, who had an Indian Motorcycle. "Take it out for couple of days and enjoy yourself," Barney offered.

I took the bike and visited and travelled with some of the guys in the motorcycle club where I had been a member.

On Thursday evening when I got home, Dad said, "Inspector Jacobs called from Toronto. He wants you to call him as soon as you're home."

I dialed the number Dad gave him.

The inspector answered, "Hello?"

"Ron Rupert, sir. You called?"

"Yes Ron, I want you to meet me in Hamilton tomorrow morning at 9:00 a.m. in front of the Bell Telephone building. I have a job that I would like you to do tomorrow night."

"Yes, sir, I will be there!"

I got up before the sun and took the train to Hamilton, meeting the inspector at 9:00 a.m. in front of the Bell building, as requested.

"Good morning, Ron, I'm glad you were able to get here at this time."

"Good morning, Inspector. Yes, it was a little early. I had to catch a train to get here. I left my bike here in Hamilton to have some work done on it."

"I would like you to go to Niagara Falls this evening and hopefully get into a poker game being operated in the back of a gift shop on Bridge Street. Do you know your way around Niagara Falls?"

"Yes, sir, I was born and raised there until we moved to Fort Erie when I was thirteen," I said.

"Very good," he replied. "You will have to go back to the office and see Sergeant Baker. He will give you some marked money to use in the poker game tonight, that is, if you are able to get into the game."

"I will try my best to get into the poker game somehow. I left my friend's bike here on Monday at the dealer to get some work done. It should be finished now. Could you give me a ride over to the bike shop so I can pick it up please?"

On the way to get the bike, the inspector said, "Sergeant Baker will tell you more about the location when you get to the office and maybe give you a few ideas about how to get in."

I picked up the bike and headed back to Toronto and the office, getting there about noon.

Sergeant Baker was waiting for me. "You got here in pretty good time," he said. "I am going to give you $75 in $1s, $2s, and $5s. What I want you to do is record the serial numbers on all the bills in your notebook. I will do the same. You do know the location of the gift shop on Bridge Street?"

I acknowledged that he knew the area.

"If you are not able to get into the game by 1:30 a.m., meet us down by the Rainbow Bridge. There is a parking lot just south of the bridge. We will wait for you there. Any questions?"

"No, sir, I guess the only thing I need to do is to find someone to help me get into the game. Hopefully that shouldn't be too difficult."

"That's about it. We hope you do get in. Just play it cool, and try your best. Good luck, Ron."

"Thanks, Sergeant. I am a little nervous about this already. I'll certainly give it a good try."

When I left the office, the guys all said, "Good luck tonight, Ron, on this, your first big job!"

I got home to Fort Erie a little after 6:00 p.m. and had a bite to eat. I couldn't eat too much because of the butterflies flying around my gut. I told Mom and Dad what I had to do for my first job as a policeman, and I was sure they were as nervous and concerned about my welfare as I was.

We sat around until I left the house about 7:30 p.m. and got on the bike and left for Niagara Falls. It was a big job for me, and my first job as a policeman. I still did not know how I was going accomplish getting into the poker game when I got there.

CHAPTER TWO

A Poker Game—My First Big Job

At approximately 10:30 p.m., Friday, July 13, 1951, I entered the men's beverage room of the Imperial Hotel on Bridge Street, Niagara Falls, where I made the acquaintance of a man sitting at the table across from me. We were the only people in the beverage room. He didn't have a match to light his cigarette, so he gave me a questioning look, as if asking if I had any matches.

I had matches, so I moved over to the guy's table and handed him a pack of matches. He introduced himself as Bill Maitland. After we chatted for a while about growing up in the city, the schools they went to, and some of the same people they each knew, the man finally asked, "What are you doing here in the fall tonight?"

"I heard there was a poker game around here somewhere. I thought maybe I could get into it and play a little poker," I replied.

He said, "It is right next door at the back of the gift shop. Just go on in."

I replied, "They don't know me, and they might not let me in. Can you take me in there and introduce me to those people so I can get into the game?"

"Sure. No problem. I can do that," he said, and I accompanied him into the China Gift Shop next to the hotel.

Maitland spoke to a man wearing a brown shirt standing outside the door and asked the guy if I could get into the game, saying I was a friend from Fort Erie. This man took me through the gift shop to a room near the rear, where I was introduced to a second man identified as Jack Graham.

Graham said, "This is a club exclusively for members only."

To join, I was required to have a sponsor or someone who knew me in order to get a membership.

I asked, "Can I join? Bill Maitland and the waiter in the hotel next door will sponsor me."

Graham was satisfied with the sponsors. We then went into the office where I filled out an application card to get my membership. On the application form, I saw the word *fee* and said, "It says on the application form there is a fee."

Graham replied, "Don't worry about it, the club pays all members' cost," and he wrote in the amount of three dollars. Graham then signed the application, stamped a membership card, and then had me sign it.

At 12:25 a.m. on Saturday, July 14, 1951, Graham took me into the back room on the main floor. The room had dark walls. There was an open door to the right, on the back wall, apparently to let in the cool night air. A large card table was to the left with the only light in the room hanging over the center of the table.

There were seventeen men in the room; twelve were seated at the large card table playing poker. The dealer was seated on the left side of the table with his back to the wall.

I learned that the game they were playing was called fish. Each player was dealt a card facedown and a second card face up. The betting started after each player received the second card. Four cards were then placed one at a time on the table in front of the dealer. Bidding continued after each of the four the cards were placed in front of the dealer. A seventh card was dealt to each player, facedown.

The four cards face up in front of the dealer were used in conjunction with the three cards dealt to each player. Betting continued as each card was placed on the table and the last card dealt facedown to each player. The pot was won by the player with the best five cards.

By 12:30 a.m., I sat in the game when one of the players left. I gave the dealer $6 for twenty-five-cent pieces and took the seat at the table. I was seated to the right of the dealer, later identified as Tom

Young. I watched as Young took twenty-five cents out of the pot when the second card was dealt and a second twenty-five cents when each of the other four cards were dealt and bets were made. The pot grew bigger as the game continued. Sometimes when the pots were bigger, two or three quarters were taken from the pots instead of just one coin. Young kept the money in front of him. He made change for the players for their bills when a player required more quarters to continue to play in the game. I also saw Young pass the bills to Jack Graham.

During the time that I played in the game, I had put $20 marked money into the game, including the $6 used to purchase the twenty-five-cent pieces when I first sat in.

The first game I played in, I lost. The second game, I got lucky and won. I then lost the next two. The next hand was dealt, and the player on the left of the dealer started the bidding, putting his money in the pot. The guy next to him put his money in and raised the bet, and two more players put their money in the pot and raised the pot. Next, three guys withdrew, throwing their cards facedown in a slush pile, and when it came to me, I called and put the required money in the pot. The next five cards were dealt, and with each card a bet was made and raised by the players coming around to me. On each occasion, I put the required amount in the pot and called.

After all the cards were played and the bets were made, I was the last one to bet or call. I called. The guy who started the betting and the last one who raised placed his cards on the table, thinking he had the winning hand. He had three aces. A good hand!

I was the last to put his hand down. I had three queens and two fours, a full house. The guy with the three aces looked at my hand and saw that I had won the pot. He jumped up and screamed at me, "You son of a bitch, you can't just sit there! You have got to bet and declare your hand. You just can't sit there and call each time a bet is made."

"I'll play my cards any way I want to. There is nothing that says I have to make a bet if I don't want to. You guys kept raising the pot. I was satisfied with that. The pot was growing nicely. You guys were making the pot bigger without my help. I was happy. Why jump in and spoil what you guys were doing? The pot might have ended up smaller than it is now," I said.

The dealer backed me up and said, "A player can play his cards any way he wants. He can bet or pass. It's up to each player to decide whether he is going to bet, raise, or call."

One of the other players said, "Why are you here in the Falls tonight?"

"To play poker. What other reason would I have to be here?" I responded.

"Why did you come here to play poker when you could probably play in Fort Erie?"

"Well, like the guy across the table bitching and complaining about my not bidding in this last hand, I bid the same way when I play in Fort Erie, and some of the guys there I played with didn't always like it either. So I thought I would come down here and give it a try."

That ended that conversation.

The game continued with one pissed-off player still in the game. The next few hands that were played, I made some bets, but whether I bid or not, I called on the last card. On two of the games that were played when the winning hands were put on the table, I threw my cards facedown in the slush pile of cards. If I had placed my cards face up, I would have won the pot with the winning hand. I threw in the winning hands so I could get rid of some more of the marked money.

At 1:00 a.m., a man I heard called Jim (and later identified as Jim Green) replaced Young as the dealer until 2:00 a.m., when he was replaced by the return of Young as dealer. Green operated in the same manner as Young, taking the same amount of rake-off from each of the pots he dealt.

At 2:10 a.m., I asked Young, "How often is the game operated here?"

"Every night of the week," he said. "This game may last until Sunday, you just never know."

At 2:20 a.m., Graham called to Mike (a player later identified as Mike Carson) and beckoned him over. Graham was at the doorway to the second room behind the gift shop. Mike went over to

Graham. Graham gave him a roll of bills, and Mike put them in his shirt pocket. I did not hear what was said between the two of them. Graham then left the premises, and Carson went back to play in the game.

At 2:45 a.m., Sergeant Charles Baker—accompanied by Corporal Ernie Black and Constables Merv Talbot, Henry McDougal, and Roy Tenant—entered the premises through the back door, which was still open. Sergeant Baker announced, "Canada police. Stay where you are!"

Confusion overtook the players. They grabbed at their money, and some jumped up from the table. Under the impression that a hold-up was taking place, Terry Duncan struggled with Constable McDougal and had to be handcuffed before he calmed down.

Sergeant Baker asked, "Who is in charge here?"

There was no reply.

He then said, "Who is in charge here, Ron?'

I stood and pointed to each person I named. "Young and Green were the dealers in the games. Both, when dealing, were taking rake-offs from each pot as that game progressed."

Young and Green were shown the search warrant.

I then said to Sergeant Baker, "Jack Graham left the premises earlier. Before he left, Graham turned over a roll of bills to Carson. Graham was the one who signed me in as a member. I was told by Graham you have to be a member of the club to get into the game. He had me fill out an application form. After I filled it out, he gave me a membership card, which I had signed."

Constable Talbot searched Carson and, from his left shirt pocket, seized $178, which included marked money he had used in the game. Also found were a Canada Hydro check in the amount of $12.84 endorsed by P. Tichota, and from his right front pocket was $72 in cash. A key was also found on him to a Yale lock on the back door of the premises.

Sergeant Baker seized $18.75 in twenty-five-cent pieces from the table and $29 in bills, which had been in front of the dealer. Five $1 bills were found on the floor.

Young, when searched, was found to be in possession of $37 in bills, $6 in twenty-five-cent pieces, and forty-two cents in change. He also had a key for the Yale lock on the back door. Green had in his possession $104 in bills and $1.50 in twenty-five-cent pieces. All the money found in their possession was seized.

During the investigation, Constable Talbot had a conversation with Todd Smith, who stated, "I am the proprietor of the Flamingo Gift Store."

Talbot asked, "What are you doing here?"

"I sell coffee, sandwiches, and soft drinks to the persons in the back room."

In view of the fact that all persons participating in the game had entered through the gift shop, which was in darkness, the four men—Tom Young, Jim Green, Mike Carson, and Todd Smith—were informed by Sergeant Baker they would be charged jointly with "Keeping a Common Gaming House" at the premises, rear room, main floor, 232 Bridge Street, Niagara Falls. Each were given the official caution, to which they all replied, "I have nothing to say."

Jack Graham was arrested out on Bridge Street at 5:45 a.m. and brought into the premises by Sergeant Baker and me. He was given the official caution and advised that that he would be charged, along with the other four persons, with "Keeping a Common Gaming House."

Graham asked, "Was there gambling going on in the back room while I was away?"

"I'm referring to the time you were here," Sergeant Baker said.

Graham then asked, "How many are you charging?"

"Five for the time being. The other seven persons in the room will be charged as found-ins.

Graham responded, "I am the manager of this place. I assume the responsibility."

Seized from the room was the money and checks taken from Young, Green, Smith, and Carson, along with the cards that were used in the poker game and two other decks. Seized from the office were twenty-five new decks of playing cards in a locked box, 126 membership application cards, two bundles of used playing cards, seventy-two blank membership cards, and nineteen completed application forms. One of the applications was in the name of Ron Rupert—the undercover police officer.

Jack Graham, Todd Smith, Mike Carson, Tom Young, and Jim Green, were charged jointly with "Keeping a Common Gaming House" at the premises known as Rear Room, city of Niagara Falls. The charges were preferred by the chief of police, Cecil R. Pay.

Later that day, the accused appeared in Magistrates Court and were released on bail of $500 each. The seven found-ins were released on bail of $25 each and instructed to appear in Magistrates Court on July 19, 1951, at which time it was put over to August 8 for trial and then to October 25 for judgment.

When the case came to trial, fines and costs amounting to $476 were levied by Magistrate John B. Hodgkins on the four men he found guilty on a joint charge of unlawfully keeping a common gaming house contrary to section 229 of the Criminal Code. Tom Young (56), Mike Carson (62), and Jim Green (23) of St. Catharines were fined $75 and costs of $17, making a total of $92 each. Jack Graham (37) was fined $180 and costs amounting to $200. The charges against Todd Smith jointly charged with the other four men were dismissed.

Six of the seven men charged as found-ins were fined $12 and costs amounting $15. A seventh man failed to appear, and the magistrate said a warrant would be issued for his arrest. Although it had been my very first case (and the first time seeing my name as a police officer in the newspaper), Magistrate Hodgkins said in delivering judgment, "I can't regard it as extremely serious," adding that the rake-off was small, according to the evidence.

CHAPTER THREE
A Month Undercover and Working Two Jobs

I left Niagara Falls that Saturday morning at 7:00 a.m., heading back to Fort Erie, quite pleased with myself that my first assignment on the police force was successfully completed. I was looking forward to getting back to the office in Toronto to find out what this next assignment was that the inspector told me would start on Monday. At this stage of the game, I had not been told where I was going or what I would be doing when I got there.

When I got to the office, I was called into the staff inspector's office. He thanked me for the job I did in Niagara Falls, getting into the poker game on Friday night. He also said that the other officers waiting near the bridge for me didn't think I had a chance getting in, being a rookie. He also said because I did not show up at the rendezvous with them at the Rainbow Bridge parking lot, they thought I was lost somewhere in Niagara Falls. I had to laugh over that comment.

I was then advised by the inspector that my next job was in the city of Brantford. I was told that there were a lot of gambling machines in stores, restaurants, and other places in that city. There were also some bookies taking bets on thoroughbred horse racing and poker games, all doing a thriving business. It would be my task to find them and obtain the evidence so that charges could be laid on those persons operating these gambling places.

"You can ride your bike to Brantford. When you get to Brantford, go to the detachment office, and I will meet you there.

You can park your bike in the detachment garage as it will not be needed. I will then take you to a business where you will have a job that has been arranged," Inspector Davidson said.

There were three Massey-Harris company factories in Brantford. After meeting Inspector Davidson, he took him to the main plant known as the Verity Works where they were ushered into the office of the top man at the Massey-Harris Company, a Mr. Roberts, who knew that I was an undercover police officer. Arrangements had been made for me to have a job, so if I was asked or if I was questioned by any of the people I would be dealing with, I could say I worked in the Massey-Harris factory.

After Inspector Davidson left, I sat with Mr. Roberts, and we talked about the factory and what I would be doing.

I said to Mr. Roberts, "I was introduced to you with my name. However, I will go by the name of Bill Newman while here in the factory and in the city."

Mr. Roberts then informed me, "Your job title while working here will be safety supervisor, and you will be working out of the employment office. You will be able to work throughout the factory, looking for any safety hazards that you may find. When you find a safety problem, go to the maintenance department and have them rectify the problem."

While working in the factory, I found several hazardous problems throughout the working areas, which I brought to the attention of the maintenance department, and they were then quickly resolved. I also called the office of Industrial Accident Prevention in Toronto and ordered safety posters, which I tacked up on the bulletin boards throughout the factory.

I was also told that I could come and go as I needed to in order to gather the evidence of gambling in the city. I stayed in the factory most of the day, only traveling outside when I tried to get to a place that closed earlier and also to place bets on horse racing at the bookies.

After leaving the factory at the end of day, I walked the streets, going into stores and restaurants and any other place looking for pinball machines, bookies, and poker games. When I found a pinball machine in a place, I played until I had a large number of free games on a gaming machine, which I then cashed in for the money they were worth.

A pinball machine is a type of arcade game, usually coin-operated, in which points are scored by a player trying to manipulate one or more of the steel balls on the playing field under a glass-covered cabinet playing area. The primary objective of the game is to score as many points as possible. Points are earned when the ball strikes the different targets on the playing field under the glass. A drain is situated at the bottom of the playing field, protected by player-controlled plastic bats called flippers that the player could control to help keep the ball in play and to obtain more points. A game ends after all the balls fall into the drain. Secondary objectives are to maximize the time spent playing (by earning extra balls and keeping the ball in play as long as possible) and to earn bonus games (known as replays). These replays can then be cashed in by the proprietor of the business or his or her employee working at the business.

After I had been in the city for three weeks, another member of the gambling squad, Doner Grimshaw, came to Brantford to follow me around and corroborate the evidence of the payoffs I was getting from each of the businesses with which I was dealing. This payoff was the evidence required for a charge to be laid.

On September 1, members of the police raided all the premises where the evidence had been obtained of gambling taking place. Two-inch headlines appeared in the papers that night and read as follows:

36 POLICE IN 20 RAIDS CLEAN UP BRANTFORD

BRANTFORD, Sept. 4 – (Special) – Following a recent "gangland" murder here when charges were published that gambling and vice were allowed to run wild in this city, Provincial Police last night cracked down in one of the biggest gambling raids in Canadian history.

Four squad cars carrying 36 Provincial Police officers snatched 30 pinball machines and arrested 24 *gambling house operators in 20 separate raids carried out almost simultaneously. It took two trucks to pack the seized gambling equipment to the city jail. The accused were charged with every gambling charge from cards and dice games to pinball machine operators. Bail ranged from $16 for "inmates" to $200 for the house operators.*

Some Brantford sources say they believe the anti-gambling drive resulted from newspaper stories on the lax gambling law enforcement in Brantford, after Edward Barbarian would-be operator was found shot to death in his car about two months ago.

A few city police officers assisted in the raid, but on the whole it was the police show.

Staff Inspector W. G. Davidson, head of the Provincial Police anti-gambling squad, said 24 arrests were made for various gambling offenses. Inspector Davidson directed the well-planned raid personally.

Zero hour was set at 2:20 pm Saturday afternoon. There was no warning of the impending raid until the Police cruisers rolled into Brantford. Inspector Davidson lauded the work of Sergeant Fowler of the Brantford City Police.

PAY $1500 FINES AS 15 CONVICTED FOLLOWING RAID

Brantford, Oct. 26 – Provincial Police anti-gambling squads hit the jackpot when they swooped down in Brantford in a series of speedy raids Sept. 1. Of 41 charges laid, 15 were heard during an all-day police court sitting yesterday. Convictions were recorded in all cases. Fines totaled $1500 and costs $225.

Sixteen pinball games and slot machines from $110 and up were ordered confiscated for destruction. Also confiscated was the money found in the machines. – except the sums put in by plain clothes officers

> *who spent July and August in Brantford playing the machines, obtaining cash payoffs when possible, and thus obtaining the evidence which lead to the mass raids.*
> *Still to be heard are five machine cases, five charges of gaming by means of a poker game with rake- off and 16 betting house charges, inclusive of found-ins. Evidence was given that the proprietors of the premises, and the owner of the machines, split the revenue on a fifty-fifty basis.*

During the trials, I was standing outside the courtroom when I was approached by one of the owners of four pinball machines, which he had just recently purchased and which were also seized in the raid. He was not happy as these were his first machines that he had purchased, getting him into the business. With a nice smile on his face, he invited me out for a coffee.

I asked, "When?"

"Tonight at 11:00 p.m."

"Where?"

"I know a nice dark alley."

"You can't get coffee down a nice dark alley."

"I will have it delivered just for you."

I responded, "Why?"

"So I can carve my initials in your fucking face." I laughed and walked away.

Another day while downtown, I went into the smoke shop to get a package of cigarettes. I had been there a few times before, getting evidence on bookmarking and on the pinball game. Jerry, the clerk behind the counter, started talking about the Fort Erie racetrack where an investigation was being carried out by the Ontario Racing Committee, assisted by the police gambling squad.

He then showed me the front page of the *Toronto Star*, an article about how they thought the jockeys were mixed up with fixing races. I looked at the article and made some derogatory comment about the cops doing the investigation.

Jerry said, "I've met some those guys. From what I have seen, they're not a bad bunch of guys. Just like you and me, we are just doing our job."

I had to look away so he wouldn't see the grin on my face.

Another time, on a Sunday, I met one of the fellows I worked with at the Massey-Harris factory. We chatted for a while about the safety program that I had started in the factory, and then he suggested we should go for a beer.

"We can't do that today," I said. "It's Sunday. There's nothing open."

"Well, I know a place where we can get a beer anytime. It's a bootlegger I know."

I said, "Okay, let's give it a shot."

I was driving, so we got in my truck and headed to the bootlegger. As I was driving down a dirt road, there was a car on the road in front of us. I said, "I don't like going down this road behind another vehicle. You never know about that car, it might be the police going to raid the bootlegger we are going to."

I had to look out the window so he couldn't see the smile on my face and keep from laughing at my comment.

During the rest of my time on the gambling squad, we visited and/or raided other establishments with pinball machines, bookmakers, poker games, fall fairs, amusement parks, bawdy houses, and any other places where illegal activities were thought or found to be going on.

On one occasion, Roy Tenant and I drove around southwestern Canada on my motorcycle, looking for more pinball machines. We checked out many country stores, convenience stores, gas stations, and any other places that might have had a gaming machine. We found a few. The evidence was obtained, charges were laid, and the machines were seized with charges being laid at a later date.

They checked fall fair amusements as they had complaints about some of the games in the amusement section. In some cases the games were not being operated in an honest manner because those operating the game were cheating. In one case the operator of the booth would demonstrate how easy it was to throw a bowling ball hanging on a cord from above, attempting to knock over a bowling pin. The operator of the booth would demonstrate how the game worked and show how easy it was to win. When a player paid his or her money to play, the person playing could not possibly hit the bowling pin because the pin was not in the same spot as it was when the operator demonstrated it. You had to look carefully to see how the operator located the bowling pin. They checked a number of fall fairs throughout Canada to make sure the operators were not cheating their customers.

In the fall of 1951, I got into a poker game in Fort Francis, Canada, where we played a few weird poker games including a three-card, high-low split pot. A raid was made by Fort Francis police and the other two members of the gambling squad while I was sitting at the poker table playing the game. The operators were charged and were convicted a week later. They were each fined, and the equipment used in the room was confiscated.

CHAPTER FOUR

Another Poker Game in the Cold North

In February 1952, Inspector Davidson came into the back office where the squad spent our time when at the office and said to me, "I would like you to go up to Sudbury and take over from Frank. He has been up there now for a month and not having any luck trying to get into a big poker game. He is apparently working in a supermarket out on Riverside Drive. Give Frank this letter." He handed it to me. "It is instructing him to return back here to the office. Then you can take over from him and try to get into the poker game as he was sent there to do."

After getting to Sudbury, I found out where the grocery store was located, got on a city bus, and went to the store to meet Frank and give him the letter. After the surprise of seeing me and after reading the letter, Frank went to the manager, made some excuse, and quit. I then applied for a job at the store about an hour or so later and told the manager I had worked full-time for A&P stores in Fort Erie and Welland in the past. I got the job as grocery clerk, but I did not tell the store manager I was a police officer.

I had been in Sudbury for three weeks and had as much luck as Frank in trying to get into the poker game. Each morning on leaving the house where I rented a room, I walked down to the corner restaurant where I usually had breakfast before heading out to the store on Riverside Drive. The same waitress served me each morning.

After three weeks in Sudbury and not having any luck getting access to the poker game, I asked the waitress if she would like to go to a movie that night. She said yes.

When we got out of the movie that evening, I found out she lived in a small town about five miles outside the city. I took her home in a taxi. On the way back to the city, I sat in the front seat of the cab and talked to the driver. He asked what I did for a living. I told him I worked in the grocery store out on Riverside Drive, and we talked about the city in general.

I casually mentioned to the driver that I had heard there was a good poker game being held somewhere in the city and that I liked to play poker but didn't know where.

He told me where it was and said, "Just go there, ring the doorbell, and they will let you in."

"I doubt that. They do not know who I am. I've only been in Sudbury for a month, and I am sure they would not let me in."

"Meet me tomorrow night at the cabstand. I'll take you there and introduce you to John, he runs the place."

"Sounds good to me. I'll see you tomorrow evening."

The next night, February 27, the taxi driver picked me up at the cabstand and took me to a service station at 48 Becker Street West. We went up to the second floor where the poker game was being held. The cabbie then introduced me to Bob Hogarth, who was in charge. I was allowed into the game and played poker for a couple of hours or so, but when the games ended, I left.

The next morning, I phoned our office in Toronto to let them know I had gotten into the poker game. I met with Sergeant Baker, Sergeant MacClaren, and Corporal Black when they drove up from Toronto that afternoon. I told them how I got into the game, the location where the game took place, and the names of the persons running the games. I was told to go back into the game that night, and if there was not going to be enough guys around to make it worthwhile to have a game, I was to leave the building and meet up with the raiding squad a few blocks away from where the games were played.

On that night I went back to the club, and as it turned out, there was not going to be a game. I chatted for a while with the guys who were there, and then I left and headed over to where Sergeant Baker and the others were waiting. The raid was called off, and we would try again the next night.

The next night I was back into a good poker game. The doorbell rang at 2:30 a.m. Bob Hogarth, who had been standing beside the chair I was sitting in and talking to me, pushed a button on the wall behind him, which opened the door at the bottom of the stairs.

Sergeants Baker and MacClaren and Corporal Black entered the building and came up the stairs to the second floor where the poker game was taking place. Sergeant Cronin announced, "Provincial police."

I attempted to stand.

Bob Hogarth, who was still beside me, had watched the three men enter through the door, come up the stairs, and enter the room. He put his hand on my shoulder and told me to sit down. He then said, "Everything will be okay, Ron."

So I sat.

Sergeant Baker said, "Who is in charge here, Ron?"

I stood and indicated Mclare and the three others involved in running the games.

All four were charged with "Keeping a Common Gaming House." The other nineteen men who were in and around the room were charged as found-ins.

The papers read as follows:

Anti-Gambling Squad from Toronto Raids Sudbury Club; Four Men Charged

A raid by members of the Provincial Police Anti-Gambling squad from Toronto, on a Becker St. Club, resulted in the arrest of four men on charges of operating a gaming house and 19 others for being found-ins early today. The crack-down was the result of a request from Sudbury Police Chief J. D. Burger, during the first week of February for assistance in obtaining direct evidence on a suspected gambling establishment.

Facing the operating charge are Sudbury promoter Bob Hogarth, 31, of 85 Samuel St.; George Simpson, 56, of 211½ Shaughnessy St.; Tod Timkin, 31 of 207 Louis St.; and Henry Franklin of 83 Beech St.

Sergeant Charles Baker, of the Provincial Police Anti-gambling Squad, led the raid at 2:30 o'clock this morning on premises of Becker Private Social Club, over a service station at Becker St. and Flood Rd.

The raid climaxed investigation begun at the instigation of Chief Burger, who contacted Provincial Headquarters in Toronto on Feb. 7, with request for assistance in bringing suspected gambling operation to court.

The Chief said he had information from a reliable source that gambling was going on at the Becker St. club, operated by Hogarth, well known in Sudbury sporting circles as boxing promoter with the Northland Athletic Club.

Since all men on his morality squad were known to operators of the suspected gambling place, the Chief stated in his letter, it was impossible to secure direct evidence to back up suspicions.

He requested aid from the Provincial Police Force's Anti-gambling Squad to secure the evidence.

Other members of the gambling squad were Sergeant MacClarin and Constable Rupert.

The police contacted Sudbury police immediately the raid got under way for assistance in herding operators and found-ins to City Police Headquarters for booking in.

All those arrested were remanded until Monday for a court appearance.

The four charged as operators were released on bail of $400 each; bail for found-ins was $25 each. Chief Burger said today the raid is part of his continuing drive to clean up bootlegging gambling and disorderly houses in the city.

A week later the trial was held in the Sudbury Court and was reported in the paper that night:

Bob Hogarth Jailed, 4 Fined $200

Sudbury boxing promoter Hogarth was sentenced Tuesday to serve one month in jail for operating a gambling house in the Northland Boxing Club, at 48 Becker St. West. Hogarth and three others were also fine $200 and costs each or two months in jail. Nineteen men charged as found-ins were fined $10 and costs each.

Hogarth, along with Henry Franklin, 83 Beech St.; George Simpson, 211 1/2 Shaughnessy St., and Tod Timkin, 207 Louis St. were arrested by members of the Anti-gambling Squad of the Provincial Police early on the morning of March 1st.

The arrests followed a month of investigation by a member of the police. The constable had come to town obtained a job as a grocery clerk, and spent his off hours attempting to gain entrance to suspected underworld circles in Sudbury and district.

The police undercover man Constable Ron Rupert, of Toronto, testified Tuesday that he gained admission to the poker sessions held at the Northland Boxing Club premises. He made his first visit there Feb. 29, when the constable again played poker. About 1:40 am that night, four other members of the anti-gambling squad had raided the establishment and arrested Hogarth and Franklin, partners in the operation of the club McCallum, Simpson and 19 other men.

Cons. Rupert had engaged in playing a variety of poker call "44," and had lost $26 the first night and $58 on the night of the raid. He testified that on different occasions Fay & McCallum acted as dealer at the game and the dealer took out chips from each pot. This, the Crown contended, was a house rake-off.

Chips in the poker game were sold for 25 cents, Cons. Rupert said, and the pots as high as $50 to $60. The dealer took chips out of each pot before the hand was completed.

Members of the raiding squad, Sergeant Charles Baker, Sergeant Tim MacClarin, Corporal Ernie Black and Const. Roy Tenant. All but Corporal Black testified Tuesday. The two sergeants had collected the money found on the table in front of each of eight players. Introduced as evidence it totaled more than $150. Hogarth's lawyer, Harry Waberg Q:C. continued to do most of the talking for the defence on Tuesday.

Cons. Rupert had testified that the dealers removed chips from the pot, Waburg said, but he had not said whether these chips were used for the house or making change or some other purpose.

The Northland Boxing Club was organized to promote sports events, Waberg said The poker games had been held only as a friendly gathering.

Crown Attorney E. D. Williams, Q:C. stated that the evidence had shown conclusively that the money taken from pot was a rake-off which went to the house.

Hogarth had been convicted of a similar offence, court records showed.

CHAPTER FIVE

A House of Ill Repute

They got a report that a bawdy house was being operated in Charlotte Township, two miles south of Delhi. From September 8 to 14, observation was kept on the house by Sergeant MacClarin and Constable Price. During this time period, they observed thirty-two cars entering. Twenty-four of the cars transported fifty-one men to the house, and then the cars left with twenty-seven men. These cars were observed from late in the evening to early in the morning while MacClarin and Price were standing in a tobacco field, watching the house and the coming and goings from the place. The cars entering the yard were directed to a place to park by a man with a flashlight.

Constable Jim Ward from the Anti-Gambling Squad, delegated by Sergeant Baker, was to enter the premises to obtain evidence. He walked to the house on September 12. He was led into the house by the man from the yard with the flashlight. He was Mike Franchetto.

While Jim was in the house, he purchased two bottles of beer, paying fifty cents each. He also bought a bottle of beer for Louise Boyd, one of the girls in the house. He watched as several of the men also purchased beer and watched as they paid for the beer. He also observed George Summers behind a bar-like structure where he was selling the drinks.

Ward went into the house again the next night. He went down the stairs into the basement where Summers was behind the bar again selling drinks. Also in the basement, the three girls were there. At 12:45 a.m., after seeing what was going on, he went outside and signaled to Sergeant MacClarin and the rest of the squad waiting in the tobacco field.

A few minutes later, the house was raided. Summers, who was in the basement, heard the commotion upstairs and ran up from the basement.

After entering the house, the squad found three bedrooms on the main floor, all three of them occupied. In the kitchen they found 678 empty beer bottles. In one of the bedrooms they found a medical certificate. In the basement there were thirty-four found-ins. At the bar-like structure, they found ninety-seven bottles of beer, part bottle of whiskey, ten shot glasses, and ninety empty beer bottles.

Charged as operators of a common bawdy house were George Summers and Mike Franchetto, RR 1, Delhi. Franchetto was also charged with keeping liquor for sale. The three women—Bernice Jacobs of Ingersoll, Mary Wannamaker from Noranda, Quebec, and Louise Boyd from Sudbury—were charged with being inmates of a bawdy house. Thirty-four men were charged as found-ins. Twenty-six of the found-ins were released on $25 cash bail. All the others were remanded in custody. The operators were remanded in custody until the next week, at which time they were sentenced to one month in jail.

This was what came out in the newspaper:

"Stamp Out Crime" Provincial Police Aim - Inspector Declares

> *A lightning raid by Provincial Police at a Charlotte township residence early Sunday morning resulted in the arrest of 84 men charged as found-ins, and two men and three women, who face more serious counts.*
>
> *Led by Staff Inspector Scott Jacobs of the Provincial Police Anti-gambling Squad, 10 officers closed in on a house, located two miles south of Delhi on the Pine Grove Road. They blocked all exits and placed the occupants under arrest in short order.*

The transportation problem was solved when a Simcoe bus was procured to bring the men charged to Simcoe. Of the 84 found-ins, 26 were released on $25 cash bail each and the remainder were remanded in custody after Justice of the Peace L.R. Eastdown read charges, and Sergeant Ben Peters, of Simcoe detachment laid information's at the court house.

Charged as operators of the "Common Bawdy House" were George Summers and Mike Franchetto, an additional charge of keeping liquor for sale being laid against summers. Police confiscated 130 pints of beer in the course of their investigation at the scene of the raid. $500 Bail Each.

Three women, Bernice Jacobs, Mary Wannamaker and Louise Boyd, were charged as inmates of a common bawdy house. Bail for Franchetto and summers, and the women were set at $500 each, all five being remanded in custody.

Referring to the charges against the women, Staff Inspector Jacobs stressed to the Reformer, that the trio will get jail terms upon conviction under the Criminal Code, Section 229-4, and dealing with "inmates". He said that the Anti-Gambling Squad, was engaged in a full-scale drive to stamp out vice, illicit use of liquor, and gambling in the province.

Sergeant Ben Peters, officer in charge of their Simcoe detachment, who with l Constables John Thornton, Peter Banks and Terry Bowls were called in as the "flying squad" swooped down on the house, said that his force would continue to crack down on illegal drinking and associated offenses in the county.

Raid is a Repeat

The raid Sunday morning was the second in two weeks at the same place. Appearing in court after the first search, Bill Anderson, R.R. 1 Simcoe was fined

> *$100 and three months in jail for illegal possession of liquor. In addition the premises were declared a public place.*
> *Police would not comment on whether future raids are planned for Norfolk County, but they made it clear that a "cleanup" is underway.*
> *Indications that Provincial Police are getting tough with all types of law-breakers, which is illustrated by the policy of releasing found-ins on cash bail instead of permitting them to plead guilty and pay fines out of court. All found-ins at the Charlotte house will appear in court Thursday.*

After the court appearance, the following appeared in the paper:

Three Girls Fined, Men Are Remanded In Raid Aftermath

> *George Summers and Mike Franchetto, R.R. 1, Delhi, were convicted in local police court on Thursday on joint charges of keeping a bawdy house. Bernice Jacobs, Ingersoll, Mary Wannamaker, Noranda, Quebec and Louise Boyd, Sudbury were convicted on charges of being inmates of the house.*
> *They appeared before Magistrate E. Donald Smith, St Thomas, in the local courthouse which was filled to capacity. Summers and Franchetto, were remanded in custody one week for sentence, and the three girls were fined $50 and costs or one month in jail. Summers pleaded guilty to an additional charge of "keeping liquor for sale and was sentenced to two months in jail."*
> *The charges arose following a raid on a house on the Pine Grove Road at part of Lot 6, Concession 11, Charlotte, on September 15th, by members of the Provincial Police anti-gambling squad Toronto, led by Staff Inspector Scott Jacobs.*

Sergeant Tim MacClaren and Provincial Constable Price told of keeping watch on the house from September 8th until September 13th. During this time they counted a total of 32 cars entering, with 24 known to be carrying 51men, and cars leaving with a total of 46 men. They kept this tally from late in the evening until early in the morning, while standing nearby in a tobacco field. On most occasions there were cars already in the yard on their arrival and cars still in the yard when they left. During their watch a man was seen in the yard with a flashlight directing the cars to parking spaces.

Officer Bought Beer

Provincial Constable Jim Ward, said that on September 12th he walked to the house and was let in by Franchetto who was in the yard with a flashlight. Ward told of buying two bottles of beer for 50 cents each. He also bought Miss Boyd a drink for 50 cents and saw several men getting drinks and making motions of paying for them. He said Summers was behind a bar-like structure where the drinks were sold.

The next night he again went to the house and this time walked in a door and went down to the basement. Summers was behind the bar and the officer bought a bottle of beer for 50 cents. This time he saw three girls. At 12:45 a.m. Sunday morning, he went outside and signaled Sergeant MacClaren and a few minutes later the house was raided. When Summers heard the commotion upstairs he ran up from the basement.

Summers was in Charge

Sergeant MacClaren again took the stand and told of going through a door leading into the kitchen. Franchetto was just inside the door with a flashlight in his hand. Witness also described the layout of the house consisting of three bedrooms, two of which were occupied, a kitchen, living room and another room with no furniture. Summers said he was in charge and later a rent receipt for $30 was found in his pocket.

In the kitchen, Sergeant Charles Baker told of finding 68 empty beer bottles. In one of the bedrooms he found a medical certificate. From Summers he took $111.20 consisting of two ten dollar bills, five fives, 14 twos, 25 ones, 42 quarters, six dimes and two five cent pieces and taken from Franchetto were three $20's, 2 tens, nine fives, three twos, nine ones, two 25 cent pieces and two five cent pieces.

In the basement Corporal Bailey and Provincial Constable Ron Rupert found 34 found-ins. They also found 97 bottles of beer, and a part bottle of whiskey, 10 shot glasses and $3.50 in silver from a glass tumbler. The Constable also said he found three men outside in cars.

CHAPTER SIX

One for the Birds

Our office had been advised that a cockfight was going to take place on a farm in London Township, just a short distance north of the city of London. We were going to raid the farm with all our members taking part and with the assistance of the London Township Police Department.

I had never been to a cockfight before, but I had heard that they had raided one or more in the past, before I came on the gambling squad.

When we got to the farm, I saw the pit where the cockfights were taking place. Watching the roosters fighting ranks right up there with the worst things that I've seen since I started working as a policeman.

A cockfight is a fight between two roosters known as fighting cocks or more accurately gamecocks held in a two-foot-high wooden ring called the cockpit. One kills or severely injures the other one in front of the spectators. The combatants are specially bred birds conditioned for increased stamina and strength. Cocks possess congenital aggression toward all males of the same species. Cocks are given the best of care until near the age of two years old, and they are conditioned much like professional athletes prior to events or shows.

Wagers are made on the outcome of the match. Cockfighting is a blood sport due in part to the physical trauma the birds inflict on each other. While not all fights are to the death, the birds may endure significant physical trauma. In many other areas around the world, cockfighting is still practiced as a mainstream event; in some countries it is regulated by law or forbidden outright as it is in Provincial.

The fighting cocks are brought to the arena by their proud owners. Time is spent talking to the birds as if they were human and feeding them while talking to other owners about raising techniques and who will win this day's events. The owners have to wait for their birds to be weighed and inspected. Then the matching of the roosters is done to make the fights more fair, ensuring they have equal fighting abilities, weights, and temperaments. The odds are set. All that needs to be done is to wait for the fighting to start.

Seeing these birds in their cages, they all looked so calm. It was hard for me to believe that they could be as bloodthirsty as I had heard. They get shampooed, massaged, and held often. I have even heard many instances where the gamecocks actually live in the owner's home. Some of the birds are said to be better treated by the owners than their wives and children. These roosters are idolized and prized by their owners.

If a breeder gains a good reputation as the breeder of winning cocks, there is much money that can be made. Customers will come from everywhere, even from other countries, to buy their roosters. Dominicans are known to breed some of the best fighting cocks around. The United States is one of the largest suppliers of game fowls for the cockfighting industry. Just go to a farm show or 4-H gathering and see these fine birds on display. A prize fighting cock can sell for as much as five thousand dollars or more.

The better breeds of bird include miner blues, hatch, claret, black, roundhead, and white hackle. Not every rooster has what it takes to be a fighting cock. The cockfighting or battle cock has the durability and strength to fight and continue fighting instead of surrendering.

When the action starts, it's exciting. Even if you are appalled at the violence, it is something to experience. The excitement (or maybe a better word is *frenzy*) from the surrounding crowd causes adrenaline to flow.

Two roosters are placed in an enclosed boarded pit, an 8×10-foot-diameter enclosure, two feet high. The owners of each fighting cock place their birds one on each side of the pit. Strapped to each leg of a fighting cock is a razor-sharp two-inch spike, which is pointed inward and curved outward. On a signal from the organizer, the owners would let their bird loose in the pit, jumping and squealing and going after the opponent.

These games can become very loud with the owners yelling, trying to tell their bird what to do, and the spectators yelling at the birds and the owners. Spectators make their wagers on the bird they expect to be the winner. Bets are made on a rooster according to the color of its leg band, and when you want to bet, you just shout it out. Someone will hear you. Even with all the noise and commotion, nothing seems to deter the roosters from their intent to kill their opponent.

Even if you don't stay in the arena and watch the fights, the bar can also be interesting, observing the people watching the fights. Even more exciting was the mad scramble of men trying to get away when they realize that the police had arrived at the site where the cockfight was taking place. Not too many of those attending managed to get away; they were taken into custody and were released on bail.

The papers read as follows:

Police Squads Swoop on "Pit" in London Twp.

Seventy-nine men and five women were arrested yesterday in a king-size raid on a London Township farm where police charge cockfighting was in progress. By The Anti-Gambling Squad
More than 70 of the fighting cocks were seized and turned over to the Humane Society in London. Lumber brought in by truck was described as the barrier for the cockpit.
Headed by Staff Inspector G. G. Jacobs, of the Provincial Police Anti-gambling Squad, the 40 raiders included members of London Township Police under Chief Doug McGuire, Provincials from

London, Toronto, Brantford, Dundas, Hamilton, Chatham, Simcoe and Glencoe, and Morality Officers Ed Coulter and Doner Warner of London City Police.

Owners of the farm, which is at the sixth concession and Highbury Avenue, Harold and Lloyd Shoebottom, were charged as keepers of the cockpit. Magistrate Donald Menzies released the two brothers on their own recognizance of $1000 each to appear in county magistrate's court today.

The others were charged under a section of the Criminal Code which provides penalties for persons who encourage or assist in the fighting of cock-birds.

Freed on Bonds

District Property owners included in this group were released on their own recognizance of $300.

Few Escape Net

The platoon of police formed up shortly after 10 a.m. and the final charge to the clearing in the centre of the bush lot on the farm was made at 3.p.m. The clearing is 1000 feet from Highbury Avenue.

The police closed in from three sides and are confident not more than a handful of men escaped in the scramble that followed.

They came from London and district, from as far west as Windsor, and as far east as Cornwall and intermediate points. There was a man from Detroit Mich.; one from Buffalo and three others from smaller New York State centres.

Last man brought in was one whose car was left at the scene when everyone else was gone.

Corporal Charles Wilkinson, with Constables Ken Galbraith and Robert White, gained entry to the locked vehicle and started to tow it to London.

A man stood up in a hay field and said: "Hey that's my car."
"Fine" the officers answered "Come on along."

Jam Police Courtroom

After names were taken the crowd from the farm filled the county magistrate's court and the second-floor hall. The overflow perched on the stairway to the main floor of the police station in a manner reminiscent of the fowl that led them into difficulties. The five women, arrested with their husbands, were among those released on their own bail. The males arrested ranged in age from men in their twenties to white haired oldsters.
Conflicting counts indicate a possibility three men got home free after they were taken to the police station. An officer taking names as patrons arrived said there were 82 men and five women. When the information's were made out, there were 79 men and five women.
Cash bail of $150 each was posted for four of the Americans. The fifth was released on property bond of $300 posted by a London man. All the others were released on their own recognizance. The last man was freed shortly before 1 a.m.

CHAPTER SEVEN

Playing in the Park

In the summer of 1952, we went to the amusement park. This was an amusement park that came into being on 1888. It eventually had many interesting rides throughout the park, which were constantly in use. There were two Ferris wheels, one a little bigger with fourteen seats, and then the smaller one with eleven seats. Each seat could accommodate two persons. There were two roller coasters in the park, a relatively tame one and a big one called the Cyclone. The Cyclone was the biggest and fastest one in the world at the time. I rode on it in my teenage years, living not too far away from the park in Fort Erie. They even had a nurse standing by, rendering aid to any persons getting off the ride and being sick.

There were two passenger ships, the *Americana* and the *Canadiana*, that brought visitors into the park from some of the northern states in the USA. There were many times when there were more than twenty thousand visitors in the park on any given day. The park eventually closed in 1989. The Cyclone was auctioned off and sold for $210,000. It was dismantled and rebuilt at the Great Escape, Lake George, New York, in 1994 with some modifications.

In the park, a large dance hall called the Crystal Ballroom held many dances, some with big-name bands, drawing large crowds. Also in the park was our target, a large penny arcade, where they would check out the gaming machines being played. There were nine of us from the police Anti-Gambling Squad. Six of us played a number of the machines, collecting evidence these machines were strictly games of chance and therefore illegal.

On the evidence we collected, the operator of the arcade, William Jacobs (37), and his three assistants—Kenneth Hunter (21), Timothy Black (26), and Henry Foster (26)—were charged with keeping a common gaming house and were summoned to appear in court. Thirty of the machines they played were seized.

> ***Crystal Beach Gaming Charges Seen Test Case***
> *FORT ERIE – (Special) - In what will prove to be a test case opened yesterday before Police Magistrate George Masters , when William Jacobs, 37, operator of the Penny Arcade at Crystal Beach, and three men said by police to be his assistants, Kenneth Hunter, 21, Timothy Black, 26, and Henry Foster, 26, appeared charged with keeping a common gaming house. The case arose out of a raid on June 12th at Crystal Beach by the flying squad of the Provincial Police, in charge Sergeants Baker and Ramsay-, working directly out of Toronto, when thirty machines of two types, "rotary pushers" and "digging cranes" were seized at the lakeshore resort.*

> ***"GAMES OF SKILL"***
> *Joseph Sedgwick, Q:C., counsel for the three men, is seeking to show various machines under seizure are "games of skill" and not machines used for gambling. Six hours of solid evidence was taken at the opening of the hearing, and the case was then adjourned until 10:00 a.m. today. It is expected that at the hearing today, important evidence will be given for the defense by J. H. Brown of St. Thomas, who has had a number of years' experience in the amusement business, that "digger cranes" and "rotary pusher" are actually machines of a type which enable skilled*

players to obtain for their investment, a fair margin of merchandise.

County Crown Attorney Tobis F. Foster, Q:C. is representing the Crown.

The machines, stored in a local building, were viewed by Mr. Brown at the conclusion of Tuesday's adjournment to satisfy him they are the same type of machine regarding which he will later give evidence. Numerous witnesses, for the Crown and the defense, were heard at the Tuesday hearing. The chances require an investment of ten cents with everything from white plastic dogs, bronze ships, cigarette lighters, brass unicorns, to other animals in green sweaters, the possible return.

All these exhibits were displayed on the magistrate's desk yesterday.

Among the witnesses called yesterday were Constable Price, Corporal Bailey, Constable Hern, Constable Carlson, and Constable Rupert. All played the various machines on the evening of June 12, and some were quite fortunate. Constable Rupert, a native of Fort Erie, won four prizes in a return for an investment of $2.60. Some of the visiting police were not so fortunate.

It was the contention of Defense Lawyer Joseph Sedgewick that some constables were more skilled than others, explaining why some had better luck answering a question from the defense counsel if he didn't think skill was required, Constable Weaver replied: "I wouldn't say so, it's a matter of luck." Constable Grimshaw for instance won a toy revolver. After a lengthy questioning by the Crown and defense, he still contended there was a wide element of chance, and possibly some skill.

"Well, even Babe Ruth could only average a little better than one hit in three. Do you know any game,

such as bridge, golf, etc., where you can win every time?" sagely asked Mr. Sedgewick. Sergeant Baker gave evidence that he had accompanied the squad to Crystal Beach, but that play had been sharply stopped at 10 p.m., while his men were testing their chances. Constable Grimshaw said this sudden cessation had been brought about by Knapp, proprietor of the place, who told his men, "Close up, .Ramsay's here." Sergeant Ramsay also accompanied the squad to Crystal Beach.

AN IMPORTANT POINT

Defense Counsel Joseph Sedgewick brought the fact to be perfectly operated from mechanical standpoint, the machines in question require a 60-cycle circuit, whereas in Crystal Beach only a 25-cycle circuit is available, and transformers have to be used. Perhaps, he implied, that might be why a little more skill was required to bring a fair return. Kenneth Hunter, employed by the Canadian Amusement Company for the past two years, said the machines would pay off in three plays of five if operated by a skilled player. He said on Memorial Day for instance, when many experts were on hand, experience of the operators showed them in more than 200 cases operators had had that ratio of success- three of five, indicative of the fact they are games of skill.

Timothy Black, another employee placed the ratio by which skilled winners might win merchandise, at even as high as seven of ten. He said he placed about 75 mixed prizes in ten machines every morning and on busy days, reloaded them in the afternoon. The particular day on which the police came saw the machines nearly empty of prizes because he had failed to notice the supply was dwindling and was engaged in fixing wires. He himself said he played

for amusement, and being an employee, always placed the articles he won back on the shelves.
Miss Beatrice Becon, a resident of Crystal Beach and a frequent player, gave evidence corroborating the fact that as one's skill increased the percentage of merchandise prizes increased. She displayed a necklace she had won and said it was only one of many prizes. Her sister, Miss Victoria Lazarin, also gave similar evidence and proved herself a very capable witness for the defense, despite a strong cross examination by Crown Attorney Foster.
John Jones, another witness caused some merriment in court with his quips. speaking in a distinct foreign accent, Sunday was quite positive the more one played, the greater the chances to win were. He was also quite positive the machines required skill, and were not solely guided by Lady Luck. Peter Hemsworth, another witness, said he played the machines for his own amusement. He get a distinct kick out of practicing on them. A skilled player has a very fair chance of a return," he declared. Under cross-examination by Crown Attorney Foster he said he did not know how often he played, how many he won proportion to losing. "I like to try my skill. I don't play for profit but for amusement. If he win something, it's so much the better. After all, these machines are in an amusement park, where people go for recreation and amusement. I don't think they are gambling devices."
When it was suggested by Defense Counsel Sedgewick several of the machines be brought into court, to be tried out for the edification of all, the magistrate commented; "It is too late in the day. They will continue tomorrow morning at ten o'clock.
The case presents many interesting angles, and should defense succeed in proving the machines under sei-

zure are games of skill, and not gaming machines, an important issue will be before the court.

DECISION RESERVED INPENNY ARCADE CHARGES

FORT ERIE (Special) - Magistrate Johnston Roberts at the conclusion of a long hearing extending most of Tuesday and up until Wednesday forenoon, reserved decision in the case of William Jacobs, 37, operator of the Penny Arcade at Crystal Beach, and three men said to be his assistance, Kenneth Hunter, 21, Timothy Black, 36, and Henry Foster, 26, all charged with operating a common gaming house. He will give decision July 16.

The last day of the hearing was largely devoted to technical evidence given by Elmer Brown of St. Thomas in regard to the possibility of the machines returning a merchandise prize for an average ten cent investment. In an able summation, Joseph Sedgewick, Q:C., of Toronto, representing the accused, maintained there was no violation of the criminal code in the operation of the machines. The accused are charged with keeping a common gambling house. Thirty machines under seizure represent an aggregate investment of approximately $27,000 by the owners. Mr. Sedgewick contended they are not automatic or slot machines as prescribed in the act. Persons who play them give ten cents, to an operator or attendant. They are chiefly games of skill.

Crown Attorney Tobis Foster Q:C. said under the act, to escape a charge of gaming, the machines must be entirely games of skill unless they are fully such, the act has been violated, "I realize this is a very important case," commented Magistrate Masters, and "I will reserve judgment for a week to review all facts.

One week later the Magistrate and gave his judgment in the case. The following appeared in the paper.

Machines Seized At Crystal B. Thirty said valued at $25,000 confiscated on order by Magistrate; Regarded as a precedent

FORT ERIE – (Special) – Magistrate George Masters this afternoon, ordered confiscation of 30 amusement devices from the Crystal Beach Park Penny Arcade, valued at $25,000 and placed fines $25 each on Eldon Knapp, 37, arcade operator and three men employed by him identified as Kenneth Hunter, 21, Timothy Black, 26, and Henry Foster, 26. All are summer residence at Crystal Beach. They had been charged by the Provincial Police anti-gambling squad with keeping a common gaming house at Crystal Beach Park.

In his written decision, the caddie maintain that "play on these machines constitute games of chance with chance predominating. Therefore they are in violation of the Criminal Code in respect to games of skill only being allowed to operate to preclude gambling."

The devices were listed as 10 holly cranes, 10 rotary merchandisers, and 10 pusher-type machines.

Joseph Sedgewick Q:C., of Toronto, told the court that this type of machine has been used in Canada amusement parks for some time. He would not commit himself as to whether or not he will enter an appeal. He termed Magistrate Masters decision" a precedent.

There were many other cases where they raided more poker games, dice games, bookies, and gaming machines, collecting evidence on illegal gaming throughout the Province. They checked fall fairs, going through the midways to make sure the peo-

ple visiting and participating in the games were not being cheated by the carnival people.
He remember being at the Rockton fair on Highway 6 which was being run by a bunch of farmers. After checking that all the gaming booths that were ok, they came across a booth selling slices of homemade pies. They stopped at the booth and the three of us each bought a slice. He bought a slice of apple. It had to be best piece of apple pie he ever had, so he bought a second piece. It was a bad move; it had to be the worse piece of apple he ever had.

CHAPTER EIGHT

Watch It, We Are Being Watched

In the early 1950s, there were thirteen municipalities (including Toronto, the largest) who all had their own police department. We got a call from the police chief of one of these municipal police departments, requesting our assistance to go after a bookie who was operating from his home. They wanted the gambling squad to get the evidence, lay charges, and put that person out of business.

We observed the residence for a few days to watch the comings and goings. It was decided that to get into the residence, we would send a registered envelope to that address. There were five members of the squad participating on the raid. One member was in the back lane behind the bookie's house to keep an eye on the back door. Three were down the street a short ways. The other member followed the mailman, who knocked on the door to get a signature for the registered envelope.

When the door opened, the officer following the carrier ran up the steps, barged past the carrier, entered the house with the search warrant, and shouted, "Police!" The other three members of the squad ran across the lawns to get to the house. One member of the raiding party carried a crowbar in case the dog, which they heard barking the day before, might attack and bite one of the raiding party officers.

While the squad members were running across the lawns on their way to the house, we passed a telephone lineman up on a pole, working on some of the lines. He happened to see the officer following the mailman and rushed past him and into the house. Then he saw the rest of the squad racing across the lawns and going to the house. He had heard earlier that there had been several break-ins in the area. So being a good citizen, he called the local police to let them know that what he thought was a criminal act was taking place.

The local police arrived quickly and quietly in force. Our guy in the lane behind the house was watching the back door to make sure no one ran off with the betting slips. Suddenly he felt something pressed into his back and was told to put his hands together on top of his head. It was one of the local police officers.

Other police officers went to the front of the house and "raided" the police officers who had entered the house to get evidence on bookmaking. All was straightened out with the local police when they understood it was their chief who had requested the assistance of our squad.

The guys from our squad had a good laugh back at the office about the telephone lineman having called the local police, thinking we were bad guys breaking into the house. As the headlines in the local Toronto papers summed it up: "Police Raiding Squad Gets Raided."

CHAPTER NINE

Gambling Days Are Over

My time on the gambling squad came to an abrupt end in the middle of October 1952. I decided on the weekend to visit my parents in Fort Erie. On Friday after work, I jumped on my big Harley (for which I had traded my Triumph) and headed home.

On Saturday afternoon, Mom asked if I would run down to the drugstore and pick something up for her.

I picked up what I went for and headed back up Bertie Street behind a pickup truck, which was almost in the center of the road. It made a move as if to make a right-hand turn on to Aberdeen Street. Not seeing a turn signal on the pickup, I went to pass it. Instead of making the right turn, the driver made a sudden left turn into a driveway.

I had nowhere to go, hitting the left rear fender of the pickup, my right leg trapped between the fender of the truck and the gas tank on the bike. As a result, I broke both bones in my right leg above the ankle.

After six months of not healing, I went to the Toronto General Hospital to have a sliding bone graft done.

I finally went back to work eleven months after the accident, doing light duties at general headquarters in Toronto at a desk in the office of the Accident Recording Division. After three months there, I was in uniform for the first time working at Toronto detachment, which was part of general headquarters, answering the phone at the switchboard, escort duty for the treasury department and on

Provincial paydays, and guard duty outside the Canada Savings Bank in the Parliament building.

One day while working on the day shift, I decided I had had enough of working in Toronto. I wanted to get out of the city and out of general headquarters to work in one of the many detachments located in the Province. The commissioner's office was about twenty-five feet from the switchboard where I was working at the time, so I decided to approach the commissioner and request a transfer.

The first question he asked was "Where would you like to go?"

I had thought about it prior going into his office and replied, "Peterborough, sir. I would like to go there if at all possible."

Two weeks later, my transfer came through, but I wasn't going to Peterborough. They transferred me instead to Dundas, no. 3 district headquarters, just outside Hamilton to the north.

As I had spent a lot of the time on the switchboard at GHQ, they put me on the four-to-twelve shifts, answering the phone for the first four weeks. Then I went out with one of the officers for a week to learn the area covered by the Dundas detachment.

I finally got to work by myself, patrolling the area to the south and east of the city of Hamilton. It was interesting and fun some of the time. I investigated accidents, charged drivers for traffic violations, stopped and arrested impaired drivers, and got called to investigate break and enters and other crimes.

On one occasion, I was dispatched to a particular accident on Highway 56 immediately north of the village of Binbrook. A farmer in a pickup came north out of Binbrook on a side road after dark to a slight left-hand curve on Highway 56, where a transport truck was proceeding south on the highway and was about to make the slight turn curve on the highway. The farmer driving the pickup thought the truck was going straight into Binbrook on the side road, so the farmer drove out onto Highway 56 and ran head-on into the truck, causing the truck and trailer to flip over.

The trailer was loaded with cattle that spilled out onto the road and disappeared in the darkness around the area. It was round-up time in Binbrook. The farmer was taken by ambulance to St. Joseph's

Hospital in Hamilton, while I stayed at the scene until the road was finally cleared and I had completed his investigation at the scene.

However, the accident had attracted a few spectators. Gas was leaking out of the tractor—fast. One of those spectators, almost standing in the gas, was about to light a cigarette. I grabbed the cigarette roughly from his month just in time and had some harsh words for him.

After the road was cleared, I headed in to St. Joseph's Hospital to see and talk to the farmer, the driver of the pickup truck. When I got to the emergency room at the hospital, the farmer was lying on a gurney fully clothed. I asked the farmer where the nurse or doctor was.

He replied, "She took off my boots then left."

I could understand why. He was wearing at least three pairs of socks, and he must have been wearing the socks and boots for many days. The odor was sickening.

The nurse came back into the room looking a little pale. She told me, "I had to get away from the farmer. I was almost sick when I took off his boots. The smell was terrible."

The statement I got from the farmer indicated he thought the truck was going straight into Binbrook, so he proceeded out onto the highway in the direction of Hamilton, thereby causing the collision.

Three days later, I made out the information, charging the farmer with careless driving. Before I was able to get to the Justice of the Peace to have the information and a summons signed and issued so I could go to the hospital and serve the farmer with the summons, I got a phone call from the hospital informing me that the farmer had died. Case closed.

CHAPTER TEN

A Car Thief, a Dumb Little Joker

Another time I was proceeding north on Highway 53 to Duff's Corners when I was dispatched to a variety store gas station. As I was just about to go by the store, I pulled into the lot in front of the gas pumps and went inside. The operator of the store was still on the phone talking to our office. He hung up, turned around, and was completely surprised to see me standing there.

There was a young man standing in the store. The operator advised me that this young man did not have any money to pay for the gas he had just put in the car. He had offered to give the owner his wristwatch until he could return with the cash. This lad was driving a big car with Florida plates.

I asked him, "What is your name, and where are you from?"

"I am John Swift, and I am from Florida."

"What are you doing here?" I asked.

"I am visiting my aunt in Windsor. I was in Toronto, and I am on my way back to her place."

"Okay," I said, "again, what are you doing here?"

"As I told you, I am coming back from Toronto and heading to my aunt's place in Windsor."

"Being at this location, you are way off the route to Windsor. You come with me, and we will get this straightened out at the office."

I put the young man in the back seat of the cruiser and drove back to the detachment office. On the way to the office, I asked again a few times why he was at this location, but he pretty well stuck to the same story he had given me at the store.

I took him into the office and sat him down. There were a couple of other officers in the office typing out reports who kept an eye on John Swift while I went into the radio room to talk to the dispatcher.

Just as I got in there, I heard Hamilton police broadcast a stolen vehicle from their area matching the car Swift was driving. I got on the phone and called Hamilton police, advising them I had the car and the person responsible for its theft.

I put the handcuffs on John Swift and delivered him into the Hamilton police headquarters. The owner of the car was an entertainer and had been doing a performance in the city. He was certainly surprised that he got his car back so fast.

CHAPTER ELEVEN

Drinking Early in the Day Doesn't Pay

Another day I started work at 8:00 a.m. and was out on patrol shortly after. About 9:45 a.m. I was at Duff's Corners, the intersection of Highway 2 and 53, when I decided to go back into the city and get some gas as it was running low. I was about halfway between Duff's Corners and Ancaster when I saw a car coming west on Highway 2 toward Duff's Corners crossing the white line onto his side of the road a number of times. I had to go off the road onto the soft shoulder to avoid a collision. I made a U-turn and went after the vehicle. I pulled alongside the car with my stop fender light flashing. He didn't stop. The car came again into my side of the road, and I had to brake quickly to avoid being hit. I had my headlights on and also my rotating red roof light on. Other cars coming toward me realized what was happening and pulled over onto the shoulder as I was now on the wrong side of the road with my siren blaring, trying to get the driver to stop.

The car finally stopped in the driving lane. I got out of the cruiser, still on the wrong side of the road, and ran around and opened the driver's door. Reaching into the car, I shut it off and took the keys. I then went back and parked the cruiser on the shoulder on the proper side of the road ahead of the vehicle I stopped. Back at the stopped car, I got in and pushed the driver to the passenger side so I could drive his car onto the shoulder of the road behind the cruiser.

In those days, to purchase liquor, you had to have a liquor permit book issued by the Canada government. When you purchased liquor, your purchase was recorded in the permit book. When I checked in the car and found his liquor permit book, it showed that two forty-ounce bottles of rye whiskey were purchased at nine that morning before he left Toronto. I found only a bottle and a half remaining in the car, which I seized as evidence.

He failed the sobriety tests I gave him there on the side of the road, so I placed him under arrest, and he was charged with impaired driving and lodged in the county jail. He was convicted, fined $100, and sentenced to seven days in jail for the impaired driving charge. He was also fined another $100 for possession of liquor in the car, and his driver's license was suspended for a period of three months.

CHAPTER TWELVE

Patrolling a Town, a Mixed Bag

I was stationed in Dundas for about a year, and then I was transferred to the Milton Municipal Detachment, where I spent the next five and a half years.

In May of 1955, I reported for duty at the Milton Municipal Detachment, a town with a population (at that time) of approximately 2,700. I was met at the detachment office across the hall from the municipal offices in the town hall by Constable George Brent, the officer in charge. A short time later that day, I met Constable Bill Dresden, the other of the two with whom I would be working with. In the future, other officers would come and go, including Calvin Smith, Jim Ross, Ted Jordan, and Henry McNaught.

Bill gave me a tour of the town, showing the locations of the different subdivisions, important factories, public schools, the separate school, and the high school. We patrolled the town on three shifts, six days a week. We also patrolled the main street on foot during peak shopping periods and some evenings.

While patrolling the streets of Milton, we had a few accidents to investigate, impaired drivers to arrest, and a few family quarrels, among other assorted calls.

In December of that first year, I was working evening late shift on a Sunday. It was around midnight when I decided to go up Main and Bronte Streets and check out the co-op before going to the office and typing out my weekly report, which showed the work I did for past week.

I checked out the co-op and found it was secure. I headed out of the parking lot to go back to the office, but instead, for some reason, I made a left-hand turn and headed north on Bronte Street to check the abattoir.

When I had arrived in town in May and been shown around the town, I was told that for the past three or four years, just before Christmas, the abattoir had been broken into, and a couple of sides of beef were stolen. No one had ever been caught for the theft.

There was a butcher shop on the Main Street called Haley's Meat Market. The owner, Stanley Haley, also had the abattoir on Bronte Street where most of his butchering was done for the meat products sold in the store. The driveway was about two hundred feet long leading east from Bronte to the abattoir. This area of the town was just open land with a few buildings.

Approaching the area, I saw a car parked on the road at the end of the driveway. I parked behind it, quickly jumped out of the cruiser, and ran up to the car. I opened the door, reached in, and pulled the keys from the ignition before the occupants realized what was happening.

I saw two hind quarters of beef lying on the back seat in the car. I hustled the two men in the front seats out of the car and placed them in the back seat of the cruiser. Because we had no cells available in the detachment, I took them to the county jail, which was also located in the town. The suspects would be held there by the guards until I could go back and investigate further.

I called Ray from the jail to have him come out and assist, then called Stanley Haley to come out and identify the hind quarters and to secure the slaughterhouse.

I picked up Bill, who was glad the meat thieves had finally been caught. When we got back to the slaughterhouse, Stan was waiting there for us. He identified the two hind quarters as taken from his slaughterhouse. He showed us where he had made cuts on the leg above the hoof in a special manner so that they could be properly identified if they were stolen and the culprits were caught. The hind quarters were returned and hung back in the cooler, and Stan locked up and secured the slaughterhouse again.

Stan went home happy while Bill and I went to the jail, picked up the thieves, and took them to the office to be fingerprinted, cautioned, and a statement taken. They did not have much to say; they were still stunned at being caught.

They appeared in court and were remanded in custody until January, where they again appeared for trial. As a result of the evidence, they were found guilty and sentenced to six months in jail.

CHAPTER THIRTEEN

A Loaded Gun, a Bad Scene

A very sad case came up. Although it was on Main Street just outside the town limits in Trafalgar Township Police area, our office was called, and I attended at the residence.

Two brothers lived beside each other on the south side of the road on the continuation of Milton's Main Street. Tom was on the left, and Jerry was to the right.

Tom had a son named John, and Jerry had a son named Timothy, both eleven years old. The two boys were like brothers, always playing together. Because it was very hot on this beautiful summer day, in the upper 90s in July, they were playing in the basement at Tom's house where it was cooler.

John's father was an avid hunter. His .308 caliber rifle was hanging on hooks above his workbench. John climbed up on the workbench to get the rifle and said to his cousin Tim, "Look at this." As John said this, he pulled the trigger of the rifle. The rifle fired a bullet, which ricocheted off the east wall of the basement, then off the north wall, and into the head of Timothy, blowing his head to pieces. A large pool of blood was on the cellar floor under the body of the boy. It was a bad scene.

I called the office and had Jim call the Trafalgar Township police to attend. I left the house shortly after the Trafalgar police arrived.

Sometime afterward, I found out that the parents of the dead boy, Jerry and his wife, sold their house and moved away, and as far as I know, Jerry never communicated with his brother again. The owner of the rifle was charged and convicted with unsafe storage of a firearm.

John was devastated and in shock about killing his cousin. He received physiotherapy evaluation and post-traumatic therapy for a year after the incident.

CHAPTER FOURTEEN

Wherever You Hid the Car, I'll Find It

I was on patrol on the afternoon shift when I saw four boys walking west on Main Street. When they saw the cruiser, they turned and walked south on Fulton Street. I also turned south and stopped beside them. I asked, "Where are you guys coming from, and what are you doing here in Milton?"

"We are from Toronto," one of the boys responded.

I asked again, "What are you doing here in Milton?"

"We just dropped by to see what was going on around here."

"Well, you better turn around and leave this town now and go back where you came from. There is nothing to do around here for you guys other than getting into trouble," I said. "Go now, I'll be watching."

I went back out onto Main Street and watched them. I figured it was odd that they came to Milton for no apparent reason other than to get into trouble or to commit a crime. It was likely they had already gotten in trouble before getting here; they would have needed transportation to get here. I assumed they must have had a car to get here, and likely a stolen one. So I called the dispatcher and asked if there were any reported stolen vehicles from the west side of Toronto or in Peel Region, and if so, to give me the license numbers.

It was a very short period of time before I found one of the cars that had been stolen. It was in the empty parking lot at the Canadian Tire Store, two blocks from where I first saw the boys. I went to go after them and saw they were hitchhiking south on Ontario St.

(Highway 25). Just before I got close to them, they were picked up by a passing vehicle heading south.

I called the dispatcher at Oakville detachment and gave him the description of the car and the four boys. I also told him about finding the stolen car from the Toronto area in the parking lot next to the Canadian Tire Store here in Milton.

An Oakville officer stopped the car the four boys were riding in. They were taken to the Oakville detachment where they were questioned and were finally charged with auto theft. The charge was also supported with fingerprint evidence found in the car by an identification officer from our headquarters in the Dundas office.

CHAPTER FIFTEEN

Seniors, Not a Good Scene

I was working the day shift, sitting in the office in the late afternoon, when I got a call from a concerned citizen. They hadn't seen their neighbors for the past couple days, which was unusual.

I went to the caller's residence, and the woman pointed to the house next door, saying, "That's the house."

I went across the lawn to the back door, on the west side of the building, closer to the rear of the house. I looked through the door window. The old gentleman who lived in the house was sitting in his rocking chair, slowly moving back and forth. I knocked on the door, to which there was no response. He just sat there and kept rocking and staring forward.

The door was locked, so I had to force it open. The old fellow just kept rocking slowly and staring. His wife was lying on the floor with her stomach up against the side of the woodstove with a wood fire that was just about out.

I called the coroner and then called the undertaker for a removal van. The coroner advised that the woman had died the day before, probably from a heart attack. An autopsy was performed the next day confirming that she had indeed died as a result of a heart attack.

The husband had apparently gone into shock seeing his wife on the floor up against the woodstove and just sat in his rocking chair rocking back and forth since she fell.

CHAPTER SIXTEEN

How Many Can You Steal in One Night?

It was another February day, and I was working the afternoon shift. It was now about 10:30 p.m., and I was on Main Street and was about to pull into the car lot of Milton Motor Sales when a four-door Ford came out of the lot and headed north on Main Street, moving fast. I checked the doors at the dealership and found that they were all secure.

A short while later, the theft of a 1950 Ford stolen from Hamilton was broadcast over the radio. The description matched the car I had seen drive out of the car lot, so I kept checking all the cars I saw.

At 2:30 a.m., John McKinnon advised me that two damaged vehicles were sitting on Base Line Road near the Bell School Road, northwest of Milton. One of the vehicles was described as the 1950 Ford stolen from Hamilton.

I drove to that location, but before I had a chance to get out of the car, a 1955 Chevrolet Sedan Delivery came up the hill and turned right onto the Bell School Road. I went after the vehicle. It turned off the road into the laneway leading to the farmhouse of W. G. R. Gervis, where the car slid off the lane and into the ditch. The driver jumped out of the vehicle and took off running into the woods.

I left the laneway and went back to where the two cars were parked. There was only one car left there, the stolen Ford from Hamilton. I contacted Toby McGaw on the police radio. I was working out of the Milton County detachment and told him about the three cars. He called the other county car on duty and told him to stop and check any moving cars he saw. As I already had accounted for two cars, there was a third one somewhere in the area.

With the cruiser headlights off, I drove back up the Bell School Road and down the laneway. The taillights of the Sedan Delivery were on, and a male person was in the driver's seat, trying to get it unstuck. I opened the car door of the Sedan Delivery, much to the driver's surprise. I proceeded to arrest him, cuff him, and put him in the back seat of the cruiser.

I then went looking for the other two cars. The damaged Ford was still parked where I had left it, and I found the other vehicle, a 1949 Plymouth stolen from Milton, on the Appleby Line with a second person asleep on the back seat. So I arrested him as well and put him in the back seat with the other one.

Dave met me at the office. The two—who were identified as Glen Jenson, age 20, and Nichol Macally, age 19—were both from Hamilton. They were cautioned, and a statement was taken. They stated that Glen stole the Ford in Hamilton, and when they came to Milton, Glen was going to steal another car at Milton Motors until I drove on to the lot, so they took off. They stole a 1949 Plymouth, which belonged to Bill Timkin, from his driveway. They then drove up onto the escarpment where the Ford had stopped running, so they attempted to push it with the Plymouth, but smashed it in the front. (I found out later it caused $350 damage.)

Macally walked down to Bell Brothers Service Station and GM Dealer where he stole the 1955 Chevrolet Sedan Delivery. Meanwhile, Jenack headed over to the Appleby Line where I found him. All three cars were towed back into town. The next week the car thieves appeared in court, pleaded guilty, and received a sentence of six months each.

CHAPTER SEVENTEEN

Trains Don't Run After Midnight

Calvin Smith and I were heading east on Main Street in our patrol car when Cal said that one of the other guys we worked with had mentioned an attempted break-in at the railroad station the night before. It was about 11:30 p.m., and we were on Main Street, close to the train station, so I turned left and headed over to see if there were any signs of the attempted break-in left to be seen at the station, so we went back to check it out. We got out of the car and went around to the front of the station where two guys were standing.

"What are you two doing here?" I said.

"Waiting for a train so we can get back to Toronto," one of them replied.

"There aren't any trains running at this time of night. You both come with us. They'll get this straightened out at the office."

We put them in the back seat of the cruiser and took them to the county jail while we went back to the train station to do a little investigation. At the west end of the station, partially buried in the snow, I found a partially concealed small jar of a white-colored liquid, which I assumed to be nitroglycerin. I also found percussion caps and a fully loaded automatic handgun. I left the nitroglycerin hidden (at a little better and safer location than it had been when I found it) as it was too dangerous to be hauling around.

We took the percussion caps and the handgun back to the office. We called the dispatcher by phone and requested an identification officer attend to dispose of the nitroglycerin properly.

Back at the county jail, we picked up the two individuals and brought them to our office to caution and take a statement from them. It took some time, but eventually they gave us a statement admitting that they intended to blow the door off the safe in the station. They were taken back to the county jail and booked in.

Corporal Tom Feaver, the officer in charge of the identification unit in Dundas, arrived and requested we obtain a bale of hay. Lou had us spread the hay out in a line. He then poured the nitroglycerin over the length of hay and set fire to it, thus burning the nitro to destroy it. This is the safest way to dispose of nitroglycerin—burning it.

The two would-be thieves were remanded in custody for one week to plead to the charges. They pleaded guilty, and because of their criminal record, they both received four months in jail.

CHAPTER EIGHTEEN

Elmer Arrives in Town for the Kids

In the summer of 1956, I decided to introduce a safety program into the elementary schools in town, but I needed a person or organization to sponsor and pay the costs, if any, for the safety program that was undertaken.

The starting point would be to introduce Elmer the Safety Elephant to the schools. This program was started by the Ontario Safety League (OSL) and had been operating in many schools throughout the province. The OSL supplied a variety of safety pamphlets, at no cost, designed with Elmer's safety messages on them to be handed out to children in the schools.

At a special meeting, the Kinsmen Club of Milton agreed to became the sponsors of the "Elmer the Safety Elephant Who Never Forgets" program to be inaugurated in three elementary schools. At the meeting, I outlined what I had done to bring Elmer and my school safety program to Milton. I also reminded the Kinsmen members that a six-foot green Elmer flag would be flying below the Union Jack on each school's flagpole and would come down if a child in the school was found to have broken one of Elmer's five rules. If Elmer came down from the flagpole, the child being held responsible (they found) would be ostracized by the rest of the children for thirty days because Elmer was missing from the school's flagpole.

Elmer teaches his five rules of safety:

1. Look both ways before you cross the street.
2. Keep out from between parked cars.
3. Ride your bike safely, and obey all signs and signals.
4. Play your games in a safe place away from the street.
5. Walk when you leave the curb, don't run.

At 10:30 a.m. on the second Monday morning of the new school term, the children assembled outside the Bruce Street school looked up to see the police car, siren wailing, leading a short parade toward their school. Following the cruiser came a sound truck carrying the public address system, sending strains of "The Land of the Isles" through the crowd. Next came the Kinsmen Club's Clown Town Wagon with three chubby clowns who circulated among the small-fry crowd and amused the curious onlookers by calling a few of them by name.

Last in the parade came a station wagon with a four-foot statue of Elmer mounted on top. Elmer had finally arrived, smiling down at the cheers and roars from the assembled crowd.

Principal E. W. Foster introduced the Mayor, E. Ross Porter, who welcomed Elmer to the town on behalf of Milton Council. He thanked the Kinsmen for sponsoring the event and the local police constable for his efforts in bringing the safety program to the town.

The mayor urged the children to learn their safety rules and impressed the rules upon both the children and their parents.

I was next to speak and warned that the pennant of Elmer flying on the flagpole would stay on a flagpole only as long as there were no accidents or incidents in which one of the children were found to be at fault. I explained that Elmer would come down off the flagpole for thirty days if any child were found negligent in an accident. I also showed the children and the parents the small pennant to be displayed in a classroom where all the children could learn and recite Elmer's five safety rules. I also displayed special jacket crests that would be given to the children, and they could wear them.

Next came the most important part of the whole program: raising the Elmer pennant on the flagpole. Once Elmer's six-foot pennant reached the top of the flagpole, three rousing cheers were given for the green elephant that would help prevent accidents from happening to the children.

At 1:15 p.m. that afternoon, the same ceremony was carried out at the Holy Rosary School where Father J. P. Larson said a few words in support of the program and again at the J. M. Denyes School, where the principal, William Siddall, thanked the Kinsmen, the mayor, and the police officer.

Only two mishaps occurred in the three ceremonies. The Kinsmen clown wagon got a flat tire, and at one school, the Union Jack already on the flagpole was flying upside down.

In the next few days I visited all the classrooms in each school and handed out safety pamphlets, talking about Elmer and stressing the importance of his five safety rules.

In each of the next four years, I ran a bicycle rodeo with the help of some parents and the Kinsmen Club. I held a free bicycle licensing program for the kids' bicycles, where they first had to pass a safety inspection. The program paid off over time. We were able to recover two bicycles that been stolen and returned them to the children because we could identify the owner through the license serial number.

Safety patrols were organized at the schools, also sponsored by the Kinsmen. I organized a safety council whose volunteer members helped instruct a driver education course, which was held during evenings in a high school classroom.

CHAPTER NINETEEN

You Can't Win All the Time

In June 1957, thirteen days after my first child was born, we had company on a Saturday evening. They left around 11:00 p.m. We lived in an apartment over a Simpson Sears order office. I was in bed with the lights out when I heard a car parked on the road outside and beside the building, revving the engine up directly below the bedroom window. There were three guys standing around the car. I heard one of the guys say, "Go around the corner and see if the coast is clear."

This situation didn't sit well with me, so I went down the back stairs and out the back door. The back door to the order office was about two feet from our back door, and it was wide open. I guessed that the guys I saw and heard from the bedroom window had forced the door open and were planning to come back and rob the store.

I went into the store, looked around, and then used the store phone in the store to call our radio dispatcher. I told him what was going on and advised him to call the two officers who were on duty and have them park across the road beside the United Church, in the darker area of the church parking lot. From there they could watch for the thieves to come back to the store to help him.

Little did I know that the two officers working that evening were five or more miles out of town when they were supposed to be only patrolling within the town limits. I, however, assumed they were parked by the church as backup for me, as I had requested.

I also called an off-duty officer, George Brent, to let him also know what was going on and notified the owner of the building to come down to the store in about half an hour to secure the premises. George left his house and mistakenly went down to the Eaton's order office instead of the Simpson office.

So there I was, thinking I had backup in place and close at hand. I sat there in the back room of the store and waited. I didn't have to wait long before two of the culprits came in through the back door. I hollered, "Police! Stop, put your hands on your head, and don't move!"

They turned fast and took off running, so I went after them. The one guy was probably twenty-five feet away as I was jogging toward him. The third guy had remained in the car, which must have been parked on Main Street. The car came around the corner and headed straight for me. I jumped back to get out of the car's path, turned, and took a shot at the car.

The guy that I had been closing in on turned and came at me, taking me by surprise. We tussled. The gun went off, and I was shot in the stomach area. He took off with my gun in his hand. It was about forty feet from my apartment building, and I walked back to the bottom of the stairs.

My wife hollered out the hallway window, "What's going on?"

"Call a doctor!" I hollered back.

She went back into our apartment and called the hospital to get a doctor to come and look after me. Then before coming back out, she went to the neighbors across the hall to have them look after our twelve-day-old baby for us. Then she came outside and helped me sit down on the back outside stairs and then helped me lie down on the grass.

Dr. Hudson arrived, and a few minutes later, so did John Thomas, the local undertaker, who also provided ambulance service. I was taken to Hamilton General Hospital, and a detective inspector arrived shortly after I landed in the emergency department to get my information about what led to the shooting. I was in surgery and operated on at about 3:00 a.m., and I woke up again sometime on Sunday in a hospital ward with five or six beds.

A visitor was talking to a patient in the bed by a large window. The visitor asked, pointing at me, "Who is that guy over there, and when did he come in?"

The patient said, "I was told that's the policeman that got shot last night in Milton."

I heard the visitor say, "They should shoot more of the pricks."

It was three and a half months before I got back to work.

Between the police and the Toronto Police Department, the investigators got word from an informer that the revolver was apparently disposed of by being thrown into the Don River. Two suspects were picked up and questioned a great length by two inspectors from the police criminal investigation branch. They were not able to break their alibis and the statements from their witnesses they produced. The officers were certain that these two were involved with a third person that was involved in the shooting in Milton on that night.

CHAPTER TWENTY

Game Over in Milton

In early 1960, the town of Milton decided to have their own police department and did not renew the contract they had with the police. As a result, we were all transferred out of the town to another detachment. The only exception was Bill Dresden, who was hired by the municipality to be the chief of police of the new Milton Police Force.

Having spent five and half years in the Milton Municipal Detachment, I was transferred up the road to the town of Acton, another municipal detachment. Acton was a detachment of four officers. Fred Domino was the corporal in charge of Vern Capston and Allen Mitchell and now me. My hobbies at the time were photography and amateur radio. As in all the other places I lived, I built another photographic darkroom in the basement, the biggest and best one yet. The darkroom was where I developed all my film and printed all the pictures that I had taken for myself and for other people in the community. Outside the darkroom, I had my amateur radio station set up. From here I talked to other amateur stations around the world.

Besides doing my normal police duties, I managed to fit in safety lectures to the children in the schools and other safety projects similar to those that I had done in Milton.

One thing I had not done in Milton was to have the Department of Highways, Motor Vehicles Branch, set up their portable safety lane. To arrange this event in Acton, I had to go to the different garages and get owners or managers to volunteer a mechanic for one to three days to help inspect the vehicles I directed from Main Street into the safety lane on the side street. We had a number of safety problems with quite a few vehicles tested, most of them of a minor nature, but they had to be corrected. After the problems were corrected, they would return to the safety lane and have their vehicle rechecked and pass the second examination.

One of the cars that I directed into the safety lane caused the driver to be somewhat annoyed. The owner told me that he had just bought the used car from a dealer in Guelph. The car was put through the safety lane but did not past the inspection. On checking the car's front end, the mechanic found the front right wheel assembly was not safe and could come apart and cause a major accident. The owner of the car was told that his vehicle was unsafe to drive, and he would have to get a tow truck to remove it from the safety lane area.

He said again, "I just bought this vehicle at a car dealership in Guelph. It was supposed to have been mechanically checked over before I bought it and drove away."

The mechanic told him, "Call the dealership in Guelph and talk to your salesperson. Tell him your car was examined in the safety lane and is not allowed to be driven on the road, and to bring a tow truck here and take the vehicle back to the dealership to fix the problem."

The car salesman from the dealership arrived, mad as a hatter, hollering and screaming at him and the mechanics. The mechanics told the salesman that the front end on the passenger side was going to come apart, which could quite likely cause a serious accident if driven on the road.

The salesman was still fuming, but he told the tow truck operator to load it up. The tow truck operator attached the car onto the lift of the tow truck. As he lifted the front of car off the road, the passenger side front wheel assembly came apart, and the right wheel fell to the road.

The salesman was horrified and apologized to the mechanics, to the owner of the car, and to me. He said he would put it in the garage in Guelph to be fixed, and while at it, he would have the other side checked over as well.

The next day the owner of the car brought it back, fixed. He thanked us for having him go through the safety lane as it had potentially saved his and others' lives.

CHAPTER TWENTY-ONE

Sometimes You Get Lucky Like I Did

At the end of September of 1964, I was invited to attend a dinner meeting of the Queens Park Amateur Radio Club, which was being held in Toronto near Queens Park. The invitation had mentioned that the commissioner of the Ontario Provincial Police, also an amateur radio operator, would be attending the dinner.

I went over the corporal's house and showed him the letter I received. When he saw the commissioner's name in it, he said, "By all means, go and enjoy yourself."

I attended the dinner meeting, and much to my surprise, the commissioner, Ernie Cotton, who came in a little late, sat in the seat next to me. After introductions were made all around, he turned to me and said, "Where do you work?"

"I am stationed at a municipal detachment in the town of Acton."

"How do you like it there?"

"I don't," I said honestly.

"Why is that?"

"I have been in Acton for the past four years, and prior to that I was in Milton municipal detachment for five and half years. I feel that's more time then I really need in a municipal detachment."

"Where would you like to be?"

"I would like to get into an identification unit," I said. "About twelve years ago I talked to Staff Sergeant Don Stinson. He was the officer in charge of the identification unit in general headquarters at the time, and he was also head of the identification units throughout the province."

I also told the commissioner that I had taken a correspondence course from the Institute of Applied Science in Chicago dealing with fingerprints, handwriting analysis, typewriter analysis, and footprint and physical comparisons.

I also added, "I have been interested in and studied a lot about photography, since I was fourteen years old."

At this point, the commissioner turned from me and started talking to the other members present at the table. I thought that was nice, a little disappointing, but I did get to meet and talk to the commissioner.

It was two weeks later, almost to the day, that I received a memo from our district headquarters in Burlington saying that I was being transferred to the Identification Unit, No 2 District Headquarters in London. I was happy to be out of Acton and municipal duties. The commissioner had put me in a position that just opened up in London, and all my dreams finally came together. I was going to the job I longed to do—crime scene investigations. I was finally able to make use of my photographic skills and the knowledge learned through the Institute of Applied Science.

PART 2

LONDON IDENTIFICATION UNIT, CSI

CHAPTER TWENTY-TWO

I Finally Made It

In October 1964, I was to report to the inspector in charge of no. 2 district headquarters (DHQ) in London. On entering the building, I went to the receptionist at the counter. In the office in the far left-hand corner, I saw Tim Morris, who had been recently promoted to Sergeant Major and transferred from Brantford to no. 2 DHQ: I first knew Tom when he was stationed in Dundas, where he was a corporal.

I went over to him and said, "Hello, Tom, and co—"

"Sergeant Major to you," he said sarcastically, remembering what happened back in 1957. I had been shot and was lying on a gurney at the Hamilton General Hospital around midnight waiting to be operated on when Tom came in to the emergency room. He came in and demanded that I tell him what had happened to me.

I said, "A CIB inspector from the Criminal Investigation Branch at the GHQ Toronto just took my statement."

He was not satisfied with my response and struck me. It was quite apparent that he had been partying and had consumed a quantity of alcohol.

My wife at the time and a nurse on duty in the emergency room saw this transaction between Tim Morris and myself. They both took offense to his actions, and apparently, both wrote letters to the commissioner describing Morris's behavior in detail. A hearing was held later, and evidence was heard from my wife, the nurse, and myself. As a result of the hearing, Tom was assessed nine days' loss of pay.

Sometime after meeting Tom at no. 2 DHQ, I heard that the members of the Brantford detachment held a stag party for his promotion and transfer. During the night of the stag and after drinking a quantity of alcoholic beverages, he got himself into another situation where another hearing was held. As a result of this hearing, he was demoted from the rank of sergeant major back to the rank of staff sergeant in charge of London detachment.

I was given directions by the inspector, which would get me to London detachment where the identification unit (known as the ident unit) also was located. I was greeted by the officer in charge of the ident unit, Corporal Donald "Don" Adam, and Constable Charlie Drew, the two guys I would be working with.

I talked to Don and Charlie for a while, explaining how I had been interested in photography at a young age and had built my own photographic darkrooms in each of the houses I lived in. I also told them how I had taken wedding photos over the years and how I did some commercial photography and portraits. I also told them about my diploma from the Institute of Applied Science, dealing in the science of fingerprinting, handwriting and typewriting identification, and other related subjects.

They both appeared equally satisfied that they were getting someone knowledgeable in what was expected of a person coming into the ident unit.

Over the following years, I went to break-ins, car accidents, suicides, accidental deaths, suspicious deaths, bank robberies, murders, police publicity photos, and anything else that came my way, including bomb threats. At this time, no. 2 DHQ was comprised of Middlesex, Elgin, Oxford, and Lambton counties in southwestern Canada.

When called to the scene of a murder, the CSI work during the investigation would be done by one of the two officers. The other officer would assist the other officer by taking notes for him while he was doing the work.

After arriving at the scene, the two officers would survey the scene, the location of the body or bodies, to determine whether there are any exhibits either close to the body or somewhere near that needed to be picked up.

Photographs would then be taken from all corners of the room. If the body had been found outside in the open, photographs would be taken from all directions. Close-up photographs would then be taken of the body and also from different angles. Any weapons or other items relating to the death of the deceased person would also be photographed close up, showing their location, with and without a ruler in the photograph.

Any items found in the room or the area outside of a dwelling that could be related in some way to the death of the person would also be photographed with and without the aid of a ruler. If the body had been found in a room, they would take measurements from each wall in the room to the body's feet and head and also from the position of the hands to the walls.

The body would not be moved or removed until the arrival of the coroner, at which time it would be determined if there are any marks on the body that should be photographed with or without a ruler.

During all this time, the second officer would take notes regarding all the photographs and measurements that were taken. When all this was complete (or at a later time and date while the area was still sealed off and guarded), measurements would be taken of the area or of the whole house where the body was found so that a detailed drawing could be made of the house or the area.

Usually the next morning, the working officer (sometimes with his assistant) would attend the postmortem at the hospital, where further photographs would be taken. The clothing of the victim had been taken, bagged, and tagged separately for examination. Exhibits received from the pathologist would also be received by the working officer. Also at the postmortem, the working officer would take the fingerprints of the victim and would also take their fingernail scrapings to determine if the assailant had been scratched by the victim before death, and if so, their blood type would be found in the scrapings.

All these proceedings were critical to my first and all murder investigations for the London ident unit.

On my arrival at the ident unit, I brought along the little fingerprint kit I received from the Chicago Institute. It contained a small cheap magnifying glass, two or three little brushes, a couple containers of fingerprint powder, some fingerprint tape, and some fingerprint lifts on which the fingerprints obtained at a scene would be taped and placed on the lifts.

Don and Charlie looked at this and laughed hard. I was then issued with good quality fingerprint brushes, jars of fingerprint powder, a good fingerprint magnifier, fingerprint tape, fingerprint lifts, and a few other incidental items. These were handed to me in a small box. Later that day, I went out and bought a briefcase. I got myself a three-inch-thick piece of foam, which I cut holes in to hold the items given to me. I got a few other little things relating to the work.

Don and Charlie both realized that I was a qualified fingerprint searcher and was great at identifying the found fingerprints.

As I was a new member of the ident unit, Charlie was delegated to travel with me a few times until I got accustomed to crime scenes. The third time out at a scene, with the fingerprints I found, I was able to come back to the office and identify them to the culprit causing the break and enter.

After a few months working in the office, I was classifying the fingerprints taken from persons charged with crimes and filing them, which I found to be a long process. It takes anywhere from five to ten minutes to classify one set of fingerprints of the criminal. If you needed a set of fingerprints to compare with fingerprints found, you had to know that person's fingerprint classification assigned under which the fingerprints were filed.

I suggested to Don about the time lost classifying fingerprints and suggested that the entire criminal fingerprint should be filed alphabetically, which would save us a lot of time. During the next two months, Don, Charlie, me, and our part-time secretary refiled all the fingerprint files. We had them all now into an alphabetic order, which made things go a lot faster locating a set of fingerprints for comparison purposes.

I took a look at the camera equipment that was being used. We were using a 4×5-speed graphic press camera. We had to load our sheet film and fill holders that held two sheets. At some cases we would take over a hundred pictures or more at a crime scene. We carried about three or four different types of film because we had to photograph crime scenes, footprints, and fingerprints—that was the reason for the different types of film.

A couple years later we were able to get a Pentax 35mm camera, which we used to take pictures of the occurrences we were at, including fingerprints when found. With a one-to-one lens, we could fill the picture frame with the entire fingerprint, showing actual size.

A number of years later, we were able to get and use Bronica cameras with several lenses, which were a bigger negative size than the 35mm. It was a damn good camera. They had interchangeable lenses and interchangeable film backs.

CHAPTER TWENTY-THREE

My First Murder: Nag, Nag, Nag, Dead

At 2:10 a.m., Sunday, March 21, 1965, Constable R. G. Malard, working the midnight to 8:00 a.m. shift out of the Forest detachment of the Ontario Provincial Police, received a call from Mrs. Charles Doxtater, who was the wife of the Special Indian Constable on the Kettle Point Indian Reservation. She advised Constable Malard there was trouble at the home of Wellington Elijah. He proceeded immediately to the Elijah residence located on the main road at the Kettle Point Indian Reserve.

On arriving at the residence, Constable Malard walked around to the rear of the house, where he observed Henry Leroy Hanks, age 23, standing at the back of a house. Malard asked him, "What's up?"

Hanks replied, "I think I killed my wife. She is upstairs."

Constable Malard entered the house, where he observed Wellington Edwards, age 64, lying on the floor beside the stove in the kitchen. He then checked upstairs and found Sandra Hanks lying on her back on the bed in the bedroom and ascertained that she was dead.

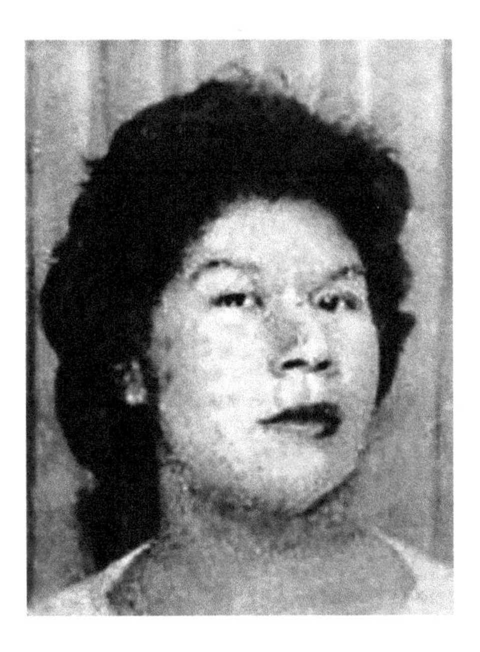

He radioed for medical and police assistance. Dr. John Jeans of Forest arrived at the scene at about 3:00 a.m. Dr. Jeans attended to the injuries of Wellington Edwards, and on examining him, he felt that the injuries were so severe that he may die. Because of Wellington's severe condition, he took a dying declaration from him. Wellington stated that his son-in-law, Henry Hanks, had attacked and injured him.

When Dr. Jeans advised Malard that Sandra Hanks was dead, Malard placed Hanks under arrest, handcuffed him, and cautioned him, at which time Hanks said, "I have nothing to say."

At approximately 3:30 a.m., Constable R. Small, investigating officer from Forest detachment, arrived with Constable D. Stone of the Ipperwash detachment. The accused, Hanks, was placed in a police car and kept under constant observation by Constables Malard and Small while Smith carried out his preliminary investigation.

Hanks was taken back to the Forest detachment office where he was briefly interviewed by Detective Sergeant Dennis at 6:45 a.m. Hanks consented to and was given a breathalyser test by Constable Don Green, who arrived from the Sarnia detachment. After three tests were taken, an average reading of .01 was obtained. This is a very low reading and is negligible.

At 11:09 a.m., Hanks was further interviewed by Detective Sergeant Dennis and Constable Malard, and he gave an inculpatory statement: "You are charged with murder. Do you want to say anything in answer to the charge? You are not obliged to say anything unless you wish to do so, but whatever you say may be given in evidence. Do you understand the warning as given to you?"

"Yes."

"What do you wish to say about the events that happened just before your wife died?"

"Do I have to tell that?"

"You do not have to tell it, but we'd like to know so as to complete our investigation."

"Well, they were over to the neighbors place there. When they all came back home, our two girls were up. I told my wife to put the girls back to bed. She was kind of drunk, so I gave her heck about changing the baby before she went to sleep. She got mad, so I brought the kids back downstairs again and put them in a bed downstairs. She came down and got the kids, and she started hollering, called me names, so I went upstairs. As I went upstairs, I asked her what she had said before, as I didn't quite hear her. I told her I don't know why she drinks if she couldn't watch the kids. Then we got into an argument, and I hit her. Then her dad, who was in the other bed, started hollering at me too, so I hit him. Then I picked up an old lamp, and I threw it at him. I did not know where I threw it for it was dark in there. Then I was real mad for I always had to take the calling down all the time. So I had gone downstairs, and the wife came halfway downstairs, still hollering at him. So I...I don't remember, it was madness, I guess. Then I think I grabbed a paring knife, I think it was. The next thing I remember, she was laying on the bed. I think after I had seen her laying there, I went back downstairs. Then her dad came down with his head bleeding, so I told John to go to Charlie's to phone for the police. I think that is all."

"You mentioned that they were over to the neighbors. Who do you mean by 'they'?"

"Me and my wife. Yeah, I was working every day. It was nagging, nagging every day. I couldn't seem to please her. I got a pretty bad temper. I blew right up, I guess."

He, Hanks Leroy Hanks, did hereby declare that the above statement was made by him, it was read by him, that he had been given the opportunity to alter it, and that he fully understood it.

The statement was signed by Hanks Hanks, witnessed by Robert G. Malard, with the officer in charge being Detective Sergeant D. Dennis.

Sergeant Dennis then contacted the Crown attorney, S. A. K. Logan, QC, Sarnia, and advised him of the details pertaining to this murder. On his instructions, a charge of noncapital murder was laid against Hanks Leroy Hanks. He was lodged in Lambton County Jail in Sarnia, at which time all his clothing was seized for the possibility of further evidence being obtained at the Center of Forensic Science.

On that same day, I received a phone call at 3:45 a.m., at which time I was dispatched to Kettle Point Indian Reservation in Lambton County. I arrived at the residence of Wellington Edwards at 6:30 a.m. with Corporal Adams. There were always two attending a major crime scene, one doing all the necessary work at the scene, the other taking notes for the one doing the work. After looking over the crime scene, I photographed from all angles the body of the deceased Sandra on the bed and took close-ups of the wounds to the body.

Measurements were taken from all points of the body to the four walls of the room so that when the photos were shown in court, the jury would get a clear picture of the body position and location. Photos were also taken of the injuries to Wellington Elijah and throughout the house, showing the layout of the house and the trail of blood from the bed, down the stairs, through the living room, kitchen, and to the back door. Blood samples were taken from the bed, the floor in the bedroom, the stairs, living room, and the kitchen, which showed the trail of blood down the stairs from the upstairs bedrooms and through the downstairs rooms to the back door.

At 11:20 a.m., I left the house and proceeded to the Sarnia General Hospital, where I attended the postmortem of Sandra Hanks, which was performed by Dr. Pearson.

At the postmortem, further photos were taken of the wounds to the body. Her fingerprints were taken. The preliminary findings were that the deceased, Sandra Hanks, died from stab wounds to her left chest and into the heart. In Dr. Pearson's opinion, death was instantaneous.

At 5:15 p.m., I arrived back at the Hanks house to take photos of the exterior of the house. The clothing and other exhibits were turned over to me, those belonging to both the victim and the husband. I found the murder weapon on the kitchen counter, some blood still showing on it. I picked it up and bagged and tagged it.

Wellington Edward's story varied with regard to the time and in the sequence of certain events, but basically the facts were that the two oldest babies who were asleep upstairs had awakened and had been crying, and Sandra had gone up to take care of them, followed by Hanks. At this time Wellington was lying in the second bedroom upstairs. Hanks got into a verbal argument with him and threw a kerosene lamp at him, which resulted in him receiving severe lacerations to his head, from which he lost a large amount of blood. Hanks had been fighting with his wife, and Wellington said that he saw Hanks with a paring knife in his hand, but he didn't see him use it. Afterward, Hanks went downstairs followed by his father-in-law, Wellington, who was bleeding profusely from head wounds, and there was blood in both bedrooms, down the stairs, and through the living room into the kitchen.

On Sunday, March 22, 1965, Henry Leroy Hanks appeared in magistrate's court in Sarnia on a charge of noncapital murder. He was remanded in custody until March 29, at which time further remands would be granted, allowing the time to build his case. The accused was not represented by counsel.

Investigation revealed that Sandra and Hanks had been married for approximately four years and had three small children: Alana, aged three; Melody, aged two; and Hanks Jr., two months. They had no permanent home of their own and had lived with his brother, John, on the Muncey Indian Reservation near London. Hanks had previously lived in Detroit.

John stated, "Hanks had gotten into an argument with his father-in-law and threw a kerosene lamp at him, which caused severe laceration to him, causing him to lose a lot of blood. Hanks had been fighting with his wife and Wellington. He said he saw Hanks with a paring knife in his hand, but he did not see him use it. Afterwards, Hanks went downstairs followed by Wellington, who was bleeding profusely from head wounds, and there was blood in both bedrooms, down the stairs, through the living room, and into the kitchen. There was very little blood around Sandra's body. While this entire fracas was going on upstairs, he was still in the kitchen."

In his statement to the investigators, he said that he heard a rumpus going on upstairs but didn't bother getting involved in it. Hanks had been up and downstairs two or three time using foul language to his wife and father-in-law, and on two different occasions, Hanks was standing in the kitchen near where the utensils were kept. While standing there, it was when he no doubt picked up the paring knife.

When the dispute stopped upstairs, Wellington asked John to get his boots so he could be taken to get some medical help. At this point, Wellington advised that he was not aware that his daughter Sandra was dead, and that he was going to get medical assistance for himself. John could find only one of Wellington's boots. At this time, Hanks told John to go and get the Ontario Provincial Police. John left the house and went to the residence of Mrs. Shawkence and asked her to call the police, which she did. This was at 2:00 a.m.

After Hanks had been taken into Sarnia and the body of Sandra had been photographed from all angles and measurements taken of the position of the body on the bed, the body was removed from the premises. Arrangements were made to have the brother-in-law, Morley Pearson, look after the three Hanks children; subsequently, he came and removed the three children. The interior of the house was photographed and measurements were taken so a plan drawing could be prepared for the trial so the jurors could see the layout inside of the house.

In a brief summary of the case, it would appear there was no premeditation with respect to the killing of Sandra Hanks. They had, in all appearances, been quite happy earlier on the day of the murder. They had gone into town with Morley Best, the brother-in-law, to the laundromat and had returned home with the taxi driver, George Schouler. They had supper with the father-in-law, Wellington, and after supper advised they were going for a bag of potatoes. Instead they went into town with Marshall Best and purchased twenty-four bottles of beer in the Brewers' retail store. They then returned home to drink it with Wellington.

Sometime during the course of the evening, they had gone over to the neighbor, John Ashquabe, to get something more to drink, which they were unable to obtain, and he had given them a few cigarettes to last until the next day. They then returned home, and it was after that the domestic quarrel took place, resulting in the death of Sandra Hanks.

When the police arrived at the house at approximately 2:30 a.m., all the beer was gone, and the blood alcohol of the deceased was 1.6/1000, and her urine was 2.2/1000. A breathalyser test was taken of Hanks at 7:02 a.m. and was .01, which is a very low reading. He had been in custody for five hours before the test was taken, so his blood alcohol would have been much higher when Sandra was killed.

There had been marital strife between Sandra and Hanks through the years of their married life. Her family, the Edwards, did not think much of Hanks as he was from the Muncey Reserve near London, Ontario, and he did not have steady employment. Also, he had been in and out of jail for forging checks and theft. The last time he was sentenced to six months in the Burwash Prison Farm for theft.

In summarizing the whole course of events, the Crown would have had a good case of manslaughter rather than the charge of noncapital murder. Everyone in this affair was related, and they are prone to testify but do not make good witnesses and are likely to forget anything they may have told police on the previous occasion. They are most unreliable witnesses in any court proceedings. However, he was charged with noncapital murder, and the jury brought in a guilty verdict. He was sentenced to fifteen years in jail.

Note: Some of the occurrences I dealt with were much shorter incidents, so I put them under "Bits and Pieces" and inserted them between the bigger occurrences.

Bits and Pieces 1

There was one occasion I got dispatched to an alleged murder in Drumbo, a small community east of the city of Woodstock in Oxford County.

I entered the house through the back door where the investigating officers were there waiting for my arrival. I was told that the husband had killed the wife in their upstairs bedroom.

I went up to the second floor and down the hall to the bedroom. A female body was lying on the bed on its back. The face and neck were covered with blood. Apparently the husband had used a broken liquor bottle when the bottom third was gone, and just the sharp broken edge remained, which the husband had used that broken end. He shoved it into the wife's face and neck several times. Her whole face and neck were riddled with deep cuts. She was unrecognizable with all the cuts and blood.

After the photos were taken, I found the broken bottle that had been used. It had been a liquor bottle. The top two-thirds of the bottle had an uneven jagged and pointed end where it had been separated from the bottom third.

The husband, when I went back downstairs, was sitting inside the back door. He had a small object in hands about the size of a book of matches. It was a small piece of material, which was really nothing of interest to anyone. He kept turning it around in his hands, looking wide-eyed at it and mumbling something about how amazing it was. He just sat there, ignoring the police officers who were there.

When asked questions, he did not respond; he just kept looking at the small object in his hands and mumbling.

He was taken to the detachment office in Woodstock, where he was questioned about the killing of his wife. There was no response from him; he just sat there with the small object in his hands. He was lodged in the jail cells at the detachment office, and a careful check on him was carried out until there was a proper facility where he be looked after properly.

He was charged with the capital murder of his wife.

The next day he appeared before a judge in Magistrate Court, where he was remanded to a mental facility for sixty days where he would be examined for assessment.

Three months after the murder, he appeared in court and was represent by a duty council lawyer. It was determined that he was mentally unfit to be tried for murder and was committed to a mental hospital for treatment.

A year or so after he was committed to a mental hospital, I heard that he was getting better, and he was getting some weekend passes to spend some time visiting his children at his mother's residence.

CHAPTER TWENTY-FOUR

Murder Caused by Bottle of Wine

This chapter deals with the murder of Dennis Doggart by Thomas George Stonewall on February 23, 1967.

Dennis had been born to William Heart and Myrtle Doggart on March 20, 1925. His father was North American Aboriginal while his mother was Caucasian. Dennis had married Marie Stonewall but had been living with Rena Blackbird for the past several years. They had no permanent home, and Dennis had a lengthy criminal record.

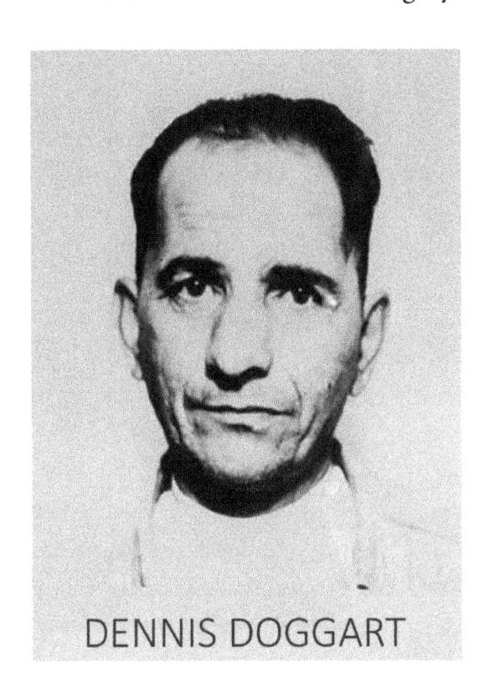

DENNIS DOGGART

Thomas George Stonewall had been born to MacAlpine and Lucy Stonewall on March 29, 1939. Thomas had a record of thefts, including numerous car thefts. He was given a complete mental and physical examination while in the Ontario Psychiatric Hospital at St. Thomas from December 2 to 29, 1961, and was diagnosed as a psychoneurotic of the mixed type. He was found to be mentally ill or mentally defective, and when under emotional stress, he demonstrated a severe stutter and muscle spasm on the left side of his face. Apparently as a young boy, he fell on his head out of a barn and developed these symptoms after the fall. He had no permanent home and for the past few weeks had been staying with his father in one room of an old eight-room house owned by Norman Hopper. Thomas's father, MacAlpine Stonewall, was allowed to live in the house rent-free, and in return, he looked after Hopper's cattle.

On Thursday, February 23, 1967, at about 10:00 a.m., MacAlpine walked to Hopper's house and asked him to order some groceries. Mrs. Hopper looked after Stonewall's money, and Mr. Hopper ordered the groceries, deducting the amount from the money held by Mrs. Hopper, and then drove Stonewall home.

Shortly before noon, Wilson Doggart (Dennis's brother) and two of his young sons drove to the home of his father, William Henry Doggart. They then drove to Rodney, came back, and then drove to Dennis Doggart's home to deliver Dennis's children's allowance check. They were met there by Dennis Doggart and his common-law wife Rena and her two small children. Then they went out for more groceries. Rena gave Dennis $1, and he bought one bottle of wine at the liquor store in Dutton, which they drank at the dump. Rena was saving $10 for rent and would not give him any more money for wine, so they drove to Stonewall's looking for some.

MacAlpine Stonewall was in the pasture while his son, Thomas, was across the road. Upon their arrival, Thomas and William remained at the house while the others left in Wilson's car. About 3:45 p.m., they arrived at Hopper's home, and MacAlpine asked for $5 of his money, which he was given. They drove to the liquor store, and Dennis bought four bottles of wine with the $5. They all returned to MacAlpine's house, and they began drinking the wine.

They had consumed three of the bottles of the wine when a car occupied by Roy Delenny and Elwood Fearce arrived from the Muncey Indian Reserve and drove into the lane. Rena remained in the house with the children and William Doggart, who was in bed in a stupor. The others were outside in the car. MacAlpine sat in the front seat, Thomas sat in the right back seat, and Wilson and Dennis remained outside near the driver's door. Fellows produced a bottle of wine and it was soon consumed. Delenny and Fellows departed, and the others returned to the house.

While the men were absent from the house, Rena hid the remaining bottle of wine under a coat on the bed against the wall. She knew that when they returned to the house, Dennis would be fighting mad and beat her up.

MacAlpine and Thomas entered the house first. Thomas wanted to know where the bottle was. As Wilson Doggart entered, Thomas pointed a gun at him, and his eyes bugged out. Dennis then entered the room. Thomas pointed a gun at him and again asked where the wine was. Dennis said he didn't have it.

Rena started to cross the room to produce the bottle of wine when she heard a shot fired over her head. The bullet must have missed Dennis because Wilson saw Thomas do something to the gun. Then there was a click, and Thomas fired again, and Dennis fell to the floor. Thomas made a grab for Wilson, and Wilson wrestled the gun away from him and threw it on the floor. Rena ran outside of the house in a northerly direction to the farm of William McAllister. Thomas obtained the gun, threw it through a window opening under the house, and continued in the direction of the BP service center on the 401 highway.

At 5:00 p.m., Leah Hauser, a sixty-year-old woman, was at the cash register of the service center restaurant as Thomas Stonewall entered. She knew him because he had worked for her a few years ago on their farm.

"Where is the phone?" Stonewall asked. "I just murdered a man and want to call the police."

Leah pointed him to the patio and said, "There are two phones in there."

"What about the one there beside you?"

"It's for private use."

He kept repeating, "I just murdered a man, and I want to call the police."

"Oh, Tommy, I don't think you did."

Stonewall kept repeating, "I killed a man and murdered the man. I shot him in the head with an automatic."

Leah Hauser went to Mrs. Manning's office and told her, "There is a man out front who says he killed a man and that we should call the police."

She came back out front where the waitresses got him a cup of coffee and made him an order of toast. She said later that they thought the food might calm him down; she told him to eat, that it might make him feel better.

"I shouldn't be eating. I murdered a man, Dennis Doggart," he repeated. When any other customers came into the restaurant, Stonewall told them, "I murdered a man." He also kept muttering to himself, "I told Dennis to leave me alone." He had been using some pretty strong language. Then he said, "Are you sure you called the police?"

Constable Don Leach was travelling east on the 401 highway when he was dispatched to the BP Service Center. He was told to proceed there directly and see one of the waitresses at the restaurant. He was told there was a person there who been involved in a serious criminal occurrence and to bring him back to the detachment. No names were mentioned, nor was he told the nature of the crime that had taken place.

Leach headed back to Currie Road where he met up with another police officer, Constable Anderson, also heading to the service center. Anderson advised him that the person at the Service Center was Thomas Stonewall, and he been involved in a shooting. No other details were given, and he was told not to question anyone there.

Leach parked the cruiser in front of the main door to the restaurant. He went inside, and Mrs. Manning, standing at the cashiers counter, pointed to Stonewall and said, "There's your man."

Lech had known Thomas Stonewall for some time and told him, "Come with me."

Stonewall had been looking at Leach as he was standing by the cashier's counter. "Are you happy now?" he said, and taking his arm, he brushed a cup and saucer and plate off the counter. He came to the restaurant door toward Leach. It appeared that he was a little unsteady on his feet. Leach could smell intoxicants as he came closer but didn't know if the odor came from his breath or his clothes.

Leach followed Stonewall from the restaurant to the cruiser. He opened the door to the cruiser, and before he got in the cruiser, Leach searched him.

As Stoneall was being searched, he said, "I haven't got a gun on me."

Leach then told Stonewall to get in the car. As Leach was driving, Stonewall turned and looked at Leach and said, "Are you happy now? A man is dead." He repeated it three more times.

On the way to the detachment, Leach was advised by Constable Anderson that there was a death involved and to call a coroner and a corporal. He was further advised to contact the London Identification

Unit. When Leach got to the office, Stonewall was again searched and then lodged in a cell. Stonewall did not make any further comments.

As the London Identification Unit had been summoned, I arrived at the at the old farm house at 7:30 p.m. with Corporal Adams. It was an old house, and it was a mess. I came in through the back door and turned left down a short hallway. There was not much of a floor left down this hallway leading to the only room being occupied in the building. The room was approximately fifteen feet wide and twelve feet deep with no windows. There was a bed on the left as you entered and two or three chairs plus a small table on the right, and the lighting was poor. There was also a small heater in the room. Photos were taken showing the body from different angles and close-ups of his face and the entrance wound. Other photos were taken displaying the room.

The body was tagged and removed to St. Joseph's Hospital, Chatham. On arriving at the hospital at 10:15 p.m., the body was taken to the morgue, which was a room on the roof of the hospital. The smell coming off the body was bad. The clothing was removed in preparation for the autopsy the next morning. After the rubber boots were removed, the clothing consisted of six pairs of socks, two pair of johns, one pair of undershorts, one black-and-white jacket, one army pullover and one red, white, and blue plaid shirt. I fingerprinted the body, and then we left hospital. The autopsy was scheduled for the next morning.

The next morning, I was at the autopsy room at 7:45 a.m. Dr. John Fellows, a pathologist from London, was there to do the postmortem. The bullet wound entered through the right eye. No damage was done to the eyelid, indicating that it must have been open. The bullet had lodged in the head, and there was no exit wound.

Thomas Stonewall was charged with noncapital murder. The trial was held in the St. Thomas courtroom in July. On the third day of the trial, it was a hot day to be sitting in the courtroom with no air-conditioning. In the afternoon it was rather dull and boring, and I suspect most people were almost asleep. The witness in the box was being asked about some of the events that took place on the day of the shooting. The Crown, Peter Gammage, asked the witness a question and received an answer. The accused, Stonewall, took exception to the answer. He jumped up in the prisoner box and screamed out loud, "You're a fucking liar!"

All the people in the courtroom—the judge, lawyers, and spectators—were abruptly jarred awake. The trial ended the next day. Stonewall was sentenced to fifteen years in jail.

Bits and Pieces 2

Physical comparisons were made involving many hit-and-run accidents. I went to many of these occurrences to photograph the scene and look for evidence left at the scene by the hit-and-run vehicle. The found evidence would be matched up to the vehicle when the vehicle was located. Here are some of those.

A fatal accident occurred on a very sandy road on the Walpole Island Indian Reserve. An elderly man was riding his bicycle along a dirt road when he was hit from behind pretty hard by a car apparently driving a lot faster than he should have been driving on this road. The old fellow, when hit, was thrown well off the road. He was found dead. The Walpole Island Police requested our presence at the scene.

After arriving at the location of the accident, the area was photographed. The vehicle and its driver did not remain at the accident scene, and the body had been removed before I got there; it was a hit and run. I checked the area where the man was hit. I spent a couple hours there checking and crawling through the sandy area.

The time was well spent. On checking through the sand, I finally found a small grayish paint chip in the sand, which they believed came from the hit-and-run vehicle. The Walpole police were shown the chip, and then they went around the reservation looking for the vehicle. They knew the owners of all those who drove gray cars. It wasn't too long after seeing the chip that they found the car and where on the car the chip had broken from. The area on the car was photographed with the chip back in its place. Later at our office, I made a chart showing the chip in place. I would use this in court when giving my evidence.

RT showing the paint chip I found after search.

Another fatal hit and run occurred west of Dorchester on Catherine Street. Two boys were riding their bikes on the shoulder of the south side of the road in single file and heading west. A car heading east on the road went off the road and on to the shoulder of the road, hitting the second boy in line, throwing him off his bike and killing him.

I arrived at the scene a short time after. Photos were taken. I then started looking for any evidence that I could find that was left by the car.

Searching for anything left behind by the hit-and-run vehicle.

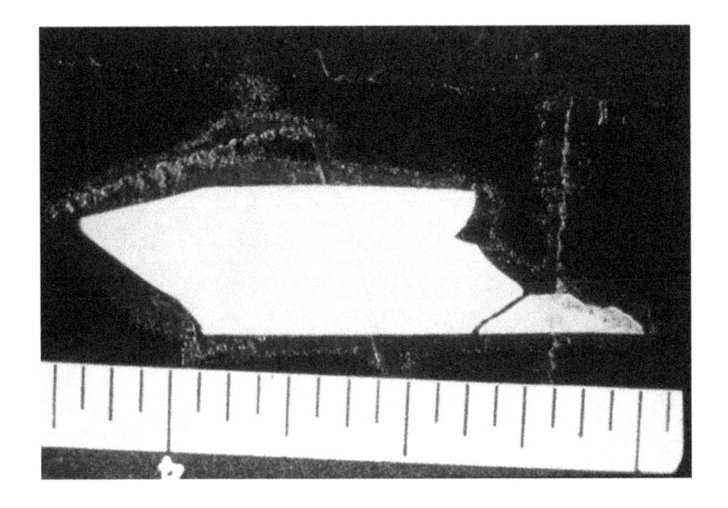

With the aid of a newspaper photographer and my photo floodlight, I was able to crawl around the area where the boy was hit to look for evidence.

A small paint chip shown on the right in this picture was found. It matched up with the bigger piece from the hit-and-run vehicle when it was found.

Late one evening, a teenager reported that someone threw a portion of a piece of grate from a small coal or woodstove through his windshield. It was wrapped in a piece of red cloth. The officers on patrol that night were advised. About 1:30 a.m., a vehicle was stopped, and the car and its occupants were checked for booze and their sobriety. Upon looking inside the vehicle, the officer who stopped the car found a piece of red cloth on the floor at the passenger's feet. The red cloth was retained by the officer, and the three in the car were taken to the office. I was advised and a short while later, I received that piece of cloth the officer found and took from the car he stopped.

I went ahead and matched the two pieces of cloth. The piece of cloth on the top was taken from the car that was stopped. The bottom piece of cloth was wrapped around the stove grate that went through the car windshield that was reported earlier.

A chart was made up showing the pieces of cloth matched.

A man parked his car on the shoulder of the road on the east side of Wonderland Road a few yards south of no. 7 Highway. He was picked by his buddy, and they headed into London for a meeting. When the meeting was over, he was driven back to his car. When he got back to his car, he found damage to it. Someone had run into his car, causing some damage to it. On the ground near the damaged area, he found a piece of metal. He called the police because it was a hit and run.

I was also dispatched to assist in the investigation. After the photos were taken, I retained the small piece of metal that was on the ground near the damaged area. The hit-and-run vehicle was located the next day through the assistance of a body shop. I was then able to match up the metal found at the scene to the vehicle causing the occurrence. The little red square in this photo shows where the piece found at the scene came from on the hit-and-run vehicle. I went to the body shop and removed the piece of metal that matched the piece found at the scene.

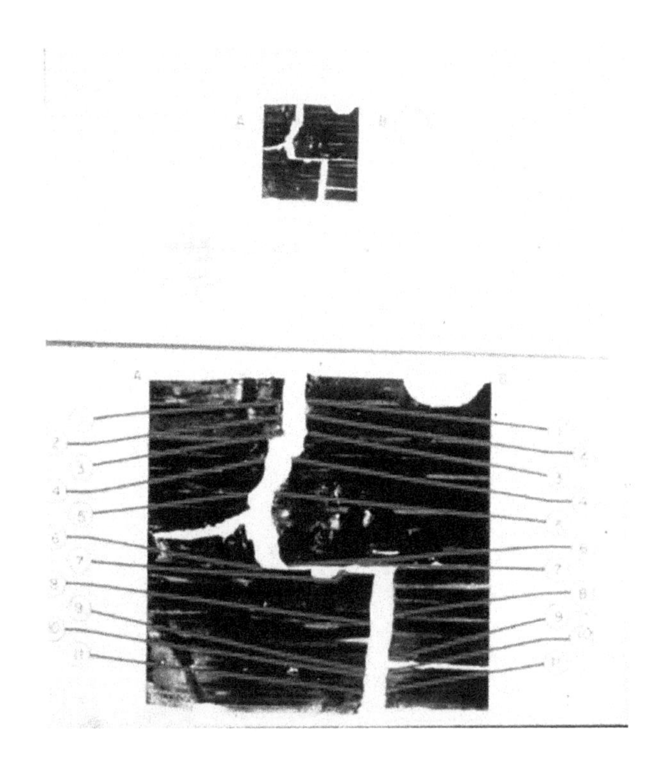

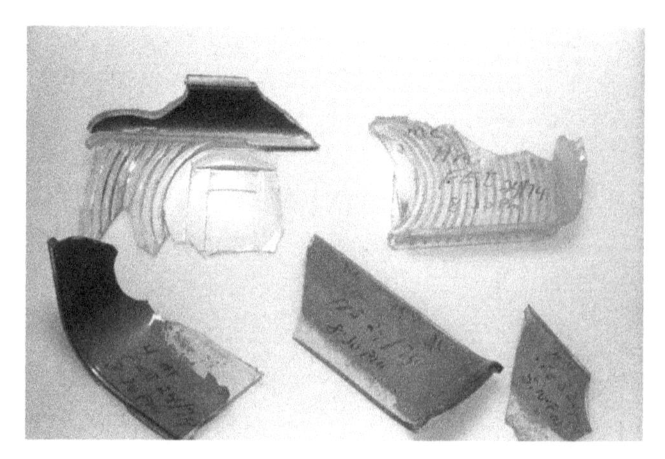

Pieces of a car's parking light was picked up at an accident scene and matched up to a piece of the parking light that was left on the car.

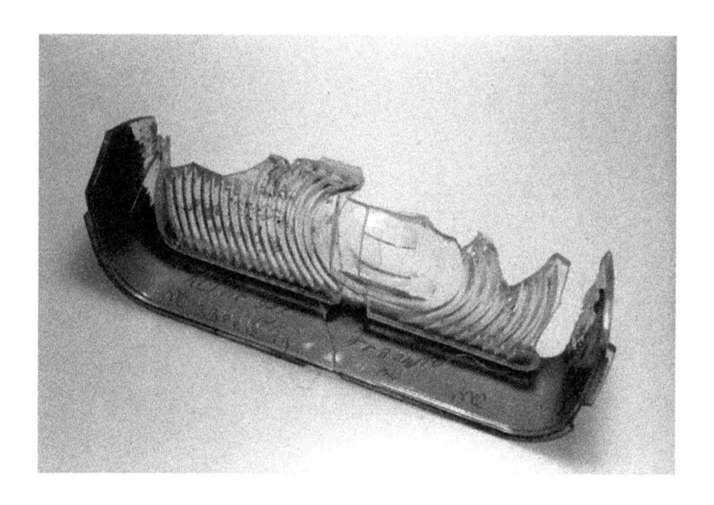

CHAPTER TWENTY-FIVE

Hit and Run, Death Fire

On August 14, 1967, at 8:00 p.m., Leonard Williams loaned his car, a 1965 Chevrolet, to John Vandy Morgan, age 26, of Hyde Park, Ontario.

On the evening of August 15, Morgan and his wife were going to a birthday party in Delaware. A short while before they were to leave the house, they got into an argument. It got so bad that John left the house in a mad rage without his wife and was on his way to the party by himself a short time after 9:00 p.m.

Meanwhile, Michael Munroe and John O'Conner left their employer's residence at 9:15 p.m. and were walking east on Sarnia Road. Munroe said to the police later that he heard the roar of a fast-moving car coming up from behind them while they were walking on the shoulder. He turned and noticed the car about three hundred to five hundred feet behind them. It left the road and started travelling on the shoulder of the road directly toward the two of them. He yelled at O'Conner to watch out, but it was too late—the car hit O'Conner. Munroe thought the car was a 1962 Chevrolet, but found out later it was a 1965, and it had not slowed down or had applied the car's brakes. The car sped away, heading east.

At 9:30 p.m., John Morgan drove through the station lot where Williams's business was located. A hired hand of Williams, Robert Richmond of Hyde Park, saw Morgan drive into and through the service station lot. Williams was watching TV at the time and did not see or hear his car.

On August 15 at 9:43 p.m., Constable Ron Botton was dispatched to a hit-and-run pedestrian accident on County Road 17 (Sarnia Road.), .6 miles west of the junction of county roads 17 and 20. He arrived at the scene at 10:02 p.m. The road at this location is a flat twenty-two feet of pavement, dry and bare, with a thirteen-foot grass shoulder. There was a broken single center line on the road that was clear and visible.

There were no visible skid marks found on the road at the scene of the accident. The posted speed limit was fifty miles per hour. When he arrived at the scene, Constable Botton learned that the injured party, John Campbell O'Conner, had been removed from the scene and transported by Thames Valley ambulance to St. Joseph's Hospital in London. At 9:48 p.m., on arrival at the hospital, O'Conner was pronounced dead by Dr. R. J. Baker.

Michael Moore, who was with O'Conner when he was hit, pointed out to Botton the location of the impact point where O'Conner had been struck by the car. The weather at the time was clear. There was no apparent reason for the car to go off the road. At the time of the accident, there was no other traffic on the road in either direction.

Photos were taken at the scene and the position of the body by Constable Botton. When he arrived and looked over the scene, he found part of a side-view mirror.

At 10:20 p.m., Constable Jackman, while on patrol on Highway 2 west of Lambeth, was advised by a motorist that there was a car on fire one mile south of the highway on the Delaware-Westminster Town Line. Jacobs proceeded to the scene of the fire where he found a 1965 Chevrolet with license number E40-899 registered to Leonard Wilkinson of RR 1 Hyde Park.

After leaving the scene of the fatal accident, Jackman went to the scene of the car fire. After his arrival, JJacobs gave him a piece of yellow cloth, which had been embedded in some of the crumpled metal of the right front fender of the burning car. He also advised Jackman that he had checked the vehicle registration and gave him the owner's name.

At 1:20 a.m. on August 16, again on patrol, Jacobs observed a male person standing at the junction of Highway 2 and Sharon Road, 1.1 miles north east of the burning car. Jacobs stopped and asked, "Who are you, and what are you doing here?"

The male person identified himself as John Vandy Norgan of RR 1 Hyde Park. He was not hitchhiking. Morgan said to Jackman, "A funny thing happened to him. I was in Delaware, and his car was stolen."

Jackman told him, "Get in the car, and you will accompany me to the office where they will get this all straightened out."

Morgan got into the cruiser, and Jacobs then drove to the detachment office.

At the office, Morgan told the desk officer, "Two masked men held me up at his house at approximately 8:30 to 9:00 p.m. and forced me to drive them to Delaware."

Jackman called Botton at the hospital to find out more about the accident. He was advised earlier that Morgan was seen at 9:30 p.m. driving through the lot where Williams worked and was seen to be by himself.

Jackman again questioned Morgan and asked about the fact he had been seen on the lot by Robert Richards.

Morgan broke down and finally admitted causing the accident. He was charged with dangerous driving.

He appeared in court at a later date and pleaded guilty to the charge. He was convicted. His license was suspended for three years and was sentenced to three years in jail.

Bits and Pieces 3

I was called to a doctor's office in Lambeth as a result of a break and enter. When the doctor's secretary arrived to start her workday, she found the safe in the office severely damaged and with the door also badly damaged and open. The safe contained only a few records. What the bad guys did not notice was the 10"×12" sign on top of the safe:

THIS SAFE IS NOT LOCKED

The staff at a flower shop in the town of Strathroy came to work and started doing their daily tasks. One of the employees needed something in the walk-in safe, which was built in as part of the building and office. The safe was a room approximately eight feet wide and about ten feet deep. The employee dialed the numbers to open the door. When the safe was open, to her disbelief, she saw the mess inside the safe. She couldn't believe what she was seeing until she looked up to the ceiling and discovered the hole.

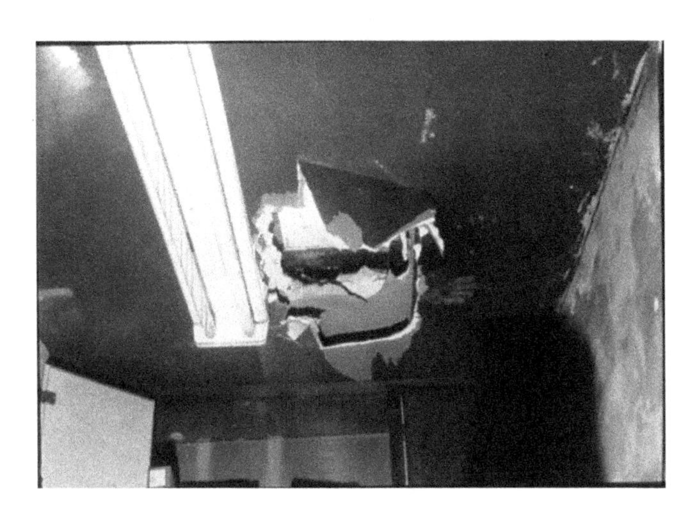

This safe was built with twelve-inch-thick walls on all four sides, which included a twelve-inch-thick ceiling through to the outside roof. I then went outside and with the aid of a ladder, I went up onto the roof. The bad guys had spent a few hours digging the hole through and into the interior of the safe. It was a small hole; I couldn't really believe how anyone could get through hole into the safe and back out as it wasn't a very big hole.

About two months after the safe job at the flower shop in Strathroy, I was called to a breaking, entering, and theft at the Tender Tootsie Factory Warehouse in Glencoe. The employees came to work that morning and found that their office was a mess as it had been ransacked. It was quite apparent that somebody had gotten into the building and had rummaged through the shelves and file cabinets. They were apparently looking for cash or anything worth stealing.

The employees went around the entire interior of the building, checking all the doors and the few windows. They did not find any damage to any of the doors, and there were no windows broken or forced open. They did, however, find a door unlocked on the north side of the building, which they knew had been locked the previous afternoon when their day's work was completed. There were no fingerprints found, other than those of the employees.

A few days after the break-in, it rained. They found how the B&E occurred. In a remote area of the warehouse, rainwater was coming in through a hole in the roof. It was then quite apparent that one of the bad guys came in through the hole, opened the door to let his buddies in, they did what they came for, and left through the door and left it unlocked.

CHAPTER TWENTY-SIX

Taxi Driver's Fare to His Death

Gerald Miller born on March 9, 1920, and at the time of his death was married with two children. He had served in the RCAF. He was discharged about five years earlier while stationed at Ontario. He had since lived in Hagersville, moving to St. Thomas in the late summer of 1967. While still serving in the air force, he was stationed at Aylmer. He had been employed on a part-time basis driving a taxi for Cox Cabs Ltd., St. Thomas. When he retired, he took full-time employment with the taxi firm in 1967. He was in arrears of his rent for his home at 66 Kains Street in St. Thomas.

On the morning of Friday, February 9, 1968, Miller received his weekly pay from Cox Cabs Ltd. in a brown pay envelope, which contained five $20s, one $10, and 69 cents in change. He gave his wife one $20 and $10 bill prior going to work. He put the rest of the bills in his pocket. About 4:30 p.m., he was picked up by a fellow worker who took him to work. Later, according to his wife, he had another $7 in his pocket and his money changer with silver money in it to make change. During the evening he made seven trips, entering the details of each trip on a worksheet attached to his clipboard in the taxi. The last trip recorded was John Bailey, who noted that Miller was sober and normal. Bailey was dropped off at 39 Joyce Street at 10:15 p.m. Miller then returned to the taxi office on Talbot Street. At that time, he had $110 in bills and his money changer.

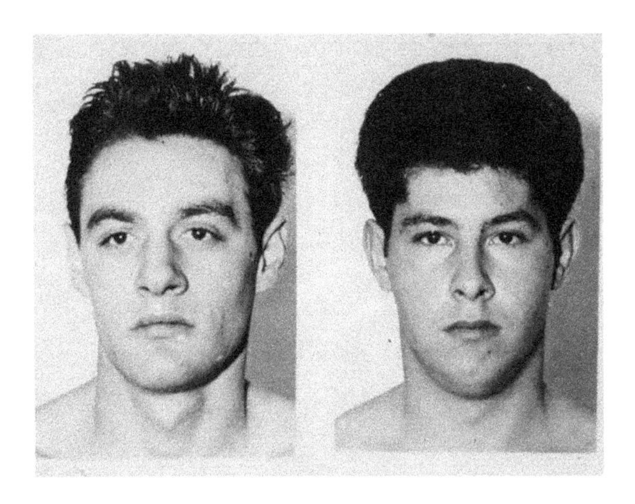

Meanwhile, between ten and eleven on this same Friday morning, Larry Wallace, age 22, and Ernie Butler, age 21, both ex-inmates of the Kingston Penitentiary and released in the autumn of 1967, were having a discussion with Wallace's cousin Larry Kinsman about his proposed trip to the Bahamas. In the conversation, Kinsman insisted that they did not need a birth certificate or a passport and would have a better advantage starting a new life in the Bahamas. Kinsman also suggested that if they could raise about $100, the three of them could go to the Bahamas together.

Wallace and Butler liked the idea and said they would see what they could do about raising some money. At this time Butler and Wallace were both wearing gloves. Butler removed one of the gloves to show Kinsman that he was wearing a brass knuckle on one hand. Butler then borrowed $2 from Kinsman.

In the evening of this same day, Wallace and Butler entered Al's Poolroom on Talbot Street around 8:30 p.m. They stayed there only a short time while they tried to borrow a dollar from the proprietor, Al Stacy. They left the poolroom and returned sometime around 10:30 p.m.

At 10:34 p.m., Cox Cabs Ltd. received a call requesting a taxicab to Al's Poolroom for a trip to Port Stanley. The cab was requested to be there immediately. The dispatcher gave the pickup to Miller.

Miller double-parked in front of the poolroom and went inside. After about five minutes, the two players at the first table saw Wallace and Butler follow Miller out and get into the back seat of the taxi, which drove off, apparently heading to Port Stanley.

A few minutes after 11:00 p.m., Mr. and Mrs.Vandepelt left a card party in the hamlet of Union. They proceeded west to no. 4 Highway on the County Road. While driving along the road, they saw what they thought was a pile of clothes on the south shoulder of the road, so they stopped the car and backed up to check it out.

What they thought was clothing turned out to be a male body, facedown on the shoulder of the road. They backed up to the first farmhouse driveway, that of Ray Anderson's. Arriving at the farmhouse, the Vandepelts told Anderson about finding a body on the shoulder of the road. Anderson then phoned the police at St. Thomas.

At 11:30 p.m., Constable J. Edwards and other officers arrived at the scene. The body was later identified to be the taxi driver, Gerald Miller. Constable Edwards got on the phone and called DHQ London, requesting that the identification unit be dispatched to the scene.

The coroner, Dr. C. A. Bell of Port Stanley, was called. He arrived at the location of the body shortly after midnight. It was apparent that Miller had suffered extensive injuries to his head, and blood was in evidence for some forty feet along the roadway from the body.

The body was lying facedown on the south shoulder of the road with his head to the west. There was a great deal of blood under his head and under the upper part of his body.

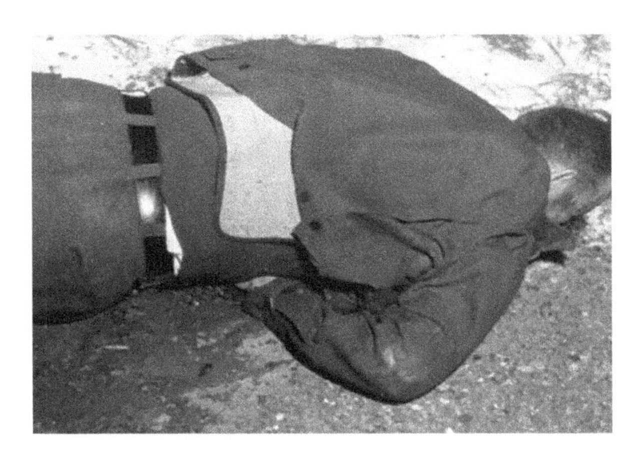

The clothing appeared to be intact, and the money changer, containing some silver, was still attached to his belt, but no other money was found on the body. Approximately forty feet to the east was a trampled area in the snow on the south shoulder and what appeared to be snow tire tracks. At this time the temperature was -20°F with a strong wind blowing from the north. Near the tire tracks, a small piece of red tinfoil was collected immediately by Constable Wild. Constable Wild is a police officer who checked things out. On the opposite side of the road, an empty bottle of with the label "Canadian Westminster Sherry" was found and also collected.

I received the call from the dispatcher requesting my presence at the murder scene. On the way, I stopped in Lambeth and picked up Corporal Adams, who would assist me at the crime scene. We arrived at the scene at 1:16 a.m. on February 10, 1968, and photographed the body, roadway, boot prints, and the tire tracks. Measurements were also taken. We were in and out of the car, which we kept running all the time because it was so cold. The camera kept freezing up, which also gave us a little chance to warm up a bit.

When the removal service arrived, the body was turned over and photographed to show his blood-covered face and the gravel on his clothes from being beaten up and dragged by the underside of the taxi.

The removal service had been told to take the body to the St. Thomas General Hospital. I strongly suggested the body should be taken to Victoria Hospital in London where there was a more experienced forensic pathologist who would do the autopsy with more accurate results.

At 11:40 p.m. Peter Farmer, a Cox Cab driver, observed taxi 17, which he knew was being operated by Miller, parked on Leila Street. The taxi appeared to be abandoned, and the roof light was illuminated, but no other lights were on. The engine was still warm and switched off with the key still in the ignition. The contents of the glove compartment were scattered on the floor. The police were called by the taxi dispatcher, and when the police arrived, the taxi was placed under guard until it could be properly checked out by the identification officers.

From the location of the taxi, Sergeants Dennis and Topper followed footprints east on Leila Street to Ross Street, then north on Ross Street to Myrtle Street, and from there the footprints led directly to 6 Myrtle Street.

Dennis and Topper went to the house and found the occupants to be Mr. and Mrs. Dunn, with three boys and one girl in the house. Their son Larry, age 16, mentioned that at 12:15 a.m. on this same morning, he noticed a man at the corner of Ross and Myrtle Streets who appeared to be intoxicated. He described this man to be approximately twenty years old, six foot one inch tall, with a thin build and dark hair, which was combed forward and back. He was wearing a three-quarter-length brown suede coat with sheepskin lining inside. This unknown person was calling Larry and his brother Gerald sea-wee pigs and was laughing at the time. This information was passed on to Inspector Dan Higley and Constable Don Wild.

We finally left the scene when the body was removed at 5:45 a.m. We went to a restaurant in Port Stanley at 6:45 a.m. where we met some of the investigation team and had a hot coffee and breakfast. We were informed that the taxi Miller was driving was found abandoned on Leila Street in St. Thomas. We proceeded to Leila Street where the taxi was found and photographed both it and the footprints leading east and south on Leila Street.

The taxi was removed from Leila Street and taken to a garage in Talbotville to be examined by Mr. W. Towstiak, who had arrived from the Center of Forensic Science in Toronto. The underside of the vehicle showed extensive traces of blood. It was apparent that the body was dragged under the taxi, causing the forty-foot trail of blood leading up to where the body was found.

Other officers made inquiries at the office of Cox Cabs. They were advised that Miller's last call was a request for a taxi immediately to Al's Poolroom. As Al's was closed at that point, further enquiries had to wait.

Witnesses were later found who reported that at about 11:15 p.m. the previous night, Wallace and Butler were observed together entering the dance at the St. Thomas arena and paying the $1.25 admission fee. They were there for twenty minutes drinking soft drinks. They were then seen leaving the arena, and a short while later, they were seen eating and drinking in the Rendezvous Restaurant.

Sometime after 2:00 a.m., both Wallace and Butler were at Butler's residence drinking beer. They requested a neighbor, Stanley

Copland, to go to a bootlegger and purchase more beer for them. It was apparent that they were now in possession of funds they didn't have earlier. They then spent the rest of the night at the Butler home drinking the beer.

During the morning of February 10, 1968, personnel cleaning up the dance hall at the St. Thomas arena found two pairs of men's gloves that appeared to have bloodstains on them. Because of where they were found, it was believed the gloves had been deliberately hidden, so they reported them to police.

The piece of red tinfoil found at the scene led the investigators to the Liquor Control Board store, where it was identified as coming from the neck of a bottle of Canadian Westminster Sherry; no other bottle of liquor had an identical red foil.

The purchase orders for this type of wine bearing the date of February 9, 1968, were checked, and it was found that on that date, two bottles were purchased in the name of Larry Doners, a person noted for his violent temper. The description of Wallace was similar to that of the drunken person who was observed by youths on February 9 in the vicinity of Leila Street. However, the person who was identified by the youths had no connection to Wallace.

Dr. John Fellows, regional pathologist, performed an autopsy at St. Joseph's Hospital, London, and the following injuries were recorded:

1. The first to sixth ribs, right side, were fractured.
2. The right scapula was fractured.
3. The lower jaw was fractured.
4. The left cheekbone was fractured.
5. The base of the skull was fractured.
6. Seven stab wounds in the upper back of minimal depth.
7. Two stab wounds in the neck, one into the interior jugular vein and the rest of the stab wounds were in his back.
8. Numerous abrasions and bruises about the face and neck.

In the opinion of Dr. Fellows, Miller died of asphyxia caused by the aspiration of his own blood due to a severe beating he received.

Although the stab wounds and fractured skull were contributory, these in themselves were not considered fatal.

At 12:32 p.m. on February 10, 1968, Sergeants Topper and Dennis arrested Larry Ross Wallace on the north side of Talbot Street in St. Thomas, between Wallace's residence at 577 Talbot Street and the city hall. The officers were parked just east of 577 Talbot Street when they saw Wallace coming out of his residence. They drove up beside Wallace. Topper got out of the car, approached Wallace, and told him they wanted to talk to him. Wallace got into the front seat of the car. There was no conversation while driving to the detachment office.

At the detachment office, Wallace was taken to the corporal's office. When the door was closed, he was asked to take off his coat and remove everything from his pockets. He removed a black wallet containing two twenty dollar bills and one one dollar bill. In the right-hand pocket of his jacket he removed one set of brass knuckles, sixty-one cents, and two keys on a chain.

"Larry, I'm Sergeant Dennis, and this is Sergeant Topper, and they are interested in what you were doing last night."

Wallace replied, "That's a good question. I had supper at home. I don't know what time it was, then I went down to a friend's house."

"What was the friend's name?"

"Ernie Butler."

"Where does he live?"

"I don't know the address."

"What did you do at the friend's house?"

"Watched television, I guess."

"For how long did you two watch TV?"

"Oh, I'm not sure."

"What time did you leave your friend's place?"

"I can't remember."

"Where did you go after you left your friend's place?"

"We went up to the pool room."

"How long did you stay there?"

"Not very long. I'm not sure."

"What was the name of the poolroom?"

"Al's Billiards."

"Who were you with at the poolroom?"

"Ernie."

"How did you leave the poolroom?"

"Walking."

"How far did you walk when you left the poolroom?"

"Up to the dance at the arena."

"How long did you stay there?"

"Ten to fifteen minutes, maybe."

"Where did you go after you left the dance?"

"Up to the restaurant."

"What did you do there?"

"I had a plate of chips."

"Who were you with at the restaurant?"

"Ernie."

"How much money did you have when you were in the restaurant?"

"I have $41 now, so maybe I would have $43, something like that."

"Where did you get the $43?"

"I was working. I worked a couple of weeks. I always had some money on me."

"Did you try to borrow money last night?"

"No."

"After you were in the restaurant, where did you go?"

"Down to Ernie's."

"What did you do there?"

"Watched the late movies."

"What time did you leave Ernie's?"

"I stayed there all night."

"Did you ride in any taxi last night?"

"No."

"Why were you carrying those brass knuckles that were found in your jacket pocket?"

"I figured that I might have to use it sometime."

"When?"

"I heard there were some guys looking for me, so I thought I might as well have something."

"You said you were in a restaurant. What was the name of the restaurant?"

"The Rendezvous."

"Where is that?"

"It is on the main street about a block from the city hall, I guess."

"When was the last time you rode in a taxi?"

"About a week ago."

"What was the name of the taxi?"

"Cox Cabs."

"Where did you go?"

"Me and my sister came back from another girl's place."

"Did you have anything to drink last night?"

"No."

"Did you buy any liquor or wine yesterday?"

"No."

"Are you working at a job now?"

"No."

"When was the last time that you worked?"

"Three or four weeks ago."

"Where was that?"

"Victor Gasket."

"When were you paid last?"

"About the same time I quit."

"How much money did you receive?"

"Sixty-some odd dollars."

"Why are you not working now?"

"Because I can't get a job."

"Why are you not working at Victor Gasket?"

"I quit for another job."

"What happened to that job?"

"I worked one day, and the boss got his brother-in-law to take my place."

"Where was that?"

"Bob Brooks, in Aylmer Heating and Oil Burner Service."

"How old are you, Larry?"

"Twenty-two."

"What grade did you go in school?"

"Grade 9."

The questions and answers finished at 2:00 p.m.

"Who is at your house now?"

"My mother, father, and my kid sister."

"We have a search warrant to search your place. Do you want to come along with us?"

"I don't care, I guess."

At 12:50 p.m. on February 10, 1968, Butler again met up with Harry Kinsman at Kinsman's home. When Butler entered his house, he was carrying a bag containing liquor. He paid Kinsman the $2 that he had borrowed the previous day. He told Kinsman that he had about $45. A further check at the liquor store revealed a purchase of a bottle of liquor for $9.90 that day in the name of Larry Doners.

On Sunday, February 11, 1968, twelve extra police officers were brought in to do a complete search on both sides of the road where the body had been found; the road was still blocked off for traffic. The items found were the following:

1. One butcher knife with wooden handle with black electrical tape, six feet inside fence, twenty-five feet from south edge of road, 2.5/10th of a mile from where body was found
2. One black plastic wallet found, nine feet from north edge of road, 4.5/10th mile west of where body was found
3. One empty bottle of Westminster Canadian Sherry in a paper bag six feet from north edge of road 3/10th mile west of body
4. Two invoice books from Carr's Grocery, on south shoulder, 212 feet from body

5. One clipboard, Cox Cabs, car 17, found on old Highway 4, two feet three inches edge of road, 21/2 feet, from body
6. One empty bottle Westminster Canadian Sherry, seventeen feet south of where clipboard was found
7. One torn seat cushion, found eight feet from west edge of road 61/2 of a mile from body

At 11:20 a.m. on Sunday, February 11, 1968, Betty Keller, mother of Ernie Butler, was interviewed by police. She said that Ernie came to her house on the Friday evening about 8:00 p.m. He left and came back about twenty minutes later and brought a dozen beers home with him. He sat, watched TV, and drank the beer for the rest of the night. She asked him where he got the money to buy the beer; he said he still owed the bootlegger the money. His buddy, Larry, was there with him. She went to bed, and Larry stayed up.

At 7:45 p.m., Constables Gibbons and Wild came to the house. They showed Betty Keller the search warrant and read it to her, then pointed out the part where it referred to a knife with black tape on the handle. She said that if it had black tape on the handle, it was her knife. She produced two rolls of tape and told them that either Ernie or Billy wrapped it. She said the wooden handle was broken when she hit it with a hammer while splitting wood for a fire. She also described a second knife missing from her home as having a brown bone handle with a white tip. At Wild's request, she went into the kitchen to look for the knives and was unable to find either of them.

On Tuesday, February 13, 1968, investigators went again to interview Betty Keller. They showed her a picture of the knife with the tape on it. She said, "That is my knife."

The Crown attorney looked at the evidence that was presented to him: When they were in the poolroom when they had no money. They ordered a taxi to go to Port Stanley. Both were wearing gloves. The taxi driver's dead body was found a short distance from Port Stanley. Later both were found in possession of money and seen going into the dance at the arena. Bloodstained gloves were found hidden at the dance hall. The knife found a few feet from the body was identified as belonging to Butler's mother. They were both in possession of brass knuckles.

Larry Wallace and Ernie Butler were both charged with noncapital murder, and when the trial was completed, the jury found them both guilty as charged. They were sentenced to life in prison and wouldn't receive parole for twenty years.

In April 1971, prisoners at Kingston Penitentiary staged a four-day revolt in protest over a number of grievances that were later conceded to be largely justified. They took six guards hostage, and to ensure the guard's safety, prison authorities allowed the prisoners to take over the cell block areas. While the leaders of the revolt were negotiating with a citizen's committee in the prison hospital, a rival faction invaded a cell block where undesirable prisoners—sex offenders—were locked up for their own safety by the rebels. The rival faction dragged these prisoners to the penitentiary's central dome, tied them to chairs, and systematically bludgeoned them. Two of the victims died of their injuries.

As news of the beatings became known, the army was sent in to restore order. The prison was heavily damaged over the four days, but the six guards were released unharmed.

Thirteen prisoners were charged with murdering the two dead victims. One of the thirteen was Mr. Miller's twenty-one-year-old killer (now twenty-four), who was described as wearing gloves and smiling as he beat helpless victims with a rod. He was convicted of manslaughter and sentenced to a further ten years.

In 1973, Mr. Miller's older murderer—the twenty-two-year-old killer (now twenty-seven)—escaped from the medium-security Collins Bay Institution with three other prisoners. The four men crawled through ventilation ducts to a service building, triggered a maintenance alarm, and surprised the engineer who showed up in response. They used the engineer's keys and car to escape.

One of the four, who exposed in the media as a sex offender after the escape, was found dead in a ditch about ten miles south of Windsor. He had been shot several times and was wrapped in a blood-soaked blanket. One of the other escapees (not Mr. Miller's killer) was later convicted of shooting him. Police captured all three remaining escapees at homes in Windsor, but not before the murderer shot a Windsor police officer in the leg. He escaped from prison again in 1979 but was soon recaptured.

Both murderers were transferred to Drumheller Institution in Alberta. In 1984, they and a third man were charged with beating a fellow prisoner to death with a baseball bat. The third man was convicted of the murder, and Mr. Miller's younger murderer was again convicted of manslaughter. The older murderer was acquitted, but while at Drumheller, he made two aborted escape attempts.

In 1992, the older murderer was transferred to Bowden prison forty kilometers south of Red Deer and in October was granted day parole from Hope Mission in downtown Edmonton. In January 1993, he failed to return to the mission and was still at large more than a month later when news of his escape was finally made public. He was recaptured in Lethbridge in April.

Despite questions raised about why he was allowed out on day parole with his record of violence and attempted escapes, the older murderer was eventually granted full parole. He married and settled in Lethbridge.

In June of 2008, now sixty-two, he fell into a rain-swollen creek and was swept away by the current. His body was found 150 yards downstream.

Marie Miller died in 2004 at the age of eighty-two.

Bits and Pieces 4

One cold fall day I got called down to the Dutton detachment regarding the death of a man. This person I found out was a "tree stumper." When a farmer or other person cut down a tree, usually a big one, this man was called in to remove the tree stump and the roots of the tree. He used ditching dynamite, which is the most dangerous type of dynamite available. He lived in a sixteen-foot travel trailer, which was near the south side of the Thames River about thirty miles west of the city of London. When he wasn't using the dynamite, he stored it in his trailer to keep it dry in case of rain. It was assumed that he had about 500 lb. of this dynamite stored in the trailer on this occasion.

He had been out removing stumps that day for a farmer a couple of miles away from his trailer. He came home to his trailer on this day, put away the tools he used, stored the dynamite he didn't use, and decided he would cook his supper as he missed lunch and was hungry.

When he lit his match to light his propane stove, he did not realize or notice the smell of propane in the trailer. When the match was lit, the propane blew up, which caused the dynamite to explode, which then caused the trailer to blow up into many pieces. The two propane bottles could not be recognized as bottles as they were also in little pieces. There was no trace of the stumper.

Photographs were taken of the damage and the area around the trailer.

We (Don and I) looked all around the area for the tree stumper. The two biggest pieces we found of him was a piece of his scalp, which, if you spread it out, would be about a six-inch square. Another piece was a little piece from around one of his ankles.

Another disturbing occasion occurred when I was working for the Woodstock Police Force. I was called out about 2:00 a.m. to a death of an eighteen-year-old male. I don't know why he committed suicide, but he did.

He went to the center of an overpass over a set of mainline railroad tracks. He waited on the overpass, and when the train was under the bridge, he jumped off the overpass in front of the train. It was a mess; his body was spread out over about five hundred feet along the tracks in a bunch of small pieces.

I never did find out why he decided to commit suicide.

CHAPTER TWENTY-SEVEN

Some Couples Should Not Be Allowed to Have Children

On May 19, 1978, we were dispatched to the residence of Vera Elizabeth, age 33, and her husband, Royden Novarre Iwon, age 54, on Dundas Street in Thamesford. Their son, Albert Royden Iwon, age 14 months, had been murdered.

The murder took place in the apartment occupied by the Iwons. It was located on the back part of the lower floor of a large two-story old brick farmhouse. The apartment was filthy, cluttered with furniture, boxes, and junk, and it wreaked of a vile odor. There were two other apartments in the house, one upstairs and one on the lower floor at the front of the house. The parents, Vera and Royden, were married in the parsonage at the Dundas Street United Church in Woodstock.

On December 8, 1972, in Tillsonburg, Vera gave birth to a stillborn baby who was to be named Lisa Anne. The baby was interned on December 11, 1972. On December 29, 1973, Vera gave birth to a daughter named Sheba at Victoria Hospital in London. Vera was discharged from the hospital on January 7, 1974. Sheba was discharged on January 21, 1974. When the baby was discharged, the Children's Aid Society of Oxford County in Woodstock took custody of Sheba as a non-ward with the consent of the parents and was placed in a foster home. This action was taken because Vera was in the psychiatric unit at St. Joseph's Hospital in London, suffering from postpartum depression.

On February 26, 1974, Vera was discharged from the psychiatric unit. She requested the Children's Aid Society to return Sheba back to her. Sheba was returned to the parents.

Within twenty-four hours after being returned to her parents, Sheba was back in Victoria Hospital suffering from a bruised palate and dehydration. It was apparent that Sheba was neglected to the point where she had become completely dehydrated. The bruised palate was caused by Vera forcing the baby food into Sheba's mouth with a spoon. On March 8, 1974, Sheba was released from the hospital into the custody of the Children's Aid and was made a society ward. The parents attempted to prevent Sheba from being adopted; however, Sheba was later legally adopted.

On March 4, 1977, Vera gave birth to a son, Albert Royden Navarro Iwon (the murdered child) at St. Joseph's Hospital, London. They were both discharged from the hospital on March 17, 1977.

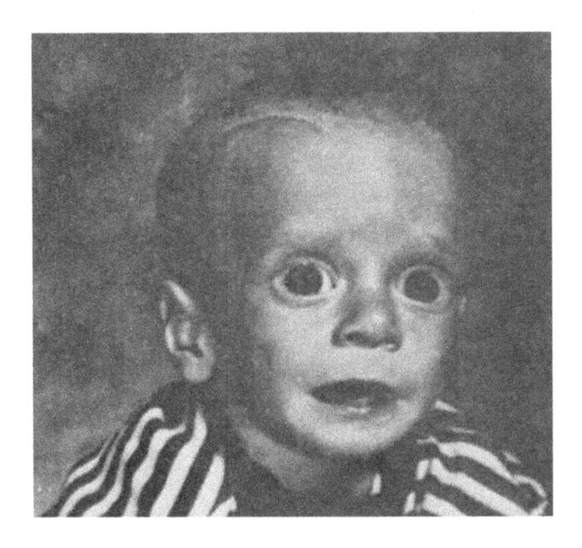

While Vera was in the hospital, Constable Clarence of the Woodstock detachment of the Ontario Provincial Police contacted the Children's Aid Society regarding the care of the baby. Clarence had been in attendance at the Iwon residence on March 17, 1977, and was very disturbed by the manner in which the baby's mother, Vera, handled her son. While Vera was in the hospital, the baby had been cared for and looked after by a woman in Thamesford, taken there by Mr. Iwon.

On March 19, 1977, Vera, having a long history of mental disorder, suffered another mental breakdown. She was admitted to London Psychiatric Hospital by her family doctor. On April 22, 1977, she was permitted leaves of absence for short periods. She was officially discharged from the hospital on August 6, 1977, diagnosed with manic depression psychosis.

On May 9, 1977, the baby was returned to the parents. Social workers from the Children's Aid Society, Oxford County Board of Health, and public health nurses from Alexandra Hospital in Ingersoll visited on several occasions prior to his death. They visited because of their agencies' concern for the baby and the mother's inability to look after him properly.

The public health nurses, concerned about the lack of progress of the baby, forced the parents to take the baby to a pediatrician in

London. On December 12, 1977, the baby was examined by the doctor, and as a result of his examination, the baby was admitted to St. Joseph's Hospital in London, diagnosed with "failing to thrive." The baby was discharged from the hospital on January 3, 1978. While in the hospital, the baby was x-rayed, but there were no fractures of the arms or of any other bones in the body.

On May 15, 1978, a public health nurse visited the Iwon residence, and she found the baby appeared to be normal.

On May 19, 1978, the father, Royden, left the house about 10:30 a.m. and went to a pay phone a short distance from his residence. He attempted to call their family doctor, but the line was busy. After several attempts trying to contact the doctor, he then phoned Bell Canada. Royden advised the operator that he had been trying to contact the family doctor for twenty minutes because his son was dying, but could not get through to his office because the line was busy. She checked the line, and it was busy, so the operator then called Alexandra Hospital in Ingersoll.

The call was received by a receptionist at the hospital. Royden told the receptionist that his little boy had been sick for a few days and that he had not been eating, and he thought that his son was going to die. The receptionist called the Woodstock Ambulance Service and dispatched them to the Iwon residence.

Arriving at the Iwon residence at 10:50 a.m., the ambulance operators viewed the boy then called the coroner and the police. While checking the baby, they observed swelling on the left side of the baby's head. The mother, Vera, stated to them it was caused by the baby hitting his head on the side of the crib.

Detective Constable D. McDougall arrived at the Iwon residence at 11:25 a.m. He met the coroner from Ingersoll and the ambulance attendants who were outside the house in the Iwon laneway. At 11:27 a.m., McDougall and the coroner entered the Iwon apartment through the kitchen. The Iwons, Vera and Royden, the parents of the child, were sitting at the kitchen table. Neither of the parents showed any signs of any emotion with regard to their son, and they were very calm.

McDougall and the Coroner entered the living room where they saw the small child lying on a couch. There was a large bruised area and discoloration on the right side of the head near the right ear and also another bruised area on the scalp just above the other one. On the left side of the head was a large protruding area, above the left ear. There were also three dark-colored small bruises in the center of the forehead. There was a small scratch on the bridge of the nose and a small scratch on the chin and one on the corner of the right eyebrow. The eyes were open, and the mouth was partially open.

The child was on a white couch. He was wearing a one-piece pink pajama outfit that was open to the waist, exposing the chest. There was a green pillow under the head and a pink blanket under the baby. There was also a Raggedy Ann doll and a yellow and pink bunny doll sitting up on the couch near the left foot. There was a baby crib in the northwest corner of the room with a teddy bear in the southwest corner of the crib. A soiled and dirty blanket was in the crib, which appeared to be covered in vomit or human excrement. The area in the room containing the child was a mess, and there was an unhealthy odor. There were three windows in the room, one on the north wall and two on the east wall. The windows appeared not to have been opened in a long time.

The parents, Vera and Royden, were still sitting at the kitchen table when McDougall and the coroner went in. They identified the child as Albert, their son, born on the fourth of March 1977. Neither parent showed any sign of emotion with regard to the death of their son.

McDougall said, "When was the last time Albert was seen by a doctor?"

"Albert was last seen by Dr. Lubell at St. Joseph's Hospital in London on April 6, 1978, for a regular checkup, and everything was OK. The doctor said Albert should be walking the next time that he saw him," Vera said.

She also said, "He was also in the hospital in December 1977 for several tests. The last time Albert was seen by anyone was on Monday, May 17, 1978, when a public health nurse saw him at home."

McDougall asked, "When was the last time Albert was conscious?"

"At bedtime, between 8:30 p.m. and 8:45 p.m. Albert was sick and throwing up. I never went to sleep. I stayed awake and changed him after a show was over on TV. He was conscious but breathing slow."

Royden interrupted, "Albert was still alive when I phoned the Ingersoll Hospital. He was making a noise from his mouth."

The parents, Vera and her husband, Royden, were arrested and charged. They both denied beating or hitting the baby. Vera stated the bruises and other injuries were caused by the baby hitting his head against the side of the crib and bumping his head into the television set. She also said the public health nurse saw the swelling on the left side of the baby's head on May 15, 1978, when she made her visit. The nurse stated there was no swelling on the baby's head.

Neither parent displayed any emotion over the death of their son. They were more concerned for the welfare of their two dogs.

The body was removed from the home to the morgue to the Woodstock General Hospital. Visual examination of the body at the hospital revealed multiple bruises about the face and head and a large swelling on the left side of the head.

The body was x-rayed. The x-rays revealed a fractured skull, a recent fracture to the lower left arm, an old fracture to the upper left arm, an old fracture to the upper right arm, and an old fracture to the rear left side of the rib cage.

Previously on December 12, 1977, when the baby was admitted to St. Joseph's Hospital, x-rays were taken at that time, and there were no fractures, old or new, that showed up on the x-rays.

A postmortem on the baby's body was conducted by the pathologist. The cause of death was determined as the result of a severe fractured skull. The severest fracture was to the left side, where a piece of the skull was completely broken out. This was consistent with the swelling to the left side of the head. X-rays also showed a recent fracture of the left arm.

The pathologist advised the skull fracture could not have been the result of a fall or self-inflicted by hitting your head. It was thought by those at the autopsy that the child was picked up at the ankles and slammed into the wall.

It was sometime later that Inspector Masters talked to Dr. Robert Bates, a pediatrician at the Sick Children's Hospital in Toronto:

> Masters: The child has a broken arm and a fractured skull. Is it possible to pick up a baby and cause the above injuries by smashing the baby against a wall?
> Bates: Yes, it is possible because of the massive fracture the skull that this child had.
> McMaster: Could these injuries occur by baby falling off a crib or table?
> Bates: Kids do not harm themselves such as this by falling out of their crib or off the table. They would only suffer minor injuries.
> Masters: Could a child live for a couple days with this fracture?
> Bates: It is possible but highly improbable. A baby would be like a vegetable and would not be responding.
> Masters: Could you tell me about aging of bruises?
> Bates: These bruises are up to about three or four days old. It's very hard to tell exactly. These didn't occur that morning of the picture being taken.
> Masters: Is it possible to cause an injury by striking the head on the right side and injuring the left side of the head?
> Bates: No, not possible in this case.
> Masters: Would these injuries occur if the baby fell off a two-foot-high step?
> Bates: No, also x-rays show injuries to the rib cage. This child was beaten, and there is no doubt about it.

> Masters: Which parent would be more likely to have killed the baby?
> Bates: Statistically it is 50-50. Normally the one usually involved in the care of a child constantly and in premature births is higher, and there are many other factors involved.

The Iwons were lodged overnight in the cells of the Woodstock detachment. At 8:40 p.m., Vera was lodged in the cells, and at 8:50 p.m., Royden was lodged in a cell. No lights were on in the cells.

Constable Carton was concealed in the shower stall in the cell block area. The purpose for him being there was to overhear any conversation between them. The following is a conversation he was able to record in writing.

They chatted back and forth all evening long. She said she did not do it. He said she put him in the crib, and he banged his head on the side of the crib and hurt his skull and brain. She had cried when she heard the results. Then she said she misses dogs. She cared for them, not the child. Instead, they must give a decent burial.

The dogs went to the pound. Somebody said they'd never see the dogs again. They must get somebody to look after the dogs, Nick and Nip. "Let's try and think of somebody to look after them at Oxford County Shelter. They might run away unless they are tied up. No way to get the dogs back," said Royden.

They talked about Royden signing a paper for the police. She didn't like that. It was the worst thing she thought he could do. Vera said she did not sign and wouldn't. She thought he had confessed; she didn't. She thought the rest of their lives, they would rot.

She wanted to know if they were proven guilty, would they hang or get the electric chair. He didn't know. They talked about capital punishment being dissolved, but she didn't know what that meant. He told her that he would take the rap.

She asked her husband if they would hang, he said no. Probably get two years.

She said she cared about the baby, but the dogs deserve better.

They talked about the autopsy at Woodstock, which showed the baby had two previously broken arms, a crack on the head, and a fractured skull. That's what killed him, the fractured skull.

They talked about going before the court, hoping their lawyer would get them remanded so they could go home to await their trial. She wanted to be at the house before the trial. He didn't know. He tried to think of the dogs, Nick and Nip.

They talked about the dogs again. They tried to identify somebody who liked dogs. Nip's a good dog. They wondered if maybe George Sanders would look after them.

She wanted to know about the London detention center, what were the female prisoners like, and how they were treated. Do they wear dresses? She said she wasn't talking about the guard; she was talking about the prisoners. Jeans and shirts, and they wear socks and underclothing. Good GI slacks. Men wear hush puppies.

She said Nick loved her and felt bad when she wasn't there. Vera said, "You heard the cop that arrested us, the fat guy with glasses, was scared of dogs in January."

Do you get smokes in the detention center in London, any tailor-mades? Now they have to roll their own.

They never knew their son had a broken arm. What's it mean? Two breaks already knit. Sometime ago his arm was broken, both arms. Knit again. Two or three bumps on forehead. One on back of head is what killed him.

They talked about the detention center, and she wanted to know if they could have a bath. He told her they had showers. She will know how many. He said about fifteen. She wanted to know if the guards watched. No, they shut the door. She said, "I've never been in prison before, but I know you have."

They talked about other things about the jail. She had ten relatives; could they come and visit? She wanted to know about the males who serve you and other things about the jail. She wanted to know about the toilets. Were there mirrors in the cells so she can brush her hair? Was there any water to drink?

They chatted again about other things. She thought they could go home for the night instead of being locked in a cell. They chatted about other things: relatives, the center, and again about the dogs. Then they both fell asleep.

At 8:16 a.m., Constable Masters removed both Vera and Roy from their cells and took them upstairs to the office, at which time Constable Carter returned to his position in the east cell block to monitor their conversation.

At 9:26 a.m., Vera was returned to her cell. At 9:29 a.m., Roy was returned to his cell.

When they were both in their cells, Vera said, "We better talk. We will be going to the detention center this morning. Now it will be soon. What about our son? Roy wants to go to the funeral home and make arrangements. He was told it was up to us. He wants to talk to Ray. He will talk to the boss and the doctor. They may think it bad for us, psychologically. He asked where he would be buried and who pays. If we were there, we could handle it. Another thing we have to worry about is Nip and Nick. We have to find somebody to look after them. Time is precious. Then it's all over. They'll never see each other again."

Roy said, "Yeah."

Their conversation carried on similarly to the colonization last evening, with short sentences and several topics.

One of the main topics they started with was with regard to Nip and Nick, their two dogs. They were concerned as they had to find somebody who would be taking care of them in the future. They talked about a nurse who lived with his wife on the outskirts of Dorchester. They had two fenced-in yards.

They talked about the funeral for their son and who will be paying for it.

They talked about the detention center. They were going to be going there this morning sometime. They knew they would be only getting sleep, meals, and smokes. They would each be in a cell by themselves.

They talked about money. They didn't know whether they were getting any money from the detention center or the province. They probably don't get the money from welfare.

They talked about their lawyers and what they would be doing for them.

They talked about their cells with the rough mattress. They would get no pop, chocolate milk, juices, apples, tomatoes, porridge, and cereal. You get breakfast at 7:00 a.m., then locked back up. Then out at 8:00 a.m. or 8:30 a.m. to walk around the exercise yard and back in the cell at 11:30 a.m.

They talked more about the dogs, the detention center, the funeral, and their lawyers.

The JP came in, and Vera and Roy were both remanded into custody for second-degree murder.

They talked about the court date coming up the next Tuesday. They would have to let their lawyers know somehow.

Vera and Roy were taken from the cells and taken to London. They were lodged in the Elgin-Middlesex Detention Center, London. They were denied bail.

On June 6, 1978, they made application again to the Supreme Court of Canada, at which time they were released on their own recognizance under the following conditions:

1. They maintain their residence at RR 4 Thamesford, unless they notified the officer in charge of the Woodstock detachment advance of any change of address.
2. They were not to leave the counties of Oxford or Middlesex for any reason.
3. No passports should be applied for or issued to them.
4. They were not to be allowed to supervise any children, or associate with, or talk to any children, and they were not to have any children in their residence at any time.
5. There was to be a curfew from 11:00 p.m. to 6:00 a.m.
6. They were to be visited weekly by the probation officer or his delegate if he could not do it at

their home by advance arrangement mutually agreeable.

7. (Mrs. Iwon only) She was to cooperate with the medical personnel and to continue taking her drugs daily. She was to be visited by the public health nurse weekly and a lab technician biweekly.

At the beginning of July 1978, Detective Inspector M. Masters interviewed and took the following statement from Arthur Iwon regarding his brother, Royden Iwon:

Masters: What relation are you to Royden?
Iwon: I'm his older brother.
Masters: Do you have any other brothers or sisters?
Iwon: They got...They call them sisters, one girl my parents raised and adopted, and the other girl my parents just raised, and she got her name changed to ours.
Masters: Can you sort of give me a brief history in writing?
Iwon: Well, as kids, there is two and a half years difference in our ages, and we never played together. He had his friends, and I had my friends. As he grew up, he got a car. I don't remember ever taking him anywhere with me. He had a car, and he never took me, but I did borrow his car at different times when mine was broke or something like that, but we never actually played together or got along together. Not that we would fight or anything like that. It was just that he seemed to have his friends, and I had mine.

Funny thing, I didn't realize this at the time, but years ago when we were in our twenties, he always hung around with people who had something wrong with them, either cripples or they weren't right or something like that. It seemed strange to me, but at the time I didn't realize there was anything wrong with them either, and I didn't realize this until our father died, and he came into the funeral home drinking pop and eating popcorn and chips and laughing and joking, and this just isn't done.

Masters: How long ago was this?

Iwon: Well, my dad died in 1963, July third. It seemed a little queer then, so it went on. They lived down here on Winnett Street, and his wife went berserk, and the police were called and asked me if I had a brother Roy, and I said yeah. So I went down, and she had wrecked the house, tore her clothes off except her panties, and was running around. Of course she was scared to death of me. I hadn't really met her until that time, so I went down, and the police couldn't get a doctor to even come near her, and so I called Dr. Blackwood, who is my doctor, and the police said, "There is no use calling him. We called him, and he wants nothing to do with it." I said, "Call him and tell him I want to speak to him." I think the only phone was upstairs. The phone downstairs was torn out.

Masters: How long ago was this?

Iwon: It would be eight or ten years, I'm just guessing. I don't have the exact date, but the city police will have the record. Anyway, I got Dr. Blackwood on the phone and told him she was my mother and what was happening, and they had to get a doctor or something, and he came down, gave her a needle to quiet her down, and then he said he thought she should be committed.

From that I went up to the hospital and got a paper signed by another doctor and brought it back, and I was driving part-time for the ambulance and had some days coming from them, so I rented the ambulance and took Vera to St. Thomas. Then I guess my brother was running back and forth to St. Thomas to see her, and I don't know whether they gave her a clear bill of sale or whether they just let her go home for the weekend, and he never took her back. This is what I heard. Like I said, my brother and I never got along with each other, so we never went out together.

So about two years after that, she seemed to take these spells about once a year, but with no warning, she'd be talking to you and bang just like that. But usually when she took these spells, she'd lock Roy out of the house, and she busted nearly every window in the house and all the light bulbs, she was trying to climb the wall when he got there, so I'm not sure whether he took her to St. Thomas twice or not, I think he did, but I can't remember for sure.

She lived out at Bob Mason's place, you can talk to Bob. I talked to him, and he's willing to talk to you. He's a salesman at Elliott Brothers Motors. He would know exactly how Roy acted. He said that in the time he knew Roy, she wrecked his house out there in the country. He'd never seen Roy violent, never, nor have I seen him violent.

Anyways, out in the country she took another spell, so Roy phoned me, and I didn't want anything to do with it, and he said, "I'm locked out, it's freezing. What am I going to do?" He added, "I went to the neighbours, and I'm calling you from the neighbours." And I said, "Well, I'll call the police." And I called the police. They said as long as she's not doing bodily harm to anybody or herself, they can't do anything about it. And just as a joke, I said, "Maybe I better take a rifle out and shoot the bugger."

By the time I got out there, I think the police had come out. I wasn't sure, but she had quieted down. Oh, that was the night we tried half the night trying to get some sleep. We called St. Thomas, and they said they couldn't do anything, and then Bob Mason took her to Woodstock Hospital and just dumped her off. They kept her there a day or two.

I'm not sure if he took her to St. Thomas then or not, he could check with Joe Pember how many times he took her because he used his ambulance both times. He's probably taken her different times. As far as my brother goes, I've never seen him violent, he's strange, in fact his youngest sister, Eleanor said, "Why don't he have him put away." Well, it's a pretty hard thing to do to have your brother put away, and another thing is he can't say, I'm going to have him put away. You have to have doctors check him out and if you can't get them acting funny, you can't get it done. I'm not trying to say his brother's crazy. He's been slow all his life.

Masters: Did you ever see them around the baby or anything, or did you ever see the baby?

Iwon: No, I never have. As I said, I haven't seen my brother for about two years.

Masters: So you've never seen this baby?

Iwon: No.

Masters: You've never seen the other baby?

Iwon: No.

Masters: What about his divorce? There was some mention about a divorce?

Iwon: Well, he called me up. I forgot where he was living. He said, "What am I going to do, the darn sheriff was here and said he had a summons, and I had to pay for a divorce." His first wife has a bunch of kids from the other guy, and he said, "I've got no money to pay for a divorce, what will I do?" And I said, "Well, I advise you to see a lawyer." The thing was at that time, he already got married to this woman at the United Church. I wasn't there. I didn't know they were married until after, but he was married, and the divorce hadn't gone through yet on the other one.

Masters: He got married to Vera while he was still married to Shirley?

Iwon: Yes. Her name was Shirley Hazen.

Masters: How long ago would they have got married?

Iwon : 1943, I think, on November 9, on Roy's birthday.

Masters: How long after he was married to this other girl would he have been served the papers for the divorce?

Iwon: This is what I can't figure out. When the records went through, and there must be records to go through when you sign a marriage certificate. A copy goes to Ottawa or someplace, how come they never noticed it? I suppose they have to have a complaint to look them up.

Masters: There was another thing that was mentioned to me, something about a baby at a funeral home. What was that about?

Roy's Mother: That's the one at Mac Smith's.

Iwon: I just did vaguely remember that.

Roy's Mother: A friend of mine mentioned it to me. I had completely forgotten about it. They never did go to the funeral home. It was premature, seven months, I think, I'm not sure, it was a long time ago. It's got to be twelve years ago.

Iwon: All of that.

Masters: There has been some allegation they had another baby, and it starved to death or something to that effect.

Roy's Mother: Well, you know, I heard the weirdest thing. A neighbor of ours worked at a restaurant down here, and she has been retired for six years. They were talking one day, and she said the girls used to hate to see them come in with that baby. They thought it was a shame that people like that was allowed to have a baby. They never saw that baby, and I don't think this lady is confused.

Masters: This is what we are trying to find out. We heard there was another baby.

Roy's Mother: This is the first I've heard of it. They never come around here. Roy would come once in a while. She'd come, but it's been years since she came.

Iwon: She'd sit across the road in the car. She came in the house once, I think.

Roy's Mother: My goodness, if they had a baby, where is it? Wouldn't there be a record?

Masters: Yes, there should be. Well, it depends on how they had it or where they had it.

Iwon: He had a baby by his first wife too, and it died as a day old. I was working for the funeral home at that time and had to go and pick the baby up and bury it—through the funeral home, of course.

Masters: And how long has this lady been retired?

Roy's Mother: Six years, and it couldn't have been Sheba. Sheba was only four, and this lady has been retired six or seven years.

Masters: Who is this lady?

Iwon: Mrs. Haskett, next door. I don't know if you saw me talking to her when you drove in or not.

Masters: Shirley Iwon, where is she living now?

Roy's Mother: Thetford, the last I heard.

Masters: What was the cause of death of the baby by his first marriage?

Iwon: Well, it never left the hospital. It was what they call a blue baby, and it died in the hospital.

Masters: Do premature babies and stillborn babies go through a funeral home?

Iwon: Oh yes, it depends on how many months the baby is when it is stillborn. I can remember back when a baby was stillborn, and they just surface and embalm it. It has no veins or arteries yet to put a needle into. You could see all the features, but it was just like a bag of liver. Of course, no one came to the funeral. They just made arrangements at the cemetery and buried it.

Masters: When he phoned you about this one at the funeral home, was this going to be a funeral?

Roy's Mother: I don't know. It's unreal that they wouldn't go, but with the two of them and the way they were carrying on, there was just no way could you feel anything for them.

Iwon: For years, friends of mine who knew Roy, like he would pull into a service station, get five dollars worth of gas out at Fred Neal's, and I'd be out to Fred Neal's maybe three or four months later, and Fred would say, "You know, your brother owes me four or five dollars, or whatever it was for the gas," so I paid him for it, and I'd say to Fred, "If he comes in again for any gas, you phone me before you give them any gas."

Well, different people, friends of mine that I worked with at the factory, he'd try to borrow money from them. Some of them gave him money once. He'd never pay them back because he never worked. Yet before the war he worked at LaFrance close to five years. He'd act strange, but he was a good worker. That was when he was married to his first wife.

After she left, he just went all to hell, and when he met this girl and got a job, he would work for three or four days, and then not come in for two or three days, and then when he got back to work again, he was not going to keep his job. It would be different if you had twenty-five years seniority and said, "Look, my wife is sick or something, and I had to stay home with her," but when you first start a job, people don't want people like that. He had a job at a truck stop on Governors Road as a short-order cook, and they liked him, but his wife just phoned up and said he wasn't getting enough money and wouldn't be in anymore.

Masters: Was there an incident with Roy when he was a baby with your mother?

Iwon: I was five or six years old, and he was two and a half years younger than me, and my dad was teaching my mother to drive, and we lived on Grace Street just off Riddell. They had a garage that was set back in, a real narrow garage, and my mother backed the car out of the garage and Dad wasn't home, told us kids to stay on the lawn, so I stayed on the lawn, and she backed the car out on the street and pulled ahead, but she was away from the curb, and she decided to back it up to the curb, and I remember just as clear as it happened today.

When she backed it in, all I heard was Roy scream, and he just lay there, and our mother jumped out of the car quick and then pulled the car ahead quick, picked up Roy, and put us in the car and took him to the hospital and left me there with a neighbor. It seemed to me it pinched his shoulder and the side of his head, between the tire and the curb. It was the big old high tire with split rims on. I can't remember how long he was in the hospital or whether he came home in a cast or what.

I just remember this one incident. It seems vague, but I remember her backing and pinching him between the curb. That was just as clear as this table, but anything else is just hazy. Different times I would give Roy money when he came here, or maybe see him on the street. One time I went out to their house. They wanted to sell their refrigerator, and my son-in-law is an auctioneer, so we went down to look at the refrigerator, and Roy was cooking dinner, and all they had was two or three little potatoes. That's all they had to eat for dinner, so I slipped him $20 then. That was six or seven years ago. I know Roy wasn't right, but I've never seen him violent in all his lifetime. You should talk to Bob Mason, the salesman at Elliott's. He said he was willing to do anything to help. Roy lived in his house in the country, you go out to #59 Ski-Hi road, down to the first corner, turn right, and it was down on the right-hand side of the road, either a mile and a quarter or three quarters of a mile.

Masters: How long ago was that?

Iwon: Oh, I had the Buick then, a '69, and it was a couple years old. Bob Mason could probably tell you more about my brother than I know could because we haven't been close. Anytime I see him, I see him for about fifteen minutes, or else I would call him at one o'clock in the morning and want a ride back to Thamesford or something like that.

Masters: Was there any conversation with Roy in regard to something that blew up at one of the places where he lived to get him out of there?

Iwon: There was a fire in Osterville.

Roy's Mother: That was the last time I saw her, I think. She came in the house and said they had it full of new furniture, and they were supposed to have been away, and when they came home, it was burnt to the ground.

Iwon: But where the house was now, I don't know, but they were going to charge him with arson, figured he burnt the house up. I don't know what happened, I didn't follow it up.

Roy's Mother: Nothing happened, they never heard anything.

Masters: How long ago would that have been?

Roy's Mother: It must have been after they left Mason's. Isn't that where they went to see the fridge?

Iwon: They went down near Tillsonburg. Glenn could tell you exactly where it was. It was near Tillsonburg someplace. Well anyways, one of his dogs burnt to death in the fire, and he was mad about that. He said, "Do you think I set the fire and burnt my dog?" Roy used to live in Ingersoll. This lady from Ingersoll phoned me and said she was a neighbor, I don't know her name.

Masters: Stirling.

Iwon: She didn't say her name, but she knew me. In fact, I just hung up the phone, and it came on television that Roy was charged for second-degree murder. They killed the baby, but she just phoned me and said that Roy's baby just died, it had choked to death on a pea, and she said, "Is there anything you can do to help them?" and I said, "I don't want anything to do with it." I took him home once, and to go to their place, you go down where Morrows Nut and Screw and the bowling alley used to be, down that street out of the outskirts of Ingersoll, and there was a dirt road where you went down over the tracks, and they lived on the right-hand side.

Masters: Mrs. Stirling.

Iwon: That would be her name, would it? She talked to me for a good hour anyways. Maybe an hour and a half that Roy felt so bad about it. Isn't there something you can do, he's got no money, Children's Aid have been helping him, and everyone else has been helping him, and I said, "I don't want to get involved in it at all."

If you know me, you know my brother, and we never had too much to do with one another, but if you wanted help, you come to me. If he'd need some money, he'd come to me. I'd give him some money, but the last couple times he came to me years ago, I said, "I've got kids going to college. I can't afford it, Roy. You've had just the same chance in life as I've had to make a living. You didn't do it, I did." But there was something definitely wrong with Roy.

Masters: In March 1977, you got a phone call from your sister, Joan Love, about something that happened. What was that about?

Iwon: She said no, it wasn't her that called, but that's the only one I could have heard from. She was closer to Roy than me. Roy always went to her place. Anyway, she said Roy was locked out, and she was trying to smother the baby with diapers and what should Roy do. I'm sure it was June who called, but she denies talking to me. I said, "We're going out for dinner date, and I don't want nothing to do with it. You call him back and tell him to get in touch with the police or the Children's Aid. I'll be down at the Shrine Club, call me back if you don't get him." I didn't get a call back.

Masters: So your sister called you and said that she had just heard from Roy, and Roy said his wife was trying to smother the baby.

Iwon: Smother the baby with diapers, putting diapers over the baby's head, and Roy was locked out. This is what she done every time she went berserk. At Mason, she locked him out, on Winnett Street she locked him out, and this will be the third time. At Mason's he couldn't get in the house, he was out just in his shirt, so they went downstairs through the outside cellar entrance and turned a registers off in their part.

Masters: One time she went up to Mason's place where they were living and something about she locked him out and was going to get him with a butcher knife?

Iwon: They had a cat and one or two dogs, and Roy said he was scared she was going to butcher the animals, and he couldn't get in because she had a butcher knife and the door was locked, and she was liable to get him too. He told me he was afraid to go to sleep when she got funny.

I have never seen my brother violent. I know he would never hurt an animal, let alone a child. He seemed to like kids. I think in this case, he was probably locked out, but on the other hand, from what you people say, if he helped cover up the evidence, it makes him just as guilty as her.

I drove him home once. He came here because his wife had a lot of clothes that were too big for her, and I had a suit I had promised him and an overcoat, so he came down to the house to get them, and he couldn't carry it home, so I drove him. I had his daughter-in-law with me, and we just stepped inside the door, that was all. Roy himself always did the housework and cooking. You wouldn't believe it, his place was just as clean as this, but Roy was always clean until he married this woman, and even then when he first married her, he did the cleaning, and their place was clean. Sure, they had dogs, but the dogs stayed in his place.

Roy's Mother: The last few years, he refers to Art as "his millionaire brother."

Iwon: This used to bug me. I'd be driving him home someplace, and he'd say to his landlord, "I want you to meet my millionaire brother. He would say things like this and really embarrassed me, and when Roy gets excited at all, he can't talk to plain. I can't believe that Roy would do anything like this because you can talk to anybody, and you won't find one person that said they ever saw him violent or heard of him being violent. But again, as he said, when this happens, he is usually locked out of the house, but he's not too bright.

My younger sister said, "Why don't you commit him?" My oldest sister said if I would do it, she'd stand behind me, but he was not hurting anybody. My uncle Artus, Dad's youngest brother, lived in London, and I got word that he died in Florida, and we were flying out that Sunday to go to Hawaii for the first time, and we had paid for tickets. There was no use in staying, so my oldest son went to the funeral and took flowers. Roy was there. My uncle always had a big diamond ring, and it seems Artus's wife, Naomi, noticed his ring missing, and Roy was in there with him by himself. I've never known Roy to steal anything. Anyway, they questioned Roy, and he said he didn't take it. So they went to where Roy lived, and they found it hidden under the rug. You can check it out because it's hearsay as far as I'm concerned. I don't think there were any charges laid against him. I've never know Roy to steal anything. He never picked up anything here or from anybody else that I know of, unless he's gone out to some farmers and stole potatoes or something to eat.

Roy's Mother: I was just out of the hospital, and I was very ill. Art was gone out the first night he had left me, so I settled myself down to watch a movie and the phone rang. It was Roy, and he wanted to talk to Art right away. I said he was down at the Shrine Club. He went on and told me that Art owed him $250. It upset me pretty much, so I called Art's sister and talked to her and got myself settled down here again.

Anyway, the story was that they had a car, no ownership, and they had gone out, and there had been a crash. They got out of the car, took the dogs, went back to their place, changed their clothes, and walked by in time to see the ambulance carry a lady away. This happened right in Thamesford. They hitchhiked to Ingersoll, wanting Art to take them home. They wanted Art to say they had been with him all night, and when Art finally talked to him, he said, "No way, I was drinking with a policeman down the club tonight, I can't say you're with me."

Iwon: But that was a lie, there was no policeman there.

Roy's Mother: At one thirty in the morning, he got a call. They were down here at his sister's still wanting a ride home. I don't know how they got home, but they watched the paper, and there wasn't a word in the paper about it, so they thought it must have been a story.

Masters: Yes, it happened.

Iwon: Did they charge him on that?

Masters: I think he was charged on that.

Masters: Do you know his previous wife Shirley's date of birth or age?

Roy's Mother: She was only fifteen or sixteen when they were married, and that was 1943.

Masters: Where were they married?

Roy's Mother: I think it was old St. Paul's rectory.

Masters: How can they find out where she lives now? Are her parents around here or anything?

Iwon: Her dad is dead, but I think her mother is still alive. The parents went from here to the Sarnia the last I heard.

Masters: Did the divorce proceedings take place in Oxford County?

Roy's Mother: The Sheriff served him in Oxford County.

Mason: Were they married on November 11, 1943?

Roy's Mother: Yes.

Masters: They have his name as Royden Novarre Iwon.

Iwon: That's right.

Masters: His stepmother's name is Vera McDonald, and she lives in RR 4, Clinton?

Iwon: Yes.

Masters: Do you have a phone number for her?

Roy's Mother: I looked for it, and I can't find it.

Masters: How do you feel? She should be able to help us?

Roy's Mother: I was going to tell you about the will. Roy and Vera went to some building in London where they keep records, and for five dollars they got a copy of the will, and they gave us a copy. In the will, the only provision for the children by the first marriage was that she had to bury Roy. They never questioned her about it, and she never wanted us to see the will. I don't know if she even knows if they did see it. When they read it, she wouldn't let Art stay.

Iwon: Another person, Delbert Smith, I don't know whether Delbert would do anything to help Roy or not, but Delbert said Roy was just like a brother to him. Like he didn't have a car, and Roy had one, so all he had to do was put the gas in, and Roy would take him anywhere. He works at the Dominion store, and he lives out near Burgessville. He was talking to me in the store, and he said if he could get enough people to say he wasn't violent, they might get him off. Well, I didn't know the circumstances or anything then. I'm trying to get him off, believe me. If he deserved to go to prison for second-degree murder, he deserves to go, but I feel sure he wouldn't do it because I've never seen him violent

Masters: I don't know if prison would do either one of them any good. I think a hospital might be a more appropriate place for both of them.

Iwon: She will never get off. I know because she's had so many spells. Been to St. Thomas twice that I know of and once in Goderich, before I knew about it, because Roy told me he had her in Goderich once, and how many times has she has been back in St. Thomas since, I don't know. Because I just told him, I wouldn't have anything to do with it anymore because he brings her out. Why not leave her there until they say she's cured? The time I took her to St. Thomas, when they got her in the hospital, the doctor started asking questions. He looked at me, and Roy said, "Oh, that's my big brother," so she asked the doctor if she could have a cigarette. The doctor gave her one. She took one puff and laid it on his desk and wanted another cigarette. He said, "You've already got one, you're burning my desk." Then Roy started talking, and I nudged Roy and said, "You better shut up. I'm not sure which one they're going to keep here." That's when I really thought there was something wrong with him.

Masters: This guy's name is Delbert Smith?

Iwon: Yes, he works at the Dominion Store on Ingersoll Road. I'm sure he wouldn't mind talking to you because he said he just feels sick about it.

Masters: Did he say when the last time it was when he saw Roy?

Iwon: He hasn't seen him for just about as long as I have, I guess.

Masters: A couple years, eh?

Iwon: Yeah. Roy used to go to the store there and bum money from Delbert, and Delbert would give it to him if he had it, and every time I go there and see Delbert, I would say, "Have you ever seen my brother around lately?" And he said, "No, I haven't seen him," and I said, "I haven't seen him for about two years," and he said, "It's just about that long since I saw him." But he could give you some history because as I say, Roy had a car, and he didn't have a car. This was years back. I'm sure he could help. I can't think of anybody else.

Masters: But June didn't think she had told you that about Roy's phone call about Vera and the diapers.

Iwon: I'm pretty sure because I'm sure it wasn't my stepmother, and it wasn't this lady from Ingersoll. She's phoned me twice that I can remember, and it wasn't Roy.

Masters: This lady from Ingersoll, is she a real talker?

Iwon: Yeah, her husband is an invalid or something. She has to drive him everywhere, or maybe he doesn't drive.

On July 5, 1978, Art Iwon was requested to wear a small recorder on his person and then visit his brother and sister-in-law, the accused, in the death of their son. This was done so they could record the conversation in an attempt to find out what actually happened to the deceased on May 19, 1978. He accepted wearing the recorder, and he then went and visited his brother and sister-in-law at their residence in Thamesford.

When Art arrived at the residence of his brother and his wife, he said he'd like to have a little chat with them because the police were asking him questions about things he knew nothing about.

Art said, "I've had people calling me, and for my sake, I would like to know just what happened because it has put me in a hell of position, and believe me, it does. Everybody is asking me about it. I'd just like to know for myself the whole thing, what happened. I mean, I can't be witness for you, or against you, or anything else one way or the other."

Vera said, "Well, I know, like in his case, his lawyer told him his sister hasn't come yet, but I imagine she eventually will come to see him, and he told him I'm not even supposed to talk to her about it. So I imagine, like being his brother-in-law and that, I better not talk to you either. I'm not trying to ignore you, I hope you understand, that's his understanding, but what Roy's lawyer told him, I don't know. He's got a different lawyer, but that's what his lawyer told him to say. If any relatives come around or anything that I wasn't supposed to talk about the case. I'm sorry you're being pestered, and I wish there was some way of stopping it. Is there any way of stopping them from coming around to see you like that all the time, the police or anything?"

"Will the police bug my phone if I wanted them to, or just tell people my phone was bugged, and then they'd hang up," Art replied.

"Oh, I see what you mean now."

"It isn't bugged," Art said.

"That's more or less, so nobody will bother you."

"Yeah."

Roy said, "That'll keep them off your back."

"I'm just on my way back from London, and I thought, well, it's been bothering me and bothering me, and I thought I'd like to come in and hear your side of the story, but if your lawyer says you can't talk to me, well..."

"Well, I know my lawyer told me, but like I say, I don't know. When Roy's lawyer talks to him, I'm not there, and when my lawyer talks me, Roy's not there, and he really don't know why. If I tell him after I'm not supposed to talk to somebody, he didn't even know I'm not to talk to his sister until the other day, did you, Roy?"

"No," Roy replied.

"He was surprised about that, but it's just what he told me."

"Like, I phoned her lawyer up and wanted to know how she was coming along, and he said, 'I'm not your lawyer, you'll have to phone your lawyer, goodbye now.' That's what he told me. I've got to go up tomorrow and see my lawyer. I've got an appointment at four o'clock in London," Roy said.

Art replied, "I have to take Lillian to London to the hospital university Monday morning."

Roy said, "Oh yeah. That's straight out Richmond Street."

"Yeah."

Vera said, "There's one thing you ought to hear. Roy mentioned about your one son that's in the RCMP. Is it true that he had gone up to the police detachment or something? I wasn't trying to contradict Roy, but I just couldn't see your son going up there, you know."

Art came back with, "No, he didn't go up over you people. He was home on business. He had to pick up a prisoner and take him back. He had to send a message to his force to pick him up in Toronto and to bring the prisoner to him."

Vera replied, "Yeah, I wasn't trying to contradict Roy, but I didn't think he would be here to see about us. He must have been here to do about something else or something of his own business."

Art, "No, he was here on business."

"No, I know when something like that happens, I imagine that I really do, like bug the family something awful, you hear so many things on TV and what you read in the paper even before anything like this occurred so that you pretty well figure it must be that way. It must be pretty hard on them too."

Vera said, "I thought that funeral was pretty good. Did you look after that, Art, or did that go through the welfare?"

Art responded, "I think that went through welfare. I looked after the grave."

"I see. We were asked by the welfare lady," Vera said.

Art replied, "They paid for the grave, but I let them use it."

"I see."

Roy said, "He had to be buried someplace."

Art came back with, "Well, the welfare lady asked us, remember that, Roy, who paid for it. She wanted to know."

"Well, she's just a worker, so I probably didn't know," Roy said.

Vera said, "Yeah, she wasn't the head of it, no, but she's just a worker."

Art replied, "The undertaker supplied the clothes for the baby and that."

Roy responded with, "Yeah, I went down and seen the undertaker. His wife said she didn't know where to get the clothes from, so she used her son's clothes for the funeral. She said, 'That's okay, that's fine, you're welcome.'"

Art said, "I don't know how it happened. I'd like to know for his own sake, not that it's going to do any good for him now. I can't be a witness for you or against you or anything else because I'm your brother, but it bugs me because I have people calling me up and really blasting me over it. Why didn't I do something? Well, I didn't even know the baby. I never seen the baby."

Vera came back with, "Yeah, it's just like people. They're ignorant. Certain place you go, like Roy was sort of in and out today, and I've had run-ins at three different places today when he wasn't home. In fact, one guy nearly plastered him up against the wall, so there's an officer here from Woodstock, not to do with the police, just a probation officer. I was telling him about it, and he said to call the police. I said I didn't see no need for it. I more or less talked to the guy and see about a washing machine he wanted us to buy. I tried to tell them I didn't want it, and he laughed at him, and now Roy's got to go over there in a few minutes, and I said, 'Now for heaven sakes, when you talk to him, don't swear and cuss, or he'll have you up for slander. Just tell him, will he please take his washing machine off our veranda, we don't want to buy it,' you know, more or less just like that. He was sort of mad because I didn't want it. He said that he didn't want to go through Roy again because Roy said he wanted it. I said to him, 'Well, we don't want it now.' He was going on, and he went right up there against the wall against him, and I just sort of backed up and just started to talk to him, and he just calmed down, and away he went. Anyway, Roy has to go over there tonight and talk to him. People are saying out in the newspaper about us and everything, what nice people they were, his father did, didn't he, Roy?"

Roy said, "What?"

"His father put an article in the paper about us," Vera said.

"Yeah, where is that paper? I was going to show it to Arthur."

"Yeah, and then you've got to get rectification on Thursday, tomorrow, about the mistake about his breakdown. I didn't have a breakdown."

Roy said, "Where's the paper, do you know where the paper went to?"

Vera responded with, "I don't know where it is right now. Well, it doesn't matter. He just mentioned that he didn't like the way people were talking about Roy, and he thought the second time I went in when I breached, that's to do with the conditions of the court, well, it had something do with his nerves, and I didn't have a nervous breakdown. I was in the courts is why I didn't have to come in, and so they had to put it in the newspaper to rectify their mistake. Don't they, Roy? They're going to on Thursday. They'll be up in arms when they hear that."

Art said, "Well, could you tell me this? How long was...was the baby still alive when you went to the phone the doctor?"

Roy replied, "As far as I know, he was, wasn't he?"

"Yeah, he was still alive. He was sick to his stomach. I'll admit that," Vera said.

"He was sick the day before, wasn't he?" said Roy.

Vera came back with, "Yeah, he was sick to his stomach. Because he was the way he went. Naturally the first thing Roy tried to get a hold of a doctor. There's no doctor around here, so he called the ambulance service."

"So then I phoned the operator, and the operator got the ambulance. I guess they come either from Woodstock or Ingersoll," Roy said.

"They probably came from Ingersoll," said Art.

"Ingersoll-Alexandra Hospital, and the coroner came from Ingersoll, and they had a guy from London?" Roy said.

"I don't know, you told me from London. I don't really know where he was from."

"Well, you seen him sitting in that chair over there."

"Yeah, I know who you mean, sort of a foreign guy."

"Chinese or Japanese or something."

"Whatever he was, I really don't know where he was from, Roy. He asked questions, that's all."

Art said, "You went down to the IGA. Did you get groceries?"

"Yeah, I went down that Thursday, didn't I?" said Roy.

"Yeah. The thing was, it really would be nice to talk about it that even though Arthur is your brother, it is none of his business what you say to him, but I'm not going to say anything because I know they did the right thing, calling and getting the doctor, that's all I know."

"Yeah, but we couldn't get a doctor."

"Naturally somebody expects the first thing you do is get a doctor. I'm just going to say that much. I'm not going to say any more because I'm not being disrespectful."

"I tried phoning the operator, and the woman operator said, 'What seems to be the trouble?' and I told her, and she said, 'Do you want an ambulance?' and I said yeah, then she said, 'What's your name and where do you live, and stay out in front, and I will tell the ambulance to come right away,' so that's what I did."

"Yeah, but first you try to get a doctor, but nobody's around. The doctor's at the hospital, so you're sort of in between, I guess, or something."

"Dr. Kosmal."

"You've seen his pictures, haven't you, Arthur?"

Art said, "Yeah, you gave me a picture. I saw the baby at the funeral home."

"Yeah, but wasn't really—like, I've heard some bad reports. It's pretty bad what he looked like," said Vera.

"No, he wasn't, he looked beautiful," Art responded.

"Well, somebody told me he looked awful because they'd taken parts out of him, that's what the cop told me."

Roy said, "No, they cut him open to check him, that's all. They cut everybody open to check them."

Art came back with, "In a postmortem, they just check."

"Here's a baby picture."

"He looked just like that picture. I saw it in the funeral home."

Vera said, "Oh, his face look good then."

"It was a respectable funeral, and I don't think an undertaker could have done any better than this undertaker did. My daughter came up to see him too," said Art.

Roy said, "Yeah, we seen your daughter at the funeral."

"Yeah, she brought the flower wreath, the heart."

Roy said, "Art said he cut the trees down."

"I cut the trees down and dug them out."

Vera said, "Yeah, see, there is a picture back there, but the other one on the other side isn't too good. The one on the right is a better one of him."

Roy said, "There's two we had done it the IGA store. We had four, didn't we?"

"Yeah."

"They took one, didn't they, or take two?"

"Oh, I don't know, it's hard to say, but I know they took one anyway."

Art said, "Well, I don't know. As I say, I'm just on my way back from London. There was so much traffic, I couldn't turn here, so I went down to the corner and turned around and came back."

Vera said, "Did you say you had been to a camp or someplace?"

"No, up to Mocha Temple. I am a Shriner. We had an election there for a past potentate, so I had to go up and vote."

Vera said, "Oh, I see now what you mean."

"So I'm just on my way back from London, and I thought maybe you people could tell me something just to ease my mind, you know."

Roy said, "Well, the best thing to do if anybody phones is tell them you don't know anything about it, and tell them if they want any further news to phone my lawyer. He's in London."

"That there army hospital up in London, what the heck do they call it?" asked Vera.

"Westminster," said Art.

"Westminster, it's run by Vic now. Are you allowed to go and visit people in there, or is there just certain people can go and visit if there's a person there? What if a person like me or Roy wanted to go and visit some of the veterans, are you allowed to do that?"

"You just have to ask at the desk if they can have visitors. They'd let you in," Art said.

Vera said, "Well, isn't there some old people that have been there for years, and if you wanted to visit as a voluntary, you know, like visit, could you be allowed to go in, or how does that go?"

"I imagine so," Art said.

Roy said, "You can if they can have visitors."

"If they're allowed to have visitors, you can go in."

Vera said, "There must be a lot of old people that never get visitors, you know."

Roy returned with, "There are a lot of hospitals that don't get visitors."

"Like me, I might soon be going back to work as a nurse's aide."

"The probation officer was here today and checked us out. He's from Woodstock."

"They've asked about jobs."

Roy said, "From Princess Street, 514 Princess Street, he comes in and checks us out once a week. Last week he didn't come around because he was on holidays. He told me he wouldn't come last week. Friday, I have to go into Ingersoll and check in with manpower to let them sign my card. Every ten days I've got to go over and let them sign my card on account of welfare."

Vera said, "That's a ten check, otherwise they cut you off of welfare if you don't check in with manpower."

Art said, "Well, I guess if you can't say anything, there is no use talking, eh?"

Vera said, "June is living with Cheryl now, is she?"

Roy said, "What is Cheryl's last name now, Jim somebody or other?"

"I don't know," Art said.

"I don't know either, works at Kelsey Hayes."

Vera said, "I always thought it was Murray, or is that his uncle?"

Roy said, "Kelsey Hayes or something."

"I don't know where. I think she lives off Huron Street there somewhere," Art said.

Roy said, "Yeah."

"Well, I guess if you can't tell me anything, you can't tell me anything, eh?"

Roy said, "We were told not to."

Art said goodbye and left.

When the case came to trial, the judge did not grant a change of venue for technical reasons, but he did allow the defense lawyers to ask prospective jurors a series of questions based around what research had uncovered. Thus, there was an attempt to weed out people who would not hear the case with an open mind. The jury was eventually chosen, and the defense counsel were satisfied that it consisted of people who would evaluate the evidence fairly. Ultimately, the jury found the father not guilty and the mother guilty of manslaughter.

Bits and Pieces 5

Late one evening, I received a call at home from our dispatcher requesting my presence at a fatal accident on the 401 highway a short distance east of the overpass on no. 4 Highway.

I headed out in the fog south on no. 4 Highway to Highway 401, where I took the eastbound lane to where the accident happened, about a quarter mile east of the overpass.

I found that a car travelling east on the eastbound lane with the father driving and the mother sitting in the front seat with their son sitting in the back. An impaired driver mistakenly was travelling west on the eastbound lane in the foggy condition. Apparently, the impaired driver did not have his headlights on for some reason or other, and a head-on collision occurred. The occupants of the two vehicles were all killed as a result of the crash.

Even though it was foggy he was able to take photographs of this mishap.

Just west of the interchange off no. 4 Highway, all traffic proceeding east was redirected off the 401 Highway on to no. 4 Highway. This included all vehicles, cars, trucks, and buses heading east on the 401.

After taking the photos and measurements at the accident scene, I headed back west on the 401, and as I was about go under the overpass of Highway 4, I heard a loud noise, which sounded like a crash of vehicles. When I arrived on top of the overpass, a transport truck had stopped in the middle of a turn to his left.

The driver of the transport truck had stopped in the middle of his turn because a nurse in a jeep was heading to the St. Thomas Hospital to begin her midnight to 8:00 a.m. shift in the fog and thinking about getting to work on time. She did not notice the transport truck coming off the ramp from the 401 and making the left-hand turn onto Highway 4 because of the fog. Her Jeep Wrangler, which she was driving, attempted to go under the center of the trailer of the transport truck, tearing off all above the hood of the engine compartment.

She ended up in the back seat with severe head injuries and multiple cuts to her face and shoulders. Unfortunately, she did not make it. She died on the way to the hospital in the ambulance.

CHAPTER TWENTY-EIGHT

Homosexual Murdered

A few years ago, a friend of mine, Dave Kinnear, had advised me of a few of the murders that he had investigated. The following is one of the cases he advised me of.

On Friday, November 2, 1984, at approximately 1:20 p.m., the cleaning ladies at 21 Kinnear Street entered apartment 2113 of Garnet Jack Bellaire. They found the apartment door locked. They opened the door with the key that was provided to them by Bellaire. They found Bellaire slumped on the living room chesterfield, apparently dead. They found no signs of life and called the police.

When the police entered the apartment, they observed that the blue pillowcase was wrapped around Bellaire's neck. He appeared to have died as a result of violence. Bellaire's right pants pocket was turned inside out, and a check of his apartment found in his bedroom dresser drawers had been opened as if they had been rifled and searched. A jewelry case had obviously been disturbed, and Bellaire's wallet was found lying on the kitchen table where it had been gone through and the contents scattered on a table beside it. There was no money in the wallet.

The scene was secured by Sergeant Black, and the identification unit arrived at the scene and commenced taking photographs and searched for fingerprints.

The coroner, Dr. John O. Martin, attended and pronounced the death and ordered an autopsy to determine the cause of the death.

Pathologist Dr. Douglas Miles attended and viewed the scene and subsequently performed an autopsy at St. Joseph's Hospital, which determined that Bellaire had died as a result of violence. Dr. Miles determined that Bellaire had received multiple blows to the nasal region, causing severe nasal fractures and hemorrhage resulting in aspiration of blood, causing asphyxia type of death.

Police investigation found that the deceased Bellaire was a homosexual and had frequented the Brunswick Hotel. Inquiries found that on Thursday, November 1, 1984, Bellaire had gone to the Brunswick Hotel at around noon and was there drinking with friends at 2:30 p.m. They were joined by a man who identified himself as Joseph Adrien François Fournair. He was not known by anyone in this group. Adrien, also known as Frank, was French Canadian, born in Montréal, and he was a cook at the Rideout Restaurant and Tavern. He was introduced around to this group of friends, including Bellaire. After several drinks, he spoke of booking sick and not going to work at the Rideout as he had had too much to drink.

Bellaire and Fournair were observed talking and whispering together, and at approximately 4:30 p.m., they were observed leaving the Brunswick Hotel together.

Inquiries at the Rideout Garage Restaurant, on November 2, found this accused was employed there and had phoned in at approximately 5:00 p.m., advising that he would not be into work the previous day. He also had not reported for work as required on Friday, November 2. The accused's address at 883 Dufferin Avenue was obtained and checked. Fournair had picked up his Walkman radio at 9:00 a.m. and had left and not returned.

The police located Fournair's girlfriend. She told the police Fournair had left her apartment Thursday, November 1, at approximately 1:15 p.m. to go to work and had phoned her later at approximately 8:00 p.m. advising he had not gone to work. He returned to her apartment at approximately 8:30 p.m., bringing with him a religious statue of the Last Supper, which he gave to her.

She advised that he spent the night there and left her apartment at about 8:40 a.m. on November 2 and saying that he had to be at work at the Rideout Garage Restaurant at 10:00 a.m. He advised that he would phone her later that night, but he did not call. On November 3, police checked the Front Page Variety Store and was advised by the owner, manager Merwan Zavis, that a man with an obvious French accent had bought the related statues from him on Thursday, November 1. The first one was bought at 10:00 a.m., and the last one, a statue of the Last Supper, was purchased at approximately 7:00 p.m. Zavis advised that this time, the man was who he subsequently identified as this accused Fournier, who stated to him that he killed somebody, and he'd be going to jail for ten years, and he would see Zavis in ten years.

Fournier's fingerprints were identified on the telephone in Bellaire's apartment.

As a result of this investigation, a Canada-wide warrant was issued for the arrest of Fournier on this charge of murder.

Sergeant David Kennear, the officer in charge of the investigation, interviewed several patrons at the Brunswick Hotel as well as the bartender, and they all gave statements to the effect that Jack Bellaire was a known homosexual. They had known him for several years. He was drinking in the Brunswick Hotel on November 1 around 2:00 p.m., where he was standing at the bar by himself for the first couple of minutes while he was there. Jack drank and rye and water. One of the witnesses had bought him a couple of drinks. He wasn't drunk, but he was well on his way.

Sometime after 3:00 p.m., they noticed this guy who came over and introduced himself to the group as Frank. He was a French-Canadian, always talked with a slight French accent. He said that he worked at the Rideout Tavern. He said he was a cook or something. He started buying a round of drinks with everybody else. He was drinking bottles of Budweiser. He said he had to be at work by five o'clock. Sometime around 4:00 p.m., he said the hell with it, he was going to call in sick.

While at the bar, they noticed Jack and Frank whispering to each other and kind of making out with each other. They were surprised since all the time they had seen Jack in there, they never saw him with anyone at the bar. They left together out through the back door that leads out to the parking lot.

The witnesses described the French guy who left with Jack to be around thirty to thirty-five years old, six feet tall, and weighed about 160 to 170 pounds. He had dark wavy hair and a mustache. He had a large straight nose with a lump in the middle of it, something like a witch's nose. He was wearing a bright blue dark velour V-neck sweater, long sleeves, and no shirt under it. He was wearing a watch on his left wrist. One witness thought he had a two-tone silver and gold expansion bracelet. His hair came just over his ears. It was full and slightly wavy and parted on the side.

Dolores Benny worked part-time as a registered nursing assistant and also cleaned a couple of friends' apartments on a part-time basis. At first she said, "I started to clean for Jim Ball at apartment 812–21 King Street last summer around late July. Jim Ball and Jack Bellaire are good friends, and around a year ago last November, I started cleaning for both of them. I have also known Jim Ball for about five or six years. Jim had told me he was a homosexual, and I believe that Jack is also one. Jim and Jack have been very close friends. They would go shopping for plants together and have drinks together. I clean Jack Bellaire's apartment every second Thursday.

"He would always have a few drinks before he went to work at 12:45 p.m. As long as I have known Jack, he lived alone, a user-friendly giving person. On November 2 at 11:00 a.m., I tried to call Jack to tell him that I couldn't come that day as my son had become ill. I wanted to pick a date the following week. I phoned his place several times, the line was always busy."

She left her apartment at 1:00 p.m. with her friend Brenda, who sometimes helped her clean the apartments. She parked her car underground at 21 King Street and got in the elevator and went up to 212. She put the key in the lock and opened the apartment door.

On entering the apartment, she checked the lower downstairs bedroom and bathroom and looked in the closet of the downstairs bedroom. It appeared that the fellow who had been living with Jack had moved out. Yesterday it was clean, and Jack did not smoke.

They went upstairs toward the second landing and with no response. They walked down the hall to the living room. She looked at the sofa, and it took her a second to register what she saw. Jack was lying in about the middle of the couch facing the kitchen area. His shirt was up, his stomach was swollen, and his face was discolored. She knew he was dead. She said, "Oh my god, Brenda, it's Jack! He's dead."

She walked closer into the room. She wanted to see if he was really dead. She noticed what appeared to be his intestines on his lower left side. She saw a towel around his neck like a scarf, and there was caked blood around his nostrils. It appeared to be a knife in the area of his intestines. She told Brenda that she had to call the police. She told Brenda to give her a towel so she could use the phone. She put down the phone and left the apartment. She locked the door. They went to the building manager's office and called 911 for the police and an ambulance.

Sergeant John Black and Constable Fournais were dispatched to 21 King Street and arrived at the apartment at 1:40 p.m. Once they entered the apartment, they were met by the two cleaning ladies who were sitting on the first landing going upstairs. They briefly informed the police officers that they had come into the apartment at 1:25 p.m., had opened the door with a master key, went upstairs, and found the occupant of the apartment, Bellaire, dead on the couch. The police officers were advised that one of the cleaning ladies had called the police.

They observed that the victim was sprawled on the couch on his back with his head pointing in the northeast direction, and his feet and legs were off the couch. He was dressed in a pair of old blue johns, which were unbuttoned, and the right front pocket was pulled out. He also had on a gray blue sweatshirt on. Around his neck was a reddish towel on the left side and a blue cloth around the right side of his neck.

Two empty Miller beer cans were on the couch beside him on the left side. A plate with meat juice was on the couch on his right side. The coffee table was at an angle, and an ashtray was on the floor, upset.

There was a black leather wallet, birth certificate, and papers on a wicker table by the west wall. The second-level lights were still on in the hallway, kitchen, and the living room.

They observed the injuries on the victim to be a cut and bruises to the bridge of the victim's nose and blood by his nostrils.

There was a half-full forty-ounce bottle of Crown Royal on the kitchen counter with some orange juice. The second floor bedroom with a single bed was messed up.

The first floor bedroom containing a double bed was neat, but there was a jewelry case open in the freezer. It contained cufflinks and tie clips. The dresser drawers in this bedroom were also partially opened. The lock on the apartment doors was a deadbolt and must be locked on the outside by a key.

The Thames Valley ambulance attendants arrived and could find no visible signs of life and left shortly after their arrival. The two officers notified the criminal investigation division of the circumstances of this death as they were known.

Cecile, the girlfriend of Fournais, received a phone call from him. He told her that he was working as a cook at the Foothills Hospital in Calgary, Alberta.

Members of the Calgary Police Department received information that Adrien Francois Fournais was wanted by the London Police Department for the murder of Jack Bellaire and was working at Foothills Hospital in Calgary.

Detectives Waycraft and Tobbins of the Calgary Police Department attended at Foothills Hospital, where they spoke to Fournais. He was told by the detectives that he was wanted by the London Police on a charge of murder. He nodded in acknowledgment.

He was arrested and given the right to counsel and cautioned for the murder in London. He was asked if he understood the caution.

He was handcuffed and was taken to the Calgary Police Department. He was taken to an interview room. After giving his name, date of birth, and other particulars, he gave the following statement.

This statement is being taken in conjunction with the murder of Jacques Bellaire in Ontario. He had been told he was not obliged to say anything unless he wished to do so. Anything he say may be given in evidence. He had also been told of his right to counsel.

He understood the nature the police investigation and made the following statement. It was signed Frank Fournais.

On that day he left his girlfriend to go to his place in London. He went for a drink first at Mingles, a bar in downtown London. This was about 11:00 a.m. He had a few beers there, and then he went to the Brunswick Hotel. He had a few more beers there with the guys in the bar, a total of fourteen beers. A guy came into the bar and talked with him. He told him he was from Québec, and his name was Jacques Belanger or Boulanger. They began talking, and he invited Frank to his place for beer. Frank agreed left the bar with him.

They got to his place. He sat on the couch, and Frank sat on the chair. They had a beer and rye. Frank phoned his boss and said he would be late. His boss was named Chris, and he spoke to Frank in the kitchen of the Garage Restaurant. Then Jacques came over and sat on the couch and started to touch him on the shoulder and face. Frank told him not to. He asked him, "What do you think I am?" Jacques kept on touching him, and they got into an argument.

Frank finished his beer and went to the kitchen to get another one. Then he went and sat on the chair. Jacques came and sat on the arm of the chair, and he got angry. Frank pushed him and repeated, "I'm not like that." He lost control. He pushed him and hit him in the face. The next day his right hand was sore. After he hit him, Jacques fell. He didn't know what happened next. He left and woke up at his place at about 9:00 p.m. What he did to him after he punched him, he didn't remember.

Signed: François Fournais

Witness: Barry Waycraft and P. Tobbins

Detective Sergeants Lucas and Mulleni flew to Calgary from London, where they were met by Detectives Waycraft and Tobbins. They were transported to the Calgary Police Department, where they presented their Canada-wide warrant for the offense of murder by Joseph Adrien Fournais after having it backed by hearing Justice of the Peace Alex Bishowf.

They then proceeded to the Calgary Remand Center, where they introduced themselves as London police officers. They wanted to speak to Fournais now and would take him caution.

Fournier: Yes.
Muiller: Frank, we'd like to record your particulars. Joseph Adrien Francois Fournais, last address 883 Dufferin Avenue, Apt. 3, London. Date of birth 13 July '54, white, 6 foot, 163 pounds, light brown hair, mustache, the lies. Last employed at the Garage Restaurant in London as a cook for a chef Frank, Mike, or the manager Chris. Employed two weeks, previously employed at Howard Jacobs for one week, then Labatt's as a packer for two weeks and laid off, Scott's Chicken, Wellington and Southdale. Lives on his own, no family contact, four sisters, one brother, married 1977 and divorced 1978 when his wife returned to Germany.
Lucas: Frank, you want to tell us what happened in London?
Fournais: I'll tell you, but my lawyer says I'm not to sign anything. I left Cecile's at 10:30 a.m., went downtown by bus to Mingles for a couple of hours.
Muller: When did you go to the Brunswick Hotel, or what time did you get there?

Fournais went on to explain that after he left Cecile's between 10:00 a.m. and 10:30 a.m., he went downtown by bus to Mingles for a couple hours. From there he went to the Brunswick Hotel somewhere around 1:00 p.m. It was his first time there; he didn't like it. He met four or five guys there. He said he left his bag in there with his working clothes and Cecile's phone. The one guy who he remembered was Jacques Bellaire, a French guy, so he talked about being in

Montréal. He couldn't remember the names of the other four or five guys he was drinking with. They were not from Montréal. The other guys were from British Columbia. They just sat around to shoot the shit, men's stuff, women, normal stuff in a bar. He had quite a few beers. He always carried pictures of him, and he didn't remember whether he showed them to the guys or not. The pictures were of Cecile's two children, Claude and Angie. He told the guys he worked as a cook, and then some guy bought another round of beers, and somebody bought a couple more. He was supposed to be at work at 2:00 p.m., and he got pretty happy.

There was a short pause, after which he said he was not trying to hide anything; he just didn't understand why it was murder. He wanted to talk his lawyer, then he will talk to the detectives about Jacques and everything. He did not try to hide it. He wanted to know the truth but what happened also. It was important to him and to Cecile. He loved her, so he wanted her all the time, her and the kids, not just once in a while. He wanted her to come with him, but she wouldn't. He knew she was very upset about this. He phoned her, and she was better now that he turned himself in. He phoned from the hospital to turn himself in when she told him he was wanted for murder in Canada. He ran from things like this before, but nothing like this. He didn't mean to do it. The guy was a fagot.

He said he had some beer and rye him. He told them he wasn't like that. He had moved to the chair away from Jacques. He called his boss to say he wouldn't be in at work. Jacques came over and sat on the arm of the chair and started to touch his face again. Fournier got up and went to the kitchen, got another beer, and when he came back in the room, Belanger touched him again. He hit with his left palm in the face, and he went down on the floor or the couch. He didn't remember which. He went blue. He was so mad, and that's it. After he hit him, he didn't know what he did after that. Then he remembered the elevator, and then he remembered being at home and then woke up at Cecile's.

When he left Cecile's, he went to the bus depot. He bought a ticket to Vancouver. He went and stayed at the Salvation Army Dunsmuir house. He had stayed there before. Then he hitchhiked to

Calgary, and he was depressed without Cecile. He went to the hospital, and the doctor talked to him, and he stayed there.

Fournais was charged with murder and appeared in court in 1985, where he pleaded guilty and received a sentence of fifteen years.

CHAPTER TWENTY-NINE

It Happened in a Mental Hospital

On October 29, 1968, I was dispatched to the St. Thomas Psychiatric Hospital where an inmate had been murdered. The hospital was a large complex consisting of fourteen interconnecting buildings. These buildings catered to the many inmates residing there.

On our arrival at the main building at the front of the complex, we were informed that the deceased, an inmate, James Arlington Haynes, age 76, was found dead in a washroom. He had been an inmate at the hospital for most of his life, being mentally defective since birth. He lived in Ward 3C at the hospital.

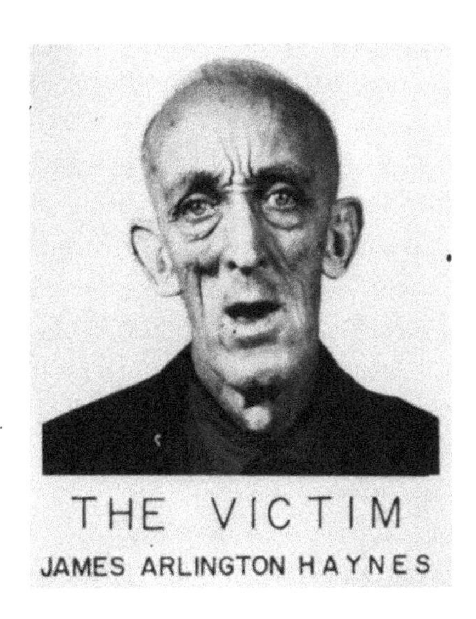

THE VICTIM
JAMES ARLINGTON HAYNES

The accused, William Robert Brown, age 23, came to the hospital from Windsor on a warrant of remand for observation. He had been charged with theft over $50. Brown was certified mentally ill on May 7, 1964, by Dr. T. G. Ing and Dr. W. G. Wallacer, and he remained at the hospital, living in ward 1C.

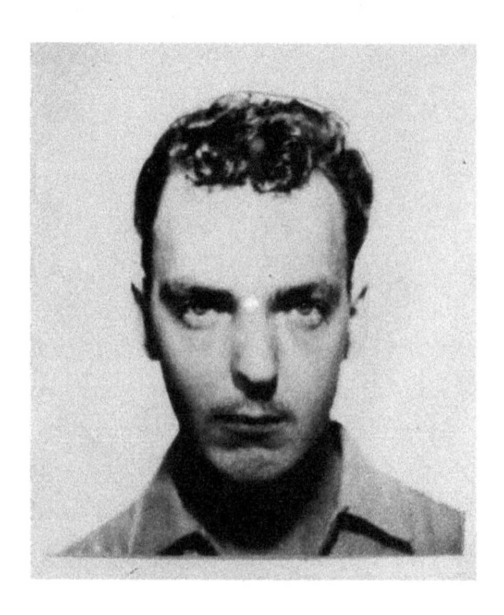

The history indicates that patient Brown was a middle child in a family of five whose father died when he was five years of age, and his mother remarried when he was nine. He did not get along well with his stepfather or the younger siblings in the new home. He attended school until age fifteen, completing grade 7, and then was employed at numerous different jobs: working in a car wash, a canning factory, and eventually at the National Auto Radiator Company in Windsor.

He attended a child guidance clinic from February 1954 to June 1955, accompanied by his mother. Reports on file indicate that psychological testing gave him an IQ of 100 at the age of nine, which is within the normal range of intelligence.

He came to the hospital on April 27, 1964, as a result of the following incidents. On April 16, 1964, his mother, Mrs. Gladys Curtis, laid a charge against him of theft over $50. The patient had apparently taken some money from his mother's purse and from a dresser drawer. He then closed out a bank account that he had and left Windsor. He returned a few days later, but his mother did not press the charges at that time.

On April 22, 1964, there was an argument in the home between Brown and his mother, father, and younger siblings. He threatened to kill his mother, and as a result, the police were called and proceeded prosecution of the previous charge of theft. The patient was examined by Dr. Pinder on April 26, 1964, at the request of the court in Windsor. Dr. Pinder recommended his remand to the Canada Hospital in St. Thomas for further investigation, feeling the patient was probably subnormal IQ or with a personality disorder of inadequate type. In either case, his judgment was defective, and he might be dangerous.

The patient was examined by Dr. Kennedy with psychological testing, skull x-rays, and an electrocardiogram being carried out. The psychological testing indicated that he now obtained an intelligence quotient of 79. The patient was felt to be psychotic by Dr. Kennedy, and certification as mentally ill was carried out on May 8, 1964, with Dr. Wallace describing the patient on his certificate as suicidal and hostile, and Dr. Kennedy stating the patient was delusional. The electrocardiogram was reported as normal, as were the skull x-rays. A conference note of May 7, 1964, describes the patient as "psychotic," divorced from reality, exhibiting violent behavior in apparent response to hallucinatory and highly delusional experiences. The conference note made a diagnosis of pathological personality—schizoid personality, limited intelligence. The patient was started on chlorpromazine, Stelazine, and Cogentin, to which he apparently showed some improvement.

He went home on probation on October 11, 1964, but returned on October 25, 1964, being probated again from November 23, 1964, to December 8, 1964. During his hospitalization, he underwent a two-stage right orchiopexy operation. He was lodged on various wards within the hospital, some of them closed, some of them open. He worked in the hospital, in the laundry, and in the kitchen and worked in St. Thomas in a bowling alley as a pin setter.

He was again at home on probation from August 10, 1966, to October 7, 1966, when he was returned. He had eloped from the hospital in February 1967, going to Toronto, eloped again in April going to Windsor. Subsequent to these elopements, he was placed in a closed ward. He regained his privileges but eloped again in October 1967 on two occasions.

On December 23, 1966, he was taken home on probation by his family but returned on January 18, 1967, after an argument with his parents, and at this time he had two or three superficial cuts on his right wrist, which he stated were self-inflicted with a razor blade. He came under the care of Dr. McLean on October 17, 1966. During the period of his hospitalization and his probations at home, he was at all times continued on various medications of the phenothiazine group.

In January 1968, while in ward 1B, he started to work with the paint party and was transferred to pavilion 1C, an open ward, on May 9, 1968. His work with the paint party was satisfactory throughout the spring and summer, and he apparently corresponded with his family who had promised to take him home on a holiday for two weeks during July 1968. These arrangements were not completed due to the mail strike. The patient continued on ward 1C until August 27, 1968, when he was lodged in 1A overnight following some sexual advances to female occupational therapists working in 1C.

On August 28, he was lodged in 1B, a closed ward, and continued there until October 11, 1968, when he was returned to pavilion 1C. Once the summer occupational therapy students left, he was allowed to return to the paint gang, but remained lodged in 1B without privileges. For two weeks he worked on the paint gang with privileges and then returned to 1C. On his return to 1C, he was quiet and cooperative, but later he appeared to be rather tense and anxious, and his medication was increased. He apparently made crude suggestions and advances to the occupational therapist in 1C on October 23. An attempt was made to inform Dr. McNiven, but he could not be reached until October 24, 1968, when the patient was interviewed.

At this time he stated he had no friends in the hospital and that he wanted to leave the hospital to go to Penetanguishene. He felt there was no hope of him ever getting out and getting home, that everyone in the hospital knew about his behavior, and that the patients in the ward were teasing him about it. Despite the fact that he was over six feet tall, he was not a good fighter and could not make them stop teasing him. He stated as well that he was not sleeping. It was suggested to him that he could be transferred to 1A and locked up there instead of Penetanguishene, but he stated that he was afraid to go to 1A because he feared some of the patients there.

His medication was changed, and he was left in 1C to continue his employment with the paint gang. There were no further reports of any sort of upset until October 29, when he was found in the hall by an attendant with blood on his clothing. He was taken to the male person at reception A, where he was held. He stated at that time that he had stabbed another patient with a knife. When Dr. McNiven interviewed him, he stated that he stabbed a patient in the washroom with a jackknife, and he hoped that he was dead. He could not identify the patient other than to say he was from 3C, the defective ward. He stated that he obtained the jackknife from another patient named Robert in pavilion 1C.

During the interview with Dr. McNiven, Brown appeared to be very cool, calm, and collected. He showed little concern for what he had done, stating that he had nothing specifically against the man he had killed and had only done this to get out of the hospital and be sent to Penetanguishene. Later in the day, the patient was transferred from male reception A to pavilion 1A for security reasons. During the transfer, he stated to Dr. McNiven that he was sorry that he had caused so much trouble.

Haynes's body was found in a small washroom on the ground floor of the hospital at approximately 10:50 a.m. on October 29, 1968, by John Delaney. Delaney was a former patient at the hospital, who, after being just decertified, had remained living in the residential section of the hospital for released patients. Delaney immediately went to the male infirmary and advised the nurse on duty, Mrs. Alice Hinds, and a cleaning man, Frank Taitham.

They both went to the washroom. They saw that Haynes was obviously dead. It was noted that a broken pocketknife was lying on the floor beside the body. The washroom was closed, and the senior officials in the hospital were notified. Dr. W. E. Ing of the hospital's staff arrived at the scene and pronounced Haynes dead.

Donald K. Fryer, a ward attendant at the hospital, passed the washroom moments after the body was discovered. He saw the body and was informed the man had been stabbed. Fryer left the area between 11:10 a.m. and 11:15 a.m. Upon approaching the kitchen area, he saw William Robert Brown standing in the corridor. He noticed what appeared to be blood on Brown's trousers and therefore approached him.

Brown said, "You have come to get me, have you?" K. Fryer asked Brown why, and Brown stated, "I have just knifed a man."

K. Fryer told Brown, "You come with me."

Brown agreed and said, "I told him I was going to kill him."

Brown was taken to reception A in the hospital and turned over to two attendants, Patrick Glynn and Stuart Morgan. All of Brown's clothing was removed from him and placed in a plastic bag and labeled. Brown was then locked in a special observation room where he remained until interviewed by Dr. John McNiven, a psychiatrist on staff at the hospital.

Brown admitted to Dr. McNiven that he stabbed an old man in the washroom. He stated that he had obtained a pocketknife from another patient, one Robert North. He made it known to the doctor that his reason for the murder was so that he would be transferred to the Canada hospital in Penetanguishene.

On Wednesday, October 23, 1968, Brown had indicated to attendants on his ward that he was depressed and unhappy with his existence at St. Thomas. He thought he was a sexual pervert who might become violent and suggested he should be transferred to Penetanguishene. The sexual pervert feeling apparently originated because of two vulgar approaches he had made to young female occupational therapists working in the hospital. Dr. McNiven was informed and was interviewed by Brown. As a result, daily medications were changed. Brown appeared to return to a quiet cooperative manner in the following days.

The Ontario Provincial Police were called. Corporal Charlie James and Constable Don Wild of the St. Thomas detachment were the first police officers at the scene, arriving at 12:15 p.m. I arrived at the hospital with Charles Drew to photograph the scene and collect exhibits.

Photographs were taken showing the location of the body on the floor and the location of the knife near the head of the body. Blood samples were also taken from the locations on the floor. At 4:15 p.m., the body was removed from the washroom to the hospital morgue. The postmortem was performed by Dr. Adilman. The clothing of the deceased was taken and turned over to him. Other exhibits from the postmortem were also turned over to him. The examination revealed there were fifteen stab wounds that penetrated the back and chest, three of which entered the heart. Death was due to the stab wounds.

At 9:55 p.m., William Robert Brown was taken into a room by Detective Sergeant Dennis and Constable Wild, where he was advised, "You are charged with noncapital murder of James Haynes. If you have spoken to any police officers or anyone with authority or if such person has spoken to you in connection with this case, I want it clearly understood that I do not want to influence you in making any statement. Do you wish to say anything in answer to the charge? You are not obliged to say anything unless you wish to do so. Whatever you say may be given in evidence. Do you understand this warning?"

Brown responded, "The only thing I can say is that I killed this guy."

The warning was repeated, and he was asked again if he understood.

> Brown: Not quite the whole thing. The only thing I can say is I wanted to do it, not specifically that guy, but anyone.
>
> Dennis: What did you want to do?

Brown: I wanted to murder him, not just him, but anyone who came along from ward C. As far as it is on my conscience, it doesn't bother me a bit.

Dennis: Why did you want to murder him?

Brown: Do I get a trip to Penetang out of this, or is this just a routine check?

Dennis: It depends on the court if you go to Penetang or not. Why did you want to murder him?

Brown: I don't give a shit where they send me. I just want to get out of this place.

Dennis: Why did you want to murder a man?

Brown: I had no intention for this man. I just wanted kill somebody. They were picking on me. I just wanted to get out. It did not have to be that man. How long will the court take before they sentence me, sixty days, three weeks?

Dennis: I really couldn't say how long. What did you use to kill this man?

Brown: A brown-handle jackknife with blade, two inches long. I think it was a Boy Scout knife. It had a sharp point on the end of it.

Dennis: Did you know the name of the man who was killed?

Brown: No, not until he told me. John somebody, I think it was. Like I said, I just picked him. It could have been anyone. Would any of you gentlemen have a smoke on you?

Brown was given a cigarette and a light. He then said, "This is all evidence for the trial, is it?"

Dennis: Yes, it is. I will read this statement to you, and then I want you to read it aloud to me. If you agree with it, will you please sign it? Before I read the statement to you, I would like to ask what you did or didn't understand about the warning.

Brown: Will you go over to the warning again? I don't give a shit about the warning or lawyer or anything like that. I just want to go to Penetang. It doesn't mean a thing to me. Ask all the questions and write all night. In other words, I don't want any help.

Dennis: I will read the warning to you again.

Brown: I am guilty of murdering a guy. The staff is asking why I did it, and I told them. Like I said, I want to go to Penetang. If they want to hang me, go ahead. I have no fucking use for this world.

Dennis: I'll read this statement to you again.

Brown: The only one I spoke to was one of the staff. Before this happened, I was upset about something. I told the staff all about it. It could have been anyone from ward 3C. I hate those guys.

Just a minute, he never said anything about any person picking on him. He was just upset, went down the hall, had a knife in his pocket, opened up the blade. He happened to see this guy standing there. He went down to the four corners, looking for any of the 3C fellows. Saw this one man there, lured him into the washroom. He asked him to roll a cigarette. When his back was to him, Brown started to stab him. He kept yelling, "Leave me alone!" The more he yelled, the more he stabbed him. That is all he can remember, except seeing the blood gush all over the floor.

He said it looked like a Boy Scout knife, blade two inches long. Cigarette. Oh, come on now—you're not going to write down about the cigarettes. You are not going to make a jackass out of him. If you want to take him to court, go ahead. He just wanted to say he killed a man and wanted to go to Penetang for it. I'm damn proud that he did it. He knows they can't hang him, and he knew he would go to Penetang. He was upset at the time. He didn't want to repeat himself, but he lured this man in the washroom and offered him some tobacco. The funny thing is, he saw him take the knife out. Then he killed him.

When Dennis asked Brown to read the statement, he said, "That is okay. It sounds screwy, but that is what happened. I am tired now."

William Robert Brown signed the statement, and it was witnessed by D. J. Dennis, Detective Sergeant, and D. K. Wild, Prov. Constable.

On October 30, 1968, at 10:30 a.m. in the doctor's office at the county jail, a further statement was taken from William Robert Brown, age 22, single, patient at the Psychiatric Hospital St. Thomas. Charged with noncapital murder of James Haynes.

After the warning was given, Brown said, "All I got to say is I am guilty, guilty of the charge."

Dennis: What charge do you refer to?

Brown: Murder charge. I killed a guy yesterday. There is no way of getting away from that. I might as well plead guilty.

Dennis: You tell us what happened yesterday.

Brown: I was on his ward yesterday. I was upset about something. It got to me later on. I went downstairs, and when I went downstairs, I was pretty peeved about things. Had this jackknife out of my pocket, opened it up, and then put it back in my pocket. After I went down the hall toward the square, I looked down the square to see if anybody was around. I went down toward the canteen. There are four corners down there, you know. I stood there for a few seconds, then after I stood there, I met this guy off of 3C. I asked him if he wanted to buy some tobacco. He said no, so I said I would give him some, so I let him follow him. I didn't make him follow me down to the washroom. While I was at the washroom, I took him inside, handed him the tobacco. While he was holding the tobacco, I knifed him, must have laid it on four or five times. That is that. It could have been anybody. I was pretty upset, walked down the corridor, had blood on my hands where I cut myself. Remember this guy with a wheelchair came up to me. He said, "How are you feeling?" something like that. When I said a smart remark, "Do you know what I done?" He said no, so he took me down to reception. Then I saw Dr. McNiven. When I went downstairs, it could have been any one of those retarded kids. That is how mad I was.

Dennis: I will read this statement to you, and then I want you to read it aloud to me. If you agree with it, will you please sign it?

Brown: I will agree with it, for that is exactly what happened.

It was then signed by William Robert Brown and also by D. J. Dennis, Det. Sergeant, and by D. K. Wild, Constable.

Brown appeared in St. Thomas Court represented by defense council Bill Jacobs and pleaded not guilty to the charge. After the evidence was presented by the Crown attorney Peter Gammage, Brown was convicted to life in jail.

Bits and Pieces 6

I had attended a "break and enter" at a Brewers Retail Beer Store in the village of Courtright. On my arrival on that Thursday morning, a search for fingerprints was done at the point of entry, the smashed entrance door, which was used by the customers to gain entry to the store. I searched around the cash register and counter beside the register. One fingerprint was found on the counter. I identified the fingerprint as being left there by George Green from his criminal record that was on file.

A month or two later, I was called to appear in the Criminal court in Sarnia to give evidence regarding the BE & theft that had occurred at the beer store in Courtright.

The Crown attorney stood, and I was called to the witness stand to give my evidence.

Crown: Are you a member of the OPP?

Me: Yes, sir. I am a member of the Technical Identification Unit, stationed at no. 2 District Headquarters in London.

Crown: What are you qualifications in this field?

Me: I am a graduate of the Institute of Applied Science, Chicago, and dealing in fingerprinting, photography, handwriting and typewriting identification, ballistics and physical comparisons. I have had several other courses dealing with fingerprinting at Police Headquarters School, the Ontario Police College at Aylmer, and the Canadian Police College in Ottawa. I received a course of instruction in photography at Eastman Kodak Co., Toronto, and also at Eastman Kodak in Rochester, New York. Also other courses in other locations in the province, including Camp Borden Army Camp, Canada, in regard to bomb disposal. I am a designated fingerprint examiner by the solicitor general of Canada.

Crown: What can you tell about a break and enter that occurred at the Brewers Retail Beer Store in Courtright?

Me: I received a phone call from our Sombra detachment at 8:20 a.m. on the Thursday morning. I arrived at the beer store at 9:35 a.m. The store had been entered through the main entrance by smashing the locking system on the entry door of the store with a heavy hammer. After entering the store, I conducted a search for fingerprints at the point of entry to the store, then the other areas in the store. One fingerprint was found on the counter near the cash the register. Other areas were searched, but only the one print was found. It was on the counter two or three feet from the cash register.

Crown: Were you able to identify the found fingerprint?

Me: Yes, I later identified the fingerprint as the middle finger of the left hand from the criminal record of George Green, living on the Walpole Island Indian Reservation.

Crown: I have no further questions for this witness.

Defense: You said the fingerprint was found on the counter. Isn't it possible that this print could have been on the counter for days or even weeks, left there when George Green went to the store and had bought beer there in days or weeks prior to this break and enter? Isn't it likely that the fingerprint had been there from one of those visits when he purchased his beer?

Me: No.

Defense: How can you stand there and lie like that? You have no idea how long that print had been there. It could have been there as I said for days or weeks.

Me: It had only been there since he put it there during the night when he broke into the store.

Defense: (raising his voice) How the hell can you stand there and say that? You don't have any idea or know long it had been there. You are lying about that.

Me: I'm afraid I do know it was put there on that night. This BE & theft occurred on the Wednesday night when Green broke into the store, and he left the fingerprint on the counter. On the Wednesday morning I received call from the Sombra detachment, requesting my presence at a BE & theft that occurred on the Tuesday, the previous night, at this same beer store. After finding no fingerprints on that occasion, I washed and wiped down the counter to get rid of the black powder I used searching for fingerprints, which I didn't find, leaving the counter clean. The store was closed for the rest of the Wednesday so the employees could do an inventory to determine if any of the beer cases had been taken.

The defense council sat down, shocked and embarrassed by my last statement. He now knew he should not ask the question if he didn't know the answer.

CHAPTER THIRTY

Don't Mess with My Sister

At 2:58 a.m. on Sunday, January 2, 1972, a telephone call was received at the police Tillsonburg detachment from Mrs. Anna Pepino, who was living at the residence of her brother, Gerhard Fox, in RR 1, Port Burwell, located in Malahide Township. Mrs. Peters advised she was anticipating trouble from her estranged husband, George Pepino, who she believed was drunk.

At 3:05 a.m., only seven minutes later, a further call was received at the Tillsonburg detachment office from the Wolf residence. This time from Mrs. Margaretha Fox, wife of Gerhard Fox, who advised that George Pepino had been there and that her husband, Gerhard, had shot George. She further stated that Pepino had then left the premises with an unknown male person in a car, license A61441.

Constable Hardy was dispatched to the Fox residence from the Tillsonburg detachment. The St. Thomas detachment was also advised of this occurrence and sent Constable Pittman from the St. Thomas detachment to the Fox residence, who arrived at 3:40 a.m. The car in which Pepino had departed the scene was a green 1967 Chevrolet sedan registered to John Martin of RR 2, Glen Myer.

A search for this vehicle was instituted, and a check of the area hospitals was also made without results.

The Fox residence was a two-story brick building. For some previous time it was a pretentious farmhouse, now in a state of disrepair, located on lands owned by the McConnell Nurseries and provided Gerhard Fox as an employee of that firm.

The ground floor consisted of a kitchen, living room, and two other rooms serving as bedrooms. There was a center front hall from which ran a staircase to the upper floor. This upper floor appeared be used solely for storage. Entrance to the house was gained by means of a rear door into the kitchen and was approached by means of wooden steps to a small porch with no railing. The house was located some five hundred yards south from the road.

The first officers arriving at the residence learned from the residents that sometime before 3:00 a.m., a telephone call had been received from George Pepino indicating that he was coming to the house to see his wife and children. Being alarmed, Mrs. Pepino telephoned the police.

Almost immediately, a car drove into the yard at the rear of the house, and there was banging at the rear door. Mrs. Fox opened the door and told George Pepino, who was standing on the small porch, that he couldn't come in and asked him to leave.

Pepino pushed his way in and called to his friend who was outside, who also then entered the house. Mrs. Fox walked to the telephone in the front hall, followed by Peters and the other man. She stated she was going to telephone the police. Peters did not allow her to make the call.

Gerhard Fox, upon hearing Pepino and his wife talking at the back door, went upstairs and removed the padlock from a door to one of the rooms. In the room he loaded his .22 caliber rifle. Gerhard then walked to the top of the stairs and observed his wife and Pepino near the telephone at the foot of the stairs. Wolf pointed the rifle at Pepino, fired, and immediately reloaded the weapon. Pepino then walked through the house to the back door and was followed by Mrs. Fox and her husband, who was still carrying the rifle.

Mrs. Pepino, who had been watching the events in the front hall from the bedroom doorway, followed the Foxes. At the back door, Pepino hesitated and then threw a beer bottle, which he had been carrying since entering the house, into the corner of the kitchen, and then Fox pushed him out.

Pepino fell down the rear steps and lay on the ground. He called to his friend, who was already in the car at the time, to take him to the hospital as he had been shot. He then got up and walked to the car and entered the right front passenger door of the vehicle. Mrs.

Fox followed him down the steps and, with the aid of a flashlight, looked at the front license plate of the car. The vehicle then left the premises, and Mrs. Fox telephoned the police to report the incident.

At 9:07 a.m., a telephone call was received at the Tillsonburg detachment office from John Martin. He advised that his car had gone into the ditch and that his friend, "Mexican George," had been shot and was dead. The call was made from Port Burwell. An officer from the Port Burwell detachment, Constable Pepper, responded and accompanied Martin to a dead-end road in Bayham Township where Martin's car was found in a shallow ditch with the body of a man lying beside it.

John Martin gave a full account leading up to him going in the ditch. During the preceding evening of Saturday, January 1, 1972, he met George Pepino, who he knew as "George the Mexican" in the Imperial Hotel in Tillsonburg. After a few drinks together, the two men then drove to Vienna and spent some time in a hotel there. At closing time they drove around the area seeking a house party that was supposed to be going on, but were unsuccessful in finding it. They then stopped at a local bootlegger where Pepino had purchased a case of beer.

Then at Pepino's suggestion, they drove to the Fox residence because Pepino said that he wanted to see his wife and kids. On arrival there, Pepino knocked on the rear door for some time without any response. He returned to the car and asked Martin to drive into Port Burwell where he would telephone the house. He made the phone call and then returned to the Wolf home.

This time, Pepino's knocks were immediately answered by a woman. Martin followed Pepino into the house. Standing in the living room, Martin watched Pepino and the woman standing in the front hall by the telephone, but was unsure of the conversation that took place between them because they spoke in a foreign language at the time. According to Martin, there was no violence or even anything menacing about Pepino's behavior.

Suddenly, he heard a shot, and he ran from the house and got into the car. He saw Pepino come out the back door and fall down the steps. He observed a woman standing on the porch with a man carrying a rifle. Pepino got up and then walked over and got into the car. He told Martin that he had been shot and asked to be taken to a hospital. The woman came down from the porch and went to the front of the car with a flashlight.

With Martin driving, the two men left and proceeded toward Port Burrell. At Pepino's request, they turned off onto a gravel road, supposedly a shortcut to the hospital in Tillsonburg. Martin contends he drove into a curve too fast, and the car went into the ditch. Unable to get the car out, Martin believed that Pepino then must have gone to sleep for when he was next aware of events, it was beginning to get light. Pepino was conscious and asked to be taken to the hospital. Martin walked along the road, only to come to a dead end. He returned to the car and then continued to a farmhouse where he was unable to arouse the occupants.

Martin returned to the car once again, finding Pepino in the same condition and partly lying on the front seat. Martin then claimed to have set off cross-country, eventually coming to Port Burwell where he went to the residence of a friend, Reginald Haley, for help. Admitted by Haley's wife, he waited in the living room for his friend to get up. It was his opinion that he may have dozed off there as well. Eventually, his friend did get up and agreed to Martin's request for aid to help get his car out of the ditch and help his friend who had been shot and was still in the car.

The two men proceeded in Haley's car, only to find Pepino lying on the ground beside the vehicle, apparently dead. They then returned to Port Burwell to call the police.

John Martin's car was located on a side road in Bayham Township, about three miles from the Wolf residence and some three to four miles from Port Burwell. The body of George Pepino was lying on the ground beside the open passenger door with his head against the door. It appeared that he tried to get out of the car and had fallen.

I arrived at the scene just after eleven o'clock, and photographs were taken of the vehicle in the ditch and the road in both directions. A close-up was also taken of the body and its location.

The body was removed from the scene and transported to Tillsonburg District Memorial Hospital. An autopsy was performed by Dr. J. D. Mull, the regional pathologist of Simcoe. Death was attributed to a gunshot wound to the left breast, where the projectile traveled to the lower right side of the torso. It was recovered intact, directly beneath the skin. The liver had been lacerated, causing considerable internal hemorrhage. The time of death could not be established. The doctor believed that if medical treatment had been obtained following the injury, the deceased person may have survived.

The Fox and Pepino families are known locally as Mexican Mennonites. These people originally emigrated from Europe to Manitoba around the turn of the century and in the early 1920s. There was a further migration from Manitoba to Mexico. As a result, the parents of Fox, Pepino, and their wives were born in Canada and were Canadian citizens. Gerhard Fox was born in Cuautemoe in the state of Chihuahua, Mexico, on November 4, 1932, and came to Canada in May 1966. The Foxes were the parents of six children ranging in ages from one to fifteen, all living in the family Malahide residence. This family followed the teachings of the Mennonite religion, and the children were educated by the church. The language used in the home was Low German.

George Pepino was born on June 28, 1939, also in Cuautemoe, Mexico. He came to Canada with his wife and children about the same time as the Fox family. There were six children in the Pepino family, ranging in ages from three to ten years. During the year of 1971 until November, Pepino worked as a waiter at the Vienna Hotel in the village of Vienna, where he was known as a good worker. He got along well with everyone. Coworkers insisted that he was neither violent nor belligerent.

In March 1971, he met a married woman, Mrs. Irene Clarkson of Vienna. This friendship developed into a common-law relationship in October, when Pepino left his wife and family to live with her. He did take his wife and children on a holiday trip to Mexico in November but abandoned them on their return. Mrs. Pepino then moved into the residence of her brother, Gerhard Fox, with her six children two weeks before the end of the year.

On Christmas Eve, Pepino and Mrs. Clark visited at the Fox residence, although most conversations were carried on in German. Mrs. Clark believed and was of the opinion that the relationship between George Pepino and his brother-in-law Gerhard was friendly. On New Year's Day, Pepino and Mrs. Clark went to the Vienna

Hotel in the late afternoon. Pepino asked her to take him to the Fox residence to visit his children. She declined because she felt there would be company at the house and because she wished to rest before going to work at 11:00 p.m. in a nursing home. Pepino, against her advice, said that he would arrange to go to the Fox residence after she went to work.

During his visit to the Vienna Hotel that night with John Martin and at the hotel closing time about 12:30 a.m., Pepino spoke with the bartender, Lewis Quigley, for some time, and according to the bartender, Pepino was in a good mood and not intoxicated. Martin, on the other hand, was considered drunk by the bartender. Although Pepino had the reputation locally of being a violent troublemaker, little evidence was found to support this allegation. His wife had reported on numerous occasions to both the police and the Children's Aid Society that her husband had assaulted her, but those responding to these complaints have found no evidence in support of her contentions. There may, however, have been some animosity between Wolf and Pepino because Fox did resent having to support Pepino's wife and six children.

A statement was taken from Gerhard Fox:

> Hickey: You will be charged with a criminal offense involving the death of George Pepino. The charge may be murder or manslaughter, depending on his investigation. Do you wish to say anything in answer to the charge? You are not obliged to say anything unless you wish to do so, but whatever you do say will be taken down in writing and may be given in evidence. If you have spoken to any police officers or anyone with authority, or if such person has spoken to you in connection with this case, I want it clearly understood that I do not want it to influence you in making any statement. Do you understand what I have just read to you?

Fox: Yeah.

Hickey: Do you understand that you may tell us what occurred only if you want to do so?

Fox: I'm not sure what you mean.

Hickey: I'm telling you that you may tell us only what you wish to tell us, if anything. Do you understand?

Fox: George Pepin called about twelve o'clock, and he said, "I'm a policeman. I want to talk to Mrs. Pepino." Then my wife, she answered the phone, and she handed the phone over to Mrs. Peters. Then George Pepino, he speaks just English, and later he speaks German, and he told us he was George Pepino. I don't know what he asked his wife. At 2:45 a.m. he called again. His wife answered the phone, and he told his wife he'd come out. My wife took the phone, and she told him he'd have to stay out. If he wants to come over, he has to come in daytime. He said he'd be right there, and his wife, she called the policeman in Tillsonburg. She still has the phone in her hand when George Pepino came up his driveway. She say to policeman, "He's coming now," and the policeman say, "Just tell them to stay out." He hit the door with the feet, and my wife opened the door, then he came in. Then his wife tried to push him back, but he just comes in. Then he said to his partner, "Come in," then he came in too. Then my wife tried to push him out, and she couldn't do it. My wife said, "if you don't go out, I'm going to call the policeman." Then he said, "You better not." Then my wife dialed the phone and just called the operator, but she couldn't talk because he put his hand down on the hook. Then he said, "You better don't call the policeman." I was upstairs already. I unlocked the door where my rifle was. I took the rifle. I load him, and George Peters, he is still there by the phone. I point him, then I guess he started to walk, but I was scared. I pulled the trigger. If I'm right, I shoot him in the left arm. Then he walked out slowly. Then he stands in the door. Then I told him, "I mean to stay outside the nighttime." And I pushed him out, and he rolled from a step down. He said to his partner he had to bring him up to the hospital, then he walked in the car, and my wife go down from the step, and she took the license plate number. Then he took off. I think that's all.

Hickey: When did George Pepino come here to the house?

Fox: Last night.

Hickey: You know George Peters's partner?

Fox: No.

Inspector Hickey read the statement back to Gerhard Fox, who stated he does not read.

Hickey: Do you wish to make any corrections or changes?

Fox: Yes, I said I was scared, not wasn't.

Hickey: Do you wish to add anything to what you have told us?

Fox: No.

It was then signed Gerhard Fox.

The exhibits consisting of the rifle, ammunition, and bullet were examined by Mr. N. Neilson, while the blood alcohol sample from the deceased, which I had taken to the Center of Forensic Sciences in Toronto, was examined by Mrs. Libres.

Gerhard Fox appeared in court and was represented with his lawyer and pleaded guilty to a charge of manslaughter. He was convicted and sentenced to six years in jail.

Bits and Pieces 7

At 11:00 p.m., three teenage boys watched a clerk in a small service station store where the customers paid for their gas and other items were sold. The store and the office were closed. He locked the front door, jumped in his car, and drove away. The three boys waited another couple hours and then broke into the office of the service station. They hauled a large quantity of cigarettes and other assorted items from the store's office and piled them in their car. While in the store, one of the boys grabbed a package of Juicy Fruit gum from the counter. He tore off the end, dropped it on the floor, opened up a stick, and started chewing away.

What the boys did not know, the office had a silent alarm that activated a call to the police. The officers who were patrolling the area were advised of the BE and started stopping and checking vehicles traveling in the vicinity. An identification officer arrived at the service station. No fingerprints were found, but the torn-off piece from the Juicy Fruit gum wrapper was found on the floor and was picked up and saved.

It was later in the early morning and after driving some distance away, the teenagers stopped in a remote area and placed the stolen goods in the trunk of the car. The boys went to a restaurant to get an early breakfast. One of the officers on duty, sitting in a plain unmarked car in the parking lot of the restaurant, recognized them from a previous occurrence when they got out of their car at the restaurant, and he knew they had been in trouble in the past. They were requested and accepted the invitation to go with the officer to the detachment office. They followed the officer's car to the detachment office where they were questioned about the BE at the service station.

They were individually questioned about the BE and theft at the service station and about the cigarettes that were stolen. They denied any knowledge of the theft.

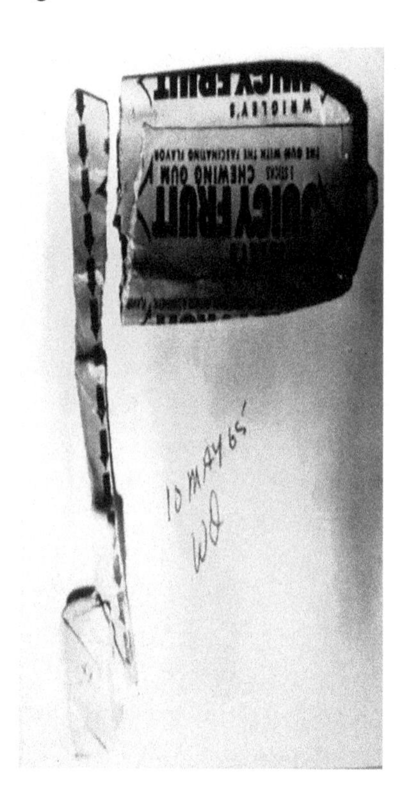

They were each told to empty their pockets onto the desk, which they did. One of the boys emptied his pockets, and in the articles he placed on the desk was a package of Juicy Fruit gum.

When the identification officer arrived at the detachment and he checked the articles the boys took from their pockets, he found the package of a Juicy Fruit gum wrapper. Then he saw the end of the Juicy Fruit gum wrapper and the torn-off piece that was picked from the floor, which was handed over to the identification officer. They finally cooperated with the police and admitted to the break-in and advised the officers where they put the cigarettes.

They were each convicted and received six months in jail.

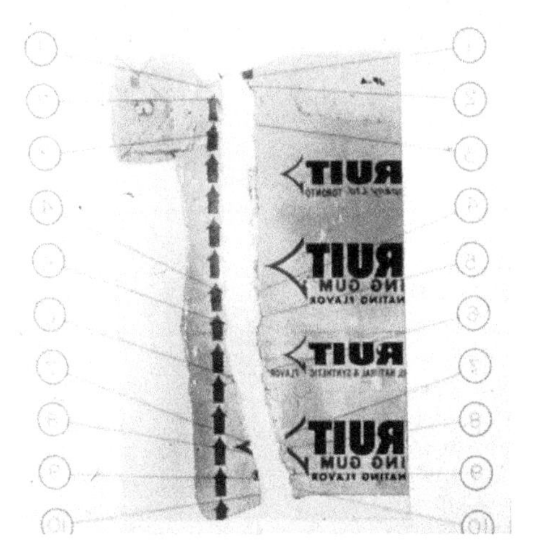

Chart to be used in court

CHAPTER THIRTY-ONE

Missing Thirteen-Year-Old Girl Found Dead

The victim, Brenda Fern Heehren, was the daughter of Pierre Frank and Betty Yvonne of 1 Avenue, Lambeth. Brenda was born at Teresita Hospital, Canada, on March 13, 1959. She was a grade 8 student at the public school in Lambeth. She was in good health and was a very quiet child. She had few friends, spending the majority of her time at her home.

The accused, Howard Frank Sambell, resided at 26 Mary Anna Drive, Lambeth. He was born on January 2, 1924, and was age 48.

Sambell was married with three children. At the time of his arrest, Sambell was the head custodian at the M. B. McEachern Public School and also did custodial work for the Lambeth branch of the Royal Bank. He had been a resident of Lambeth for sixteen years. Speaking with many residents of Lambeth, Sambell was described as a quiet family man. It was also learned that he and his wife had cared for ten foster children over the past several years. Sambell had a fingerprint record with the RCMP in Ottawa. The police records showed that he was charged and convicted of theft, which occurred in Berilium, Canada, in 1948.

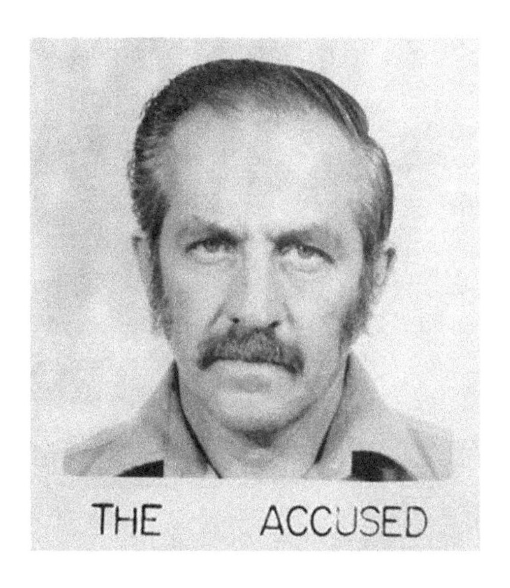

THE ACCUSED

Brenda was first reported missing to the London detachment of the police at 11:10 a.m., August 27, 1972, by her father. Brenda left her home that morning at nine to collect soft drink bottles, which would have taken about fifteen minutes. At approximately 9:30 a.m., when Brenda failed to return home, her mother became alarmed. Mrs. Heehren explained that when she was nine and eleven, she had experienced two sexual-type assaults, and because of this, she feared the same might happen to her daughter. Because of her experience, she became more protective of Brenda, keeping close watch on her movements. It was a standing policy in the home that should Brenda wish to extend her absence from home, she would first telephone for permission.

On the date Brenda went missing, O.P.P. constables J. Cruz and M. Montana from the police detachment investigated. Through their inquiries, it was learned that Brenda had last been seen in front of the Royal Bank at the southeast corner in Billsborg between 9:15 a.m. and 9:30 a.m. by Mr. William Duncan of Stephen Street in Byron. Mr. Duncan was on duty at the Blendi Service Station situated at the northeast corner of the two highways when he observed Brenda. She was in possession of a large-size pop bottle. Mr. Sambell, the accused, also informed Constable Smith that he was working in the Royal Bank. Sambell said Brenda was in possession of an empty pop bottle.

On that same day, August 27, 1972, many local residents, including members of the Lambeth Volunteer Fire Department, made a search of the Lambeth area for the missing girl without success. The search was commenced about noon on August 27 and terminated on the late afternoon of August 28. The main reason for the search terminating was due to the report received by Constable A. Loyola from Linda Potter. Ms. Potter, from London, reported that on August 27 at 7:30 p.m., she had met Brenda Heehren who she had known in Westside of Lambeth, London. According to Ms. Potter, Brenda told her that she had run away from home. Ms. Potter did not inform the police.

A month and a half later, on October 14, 1972, at 2:15 p.m., Arie Osman, age 18, from RR 2, Lambeth, was hunting pheasants at the Dingman Creek Conservation Area Park. Along the east bank of the Dingman Creek near the Westminster Delaware Township Line about five kilometers northwest of Lambeth, Osman detected a foul odor and, upon exploring, found the decomposed remains of a human body. The body was contained in green plastic garbage bags floating along the creek's edge, with the feet exposed. Osman returned to his home immediately and told his father, Aart Osman, who in turn notified the police detachment at 3:10 p.m.

I was dispatched to the Osman residence. Accompanied by Arie Osman, we proceeded to Dingman Creek Conservation Area Park, where the body was found. We arrived at the location at 3:48 p.m. On entering the park, you travel seven hundred feet east along a dirt road to the main park area, a large open area approximately 300 feet × 500 feet to the left at the end of the road. Farther east and 225 feet from the end of this road is the creek and a foot bridge across the creek.

At this point, the creek runs northeast from the southwest; 200 feet southeast of the bridge, the creek turns and runs north and south. From the end of the dirt road to the south, another road travels approximately 950 feet to a turning around area. The road on the west side of the creek is approximately 40 feet above the water level.

Other officers of the detachment attended included Constable Paul Edmans (the investigating officer), Det. Sergeant D. Dennis, and Sergeant Major A. H. Baker. South of the road in the park area was open farm fields. Osman led us across the foot bridge in a southeast direction for 125 feet, and then south for 300 feet, then approximately southwest for another 325 feet, where they arrived at the bank of the creek and where Osman pointed to the water and what appeared to be green garbage bags.

At this point the water was seven inches deep, and the bank was seventeen inches above the surface of the water. A small tree or bush was parallel with the water surface partially in the water running west from the bank. The body was on the north side of this bush. The top end of the bag was near the edge of the creek. The feet were protruding from the bag and appeared to be running northwest from the edge. It also appeared the ankles were tied and flexed back to the buttocks. One green and white thong was floating in the water upside down southwest of the body. The center area of the plastic bags was open, showing the left hip, wearing what appeared to be brushed denim jeans.

A quarter-inch rope was tied around the middle of the plastic bag just above the blue denim jeans at the waist of the body. The rope came up from both sides of the body, up and over a small three-quarter-inch branch where the end was tied with three half hitches from the left side of the body. The loose end was tied around another piece of rope eighteen inches farther along with a turn and two half hitches, leaving another three-and-a-half inches to the end.

The second rope was five feet long and tied fifteen inches from one end. The main rope was tied to the base of a milkweed plant, approximately four feet high and a half inch in diameter. The loose end of the rope was hanging in the creek. The creek was approximately thirty-three feet wide and flowed south to north. The body was found seven hundred feet south, upstream from the bridge. The area on the east side of the creek where the body was found was heavy bush with light paths.

I took the appropriate photographs and measurements. The body was then removed from the creek at 7:30 p.m. by the attendants of the Thames Valley Ambulance Service. The coroner, Dr. Robert Sherman, and the resident pathologist, Dr. M. S. Pembrook, from Victoria Hospital also attended the scene and supervised the removal of the body.

I proceeded with the body to Victoria Hospital, where it was placed and sealed in a locked locker, and I retained the key for the locker.

On October 15, 1972, at 8:00 a.m., I arrived at the morgue with Dr. Pembrook. I unlocked the locker, and the body was removed and placed on the autopsy table. CIB inspectors John McPherson and D. F. Carrie also attended at the morgue at Victoria Hospital. It was observed at this time that the body was actually enclosed in three plastic bags; one was covering the lower area, which had split exposing the feet, and two plastic bags covered the upper torso. The plastic bags were securely tied with white cord, referred to as butcher's cord.

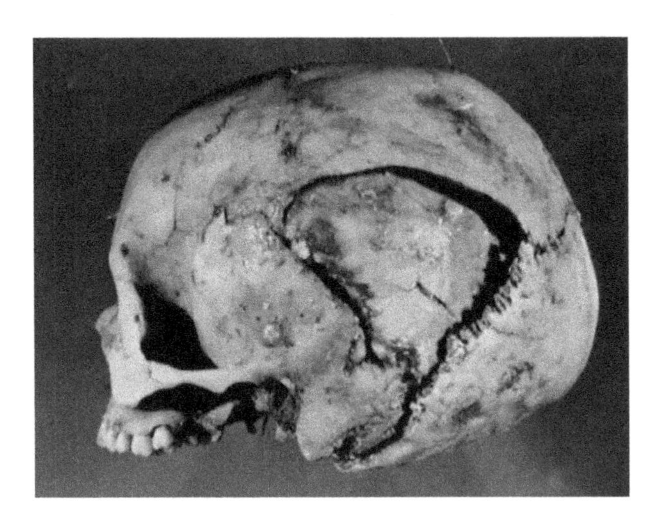

Dr. Pembrook arranged for x-rays to be taken of the body before it was removed from the plastic bags. The x-rays revealed to Dr. Pembrook that the following parts of body were missing: (1) large section of the skull (base portion), (2) complete left hand, (3) lower mandible.

Following the x-rays, Dr. Pembrook decided to leave the body as it was found and return to the scene in search of missing parts.

At 11:00 a.m. Dr. Pembrook, assisted by the coroner and myself, returned to that area where the body was found at the scene. Two police divers arrived and searched the shallow area. The divers recovered the missing portion of the skull and the lower mandible. They also found most of the teeth from the mandible and the missing bones of the left hand.

On October 16 at 8:00 a.m., Dr. Pembrook commenced the postmortem examination on the body of Brenda Heehren. I was also there taking photographs. All the cords tied around the bags were cut and the knots preserved. The three plastic bags were removed by Dr. Pembrook, exposing the body. The body was found clothed in blue jeans, panties, bra, and a sleeveless sweater. A red and white candy stripe cotton cloth, when put together, formed the lower portion of a child's sleepers. It was found in the upper portion of the body. This item was not part of Brenda's clothing.

Dr. Pembrook utilized the services of Dr. K. B. Peters, DDS, Canadian Society of Forensic Odontology, Dental Service Building, University of Western, London, for the purpose of identifying the victim through the teeth. Dr. Peterson obtained Brenda's dental chart from the family dentist, Dr. James Bell of Lambeth. Dr. Peters was able to identify the body being the body of Brenda Fern Heehren.

The postmortem was performed by Dr. Pembrook, which lasted for five days and was very extensive and detailed. The cause of death was determined to have resulted from two separate skull fractures, each of a severe nature. In the opinion of Dr. Pembrook, the fractures were consistent with two or more heavy blows with a blunt instrument and were not consistent with a fall.

I should mention at this point that a gold ring removed from the right hand of the victim was identified by her mother as the property of Brenda. Her mother also was able to identify the blue jeans that were removed from the body.

From investigations made by Inspector Carrie and Constable Edmonds, it was learned that on August 27, 1972, the date that Brenda went missing, Brenda's father Pierre observed Mr. Sambell's car, a 1969 Chevelle, green bottom, black top, was parked at the McEachern Public School at approximately 9:25 a.m. and again at 10:45 a.m. On each occasion the vehicle was parked in a different position.

Brenda's brother, Frank, also observed Sambell's car parked at McEachern Public School at approximate 9:55 a.m. parked in a different position than noted by his father. Frank also saw a large pop bottle sitting on the front steps of the school. Knocking at the school door, he had received no reply.

Brenda's mother Betty suspected Howard Sambell, but did not reveal this fact until October 16, 1972. She knew that Sambell saved soft drink bottles at the school for Brenda. According to Betty, Brenda would not speak with strangers, nor would she accept rides unless the person was someone she knew well, such as Howard Sambell. This fact was also verified by local residents.

On October 17, Constable Edmonds and Inspector Carrie made a visit to McEachern Public School where they toured the school with the principal, Mr. Neil MacMillan. Constable Edmonds took into his possession green plastic garbage bags, white butcher's cord, and rope and two lower portions of child's sleepers of cotton material, cut identical to the foreign cloth found with the body. These items were turned over to me.

On October 18 at approximately 2:30 p.m. at the McEachern School, Inspector Carrie, Constable Edmonds, and the principal Neil MacMillan walked out of the principal's office north along the corridor, intending to locate the caretaker Sambell to obtain the key to the tractor room at the school.

They met Sambell walking west along the main corridor. He turned around and walked east and entered the washroom on the south side of the corridor. They waited outside the washroom door for a few seconds, and when he came out, Carrie asked, "Are you the janitor?"

Sambell said, "Yes."

"I understand you had the only key for the tractor room."

Sambell nodded his head and said, "Yes."

"We would like to see inside the tractor room," Carrie replied.

Sambell walked east along the corridor toward the tractor room in front of Carrie and Edmonds. MacMillan didn't follow.

"You have a tractor at the school?" Carrie asked.

"Yes, a small one. They keep the large tractor over at Duffield School."

"When did they get this tractor?"

"Sometime last July."

They went to the tractor room, where Sambell unlocked the padlock on the door. Sambell said, "You're police officers, are you?"

Carrie responded, "Yes, we are investigating the Brenda Heehren case. Mr. MacMillan has given us permission to see inside. They were here yesterday, but he didn't have a key for the padlock."

"You don't think it happened here, do you?"

"We were at your house today."

"You were?" Sambell replied.

"Yes, but no one was home."

Sambell said, "I left about one o'clock. Was there a car there?"

"Yes, a silver car."

"My son should be home, but he'd be sleeping."

Carrie said, "That's a nice swimming pool behind the house. Did you build it yourself, or was it a kit?"

"I built it. It's a cement floor and fiber glass walls."

"Do the fiber glass walls come in a kit?"

Sambell answered, "No, they're just sheets that you can buy."

"Mr. MacMillan told us yesterday that he checked this room and the other rooms in the school the day Brenda went missing. He must be wrong if you had the only key."

Sambell came back with, "I don't know, but I searched the school that Sunday afternoon for Brenda."

"Did you see any sign of her?"

"No, none."

"Okay, we'll be back to see you later," Carrie said.

Samell said, "I suppose you're just been hitting your head against the cement wall."

"No, I don't think so," Carrie said.

Carrie and Edmonds left the tractor room and reentered the school, walking west along the corridor. Sambell locked the tractor room door and followed. Carrie and Edmonds then walked away and left the school.

At 4:20 p.m., Carrie and Edmonds came back to the school and caught up with Howard Sambell.

At 4:32 p.m., Howard Sambell gave them the following statement:

"I went to the bank at 8:00 a.m. It was my weekend for doing the floors. That is at the Royal Bank. Brenda's father came around to the bank and asked me if I had seen Brenda. I told him I saw her between 9:00 a.m. and 9:30 a.m. This is not exact. The date was August 27, 1972, a Sunday. I don't know what I can add to it, I saw her there."

When he saw her at the bank, she tapped on the window, and that's when he saw her. That is through the front door window. She waved at him, and he waved back. To the best of his knowledge, she headed toward home. He should not say that because he didn't know. She might have headed down toward the water tower. Brenda was carrying an empty bottle, which was her trademark. She was always after empty bottles. She brought bottles here from the bank. He used to bring the bottles here from the bank to the school. He burned the bank garbage here.

When he left his house at 8:00 a.m. on August 20, 1972, he drove down Terry Street and around the corner onto Howard, left onto David, right on Martin, and left on Broadway to Talbot and right on Talbot to the main corner. That would be highways 2 and 4. He drove in his 1969 Chevelle. He was in the bank from 8:00 a.m. until Pierre came at about 10:30 a.m. He would've been in the bank all the time. He would've had the polisher going and would not have heard anything.

After Pierre came, he was kind of concerned. He worked for approximately another hour, then he left the bank. He drove toward home. He passed Pierre's, and he was sitting there. He stopped and asked if Brenda had been found. Pierre said no. He said he was going to drive around, and he said he would do this too.

He drove around for a while and then went home. He passed the school and saw the principal in the front parking lot just walk in. He spoke with the principal. He asked if he had seen Brenda, and he said no. He told him they were looking for her and that Pierre couldn't find her, and that was about it. He spoke to the principal between 12:00 p.m. and 12:30 p.m. He then went home for lunch; it would be just after 12:30 p.m. when he got home. That is the time they eat. Up until about 12:30 p.m., he spoke to Pierre and the principal. He spoke to no one else about Brenda.

He thinks it rained that day. "My son went to search. His name is Randy, age 16. When he came back, he was soaked. Randy would've come home around 6:00 p.m."

Sometime Sunday afternoon, he did come back to the school. It must have been when the search party was out. He can't give an exact time that he came back to school, maybe 3:00 a.m. to 4:00 a.m. No one was at the school when he came back at that time. That may have not been the hour he was at the school. He just comes and goes. He comes back to school every Sunday and Saturday. It was in the back of his mind to look for Brenda. He toured the school. He walked through the halls and all the classrooms. He saw no sign of anyone in the school. He had a pet peeve that too many keys are out and teachers not properly locking up.

The bottles that are saved are kept in the boiler room. Mostly he gave them away. Brenda seemed to get more than anyone. He gave bottles to the other children also from time to time.

Near the end of June, he would think he gave Brenda bottles. He doubted that Brenda got any bottles from him during the summer.

After he checked the school in the afternoon, he went home. He would be home the remainder of the night. He didn't recall things that clearly. On Monday morning he returned to school. He would start at 7:00 a.m. Rex Denver would also be working with him at the school. There was no further search made by him Monday or any other day after that.

He lived in Lambeth for seventeen years last May. He didn't recall what Brenda was wearing on August 27. He was not outside the bank to talk to Brenda on the twenty-seventh.

He and Rex were working in a room on the north side of the school and saw Brenda one day in the summer. Brenda had a little dog with her. The conversation was short and just joking about the dog. "I had seen Brenda several times during the summer but never spoke, just a wave."

The statement was signed Howard Sambell.

On October 19, 1972, at 4:42 p.m., Carrie and Edwards had another meeting with Sambell.

Carrie: I want to clarify a few points in connection with the statement you made yesterday.

Sambell: I don't know what I can add to it.

Carrie: You told me yesterday that you were at the bank 8:00 a.m. to 11:30 a.m. and didn't leave. My information is that your car was seen at McEachern School about 9:30 a.m.

Sambell: I don't know who would've told you that.

Carrie: You told me you hadn't been out of your house that Sunday night.

Sambell: Who said that?

Carrie: Betty Heehren claims you were at their house at about 8:00 p.m. August 27 and asked if Brenda had been found.

Edmonds: We also have information you have kissed and put your arm around girls in the school. Is that right?

Sambell: I never meant any harm.

Carrie: Inspector McPherson, who is in charge of this case, is at London Detachment. He would like to speak with you if you're willing to come in with us.

Sambell: It's all right with me.

They departed for London at 4:48 p.m.

At 5:00 p.m., Sambell was advised by Inspector Carrie and witnessed by Constable Edmonds that he would be charged with noncapital murder in connection with the death of Brenda Fern Heehren, which occurred on or about August 27, 1972.

"Do you wish to say anything in answer to the charge? You are not obliged to say anything unless you wish to do so, but whatever you say may be given in evidence. Further, if you have spoken to any police officers or anyone with authority, or if such person has spoken to you in connection with this case, I want it clearly understood that I do not want to influence you in making this statement."

Carrie: You understand the charge?

Sambell: Yes.

Carrie: Do you understand the caution I have read, that you need say nothing?

Sambell: Yes, I do.

Carrie: Do you understand the caution about persons in authority?

Sambell: Yes, I do, fully.

Carrie: What do you wish to say, if anything?

Sambell: Well, in the first place, it was not murder. We went to the school and started collecting bottles in various rooms. The last trip through the boiler room at the door leading to the steps, the same damn old story, I put my arm around her. She sort of jumped, I stuck my foot out. She went down the first flight of stairs and hit her head a heck of a whack. I went to pick her up, I guess she got frantic or something.

She pulled away. She went down the other steps. There was blood all over the place. She was out then. I tried to bring her around. I thought she was almost dead. I picked her up. I took her into where I keep the tools. I could not get her to come around. I didn't know what to do. I was almost out of my mind. I didn't know if I should report or not. I didn't think anyone would believe what happened.

I just decided to dispose of her somehow. I tried to stop the bleeding. I put a rag on her head. I could not get any heartbeat. All I could think of was to get rid of her. I put those damn plastic bags around her. I put one over the head to stop the blood. I folded her feet and tied them. I then put another bag over her feet. I think I used another bag. I didn't touch her sexually or anything like that, I couldn't. I tied her up with cord from the school.

I took her out the front door of the school and put her in the back seat of my car on the floor. Everything happened so fast. I put her in the car about nine thirty in the morning right after it happened. I drove over to Dingman Creek Conservation Area. I drove up the hill at the conservation area and put her down into the creek. I went back to work then at the bank.

Then her father came around about ten thirty in the morning to inquire about her. I thought for sure she would be found that day. The following Sunday, I went back to Dingman Creek to see why she had not been found. Her body had crossed from one side of the creek to the other. I pulled her body back. It was only a couple of feet from shore. I got some heavy rope from the trunk of my car and put it around her. I just didn't want her to be found. I tied the other end of the rope around a bit of a twig sticking up growing there. I left her. That was the last time I saw her. The rag I used, I got from the box in a custodian room. Before I went to the bank, I went back to the school and cleaned up the mess. No, that's not right, I cleaned the mess up before I left the school. I used the mop to clean up the floor. That's it.

Carrie: Now that I have read this statement aloud to you and have asked you to read the same, which you refuse to do, is there anything which you might wish to add or take from the statement?

Sambell: I can't take anything from it, that's what happened. I have nothing do with these other crimes. This is the first time I have been involved in anything like this.

Carrie: You wish to sign this?

Sambell: Yes, I do.

Signed: Howard F. Sambell
Taken by DA Carrie, Insp. CIB
Witnessed by Paul Edmonds, Constable
Completed: 5:42 p.m.

On the way to the detachment, they stopped at the Sambell residence. They brought Mrs. Sambell to the police car. Sambell was in the rear seat behind the driver. Mrs. Sambell went into the rear seat on the right side.

Sambell: It's right, I had her at the school to get pop bottles. It was an accident. She hit her head.
Wife: Oh, Howard.

She put her head on Sambell's shoulder.

Sambell: I tried to get rid of her body. I put it in the creek. I couldn't live with it much longer. I had to tell someone. I didn't do anything sexually to her. I want you to know that I just couldn't. You will have to sell the house.
Wife: Where are the keys?
Carrie: The keys were given to me by Sambell and are at the office.
Wife: How the hell am I to going to clean the bank?
Carrie: I could arrange that the keys be brought to you.
Wife: Oh, hell.
Sambell: Don't paint too black a picture to the kids. Sell the house quietly.
Wife: Can he come in the house?
Sambell: No, these fellows have been good enough to bring me here to talk to you. We have to go.
Wife: Where is he going to be held?
Carrie: London detachment.
Wife: Where is that?
Edmonds: At the corner of Wellington Road and Highway 401. Take Highway 135 and cross Wellington Road, and it's on your right.
Wife: I'll have to give the baby up to the Children's Aid.
Sambell: No, don't do that. Hold on to it. You best go now.

They soon had their arms around each other as a last farewell. The wife left the car, and so did Edwards.

They left the Sambells' home at 6:34 p.m. and drove to the junction of Highways 2 and 4.

> Carrie: Which way did you go to Dingman Creek?
> Sambell: Travel west on number 2 highway. Turn right here. Oh no, keep going.

They drove on.

> Sambell: Turn right here now, Gore Road.
> Edwards: Where now?
> Sambell: Just keep going. Turn right here into the park.

They turned and entered the park.

> Sambell: Stay on the road to the right.

They then drove the road to the right.

> Edmonds: How far?
> Sambell: Keep going right to the end of the road.

At the end of the road, they had to turn around, so they made a turn.

> Sambell: Stop here.

The time was now 6:44 p.m. They all got out of the car. Still in daylight, Sambell walked to the bank, which was a steep drop down to the creek. A guard rail was around the top.

Sambell: (Pointing down the bank) I took her down here and put her in the water. When I came back the next Sunday, she had drifted down a bit.

He pointed his left hand to his left and said she was near the other side.

They all entered the police car, drove to the main parking area, and left the car. At 6:52 p.m., they arrived at the location where the body was found. Sambell led the way from the parking lot.

Sambell: Good god, the water's down. That tree was out in the water (points to a large tree to the right). It wasn't trampled like this. There was a lot of growth here then.
Carrie: Is there anything else you left here?
Sambell: You might as well know it all. I came out to cut the cords I had tied her up with. Her head was out of the bag. Part of her face was gone. There was a terrible odor. I couldn't do it. I pulled her over to the bank and tied her with a rope to a stick about that size.

He pointed to the ground then pointed to a milkweed's stick to the right.

Edmonds: Did you get the rope from the school?
Sambell: No, it was some of my own I had in the trunk of my car. I put the knife under a big tree somewhere near here. I think I can find it.

He walked back up the trail to a tree. It was a large tree. Sambell went on his knees and pulled out some leaves from a hole at the tree's trunk. Then he pulled out a long broomstick handle. A knife was attached to cut the end. He gave it to Edwards. Time was now 6:57 p.m.

Sambell: Now you know the whole story.

They left the area of the scene, walked back to the car, and left the park at 7:05 p.m. From the park, they drove back to the McEachern School and entered the school at 7:23 p.m.

Sambell stopped at the doorway leading to the boiler room area.

Carrie asked, "Howard, is this where it happened?"

Sambell said, "We came around the corner here. I put my arm around her." With his left arm, he indicated how he put his arm around Brenda. "Brenda panicked and jumped away. I stuck my foot out, and she tripped and fell down."

Sambell walked down the steps to the landing and pointed to a second step from the bottom. He said, "She hit her head here. She was dazed. I went to help her up, and she pulled away and fell down here."

Sambell then walked down the next set of steps, pointing to the steps and landing. He said, "She hit her head again. I don't know where. She was on the landing. I picked her up and carried her into the tool room and put her on the floor." He pointed to the floor where he placed her.

Carrie wrote notes at this point and then went back to the boiler room with Sambell and went over the notes and events.

Sambell: There was blood all over her head. I got a cloth and put it on her head. She was gone.

Carrie: Where did you get the cloth?

Sambell: From over there. (Points to the center area of the west wall.) It was one that I had used.

Edmonds pointed to a shelf on the south wall above the desk and asked if this was the cord he used.

Sambell: Yes, but that's not the roll. That's new.
Edmonds: What about the plastic bags?
Sambell: I got them from the cupboard.

He walked over the cupboard northwest area of the tool room, opened cupboard doors, and pointed to a lower area in the right side where there were plastic bags.

Sambell: I put her in the plastic bags and tied them up.

Then he walked out of the tool room. He then showed Edwards and Carrie where he carried Brenda out the front door.

Sambell: I took her out the front door, the same one we came in. I put her on the floor of the back seat of my car.
Edmonds: What do you use to clean the floor with?
Sambell: (Points to a mop in the hall just outside the tool room) I used that mop. Then I left the school at 7:39 p.m.

On November 8, 1972, at 1:30 p.m. at the London County Jail, Inspector Carrie had a meeting with Sambell.

Carrie: How are you doing in here?
Sambell: Fine, I'm doing some painting at the jail to keep busy.
Carrie: I'm not here to talk about your case, Sambell, just on a visit. I told you I'd get around to seeing you again.
Sambell: I appreciate that.
Carrie: I went to see your wife. She wants to know when the car could be released. I told her we would get it back to her as soon as possible.

Sambell: Yes, she told me. She has been to visit every day.

Carrie: You have taken off your mustache.

Sambell: Yes.

Carrie: Has Reverend Elliott been to visit you?

Sambell: Yes, twice. I don't know how things will go. I'll have to wait and see.

Carrie: I spoke to your wife about welfare.

Sambell: Yes, she can't get any until I'm sentenced. We still have bonds. I wanted to use them and pay the lawyer.

Carrie: If I can assist you any way, let me know. I guess welfare people have regulations.

Sambell: I guess no one believes it was an accident.

Carrie: I believe part of your story, but not all of it.

Sambell: That's what I mean. Who will believe it was an accident?

Carrie: I guess it is up to the jury.

Sambell: I don't know. I guess they will have to prove it wasn't an accident.

Carrie: That is right.

Sambell: What time did Pierre say he came to the bank?

Carrie: About 10:30 a.m.

Sambell: It was 10:40 a.m. exactly. I died a thousand deaths when I saw him at the door.

Carrie: I guess so.

Sambell: I really had not much time. It was all over in less than one and a half hours.

Carrie: Yes, I gather that.

Sambell: I had only been back at the bank about ten minutes before Pierre came.

Carrie: You still belong to the Lodge? I saw somewhere that you are a member.

Sambell: I was. Are you with the Lodge?

Carrie: Yes.
Sambell: Which one?
Carrie: Lake of the Woods.

Howard Sambell appeared in court and pleaded guilty to a lesser charge of an indignity to a human body. He was convicted and sentenced to two years in jail.

Bits and Pieces 8

An Afghan dog breeder had one puppy left from the litter, which he advertised and finally sold for $600. The purchaser picked up the dog and paid the breeder with a check. The breeder took the check to the bank a couple days later to cash it. It bounced. He did not get the information on the name and address of the purchaser, so he was out the $600.

Six months went by. The breeder saw an ad in the local paper where a person was trying to sell a six-month-old Afghan dog for $600.

He thought that it might be the dog that he sold to the person who bought the dog with a bad check. He called the police and advised them about the ad in the paper and his suspicion that it could be the same dog that he reported to the police six months earlier and that the purchaser paid him with the bad $600 check for the dog.

He also advised the police that when the three pups were born, he had taken nose prints of each of the pups when they were three months old, which he retained. The seller of the dog was contacted by the police and was questioned about the dog and the bad check. He denied about buying the Afghan dog and denied giving anybody a bad check at any time.

I was called and went to see the dog where it was being kept until the matter was resolved. I took the nose print of the dog and then received the nose print from the breeder, which he had taken when the dog was three months old. I compared the nose print I took from the dog and compared it with the nose print that the breeder had taken. The nose prints matched. It was the dog that was sold for $600 with the bad check. The person who issued the bad check was charged, and the dog was returned the breeder. He received a jail sentence.

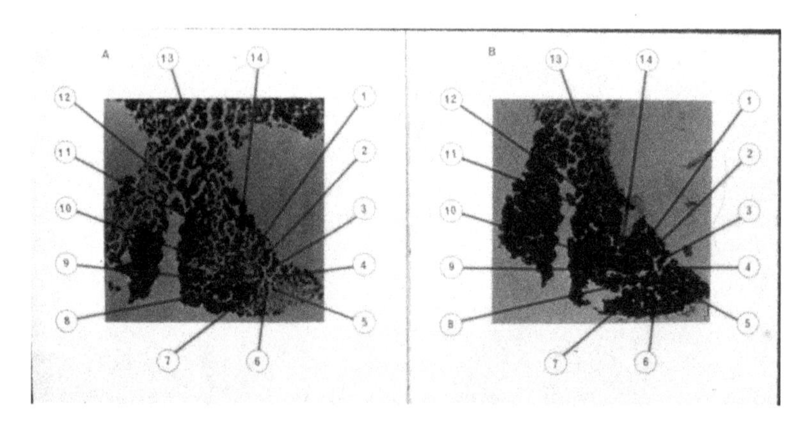

The chart showing the matched-up nose prints.

CHAPTER THIRTY-TWO

Two Fourteen-Year-Olds Kill

The murder victim, Mr. Andy Pako, age 74, owned a farm at lot 16, First Range North, and Caradoc Township. The farmer's main product was tobacco, with a lesser area set aside for vegetables on a small-scale market garden operation. Mr. Pako lived on the property in a bungalow facing no. 2 Highway with his wife Maria, age 72, and his son Andrew, age 37.

Mr. Pako was known as a quiet man who enjoyed work on the land producing vegetables. During the past two or three years, the Pakos had a number of thefts of vegetables from their garden, and their house had been broken into and money stolen. In 1973, $510 cash was stolen from the house, and subsequently, Leslie William Beam, age 14, born October 24, 1959, a neighborhood boy, was convicted at the London Juvenile Court for the theft of the money and was placed on probation. He was still on probation.

On Wednesday, July 31, 1974, at about 5:30 p.m., Mr. Pako and his wife were preparing beets for the market. Mrs. Pako was washing the beets near the greenhouse, about 150 feet southeast of the house, while her husband was pulling beets in the field west of the house and adjacent to no. 2 Highway and then carrying them back to her. He went to the field for more beets, and shortly after, Mrs. Pako heard what she thought was a gunshot. She was frightened and went to the back of the house, calling her husband's name. She found him lying on his back with blood coming from his mouth on a path under a grapevine hedge, which separated the field and the backyard. Her thought at this time was that her husband had had a heart attack and fell, as he had been found once before like this. She tried to revive him without success and then contacted her daughter by telephone.

Her daughter, Mrs. M. Goldsmith from RR #1, Mount Brydges, arrived and found Mr. Pako dead. His body was removed to Strathroy Hospital by Denning's Ambulance Service of Strathroy.

At the Strathroy Hospital, Dr. John Cunningham certified the death. The body was later examined by Dr. F. Boyes, coroner, of Blessed Court, Canada. He could not determine the cause of death and ordered an autopsy and notified the Canada police detachment at Glencoe. Constable D. Kersey was assigned, and with Corporal R. Hooker, they attended at the morgue. They found what appeared to be a bullet wound in the lips and exit wound in the back of the neck. As a result of their discovery, a murder investigation was immediately initiated.

At 12:45 a.m. on Thursday, August 1, 1974, an incident occurred in Metropolitan Toronto, which at first seem unconnected but later on revealed the identity of the persons responsible for the death of Mr. Pako. At that time, a hit-and-run motor vehicle collision occurred at Queen and Victoria Streets, where a Metro taxi operated by Mr. Henry Pyka, Toronto, was struck from behind by a 1965 Oldsmobile F 85 bearing Provincial license CYA–033, which left the scene.

The Oldsmobile was chased by the taxi and by a Provincial ambulance operated by Mr. Christopher McDonald of Thornhill, who had witnessed the collision. McDonald pursued the hit-and-run vehicle, which was finally stopped, and the two male occupants were held by Mr. MacDonald and his escort, Mr. Earl Milley, also of Thornhill, until the arrival of Constable Richard MacLachlan of number 5 District Traffic Unit, Metropolitan Toronto Police Department.

The two prisoners were then taken to #52 Division Metropolitan Toronto Police Department, where they identified themselves as Leslie William Beam of Mount Brydges and Raymond David Ransum, Thorndale. It was established that Ransum was in fact from the St. Thomas Psychiatric Facility in St. Thomas.

The two youths admitted that they had stolen the car, which Ransum was driving, from a farm near Delaware, Canada. While in #52 Division, Ransum started to talk with Beam about "shooting the old man" near Mount Brydges. Sergeants D. Yeandle and R. Barbour of the Metro Police, who at that time were handling the investigation regarding the stolen car, contacted London police and were informed there had in fact been a murder. The two boys were separated, and there were no further interviews prior to arrival of CIB Inspector W. R. Perrin at 5:20 a.m.

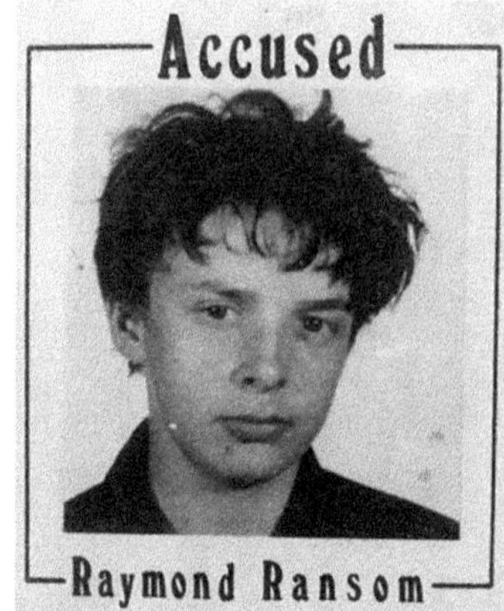

At 7:20 a.m., after obtaining information by telephone from Constable D. Kersey, Inspector Perrin interviewed Leslie Beam with Sergeant D. Yeandle. The following statement was taken.

"Leslie Beam, you are arrested on a charge of noncapital murder in the death of Andrew Pako Sr. of Stansel, Canada. Do you wish to say anything in answer to the charge? You are not obliged to say anything unless you wish to do so, but whatever you say will be taken down in writing and maybe given in evidence."

Q: Do you understand the caution which I have just read to you?

A: Yes.

Q: At approximately 5:15 p.m. Wednesday, thirty-first of July 1974, Andrew Pako was shot outside his residence at Stansel, Canada. What, if anything, can you tell me about this?

A: Do you want me to tell you everything that happened?

Yeandle: Yes.

A: We were walking toward the Pako residence and decided we should go to Toronto to visit one of Raymond Ransum's friends. Raymond was staying with us and was with me then. We decided to drop in to Pako's house and get some money for ourselves. We went down to the basement through the basement window and went upstairs to Andy's room, that is Andy Junior. We went through some of the clothes in the drawers, and we found ourselves $129.

We went through some things in another room and found about $3 in change. We left through the front door, and we saw Mr. Pako Sr. He saw the gun I was carrying and just stood there. Raymond told me to shoot him. I was kind of scared.

Mr. Pako started talking to me in Hungarian while Raymond reached over and started to squeeze the trigger. I knew the gun was approximately aimed at his Adam's apple. When the gun went off, Mr. Pako fell. Mrs. Pako came running to see what was wrong. Raymond told me to shoot her too. I told him we'd just better get going because it was bad enough.

We ran down behind the restaurant, and we went inside to get a pop. Then we walked down as far as one farm to ask for a ride down to another. We got a ride down to Delaware, and we walked towards the small road. At the end of the road, we noticed a small golf course. We walked up to the house, and an old man came out who was 'proximately forty-five years old. He asked us what we were doing with the .22, and we told him we were hunting.

We left his property, after we got a drink. When he told us that we had better leave the premises with that gun, we walked until we got to an old fruit stand, and we went inside. We stayed there for about ten minutes and divided the money up. We left and walked till we saw a farm. There was nobody there.

Raymond and I were looking for a car. We found a '65 F85 Deluxe. We got in the car and started it. We went on to the highway on our way to Toronto to visit one of Raymond's friends. We got involved in an accident by hitting a taxicab because the brakes wouldn't work. Raymond got scared, and he put it in reverse and turned up the side street. The taxicab and the ambulance were chasing us for a good five minutes until I told Raymond to pull up by the curb, put it in park as fast as he could, and shut the car off. Then we were taken outside by the ambulance crew and held until the police came. We were taken into the police station and were questioned by the police.

Yeandle: Is there anything further you wish to add to this statement or make any alterations?

A: No, everything is in there.

It was signed by Leslie Beam witnessed by Yeandle and Perrin.

At 8:30 a.m., the following statement was taken by PW Nancy LeKrow and Inspector Perrin:

"Raymond David Ransum, you are charged of the murder of Andrew Pago Sr. Do you wish to say anything in answer to the charge? You are not obliged to say anything unless you wish to do so. Whatever you say will be taken down in writing and may be given in evidence."

Q: Do you understand the caution?

A: Yeah.

Q: What can you tell me about this matter?

A: It is true, we were not really headed for Toronto, farther than Toronto. We were going past Andy Pako's, and Leslie said he generally carried about $2,000 in the house. We decided to go up there and try to find a way in. We went around to the back door, and just as we were about to go in, the old guy came, so we ducked in behind the bushes, and we went in the field. Then we tried the back door, and it was locked, so we went around the side and through the basement window.

Then we went upstairs and checked Junior's bedroom, and we found something like I think it was $130 and counting. In Hungarian money it was supposed to be 11,009,520, and that was in Hungarian dollars. Then we checked the great big dresser thing and in that we found the change purse with change in it. So then we went out the front door and went around the back and met Pako Sr.

Then he started speaking Hungarian to us, and Leslie told me what he was saying in English, and he was daring Leslie to shoot, and he told Leslie to shoot. He told him three times. I put my finger on the trigger, and he started speaking Hungarian again, and I started listening, and the gun went off. So then we took off, and Leslie said, "Let's go back and shoot the old lady" because she started hollering. Then we went back, and she was hollering and screaming at the guy. And she was saying, "Oh god."

We took off. We ran behind the service station. WE went in, got a couple drinks, and started walking down the road to a farm. We asked the guy to take us to London, and we pay for the gas, and he took us as far as Delaware. Then we tried to buy a car at some wreakers and a Ford dealer, try to get an old one. Then we walked down and across the golf course to the fruit stand. We divided up the money, stayed there for about twenty minutes. Then we went down to a house. Nobody was there.

We saw a car with the key in the trunk and the key in the dash, so we took it. We drove to a gas station, put $7.80 in gas and $2.00 in oil, and we paid them nine dollars. He didn't charge us the 80¢. We left the garage, went down to the 401 Highway, and drove to Toronto. Then we were going down a street, stopped at a couple of lights, and came up behind a taxi stopped at a light. I put the brakes on, and she wouldn't stop. We plowed into the taxi. Then I hit reverse, whipped around the car, and tried to outrun him. He chased us around the streets, and we hit some garbage cans, and that's when finally the ambulance caught up with us again. He had seen the accident. He turned on his siren, so I went around the corner, and I said, "Shall we pull over or try and get away because I couldn't get around any more corners without brakes." I couldn't control the car. So then I slowed her down best I could, put it in park, and a gear started to grind, and I shut off the engine. I got out of the car, and the guy from the ambulance threw me up against the car. Then he phoned in, and the cops came. Then they found the gun and the knife, and they said the gun was loaded, and I said the gun was not loaded because I threw it in the back seat.

Q: Is there anything more you wish to add?

A: No.

It was signed Raymond Ransum and witnessed by P. W. Nancy LeKrow and Inspector Perrin.

Note: Because the two accused were juvenile offenders, their names as well as the victim's name have been changed.

In the early inquiries, it was established that Ransum was a ward of St. John's Training School, Uxbridge, Ontario, and had been transferred to the St. Thomas Psychiatric Facility. The families of both youths were advised by Metropolitan Toronto Police Department (MTPD). An aftercare worker, Ms. Barbara McCahery of St. John's Training School, attended at no. 52 division and was present when Ransum made a statement. Also present was policewoman Nancy LeGrow, MTPD. Leslie Beam did not want his mother present.

At 8:20 a.m., August 1, 1974, as Ransum could neither read nor write, except his signature, Inspector Perrin gave a copy of Beam's statement to Mrs. McCahery, and she read it to him without comment and also the statement that was taken from Ransum after being cautioned. Basically, his statement was identical with that of Beam's.

Mr. A. A. Binnington, barrister, Aurora, attended at number 52 division and talked to Ransum.

The two youths were escorted to London at 4:00 p.m. on August 1, 1974. They appeared before Juvenile Court Judge W. H. Fox on a charge of juvenile delinquency, in that they murdered Andy Pako. There was concern that there was insufficient security at the London Detention Home to hold Ransum, and he was remanded to Hilltop Training School, Guelph, on August 2, 1974. Beam was remanded to a London detention home on August 2, 1974.

At 7:00 p.m., August 1, 1974, Dr. D. M. Wickware, psychiatrist, examined Ransum. At 10:00 a.m. on August 2, 1974, he examined Beam. Both youths appeared before Juvenile Judge Fox at 3:00 p.m. on August 2, 1974, and Ransum was remanded to Penetanguishene Mental Health Center for not more than sixty days for examination. Beam was again remanded to a London detention home.

A postmortem conducted by Dr. Elder M. Davies, pathologist, at St. Joseph's Hospital in London on August 1, 1974, revealed cause of death due to gunshot wound. The bullet had passed through the lips and tongue, severed the spinal cord, and damaged the vertebrae and exited from the back of the neck.

Examination and photographing of the scene was carried out by me. There were no prints found suitable for comparison. In the basement on a recently raked sandy area, several shoe heel prints were found and photographed and casts were made. These were examined against shoes of both accused and were identified to the footwear the two youths were wearing.

In conversation with Beam, he advised that the shell casing from the bullet that killed Mr. Pako was ejected in a bush area south of no. 2 Highway behind the Arrow Gas Station and Restaurant about three hundred yards east of Pako's residence. The brush in that area was cut, and a manual search conducted in that area was also searched using a metal detector without locating the shell casing.

The rifle, ammunition, and the knife were seized from the youths on arrest and were turned over to him to be submitted to the Center of Forensic Science. The money seized from youths on arrest was turned over to Constable Kersey.

Witnesses in the area had seen the two accused prior to and after the offense, and statements were obtained from those witnesses.

At the scene, Mrs. Pako did not see either of the youths, and this could be explained by the shocked condition of Mrs. Pako and by the fact that there was thick shrubbery in the area between her and the youths.

Both youths appeared in juvenile court and were convicted.

CHAPTER THIRTY-THREE

Fatal Accident, Three Died

The latter part of February 1971, we were moving from our office on Centre Street to our new office in a new two-story building on the north side of the 401 Highway. The DHQ was on the second floor, which included our office, photographic darkroom, and a small storage room. The London detachment was on the first floor along with the district radio room and the cells. The lunchroom, a class room, and a room for detachment files were in the basement.

Ray and I were driving into the parking lot of the office when I was dispatched to a fatal accident in the Strathroy area on 22 Highway a short distance east of the Lampton-Middlesex county line. Ray took the articles into the office, and I proceed to the accident scene.

When I got close to Strathroy, the Strathroy office called on the radio and advised me that 22 Highway was closed in some areas, and I would be better off taking the old 22 Highway, which was about a mile or so south of the new 22 Highway.

Travelling on this road with six- and seven-foot snowbanks on both sides of the road seemed like driving in a tunnel, but with the wind blowing the snow of the snowbank, it made visibility very bad. Luckily there was no other traffic on the road in either direction. With the headlights and the red flashing roof lights on, I felt a little safer.

I finally got to the scene of the accident. One police cruiser was parked on the north side shoulder of the road, and two vehicles parked behind it. A tow truck was parked behind the second vehicle, and a third vehicle was parked beside the first car behind the cruiser.

The story I got as told by the corporal from the Strathroy Detachment, who had arrived at the scene prior to my arrival, was that the two vehicles parked behind the cruiser were involved in an accident. The police officer, Constable Bill Reid from the Petrolia Detachment, who had been in the area, was dispatched to the scene.

He talked to the two drivers of the vehicles and invited them back to car where he would obtain their statements. He was leading them back to the police car when the third vehicle drove through the accident scene, hitting all three of them. An ambulance arrived and took all three to the Sarnia Hospital. They all died en route to the hospital or shortly after arriving there.

I photographed the scene as best as I could considering the weather condition; it was damn cold, windy, and snowing.

I went to the hospital where I took Bill's gun belt and his gun. I also received blood samples of all the three victims during the autopsies.

The next morning I went to the garage where the vehicles were taken. The vehicles were photographed with close-ups of the damage to each of the vehicles involved in the previous accident. Photos were also taken of the third vehicle, including close-ups of the vehicle.

I found the damage was not consistent with the Cpl's description as I was told by the corporal.

I went over to the Strathroy Department and spoke to the corporal. I told him that the accident as he described it was not correct. I explained to him how it happened indicated by the damage to the vehicles. we went over to the garage, and I showed him how the damage caused to the vehicles were not consistent with his explanation as to how it happened. I told him that he was wrong and I was right about the cause.

I left Strathroy and went back to London and to the office. I went into the darkroom and developed the film used at the accident scene and the film I used in the garage photographing the damage to the vehicles. When the film was developed and dried, I printed the pictures that showed the damage that was caused by the accident that did not go along with the corporal's explanation of the cause.

I went into the traffic sergeant's office and told how the accident occurred as I was told by the corporal. I then told him how I saw how the accident occurred and showed him the photos backing up my explanation as to the cause.

He immediately got off his chair, put on his parka and hat, and as he left his office, he said, "I'll go and straighten him out fast." And he was gone.

Days later when the accident report arrived at headquarters, It was the corporal's explanation as to how it happened. Again the traffic sergeant headed out the door for Strathroy with the accident report in his hand. He was somewhat annoyed.

It was months later when a hearing took place on a lawsuit against the driver of the car that caused the death of the policeman Bill Reid and the two drivers in the first accident.

Because of the weather conditions and the fact the visibility was really bad, no charges were laid. However, the lawsuit was initiated by the two drivers' families. They sued the driver that struck the vehicle as well as the police.

The lawsuit did not go to court as it was settled before a court date was set. The insurance company of the two drivers of the first accident who were killed when the car struck them and the police officer settled for an unknown amount. The lawsuit against the police was dropped.

Bits and Pieces 9

On one occasion, I was dispatched to the northwest corner of Middlesex County where a Chipmunk aircraft from the Royal Canadian Air Force Training Air Base at Clinton had crashed and burned. It apparently hit the ground in Lambton County to the west, went airborne about a hundred feet a few feet off the ground, and came down across the county line into where it ended up in Middlesex County.

I took photos of the aircraft, at least what was left of it, with the two dead bodies still in their seats. When we went to a crime scene, traffic accident, or any other occurrence we were dispatched to, we took close-ups showing the position of the bodies or any other item that would have been involved in that occurrence. An air force photographer from the Clinton Air Force base arrived and took photos of the Chipmunk as well.

About three weeks later, another Chipmonk came down in a wooded area at camp Ipperwash, another military facility. The same Air Force photographer arrived and took photos of this aircraft mishap. He thanked me and told me I saved his ass at the previous crash. He did not take any close-up photos of the cockpit area showing the bodies at the previous crash. I had taken several close-ups at that previous crash. I had sent him copies of all the photos I had taken, which he was very grateful for because those were the ones the inquiry board wanted.

At this second crash, he took close-ups and would now do it at all occurrences he would have in the future.

Another civilian aircraft, a crop duster, came in a farmer's field while spraying his crop. The pilot in this crash survived.

This is another civilian aircraft that apparently came straight down after having a mechanical problem. At least that's what they assumed happened. The pilot did not live to tell us what happened.

Another plane was about to fly over the Dorchester area when for some unknown reason, it came apart when it was somewhere over one thousand feet high. The plane came down in and around the Dorchester pond.

The pilot and the passenger, a well-known retired NFL football player, were both killed before hitting the ground.

I went to the morgue at Victoria Hospital to attend the autopsy, which might indicate what happened to the aircraft. It was the worst sight I had ever seen in a morgue. Both bodies were molded together into a three-foot ball of blood, bones, and guts. It was a complete mess. There was no way you could tell what belonged to whom. The autopsy was cancelled.

CHAPTER THIRTY-FOUR

Another Taxi Driver Murdered

On January 2, 1974, at 10:18 p.m., a call was received at the St. Thomas detachment from a Mr. Bill Tomas of RR 1 Union, who reported that a man was lying beside a taxicab in the laneway of Don Hepburn's residence. This location was roughly one mile north of the village of Port Stanley at the intersection of Elgin County Road no. 23 and no. 4 Highway. Both of these roads run south to Port Stanley. The Hepburn laneway ran west from no. 4 Highway.

The first officer at the scene, Constable J. C. McCaw of the St. Thomas detachment, arrived at 10:35 p.m. He was met by Mr. Donald Hepburn of Lot 2, Concession 2, Yarmouth Township, RR 1, Union. He was the owner of the property where the body and taxi were found. The taxi was a 1968 Ford, four-door, black in color, bearing Ontario license DAC 454, Checker Cab no. 349.

The taxi was parked in the laneway facing in a westerly direction, about thirty feet west of no. 4 Highway. The doors on the vehicle were closed. The motor was not running. The ignition switch was on, and the transmission indicator was in the park position. The radio microphone was torn out and lying on the floor. The taxi meter registered $12.65. There was a large quantity of blood in approximately the middle of the front seat. A spotlight lying on the front seat was also covered with blood. There was blood on the floor in the back of the vehicle behind the driver's seat, and blood also was splattered on the door post on the driver's side.

Approximately nine feet south of the taxi was the body of a male person lying facedown. A brown nylon jacket was pulled over the head, and the arms were bent around toward the top of the head. There was blood on the back of the body (on a gray pullover sweater) and on the back of the head and the neck. There were drag marks in the snow leading from the front driver's door of the cab to the body.

I arrived at the scene at 11:15 p.m. and took photographs indicating the location of the body and the taxi. Directly across a road from the laneway where the taxi was found, two sets of footprints were found on the shoulder of no. 4 Highway. One set was made by a plain flat shoe approximately size 7 or 8. The other set was made by a 7 or 8 woman's shoe with a round heel. There were no tread marks on either shoe. These footprints crossed the boulevard between the two highways.

Corporal D. E. James, London detachment, brought his canine, Arab, to the scene. Arab followed one set of tracks to the rear of a house located on no. 23 County Road, a short distance from the scene. Another set was followed south and into Port Stanley where the trail was lost.

At 12:18 a.m. January 3, the coroner, Dr. R. J. Foster of St. Thomas, attended at the scene. He ordered the body be removed to St. Joseph's Hospital, London, by the St. Thomas Ambulance Company. The body was subsequently identified by Arthur Ross Armstrong of RR 4 Glencoe as his son, Timothy Ross.

Timothy Armstrong was married with no children. He and his wife had separated in 1973, and she was presently residing in London, the exact address unknown. In June 1973, Armstrong began driving a Checker cab owned by Mr. William Marvin of London.

Following the identification of the body, Dr. D. M. Miles, pathologist of St. Joseph's Hospital, commenced the autopsy beginning at 9:30 a.m. Dr. Miles found the cause of death to be multiple gunshot wounds to the chest and back and two bullet wounds to the skull. There was massive hemorrhage into the right chest and severe laceration to the brain.

There were four bullet wounds to the body. The first projectile entered the right anterior chest, passed through the lung, diaphragm, liver, three loops of bowel, large intestine line, and lodged in the left lower abdomen. The second projectile entered high on the back just barely right of the midline. It went through the right lung, and the bullet was lying free in the chest cavity. The third projectile entered the right side of the skull near the top. It fragmented, lacerating the right side of the brain. The first and second projectiles appeared to be suitable for comparison tests.

Bill Thomas advised that he had left home at approximately 8:30 p.m. He returned at 10:15 p.m. and found the taxi and the body. Chris Ingram, RR 4 St. Thomas, stated he went by Hepburn's laneway at approximately 9:10 p.m., and there was a taxi in the laneway with an interior light on. He didn't notice anyone in the area.

Alvin Tucker of St. Thomas stated he went by Hepburn's shortly after 9:30 p.m. and observed a car in the laneway. He saw two people running across the field. One was wearing a short coat, but he was uncertain of the color. He thought one person had dark hair about shoulder length. He was unable to give any further description.

David Appleton was employed as a dispatcher at Checker National, London Ltd. On January 2, 1974, at 8:43 p.m., he received a call from a person who identified herself as Linda. This person advised she was calling from a telephone booth at Richmond and Central in downtown London and wanted to be taken to Union. Appleton called three taxis, and they were all busy. He dispatched Armstrong in taxi 349 as he was next on the dispatch list. Approximately five minutes later, he called Armstrong and was advised that the fare had been picked up.

Donald Anderson, detective sergeant, CID, London Police Force, said on Thursday, January 3, 1974, that he received the telephone call from Mrs. Alexandra Ames of 153 John Street. Mrs. Ames was a person he knew through an investigation of a subject who broke into her apartment, and the charges were still pending in that matter. She said she had some very important information for him and that she did not want to discuss on the telephone and would he please come to her residence.

At 9:45 p.m., he went to Mrs. Ames's residence and spoke to her and her husband, Wolfgang, and a friend, Mark Watson. These three persons were obviously upset and said to Anderson that they knew who was responsible for the murder of Timothy Ross Armstrong.

They briefly told Anderson the story concerning the persons they believed had committed the murder, namely John Gibbins, who had the nickname Blue and who resided at 15 Kappele Crescent, Apt. 11, Stratford, Ontario. Mark Watson and Wolfgang Ames stated that Gibbins and his girlfriend (a girl with the name of Linda, last name was unknown) had been to the apartment recently and were discussing a planned holdup of a Loblaw's Store in St. Thomas.

There was apparently some consideration given to them participating in the holdup by Watson and Ames, but Gibbins stated that when it came right down to it, he believed that they would back out.

Wallace and Ames went on to say that on the evening of Wednesday, January 2, 1974, about 8:00 p.m., Gibbbins and his girlfriend were at the apartment, and when they left, they said they were going to rob a cabdriver. Both returned to the apartment again at 3:00 a.m. on Thursday morning, January 3, and at that time said that they were in a bit of trouble and wanted to stay at Ames's apartment. At this time they were with a man by the name of Bill who resided in St. Thomas. He didn't know the last name of this person, who was driving about a 1960 Chevrolet vehicle.

Ames refused to allow them to stay at the apartment, and they left. At about 3:00 p.m. on Thursday, January 3, Gibbins and his girlfriend, Linda Recinos, again came to the apartment. Ames asked Gibbins what had happened. Gibbins stated the he was in trouble and told what happened.

Anderson did not go into the complete details with the Ameses at this time as he did not feel they should go through the story twice. He advised them that he would immediately go and get the inspectors from the police who were in charge of the investigation to come and interview them. He asked them if they had any idea where Gibbins and his girlfriend would be at the present time. The Ameses said they believed they would be in the apartment they had rented in Stratford because they had left the Ames apartment at 4:45 p.m. to catch the bus to Stratford, which would leave the bus depot at 5:15 p.m.

At 10:30 p.m., Andrews, in the company of Detective Lawrence Moss, went to the Horseshoe Motel and interviewed police inspectors William Orton and John Masters. He advised the inspectors of the information he had received and assured him that it was reliable.

Inspector W. Orton, assisted by Inspector J. C. Masters, interviewed Wolfgang Ames, age 23, of London. Ames stated that on January 2, John Gibbins, later identified as John Patrick "Blue" Gibbins, age 21, FPS no. 395946 A, and Yolanda Margaret "Linda" Recinos, age 18, both of Stratford, came to his home and were discussing plans to rob a supermarket in St. Thomas. They left around 6:00 p.m. and went out for supper. When they had supper and returned to his home, Gibbins, in the presence of Recinos, advised Ames he was going to rob a cabdriver. Ames told Orton he knew Gibbins always carried a pearl-handled .22 caliber derringer pistol with two barrels. Gibbins had advised Ames earlier that he was going to use this gun in the holdup. Ames asked Gibbins what would happen if the driver resisted, and Gibbins replied, "If I have to shoot him, I will."

He said Gibbins told him he was going to use a pay phone, and he thought Gibbins would probably use the telephone at Richmond and Central as it was the nearest payphone. Around 3:30 a.m. January 3, Gibbins returned to his home. He noticed Recinos was in a Chevrolet car parked in front of the house with Bill from St. Thomas (later identified as William James Usher, age 24, of St. Thomas). Gibbins told Ames he was in trouble and the police were looking for him. He then left.

About 3:00 p.m., January 3, Gibbins and Recinos returned to Ames. Ames asked Gibbins what had happened. Gibbins said that he told the driver to give him the money. He pointed the gun at the driver's head. The driver panicked and reached for the microphone, so Gibbins shot him in the head. He was still moving around, so he shot him again.

During the conversation, Ames noted that Recinos was interjecting and laughing and joking and thought it was quite funny. Gibbins said that Recinos had shut off the car, and then he dragged the body about ten feet from the car. Gibbins said he wanted to make sure the guy was dead, so he shot him through the heart and that he had shot the victim a total of four times.

He said they tried to start the car but couldn't, so they ripped out the wires. He said they took the money changer and threw it away after taking out the change. He said they searched the driver for a wallet but only found a billfold with around $25 in it. Gibbins advised they then ran down the road to Port Stanley. They obtained a ride with an acquaintance named Giselle (later identified as Gisele Mary Manning, age 27, of Port Stanley) to Bill Usher's house in St. Thomas. Usher then drove them to Stratford and then London.

Inspectors Orton and Masters proceeded to Stratford with the two London police officers. They contacted acting Sergeant William Forest of the Stratford Police Department. They then proceeded to 15 Kappele Circle, Stratford, and obtained a key to apartment 11 from the building superintendent. Gibbins and Recinos were asleep on a chesterfield bed in the living room. Recinos was taken to a bedroom by Detective Sergeant Anderson, and Gibbins was kept in the living room while the apartment was searched. The inspectors left the apartment with Gibbins, taking him to the Stratford Police Station at 5:15 a.m. Inspector Orton cautioned Gibbins and received an exculpatory statement.

At 5:20 a.m., the following statement was taken.

Name: John Patrick Gibbins
Address: 15 Kappele Circle, Apt. 11, Stratford
Occupation: Labourer

"You are charged with murder contrary to the Criminal Code of Canada."

Gibbins was given the police caution.

Question: Do you understand that caution?

Answer: Yes.
Question: I am investigating the murder of Timothy Armstrong, a driver for Checker Cab, which occurred on January 2, 1974. What can you tell me about this matter?
Answer: Nothing.
Question: Where were you on the evening of January 2?
Answer: I have nothing to answer to that. I am not going to say anything until I see a lawyer.
Question: Do you own or have you ever owned a double-barreled pearl-handled derringer 22-caliber pistol?
Answer: No.
Question: Were you in the Port Stanley area January 2, 1974?
Answer: I have nothing to answer to that.

Gibbins refused to sign the statement after reading it.
W. B. Orton, inspector police
Statement ends 5:22 a.m.

At 7:15 p.m., Gibbins was turned over to Detective Sergeant Anderson and Detective Moss, and they transported him to London. Recinos, while still at the apartment, admitted to Anderson before he left for London with Gibbins that Gibbins had killed the cabdriver and that she was with him at the time.

At 7:15 p.m., the following statement was taken.

Name: Margaret Recinos
Address: 15 Kappele Circle, Apt. 11, Stratford Ontario
DOB: Dec. 1/55, age 18
Married or Single: Single

"You are charged with noncapital murder in connection with the death of Timothy Ross Armstrong, contrary to the criminal code.

Police caution was given to Recinos.

Question: Do you understand the two cautions which I have read to you?
Answer: Yes.
Question: Would you tell me in your own words what, if anything, you know about this death?
Answer: Well, I guess I witnessed it, but I didn't have anything else to do with it.
Question: Would you like to start at the beginning and tell me all you know?
Answer: Well, we were over at Wolfgang Ames's place on 153 John Street, London. I saw the gun. John Gibbins pulled the gun out and showed it to everybody that was there. I heard John Gibbins say he was short of money, and Wolfgang said to rob a cabdriver. He used to be a cabdriver. He said it was easy to rob a cabdriver, just take them outside the city. He also said that the Checker Cab was a bigger cab company.
We, John and me, left Wolfgang's house to go to a phone booth to call a cab. John said for me to phone. I didn't want to, but I did. I asked for a cab to come to the corner of Richmond and Central, and I asked him how much it would cost to go to Union. I said it was Linda Gibbins calling. Then we waited around for the cab to arrive.
When it arrived, we got in the cab and drove down through Union. John said to pull over into the next driveway on the right. John told him not to drive all the way up the driveway, it would be too hard, so he stopped. It was Hepburn's Riding Stable driveway.

When the cab stopped, I opened the door to get out, and when I turned around, John asked the driver to hand over the money. I saw him. John started shooting the cab-driver from behind. I think the cab driver moved around like he was going to pick up the microphone, that's when John shot him. He shot him twice from behind while he was in the back seat.

Then John got out of the car and went around the back of the car to the passenger side, opened up the passenger door, and ripped out the wires, and then John reloaded the gun, leaned over, and shot the driver twice more. Then John stepped back from the car. I think he found some sort of a stick and then pushed the driver outside the car.

In the meantime, I was standing outside the car by the right-hand side by the back of the car, ready to be sick. John asked me to help him drag the driver away from the car, but I didn't want to help. Then John dragged him away and checked his wallet and pockets for the money. He ripped out the coin changer and handed it to me. I had it in my purse. While dragging the body away, he asked me to shut the car off. I opened the door and saw all the blood, and I said, "No, I can't do it."

Then John said, "Let's split." We kicked some snow over the body, and then we left. We went to Port Stanley to visit a friend who wasn't home, but his wife Giselle was, and she gave us a ride to St. Thomas.

We went to Bill Usher's home, but he was not there. So we went to the house where

> he used to live where some of his friends still live to look for Bill, but he wouldn't be back until 11:30 p.m. We walked around town waiting for Bill to come back. When he came back, John asked for a ride back to Stratford because we were hot.
>
> Bill said he had to pick up his girlfriend at midnight from work. We waited at Essex Wire until his girlfriend came out. While we were waiting, we talked to Bill about what happened, and when the two girls, his girlfriend and another girl, got in the car, we never talked about it again.
>
> They drove us to Stratford to pick up some money from the apartment, and then drove us back to London to see if we could stay the night at Wolfgang Ames's. We couldn't stay there, so we stayed at John's mother's house. The next day, yesterday afternoon, we went back to Wolfgang's place, and he had seen it in the newspaper. We talked about the murder, and then at 5:15 p.m., we caught a bus at the bus station and came back to Stratford.
>
> That's about it.

Signed: Yolanda Recinos
Statement concluded at 8:00 p.m., Jan 4, 1974
Inspector J. C. Masters
Inspector W. B. Ortone

At the London Police Headquarters, Gibbins made the following statement at 9:45 a.m.: "I, John Patrick Gibbins, make the following statement voluntarily after having been cautioned by Donald Anderson, Detective Sergeant."

Police caution was given to Gibbins.

Q: On Wednesday, January 2, 1974, a cabdriver was found dead in the Port Stanley area. Do you wish to tell me what you know about this matter?

A: Well, we were short of money, and that's how it all started off. I went to welfare to get some money to pay the rent, and they refused. I went around to some friends and asked if I could borrow some money, and they were short of bread. This friend and I discussed on how to raise some money, and it came up that if you wanted to get about eighty bucks, to rob a cabdriver. So I went and did it.

We called him from a phone booth, and like, we went down there and went to Union. I didn't know what to do. I was getting more confused, so I thought of Hepburn's, and when he pulled into the driveway, I pulled the gun out. Like I asked him for the money, and that's when I started freaking out. I had the gun at the back of his head. He started to turn around and grab me, and I don't know, I just pulled the trigger. He was bouncing around. I didn't know what to do, and I couldn't see him in pain like that, so I just shot him again. I got out of the car then, and Linda got out. I don't know if I hit him in the lung or not, but noises were coming up like gas, and I went around to the other side of the car and just started shooting. I went around the other side of the car and pulled him out, and like, I pulled him in the ditch there, and I threw some snow over him, and I took his billfold. I tried to take the car, but before I ripped the mike out and a light, and then I tried to start the car, but it wouldn't start. I grabbed Linda and told her to run. We went down into Port Stanley to see if we can get a ride to St. Thomas. We got into St. Thomas, and then we went to Stratford and back to London and back to Stratford again, and that was it.

Q: Who was with you when you shot and robbed this cabdriver?

A: Linda Recinos. Like, she never participated in anything, I didn't even want to rob the guy when we got there, but I didn't have any choice.

Q: How much money was in the billfold you stole from this man?

A: $20.

Q: What happened to the billfold?

A: I threw it away somewhere in Port Stanley.

Q: Did you steal anything else at the time of the commission of this offense?

A: A watch, but it didn't have a strap on it, his coin changer, and his cigarettes.

Q: What happened to the gun with which you shot this man?

A: Like I stashed it in the floor of the car under some things, where I told you.

Q: Is or anything else you wish to say about this matter?

A: Well, like, no one else was really involved, and I didn't mean to shoot him. It wasn't intentional. The people I got a ride with didn't know what was going on.

Statement completed 10:20 a.m.
Signed: John Gibbins
Donald B. Anderson

On January 5 at 11:40 a.m., Inspectors Orton and Masters located William James Usher at 44 Park St. in St. Thomas. He was taken to the St. Thomas Detachment, where he gave an exculpatory statement under caution in which he admitted driving Gibbins and Recinos to Stratford and London. Following the statement, Usher was questioned further and admitted Gibbins had told him about the murder before transporting them to Stratford.

Name: William James Usher
Address: 139 Wellington Street in St. Thomas
Age: 24
Married or single: Separated
DOB: February 2, 1949
Occupation: Assembler

"You are charged with aiding and abetting John Gibbins and Yolanda Recinos knowing they're responsible for a murder contrary to the Criminal Code of Canada."

Police caution was given.

Q: Do you understand the caution I have read to you?
A: Yes.
Q: I am investigating the murder of Timothy Ross Armstrong on January 2, 1974, and the circumstances surrounding it. Do you wish to tell me about this matter?
A: Yes, John came to my place. John and his girlfriend came to my place. They wanted a ride to Stratford. I wasn't at home when they first came. Like, I was at the horse races. When I came home, one of the persons who was living there said John was there. He said he would be back in about ten minutes, he had gone for coffee. But five minutes later, after I got home, he came back.

He asked for a ride to Stratford. I told him I had to pick up my girlfriend at work at twelve. We went up to Essex Wire and picked up my girlfriend and her sister. From Essex Wire we went to the Fina Station at the end of Talbot Street and got gas and drove to Stratford. When we got to Stratford, he asked us in for a cup of tea or coffee.

We left his place. He wanted a ride back to London, and we stopped in at Tim Horton's Doughnuts. We got some doughnuts and hot chocolate. We then drove to London. I dropped him off at his mom's place. From there I drove home. That's it, and I went to bed. After I dropped him off at his mom's home, I drove back to 44 Park Avenue in St. Thomas. Going through London, we got stopped by the police for faulty taillights. This was before we got to his mom's place. That's it. After I dropped him off, I went home.

Q: Do you mind if I ask you a few questions?

A: Yes, you can ask them.

Q: Who was it that John saw at your place before you talked to him?

A: I am not sure. There are about six guys that lived there, and I am not sure who he talked to.

Q: What time was it when you first saw John?

A: About twenty after eleven.

Q: Who went with you to Stratford?

A: Jeanette Beaman. She was married. You can also use the name Harmon, Annie Harmon, her sister.

Q: How do you spell that?

A: It starts with an *H* not an *N*. I don't know how you spell it.
Q: Who was with Gibbins?
A: His girlfriend Linda or Yolanda.
Q: What did they say about their activities?
A: They said they went out to visit Phil May, and he wasn't at home. He was down in Toronto driving a coffee truck for his brother-in-law.
Q: Where does Phil May live?
A: Port Stanley, Mitchell Heights Hotel, I forget the name of the street.
Q: Did they tell you how they got to Port Stanley?
A: No.
Q: Did they tell you how they got to your place?
A: Yeah, Phil's wife Gisele.
Q: Did they mention to you that they were in difficulty?
A: No.
Q: What do you know about the gun found in your car?
A: All I know is that two police officers came up and said there was a gun in my car.
Q: When you were in London after being stopped by the police, did you stop at any other houses other than John's mother's house?
A: No.
Q: Were you on John Street in London? This is in the downtown area.
A: I don't know the streets. Yeah, I remember we were on John Street. We stopped at a person's house there. He went in for about five minutes and back out. I didn't even think of

that. That was before we got stopped by the cops.

Q: Why did Gibbins want you to drive him to Stratford from St. Thomas?

A: That's where he lives.

Q: Why did he want you to drive him to London?

A: Because I was going to St. Thomas, and he wanted a ride back to London.

Q: This seem unusual to you?

A: No because I have driven him around before. He doesn't have a car. He comes over to my place whenever he is in St. Thomas and needs a ride, he comes to me, and if I'm not busy and he pays for the gas, I take him.

Q: Is there anything else you wish to say?

A: That's it. That's all I know.

Q: Did he pay for the gas?

A: Yes.

Q: How much?

A: Five dollars. The gas was $5.02.

Signed: W. B. Orton, police
Witness: Inspector J. C. Masters
Criminal Investigation Branch
12:47 p.m., January 5, 1974

At 12:55 p.m., he was asked again, "Do you want to tell me again what you know?"

"Just what I told him at Essex Wire. They said they had to get out of town. I asked why. He said he did not want to tell me because the less I knew, the better it was. He would read about it in the paper the next day. I told them if I was going to read about it, you might as well tell me. They told me they took a taxi driver from London to Port Stanley, and they shot him. Linda let slip out that it was a taxi driver. John said they robbed him. That's about it. Linda said there was a lot of blood all over.

Signed: William J. Usher
Ends 1:07 p.m.
Signed: W.B. Orton
Witness: J. C. Masters

John Patrick Gibbins pleaded guilty to noncapital murder and was sentenced to life in prison with no possibility of parole for ten years. The Crown attorney was unsuccessful to have parole eligibility postponed to fifteen years. A psychiatrist called by the defense testified that the killer had a treatable personality disorder and that extending the parole eligibility period beyond ten years would make treatment more difficult. In refusing the Crown's application, the judge expressed confidence "that this person at any time in the future unless is no longer a danger to the public."

Margaret Recinos was also convicted of Armstrong's murder. She was found in possession of the victim's coin changer, and her statement to the police indicated that she was aware of the plans to rob a taxi driver. The criminal code provided the main grounds for her conviction, that she participated in the planning of the robbery, and she knew the killer was armed.

The killer, Gibbins, was subsequently paroled and died in a car accident that claimed four lives. A shotgun was found in the wreckage of his car.

CHAPTER THIRTY-FIVE

Raped and Murdered

The victim, Louise Patricia Jensen, 19, was born prematurely on June 28, 1956, at eight and a half months. She was adopted by Mr. and Mrs. Jack Gilbert of Strathroy. At the time of this occurrence, she had been living at RR 2, Mount Brydges, for the past thirteen months with her husband, Denys Jensen, age 24, and their seven-month-old daughter, Rachel Amanda.

On Monday, October 20, 1975, at approximately 6:15 p.m., her husband arrived home from work and entered the house through the back door, which was unlocked. Upon entering the house, he discovered the body of his wife lying on the kitchen floor. The body was lying face up in a prone position with her head in the entranceway to the dining room. There was a black bootlace tied around her neck, and her throat had been cut.

When Denys touched her hand, he realized that she was dead. He immediately stepped over her body and rushed upstairs to the baby's room and found his seven-month-old daughter Rachel unharmed in her crib. At this time, Denys removed the baby from the house and ran to the residence of Ms. Edna Beaman, age 74, their neighbor who was immediately to the south of their home. Jensen used Ms. Beaman's phone to notify his brother-in-law and to request an ambulance. The Jensen phone had been disconnected in August 1975.

At 6:31 p.m., a call was received at the London detachment of the police from the Thames Valley EMS Service reporting the death at the Jensen residence. Ontario constable P. Weese of the Strathroy detachment, who was on patrol in the area, was dispatched at 6:33 p.m. to the Jensen residence. He arrived at the scene at 6:34 p.m. On his arrival, he found the ambulance attendants standing along with the husband outside the rear door of the house.

The Jensen residence was a storey and a half white-frame single-unit dwelling. It was situated on the east side of Highway 81 and set back from the highway approximately fifty feet. This residence was located 3.1 miles south of the town of Strathroy and 3.4 miles north of the village of Mount Brydges. While checking in the house, Weese observed the body of the deceased lying on the kitchen floor in a large pool of blood, which had already began to congeal. He also saw the bootlace tied around her neck and that her throat had been cut. The scene was secured, and assistance was requested from district headquarters in London.

At 6:51 p.m., Constable B. Lindsay, the investigating officer, arrived at the scene and commenced his investigation.

When the body was found, it was lying with the face up and with the head in the entrance to the dining room. There was a large pool of partially congealed blood under the neck, head, and shoulder area. The room temperature was 70°F. There was a ligature consisting of a black bootlace, which was tied around her neck with a double granny knot at the front left side of the neck.

There were three lacerations to the throat. Two represented hesitation cuts, which were 4½ inches in length, very superficial, and were spaced half an inch apart. The third was a deep laceration, 4½ inches long and 1½ inch above the two hesitation cuts. This deep laceration extended from the left front to the right side and passed through the junction of the larynx and trachea, lacerating the thyroid gland and the jugular vein.

I arrived at the crime scene at 5:55 p.m. I photographed the body and the interior of the main floor in the house before anything was moved. I searched the scene and the area immediately outside the back door, which led into the kitchen area where the body was found.

It was learned from Ms. Edna Beaman, the neighbor immediately to the south of the Jensen residence, that she observed a late-model cream or yellow vehicle, which entered from the north and parked in the Jensen driveway. This vehicle had a long hood and was quite shiny. The vehicle was occupied by one male subject described as being slim, walked erect, not too large (approximately 5'9" or 10"), age approximately 30, dark hair, collar length and neat, wearing a light-colored windbreaker and dark trousers. This person was observed from the back only and was seen to speak to the deceased at the back door of the house for approximately three or four minutes, then entered the house. She also noticed that this vehicle was still parked in the driveway at approximately 4:15 p.m., and about five minutes later, the vehicle was gone. The direction of travel was not known to her.

Also on this afternoon, at approximately 4:15 p.m., Mr. J. G. Mornington of London was southbound on Highway 81 in a CNR truck. As he rounded a curve in the highway, he observed a car on the left shoulder of the highway facing south. This location was directly in front of the Jensen residence, and a large white dog (Jensen's) was standing by the driver's door, which was closed. As Mornington approached, the vehicle pulled out onto the highway directly in front of him, and he had to brake suddenly to avoid a collision. This vehicle, he said, was a late-model car, tan bottom with a cream or white top, two-door model, small opera windows, with rectangular taillights that were approximately three times as high as they were wide and the same width at both top and bottom.

Pictures of all the latest model cars were shown to Mr. Mornington. He pointed to the Oldsmobile Cutlass Supreme as closest to the vehicle he saw in front of the Jensen residence.

As a result of the above-described vehicle having been seen at the Jensen residence, a printout was later obtained on all Oldsmobile Cutlass Supremes having the small opera windows. This consisted of the model years 1973–1976. This printout was obtained by the police auto theft branch and covered the southwestern part of the province.

The coroner, Dr. J. B. B. Ronins from London, attended at the crime scene and viewed the body. He then called the pathologist, Dr. D. M. Miles, who arrived at the scene at 11:00 p.m. and viewed the body before it was moved. The body was then removed from the crime scene to the morgue at St. Joseph's Hospital, London.

At 9:00 a.m., October 21, I attended at the morgue in St. Joseph's Hospital where Dr. Miles performed the postmortem on the body of Louise Patricia Jensen, who had been identified to Dr. Miles by Denys Jensen, husband of the deceased. I received exhibits from Dr. Miles, the clothing removed from the body, hair samples from her head and pubic area, the lace used as a ligature, and also blood samples and the stomach contents.

In addition to the lacerations to the throat and a ligature around her neck, there were no recent bruises to the body, and the hyoid bone was intact.

There was a considerable petechial hemorrhage of the face and eyes, which is common with strangulation. Based on the body temperature of the deceased, the nature of the clothing, and surrounding temperature, the time of death was placed between five and six o'clock the day before.

The cause of death was incisive laceration of the throat with severe laceration of the trachea, right lobe of the thyroid gland, and the right jugular vein. There was an attempted ligature strangulation of the throat by the shoelace prior to the knife being used.

Denys Malcolm Jensen, age 24, husband of the deceased, was interviewed several times and thoroughly investigated concerning this crime. He stated he was born in Windsor, Ontario, and his parents were Cyril T. Jensen and Lillian, RR 1, Thetford (Port Franks). He was adopted out of Windsor by these parents when he was about two months old.

He said he had lived in Port Franks, Sarnia, Toronto, Point Sutton, Forest, and London. In 1970, he moved to Strathroy and boarded at Merv Wain's house.

He met his wife Louise shortly after moving to Strathroy. He went out with her for two years. They lived common law for a year and had been married for two and a half years.

Louise was adopted out of London when she was a baby. Her parents were John and Helen Gilbert of Strathroy.

When Louise and Denys were living common law, they lived in Sarnia. At that time he worked for McCully Automotive while Louise did not work. They moved back to Strathroy after a year and lived on Victory Street for a little over a year. They were married during this time. They then moved out to where they were living at the time of the murder about a year previously. Shortly after he met Louise, she got pregnant. She was fourteen. They had the baby at Victoria Hospital. The baby girl was put up for adoption by the hospital. During the time Louise was having this baby, and immediately after, he was not supposed to see her. Her parents didn't want him to see her. About three months after she had the baby, they took off to live in Sarnia.

He always got along with Louise. They had just the usual arguments between couples, nothing serious. He swatted her a couple times on her rear end during an argument, that's all. He never hit her anywhere else.

They both had a grade 9 education. He received his schooling in Sarnia. Louise went to school in Strathroy. When Louise was younger, she was a tomboy type. She enjoyed playing with the boys. Since he had known Louise, she never screwed around with other guys. She was a good cook and housekeeper. She liked the baby. They were both right-handed.

On Monday, October 20, he got up at 7:45 a.m. He had shaved and made some tea. He sat and drank his tea in the living room and listened to the news on the radio. The dog was in the kitchen. The back door, on the south side of the house, was not locked.

Louise usually got up anytime between seven o'clock in the morning and noon, depending on the type of night she had had with Rachel. Lately the baby had been fussing more at night. Louise always looked after the baby at night.

The last time he had sexual intercourse with his wife was Sunday night. No, it wasn't; it was after they watched the late show on Global. It would be around one or one thirty in the morning. They had intercourse in bed. They have had intercourse on the couch in the dining room and on the couch in the living room. His wife was on birth control pills. They had sex at least twice a night. Sometimes more; it all depended on how energetic he or she felt. They normally did not have sex when she was menstruating. They usually had sex after going to bed. That Sunday night, they only had it once.

Jensen worked at Larry Smith's Sunoco garage in Strathroy all day on the Monday, from 8:30 a.m. to 5:30 p.m., with a one-hour lunch break at 1:00 p.m. to 2:00 p.m., during which he proceeded to his residence where all was in order. He was at the Sunoco garage until approximately 5:50 p.m. and then went to local stores to purchase groceries until approximately 6:05 p.m.

They had a Family Plan Life Insurance Policy, drawn up by Prudential Life Insurance Company of America, dated August 7, 1975, on which monthly payments of $18.30 were made. A settlement was made with Denys Jensen for a total of $16,980.15. This insurance plan was purchased at the instigation of Mrs. J. Gilbert, mother of the deceased.

On Monday, December 22, Denys agreed to a polygraph examination, and arrangements were made with the Michigan State Police at Detroit, Michigan, to have this examination done. On Wednesday, January 7, the polygraph examination was conducted by Det. Sgt. Stuart S. Hutchings, Second District Headquarters, Michigan State Police, in Detroit. The findings of this examination were that Denys was being truthful when he stated he did not kill his wife and that he did not know who was responsible for his wife's death.

I attended at the scene daily, from Monday evening, October 20, until the afternoon of Friday, October 24, searching for evidence and fingerprints and taking measurements to produce a plan drawing of the main floor of the house. Twenty-seven fingerprints were found in the Jensen residence, and all but five of these prints were eliminated by the husband, the deceased, relatives, and friends. The five unidentified fingerprints were found on empty beer bottles found in a beer case located in a back room of the residence and were not likely those of the person responsible for the crime. The fingerprints of 131 subjects were checked for comparison with the outstanding latent fingerprints.

The prime suspect in this murder was Christian Herbert Harold Magas, age 28, DOB April 1, 1948, of RR 3, Strathroy. This person was interviewed on November 12, 1975, with regard to the Jensen murder and had previously been interviewed on March 24, 1975, with regard to the Barker murder investigation.

Although there was no evidence directly connecting him to either murder, he remained as a suspect because he knew both of the deceased. With regard to the Jensen murder investigation, he had access to and used his father's 1969 Oldsmobile four-door hardtop (black top over yellow bottom).

Magas's fingerprints were checked against the five unidentified prints found in the Jensen residence with negative results.

The vehicle that was described as seen at the site of the crime at the approximate time of the murder was a late-model cream or yellow vehicle with a long hood, which was believed to have been an Oldsmobile Cutlass Supreme two-door hardtop.

On Tuesday, June 15, the body of Susan Lynn Shore, age 15, of 227 Platts Lane, London, was found in a farm field on the north half of lot 7 Concession 17 in Bosanquet Township, Lambton County. She had been raped, strangled into unconsciousness with her halter top, which had been knotted around her throat, and then stabbed in the throat. It was apparent that this murder occurred at the location where her body was found. This investigation was conducted by Prov. Const. D. J. Carter of the Forest detachment.

On November 3, 1975, Sylvia Holly Towers, age 14, came to London from Guelph by bus to visit friends. Sometime after supper, she started to hitchhike in the area of Waterloo and Dundas streets in London.

She was picked up in and old, noisy, rusty car, which she could not describe very well as she was not familiar with cars.

The driver she described very well.

The male driver drove around London for a while and then drove out into Caradoc Township and down an abandoned dirt road, where he stopped.

He told her to take her clothes off, and he started to rip them off.

Sylvia kicked and screamed, and he struck her in the face and had intercourse with her, causing a two-inch laceration up into her vagina and a one-inch laceration from the vagina orifice toward the rectum. He also placed his hands around her throat until she became unconscious.

She was later found lying naked beside the road by a passerby. The passerby called the police and an ambulance, who on their arrival noted that she also had bruises and lacerations over her whole body. She complained that she had been raped to Constable Weese, the first officer to arrive on the scene. At the Strathroy Hospital, she was examined and was found to have a fractured skull in addition to her other injuries.

At the time she was found, it was cold and raining. Given the weather and the remote area where she was found and her injuries, she could easily have perished if she had not been found when she was.

Several suspects were investigated but ruled out by their proven alibis.

On November 6 at 2:22 p.m., Constable P. Devon interviewed Sylvia Jessen. Sylvia said that she bought a bus ticket at 11:05 a.m. in Guelph for a trip to London. The bus arrived in London about two o'clock in the afternoon Monday, November 3. It was raining, and she bought a newspaper to find somewhere to stay.

As a result of reading an ad in the paper, she phoned Glen Wells, who owned the Trade Winds Store. He gave directions on how to get to see him. She went to the store where he had an office downstairs. He told her to go look at the room at 300 Wolfe Street. The couple who looked after the room lived at 298½ Wolfe Street.

The girl's name was Linda. Linda showed her the room. She told Sylvia she would have to put down the first month's rent of $85. Sylvia told her she had just got into town and didn't have a job, but asked her not to show the room to anyone else for a couple days since she could maybe get the money from friends.

Sylvia went back to the Trade Winds Store, not far from the city hall. She said they sold art things, really expensive. Sylvia told Mr. Wells she didn't have the money and was going to see a friend. She indicated that she would be back on Wednesday to tell him if she wanted the room for sure.

She then went to the Mascot Restaurant, which is on the same street, and had a hamburger and a cup of coffee. She finished eating about 7:40 p.m.

Sylvia then went out and walked around down by the bus depot, went to Eaton's Mall, and sat in there for a while and had a cigarette. She then walked down from Eaton's Mall and went into a variety store. She asked the girl where to find 65 Tecumseh Street, which she had written down. Her old boyfriend's brother lived there. Doug Sinfield, her old boyfriend, was supposed to be staying there. The clerk didn't know where the address was. Sylvia went down the street and turned a corner where there was a gas station, possibly a Shell station.

She asked the man at the cash register if he knew where the Tecumseh Street address was. He said it was too far for her to walk, about thirty blocks, and then turn left. Sylvia left the restaurant and thought she would hitchhike to that address.

Sylvia went to the opposite side of the street from the restaurant and started to hitchhike back the way she had come. About four cars went by before one stopped. It was raining, but not very hard. The cars had to stop at lights before they got to the restaurant. There were two lanes of traffic on each side.

When this car stopped, there were no cars behind it. It came straight to the lights. The car pulled over and stopped.

The streetlights weren't very bright at this spot. The car was dark purple or blue in color. It had two headlights on and no other lights visible from the front. There were no sidelights on. There was a stripe of chrome, about one inch wide, along the side of the car from the front fender to the back. She did not remember a mirror on her side. The car had a triangular-shaped vent window at the front of the front door, which had a hook on it. You could push the vent window open because she did so when she later had a cigarette. The car had two doors. The outside of the car was dirty. It was rusty along the bottom.

The car stopped with the passenger door at her feet. The driver leaned over and pulled up the button and unlocked the door. The top interior light came on. It was a little longer than it was wide.

When she opened the door, the driver said, "Hi."

She asked him if he knew where the Tecumseh Street address was and handed him the piece of paper. He kept it. She thought she saw him put it on the floor but was not sure. At this point, she was sitting in the car with one foot in the door and the door open. Twice she asked him if he knew where the address was. Once he said, "I pass it every day." Then he said, "I'll find it."

Sylvia then closed the door, and he drove off. She asked him if he minded if she had a cigarette, and he said, "No."

She noticed a lot of loose things on the floor. She saw a small flashlight with a button on the top; it was orange around the light, and the rest was white. There were some brown cloths on the floor, the type you would see in a garage. She said she smoked about two filter Player's cigarettes while in the car. She lit them with paper matches. He was smoking Export A cigarettes and used a pocket lighter. The floor in the front had black plastic, even over the hump. At the front where your feet would go was blue carpet.

She thought the interior was all blue. The front seat was vinyl covered. The back seat split in the middle, but the bottom of the seat was all one. The gearshift was on the wheel and was automatic. There was a hole in the dash as if the ashtray was missing. Sylvia thought there was a radio, but it was not on. The speedometer area was in an arc about a foot long. The numbers were white with a red pointer. The inside directional signal indicator was at the end of the arc with arrows that flashed green. The car was noisy, sounding like the muffler was worn out.

He asked how old she was, so she told him she was sixteen. He had a medium voice. He asked why she wasn't in school. Sylvia told him she came down for a visit. He said, "What did your boyfriend think of that?"

She said, "I haven't got one."

He asked, "Do your friends know if you have come to see them?"

She said, "No, I'm going to surprise them."

He said his brother used to be a big dope dealer around here. His brother and another guy almost got caught on or near the Mexican border with dope.

He asked if she drank.

She said, "Yes, sometimes."

He asked if she ever used dope.

She said, "Yes, I have." He asked if she had any, but she said, "No."

He said he drove to St. Catharines every day, and the street was on the other side of town, so he passed it every day.

He eventually drove out of town. She asked if the street was out this far, and he said something like it's around the next corner or over the next hill. A couple minutes out of the city, they went down a hill where there was a fork in the road, and a Shell gas station was in the center. She asked to get a map, but he said, "They don't carry them anymore."

She remembered going to a small place with a small name and seeing Township Road signs possibly in Roman numerals.

They had been driving for about three-quarters of an hour when he pulled down a side road, went for a few feet, and stopped. There were bushes on both sides and no houses around. He turned off the engine and turned off the lights. He then said, "You may as well take your clothes off now."

She remembered how he looked. He was wearing old green work pants and tan-colored high work boots. He didn't smell of anything as if he had been drinking. He steered the car with his left hand and smoked with his right hand. Hair was straight, neck length, reddish brown. He had a beard, but it didn't go to his mouth. No moustache. He looked like he had too many teeth. Some were brown. The eye teeth were sticking out more than the other teeth. His fingernails were kind of long. His hands were cold.

He pulled Sylvia's coat off and ripped at her shirt, then threw her coat and purse in the back seat. Then he opened her door from the outside. He was holding her by the legs with her head toward the steering wheel. Sylvia was kicking and fighting and screaming. She did not know if she kicked him or scratched him, although her nails were very long. He took his pants down and got back in the car. He had intercourse with Sylvia. He was very rough. When he was in her, she remembered screaming. He said, "Shut up" and hit her in the left eye with his fist. Then he started choking her with both hands, all the while forcibly having intercourse. Sylvia passed out.

The next thing she remembered was being on the ground and a car coming with one headlight. She was at the side of the road and couldn't get up. She screamed to the car to stop, and it went by and splashed her with mud. She heard the ambulance coming and thought it was going to run her over, so she tried to roll to the side of the road and started to cry.

On November 7, 1975, I went with Constable Devon to the hospital to interview Sylvia Jessen. The description she gave of her attacker was age 28 to 30, height 5'8" or 9", build medium and skinny, weight 150 lb., hair brown to neck, straight beard, and blue eyes. Using the Identi-Kit and with her description, he made a very good likeness of her assailant, which she agreed looked like him.

Investigation revealed the likeness to person of interest, Christian Herbert Harold Magas, who was in London and in that area on the night the victim was picked up. He was familiar with the area where she was found. On at least one other occasion, he picked up a hitch-hiking girl in the same area of London, drove her out to a remote road in the area of his home, and had intercourse with her. This girl, Elaine Roberts, did not report this to police because she was Indian, and at the time she was pregnant and had a criminal record.

Another girl, Rosalie Gertrude Summers, was sexually assaulted in Alexandra Park in Strathroy by Magas on June 20, 1975. She was grabbed from behind as she was walking through the park. Both of these women gave detailed statements of their attack by Magas.

On Friday, August 20, 1976, an identification parade (lineup) was held at the London City Police Department. In the parade were ten civilians and the suspect, Magas, who was in custody, charged with murder of a hitchhiking girl in Forest, Ontario, area. He was given the choice to pick a location in the lineup, and he chose to be at the end of the lineup on the right.

Jessen viewed the lineup, and without any hesitation, she picked out Magas as the man who attacked her.

Both Elaine Ranken and Rosalie Summers viewed the lineup, and when it was their turn to the view the lineup, both did not hesitate in picking out Magas.

But the charges did not end there. Earlier in the year, on Tuesday, June 15, 1976, at 1:45 p.m., James Harvey Frayne, age 16, of RR 2, Forest, Ontario, left his farm home, driving a farm tractor pulling a hay rake. He went to another family-owned farm 4.6 miles distant to cut a hay field.

On his arrival at the farm, Frayne drove into the original entrance laneway overgrown with grass and weeds. Opposite the remains of the house foundation, he glanced at a derelict water pump windmill, then looking to his right, he spotted a leg and a knee in the grass near the old foundation. He was uncertain of what he saw, at first believing someone was sunbathing, but he realized there was no vehicle around, the spot being distant from any built-up area.

Frayne revved the tractor engine and blew the horn but saw no movement from the grass. He continued to the area of an old burnt-out barn on the property and changed the hay rake for a mowing machine. He went into the hay field and cut two swatches around the outer edge of the field, but what he had seen still bothered him.

His uncle, Reginald B. Frayne, arrived at the field by car at 3:00 p.m., and young Frayne told him what he had observed. The uncle did not show any interest, and the youth returned to his tractor and cut another couple of swatches. However, he could not help wondering if someone needed help where he had seen the leg in the grass. He unhitched the mowing machine and drove back toward the property entrance where he dismounted and saw the leg still in the same position.

Approaching, he saw a girl lying on her back with blood on the body, and he was sure the girl was dead. The youth returned to where his uncle was checking fences, and together they checked the girl's body and immediately drove to the Forest detachment of the Ontario Police to report the matter at 4:30 p.m.

The location of this discovery was on the north half of lots no. 7, conc. 17, Bosanquet Township in Lambton County and contained the remains of an old farm comprising a cement foundation above ground level, about a foot high, left derelict for many years. The cement walls of a burned-out barn stood about two hundred feet east of the foundation. A derelict water pump windmill stood about fifty feet to the north. Entry to the property was gained by an overgrown driveway from the 17th conc., the north side.

The body was lying on its back, with the head pointing north about ten feet north of the foundation remains. Both knees were bent with the legs open. The arms were lying slightly out from the sides. A small area of grass was trampled down between the body and the foundation. There was no indication of a great struggle.

The body was clothed in a homemade pair of bikini swim pants. Around the neck (in a strangling position) was a halter top of the same material. The neck and shoulders were blood covered from a stab wound in the lower center of the throat.

The earth below the neck was blood soaked, and all indications were that the strangling and stabbing occurred where the body was found. However, it would appear that the sexual assault on the girl occurred in the grass-trampled area.

About six feet north of the left hand was a green T-shirt, inside out. Immediately by the right foot lay a pair of cut-off blue jean shorts.

Constable D. J. Carter of Forest police was at the office when the report was made by the Fraynes. He went to the scene with them, arriving at 4:48 p.m. Carter secured the scene until the body was removed, and the area was then guarded until Thursday, June 17, 1976, after a complete search had been conducted.

The coroner, Dr. D. McKinley of Sarnia, attended at the scene at 5:44 p.m. and certified the death and ordered an autopsy.

The body was removed to Sarnia General Hospital, where the body was identified by Mrs. I. W. Scott of London, at which time she had been residing at her cottage at Hillsboro Beach, a short distance from Forest. She identified the victim as her daughter, Susan Lynne Scott, born December 5, 1960.

Mrs. Scott last saw her daughter alive just prior to 1:00 p.m. on June 15 at the family cottage. Susan then left with her brother Geoffrey to go into the town of Forest to buy batteries for her portable radio. Geoffrey dropped her in town on his way to work. When Susan had not returned home in the evening, Mrs. Scott and her son reported her missing to the Forest detachment. It was then realized by the police that this girl could well be the victim found earlier.

A postmortem examination was conducted at the Sarnia General Hospital, and the cause of death was "stab wound which punctured the windpipe and severed two major blood vessels in the neck." Additionally, there was strangulation that would also have caused death without the accompanying stab wound. The pathologist indicated the strangling by the halter top caused unconsciousness prior to the stabbing.

Across the lower abdomen, above the pubic area, a small cut ran from the right side thigh to the left thigh. The pathologist believed this occurred after death as there was no bleeding from the tissue.

On the inside of the rib cage below the stab wound, three small wounds were visible on the flesh between the ribs, just missing the lungs. These wounds indicated the knife used had apparently been struck into that area three times, although there was no indication of more than one wound on the outer flesh. The almost circular throat wound gave the appearance that the weapon had been turned while in the wound.

The autopsy established that rape had occurred indicated by tears of the inner wall of the vagina. Semen was present. In connection with this, the pathologist's examination had also established the victim was five to eight weeks pregnant.

It was learned that the victim was seen in Forest about 1:00 p.m. on June 15, where she purchased two AA-size flashlight batteries at the variety store. She was then seen walking back out of town toward County Road 12.

On June 16, a search was conducted from where she was last seen near the tile yard, on the western edge of Forest, from there to the scene and to all adjoining roads. The search was for the two batteries and the murder weapon, believed to be a knife. As a result of further information, the area adjacent was searched for at least another two miles.

The search was conducted by officers on foot, the K9 unit from London, and was also searched with metal detectors supplied by the Canadian Forces Base in London.

On Wednesday, June 16, Mrs. V. McFarland and her son Robert McFarland, both of Forest, attended at the Forest police detachment. Mrs. McFarland was the wife of the owner of McFarlane's Tile Yard in Forest, the business being situated on the north side of County Road 12 and the last property at the western edge of Forest.

Mrs. McFarland had heard of the murder that morning on the radio. She went into the production area of the yard to tell the employees. She had seen a girl answering the victim's description walking west on County Road 12 in front of their premises at 1:30 p.m. on June 14.

Robert McFarland, who had been transferring tile from the kiln to the yard with a forklift vehicle, had noticed a girl referred to by his mother and saw her get into a truck, which stopped right alongside her. He knew the girl through her brother Geoffrey Scott, and he recognized the truck as a dead animal disposal truck. At the time he wondered what she was doing out of school and why she would get into a truck that would smell so badly. Another employee, Mr. R. Lock, saw the vehicle travel west on County Road 12.

Inquiries revealed that the dead animal truck in question was a 1975 Ford one-ton truck, dark green cab with a red metal load box, license C74911. It was owned by a dead stock dealer in the Strathroy area and was the only collector operating in the area with which they were concerned. On that Tuesday, June 15, the vehicle was operated by Mr. Christian Herbert Harold Magas, born April 1, 1948, in Strathroy. It was learned that he had ten calls to pick up stock that day with one call at the farm of Sambell Brand about two and a half miles north of the scene. To get to that call, Magas would pass through Forest Lawn County Road 12.

Two police officers were dispatched to locate the slaughterhouse vehicle and the driver. At 3:45 p.m. on June 16, Magas was located with his truck at the slaughterhouse on Highway number 22. The truck was seized, placed under guard, and removed to secure storage at the Forest Fairgrounds, later to be taken to the Center of Forensic Sciences in Toronto by the police trailer.

On being asked by Corporal Craig to go to the Forest detachment, Magas agreed and did not question the reason.

At the Forest detachment, police officers interviewed Magas at 4:25 p.m. They initially questioned him generally on his movements for the previous day. He stated he had been employed by the removal service for the past two months, and part of his job was to pick up dead animals from farms and take them to the plant in Strathroy. He drew a route map of the calls made on Tuesday, June 15, and said he returned to the plant at about 3:30 p.m.

He was told that he was seen picking up a girl in Forest, and she was later found dead. He admitted he picked up a girl who said she was going to her mom and dad's and was from London. She wanted to be dropped off at the Lakeshore Road stop sign. Magas stated he dropped the girl at the stop sign.

He was quite willing to talk about anything but the murder and stated he possibly had sexual and mental problems. He admitted that his wife complained about his sexual behavior. He seemed much attached to his two children, a boy, age 4, and a girl, age 2. The children had been living with him at his parents' home since his last separation from his wife in 1975.

During the questioning, there were a number of occasions when Magas appeared to be about to confess and gave the impression that there was a tremendous upheaval going on within him. He was extremely nervous and was almost about to break, but at the critical moment, something seemed to block him from talking.

He appeared content to be in police custody and at no time asked for any explanation or requested a lawyer or showed any of the normal reactions one expects from a suspect. The police got the impression that Magas would deliberately block out all questions when he no longer wanted to listen.

He said he had been questioned regarding the Strathroy area murders and rapes. It became obvious that he was prepared for questioning in this case. When confronted with a question that might have been dangerous, he spent a long time considering before answering. Questions he didn't want to answer, he avoided by just staring at a fixed point with no reply.

He was placed in the cells at 7:40 p.m., where he went to sleep.

On June 16 at 11:45 p.m., Magas was again interrogated. In the meantime, it had been established that a knife bracket for a fillet knife was normally kept in the truck used for the stock pickup. The knife would be used to puncture bloated animals to release built-up gas. When the truck was seized, there was no knife in it. Magas's reason for this was that he had used the knife Friday, Saturday, or Monday prior to the murder to cut an ear tag out of a calf at a slaughterhouse. His employer verified the tag was cut out on Monday, June 14, but also confirmed there were twelve to fifteen knives at the slaughterhouse.

Magas said he picked the girl up about 1:30 p.m. to 2:00 p.m. and dropped her off about fifteen minutes later. The distance from the tile yards where he picked up Susan to the stop sign is 3.2 miles. It was established from a witness that he picked her up no later than 1:30 p.m. and arrived at the Brand farm six miles away at 2:00 p.m.

June 17, 3:10 p.m., Magas was returned to the cells and went to sleep and was still sleeping at 10:00 a.m. All the clothing worn by Magas was seized and packaged separately. He said those clothes were the same worn by him on the Tuesday, June 15. His employer, mother, and the farmers on his route indicated it was the same clothing. Laboratory examination revealed human bloodstains on the shirt and pants, but not sufficient quantities for grouping.

On Thursday, June 17, at 3:00 p.m., a decision was made to charge Magas with the murder of Susan Lynn Towers, and the Crown attorney of Sarnia was apprised of the occurrence. He agreed that the murder charge should be laid. Magas was then remanded to appear in Ontario Court on Friday, June 18.

As a result of news media coverage concerning the arrest of Magas, new information came to light indicating that on the day after the murder of Louise Jensen, it was learned that Magas was alleged to have arrived at his place of employment, MacLean Elevators, with a scratch on his face.

As a result of this information and the similarity of both murders (strangulation into unconsciousness by ligature tied around the throat, causing petechial hemorrhaging to the face, and knife wound to the throat while the victim was lying on her back in a prone position), a concentrated effort was made to pinpoint Magas's every moment from the date of October 20, 1975, forward.

On Tuesday, June 22, 1976, Magas was interviewed for six and a half hours at the Ontario Jail in Sarnia by Constable Lindsay with regard to the Jensen murder with negative results.

On Friday, June 25, Magas was examined by Dr. E. T. Barker, MD, Psych., CRCP, and was then admitted to Penetanguishene Mental Health Center for assessment for a period of not more than sixty days.

On admission, the patient was given a physical examination, routine blood and urine tests, skull x-rays, and an EEG. No significant abnormalities were detected.

A number of psychological tests were given at the mental health center. The review of the personality test data suggested that Mr. Magas was a rebellious and restless individual who was also impulsive in his actions. He had a low frustration tolerance but at the time of testing was relatively well-controlled. In unstructured situations he tended to be anxious, but able to overcome his anxiety quickly. He was manipulative and experienced some sexual confusion with a high potential for aggressive acting out.

During his stay at this hospital, the patient was seen once weekly on rounds by Dr. Fleming and by Dr. J. Curtin on a number of occasions. Additionally, and with his lawyer's consent, he was given a sodium amytal interview.

On Tuesday, August 17, 1976, the patient's case was presented at staff conference, and the following conclusions were reached: (1) he was fit to stand trial; (2) diagnostically, label of pathological personality, antisocial type seemed appropriate; and (3) he was certifiably mentally ill, and from a psychiatric point of view, it was recommended that he should not receive bail.

On Wednesday, July 28, 1976, the investigating officers from the Strathroy and Forest detachments had a meeting with Dr. Barker, who was the accessing psychiatrist at the Penetanguishene Mental Health Center, to discuss all known facts about Magas and the crimes he was believed to have committed.

Later that same afternoon, Magas was again interviewed for three hours with regard to the Jensen murder, with negative results.

Over the next three years, Magas was visited and interviewed on numerous occasions. During these visits, Magus did not make any incriminating statements in regard to any of the crimes of which he was suspected or for which charges had been laid.

On Friday, May 11, 1979, Christian Herbert Harold Magas was again interviewed at the psychiatric facility at Penetanguishene by Constables Lindsay and Devon from the Strathroy detachment. At this initial interview, Magas denied any involvement in the crime that he was suspected of committing.

Ten minutes after Lindsay and Devon left Penetanguishene, they were called back to the psychiatric facility at the request of Magas. At 4:06 p.m. on this date, Magas commenced to dictate six inculpatory statements pertaining to the following:

1. The murder of Judy Barker, Strathroy
2. The rape of Rosalie Summers, Strathroy
3. The murder of Louise Jensen, Mount Brydges
4. The attempted murder and rape of Sylvia Jessons, Mount Brydges
5. The murder of Susan Towers, Forest
6. The rape of Ilene Rankin on abandoned road in Strathroy Detachment area

The last statement was completed at 7:20 p.m. Christian Herbert Harold Magas signed all of the statements. The details for each are as follows:

The Murder of Judy Barker, Strathroy

4:06 p.m., Friday, May 11, 1979
Mental Health Center

Name: Christian Herbert Harold Magas
Address: Mental Health Center, Penetanguishene
Age: 31
Married or Single: Married

Q: You are charged with the murder of Judy Barker. Do you wish to say anything in answer to the charge? You are not obliged to say anything unless you wish to do so, but whatever you say may be given in evidence. Do you understand the caution?

A. Yup.

Q: If you have spoken to any police officer or to anyone with authority, or if any such person has spoken to you in connection with this case, I want it clearly understood that I do not want it to influence you in making any statement. Do you understand this caution as well?

A. Yes. I am not under duress by any officers, and I give this statement of my free will, and I know my legal rights that I may have a lawyer present if I so wish, and I choose not to, of my own will.

Q: What is a statement that you wish to give?

A. I realize the magnitude of this charge, but it is my firm belief that I was sick at the time of the crime that I'm accused of admitting to, so I feel that no further action will take place, but even if so, my main concern at this time is for my well-being in treatment into my sickness that led to this crime.

It was late at night. I was at home watching a hockey game, and I decided to go uptown to get some raffle tickets on the game at the news depot. It was a very foggy night. After getting the tickets, I started for home. I noticed a girl walking on the street in front of me. I started fantasizing sex with her, and I was trying to build up nerve to approach her. As we walked along, I finally built up enough courage, or else my sickness was coming to a head that I grabbed her after we crossed over the tracks. I told her what I wanted. She struggled and refused. I grabbed her by the throat. She goes down, then I panicked, took my jackknife out, and stabbed her in the throat. I undid her pants and started to play with her, and then I guess reality had hit me or my morals started to come up, and I got scared, and I went into her purse and took some money. I'm not sure how much it was but runs in my mind, it was about $20 or maybe a little more. I don't know if this was trying to justify what I had just done to myself by making it out as a robbery. I could be using this as a defense to myself for my sick behavior, but after I took the money, I went home and dried my knife off. I had washed it off earlier at mud puddle on my way home.

When I got home, I'd gone up to the bathroom, and I was drying my knife off. My wife came in, asked me what I was doing. I told her I was drying my knife off, that I dropped it in a mud puddle. Subsequently, my wife was running scared because of all the talk that was around town at that time, that she had taken the knife a few weeks later and threw it out. I don't think that she truly thinks that I did it, but the fear of the unknown made her do this. At least this is my theory on the matter. That is it.

Q: The girl that you mentioned, do you know her name?

A. Yes, her name is Judy Barker. I did not know who she was till I finally approached her at the tracks.

Q: Is there anything you wish to add to or change in this statement?

A. One thing, it's not a change, it's a request. I like to request for Bart and Pete when they are investigating this further, that if possible, they be here when the wife comes up to see me in their presence and let me break the news to her as it will be quite a shock to her, and I would not want to see her try lying to defend me, thus leaving herself wide open for more problems than what she's already got for disposing of the knife, and I would hope that no charges be laid against her.

Signed: Chris Magas
Signed: B. Lindsay, P. Devon
Completed: 4:50 p.m.

The Rape of Rosalie Summers, Strathroy

5:10 p.m., Friday, May 11, 1979
Mental Health Center
Name: Christian Herbert Harold Magas
Address: Mental Health Center, Penetanguishene
Age: 31
Married or Single: Married

"You are charged with the rape of Rosalie Winters."
Caution is then given.

Q: Do understand this caution?

A. Yes (initialed CM).

Q: If you have spoken to any police officers or to anyone with authority, or if such person has spoken to you in connection with this case, I want it clearly understood that I do not want it to influence you in making any statements. You understand this caution as well?

A. Yes.

Q: What statement do you wish to make?

A. I'm making this statement of my own free will. I am under no duress by any means or by anybody. I know my rights that I can have a lawyer present, and I chose not to of my own free will. As far as the charge goes, I feel it was not rape but gross indecency assault. I feel, or that is, I know I was sick at the time. I'm getting this off my chest just so I can deal with my sickness so something like this would never happen again.

I was looking out my window up the street. I noticed this girl down at the corner heading toward the park, down by the swimming pool. I was feeling a lot of loneliness and sexual frustration at the time, so I took out after the girl. When I got down to the park, she was nowhere in sight, except somebody was way over on the far end of the park, so I headed in that direction. When I got to the far end of the park, there was nobody in sight, so I crossed over Victoria Street and started along the path leading to the hospital. At the bottom of the hill, there's a boardwalk that leads way around the other side, and she had taken this route, and we met at the bottom of the hill. At this point, I grabbed her, and her books went flying, and I pulled her off the path. She started screaming. I told her to shut up. She didn't, so I put my hands around her throat, not that tightly because after a few minutes or seconds, she indicated she'd be quiet. So I removed my hands and proceeded to undo her pants, then she started screaming and struggling. I put my hands back on her throat and started to choke her. She passed out. I got scared, dragged her farther back off the path. I fingered her a little bit, playing with her vagina, but the desire to have sex had left. I don't know if this was because my morals were getting to me or if I just was realizing what I had done, but I could not carry it out even though there was no actual sex involved. I felt sorry and remorse and deep shame for the agony and grave injustices done to this girl. That's all.

Q: Is or anything you wish to change or add?

A. No.

Signed: Chris H. H. Magus
Signed: B. Lindsay, P. Devon
Completed 4:50 p.m.

The Murder of Louise Jensen, Mount Brydges

5:40 p.m., Friday, May 11, 1979
Mental Health Center
Name: Christian Herbert Harold Magas
Age: 31
Married or Single: Married

"You are charged with the murder of Louise Jensen on October 20, 1975."

Caution is then given.

Q: Do you understand this caution?

A. Yes, I do.

Q: If you have spoken to any police officer or to anyone with authority, or if any such person has spoken to you in connection with this case, I want it clearly understood that I do not want it to influence you in making any statement. Do you understand this caution as well?

A. Yes, I do. CM.

Q: What can you tell me about the murder of Louise Jensen?

A. First, I know my legal rights. I know I can have a lawyer present. I choose not to of my own free will. I am not under duress of any means, and I give this statement of free will because I realize my sickness at the time and now, but I'm trying to get better so that I can be a responsible person once more. I did kill Louise Jensen because I was very sick at the time. She was a close friend of mine, someone that I had respected. That's why looking back on it, I can start to see how sick I was.

I went to the door that day. I don't know what excuse I used to get in, but my hidden motives were to have sex with her. Once I got in the house, I grabbed her and forced her down to the floor. She said something about why and about my wife. I told her that my wife and I were split up again and that I wanted her. I took her pants off. She had slid from the kitchen into the living room, wiggling out of her pants. I started to make love to her, and my morals and deep affection for her stopped me, so I got off her, and she went back out into the kitchen, put her pants on. At this time, I don't know if the fear of my wife finding out thus ending all chances of my wife and I ever getting back together, or if it was my sickness that made me do what I did. But if it was my sickness or my fear, I had no control over killing her. The feelings I had just a few minutes before of remorse and respect had left. There was just a rage to kill. I grabbed her by the throat and started to strangle her. She was still making sounds, so I looked around and saw a pair of shoes there, so I took the lace out of the shoe and tied it around her throat. Then I noticed a knife and took the knife and stuck her in the throat with it. I pulled the knife out. Saw a tea towel there. Dried the knife off or wrap the knife up in it, I'm not sure. I think the reason that I used the knife was to make sure that she was dead because I tried strangling once before, and it did not work. So this shows that my sickness of these crimes are all interlocking, and that's why I'm coming clean at this time and hope to get some true insight into my sickness so that this will not happen again. When I left, I took the knife and towel with mr, and I threw them out of the car a few miles away. That's all.

Q: Is there anything you wish to add or change in this statement?

A. No.

Signed: Chris H. H. Magas
Signed: B. Lindsay, P. Devon
Completed: 6:05 p.m.

The Attempted Murder and Rape of Sylvia Holly, Mount Brydges

6:10 p.m., Friday, May 11, 1979
Mental Health Center
Name: Christian Herbert Harold Magas
Address: Mental Health Center, Penetanguishene
Age: 31
Married or Single: Married

"You are charged with the attempted murder and rape of Sylvia Holly Jennings, May 3, 1975."

Caution was then given.

Q: Do you understand the caution?
A. Yes, I do. CM.
Q: If you have spoken to any police officer or to anyone with authority, or if any such person has spoken to you in connection with this case, I want it clearly understood that I do not want it to influence you in making any statement. Do you understand this caution as well?
A. Yes, I do. CM.
Q: What statement do wish to make?
A. I realize I have the right to have an attorney present. I chose not to of my own free will. I'm not under duress from anybody except I realize I was sick, and I wish to get better.
I was in London that day and was heading home from my girlfriend's, and I noticed her hitchhiking, so I stopped and picked her

up. She asked me the name of some street she was looking for. I said I knew where it was. So we started driving. I took her outside of London down to Mount Brydges and pulled down an abandoned side road, and I stopped. I don't know what excuse I used for stopping or if I use any at all, but I got out of the car, went around to her side. I opened the door and told her I wanted to have sex with her. We struggled a little bit, but she gave in. I took her clothes off. I started making love to her, and she started to complain how much it hurt, which brought her back to reality. Then I started to have some feelings for the girl, so I quit. I got off her and got dressed, and she started to get dressed, but before she had a chance to get dressed, my sickness got the best of me again. I wanted to finish having sex with her. So I grabbed her, but instead of having sex with her, I tried to kill her. I started to strangle her, and I took the pop bottle and broke it over her forehead. I don't know if the reason I went to this extreme was because I was only feeling part of a man for not being able to satisfy her the first time, not being able to go all the way. I think this fed my sickness because I didn't want to have sex with her the second time. Instead, I just wanted to destroy her. I don't like what I done, but I'm glad I'm getting it off my chest so now I can get some help. When I left, she was laying there nude. When I got to the end of the side road and turned onto the fourth concession, I noticed all her clothes were in the car yet, so I threw them in the ditch or on the side of the road. That's all.

Q: Is there anything you wish to change or add to this statement?

A. No.

Signed: H. H. Magas
Signed: B. Lindsay, P. Devon
Completed: 6:26 p.m.

The Murder of Susan Towers, Forest

6:52 p.m., Friday, May 11, 1979
Mental Health Center
Name: Christian Herbert Harold Magas
Address: Metal Health Center, Penetanguishene
Age: 31
Married or Single: Married

"You are charged with the murder of Susan Lynn Scott, June 16, 1976."

Caution was then given.

Q: You understand the caution?

A. Yes, I do. CM.

Q: If you have spoken to any person or to anyone with authority, or if any such person has spoken to you in connection with this case, I want it clearly understood that I do not want it to influence you in making any statement. Do you understand that caution as well?

A. Yes, I do.

Q: What statement do you wish to make?

A. I'm making this statement with the full knowledge that I could have an attorney present, which I choose not to have. I have been convicted of this crime. I was found not guilty through insanity. The only reason I'm making this statement at this time is so I can get help for my sickness and to relieve all doubt as to my involvement in this crime. Because I did do the crime, even though I was sick at the time. I did do it, and I make this statement of guilt because in the past, I denied it. So I make this statement to relieve all doubt of my guilt. That's it.

Q: After having this read to you, is there anything you wish to change or add?

A. No.

Signed: Chris H. H. Magas
Signed: B. Lindsay, P. Devon
Completed 6:58 p.m.

The Rape of Eileen Ranken on Abandoned Road in Strathroy Detachment Area

7:05 p.m., Friday, May 11, 1979
Mental Health Center
Name: Christopher Herbert Harold Magas
Address: Mental Health Center
Age: 31
Married or Single: Married

"You are charged with the rape of Eileen Ranken." Caution was then given.

Q: Do you understand this caution?

A. Yes, I do.

Q: If you have spoken to any police officer or to anyone with authority, or if any such person has spoken to you in connection with this case, I want it clearly understood that I do not want it to influence you in making any statement. Do you understand this caution as well?

A. Yes, I do.

Q: What can you tell me about the rape of Eileen Ranken?

A. First off, I don't believe it was rape as rape goes. I will admit it was my intention, but I don't believe that I raped her as there was no force of any means. When I approached her for sex, she was almost immediately willing. I believe that me and Eileen had a good and beautiful relationship thereafter. The only reason I'm making this statement is for some reason, Eileen chose to call it rape. As I stated, this was not my intention, but I don't think she realized this at the time. This was my intention when I had picked her up, but after talking to her, my feelings were different. I still wanted sex from her, but there was a different meaning to it. From talking to Eileen, there was some kind of a bond developed, or I feel there was, and I think Eileen felt the same. I think that's why she was so willing a partner in the act of sex and why we had such good relationships. Thereafter right up until she got back with her old boyfriend. That is why I feel there was no rape. Just two people coming together out of loneliness. That's all.

Q: Did you have intercourse with Eileen Ranken?

A. Yes.

Q: Where was that?

A. On an abandoned road across from the old number seven Metcalfe Public School.

Q: Is there anything further you wish to say, or having heard this statement read to you, is there anything you wish to change?

A. No.

Signed: Chris H. H. Magas
Signed: B. Lindsay, P. Devon
Completed: 7:20 p.m.

Epilogue

Magas was first tried in October 1977 for the strangulation and stabbing to death the year earlier of a fifteen-year-old girl near Forest, Ontario. The girl's body was in found bikini briefs with a laceration above her vagina.

He stood trial again on January 1980 for the killing of two nineteen-year-old women, the rape of a fourteen-year-old girl, and the choking and fondling of another victim.

Christian Herbert Harold Magas appeared in court and pleaded not guilty. After hearing the evidence, the jury found Magus not guilty by reason of insanity on three counts of first-degree murder, an account of rape, and another of indecent assault. He was committed to the Oak Ridge division of the Penetanguishene Mental Health Center.

After twenty-nine years in Oak Ridge, Magas says he had his treatment, and now it is time for the system let him move on. In December, the Ontario Court of Appeal heard his application for transfer to a medium-security unit in Toronto.

"You just can't hold somebody," Magas said. "There has to be a progression of better treatment and privileges...This place thinks all they have to do is house the person, but the courts sent people here for treatment. They aren't criminals. That's supposed to be different between this place and the correctional system."

Magas suffers from personality disorder and at least three paraphilias according to a psychiatric serological report submitted to the court of appeal.

"Magas's fantasies involving torture, dismemberment, and cannibalism with respect to his victims is also consistent with the diagnosis of sexual sadism, and he has a history of postmortem other sexually related activities," wrote Dr. Philip Klassen after conducting a five-hour assessment on April 16, 2004. But this man's history suggests to him that this gentleman could be managed on a medium-security unit with respect to both aggressive behavior and elopement risks.

"If Magas's transfer application to Toronto succeeds, it would be the first time a Canadian court approved a move from maximum to medium-security facility," said Daniel Brodsky, Magus's court-appointed lawyer.

"Mr. Magas, in retrospect, would've been far better off in a penitentiary. He would've either been in a minimum-security institution by now, or he would be living in the community," Brodsky said.

"I'll bet that his trial lawyer had champagne, and all his friends thought he had a great victory when his client was found not guilty by reason of insanity. Thirty years later, he's in exactly the same place as a day after he won his case." Brodsky said, "A transfer would not pose any risk to the public because the trauma facility has sufficient measure to keep him on site."

But the Penetanguishene Mental Health Center has expressed concerns over the application, arguing that moving him to Toronto would put him one step further from jurisdiction of the Ontario Review Board, which annually reviews the status of every person found not criminally responsible due to mental disorder.

Klassen also noted in his report that the Toronto facility doesn't have the recreational programs Magas currently enjoys at Oak Ridge. Magas's case highlights the complete lack of specialized mental health treatment programs in the prison system and the scarcity of such programs of mental health hospitals, Brodsky added.

The Ontario Court of Appeal overruled the Ontario Review Board, which had approved Magas's transfer from a maximum-security facility, despite over whelming evidence Magus poses a continuing and substantial risk to offend. He was therefore returned to Penetanguishene.

"This is a small victory for victims and their families," said a London man whose sister survived after being left for dead by Magas.

"I feel good about it," said the man, who feared Magas is trying to get back on the streets of London where his sister, nineteen at the time of her attack in 1975, remains traumatized by him to this day.

Bits and Pieces 10

Bill Jacobs, a lawyer in St. Thomas, was somewhat of a practical joker in and out of the courtroom. One day in court, after giving my evidence on some exhibits, he asked if I had given them a "carbon 14 test." I was a little surprised at the question; the test is only given by a scientist on an article found as a result of finding an object while doing an excavation in an old burial site. The item the carbon 14 test would be used for by the scientist knowing it would be two hundred years old or older. The Crown Attorney put one over on him aas he had the body identified as he sat down.

The Crown attorney (prosecutor) on one murder trial had the pathologist (the witness) on the stand giving his evidence. On each case, he would ask the pathologist before he was asked his findings he found while doing the autopsy, he would ask the doctor the identity of the body and who made the identification to him. On this one occasion, he did not have the body identified to the jury but went through the doctor's results where he gave the cause of death.

Bill sat there listening to all the evidence, knowing the body had not been identified. The body not being identified gave Bill a good chance of getting his client off on the charge before him.

The Crown, after getting the cause of death from the witness, was in the process of sitting down when he stood back up and asked, "Who identified the body to you and the name of the body?"

Bill thought the Crown attorney was going to miss identifying the body because this was normally done at the beginning of the doctor's examination. Because the body was not identified earlier,

Bill did not take any notes to question the doctor. He was upset that the Crown put one over him.

On another occasion, I had a BE at a cottage in Port Stanley. I was dispatched to a cottage along the shoreline of Lake Erie. The front of the cottage faced the lake. In the front of the cottage, there was a veranda.

At night, on one occasion, three young guys went up on the veranda where there was a window that was over a sink in the kitchen. The window was partially open. They opened the window more and climbed in. Before entering the kitchen, they had to remove an aluminum bar that was attached inside the kitchen to each side of the window frame.

On dusting for fingerprints, I found two prints on the aluminum bar. They were identified as belonging to one of the three.

The three were later arrested. Bill Jacobs was hired to defend the two who had not left fingerprints. Bill's lawyer buddy was Ernie Peterson. Bill had Ernie defend the guy who left the two fingerprints on the bar.

I gave his evidence and produced a fingerprint chart for one of the fingerprints I found.

Bill, very cocky, stood, asked a few questions, and then sat down.

Ernie got up and started his cross-examination. "You said you found two fingerprints on the bar. Why didn't you make a chart for the other fingerprint you found?"

"I did make a chart on the other print." I then produced it and showed it to him and the court and to the magistrate.

Ernie was, I think, a little shocked when he realized he had been had. He had been standing right in front of the witness stand. He walked back around to his side of the defense table, and as he passed Bill, he bent down and whispered to Bill and said, "I just got fucked," which everyone in the courtroom could hear.

Even the judge had a big grin on his face.

CHAPTER THIRTY-SIX

Woman Strangled and Stabbed to Death

On November 11, 1985, James Kenny went to the St. Thomas Police Department and reported to the officer on duty, Sergeant James Black. He reported to him that a friend, John Faber, had come to his address on the previous evening and confessed to Kenny that he had murdered a woman in London by strangling her and stabbing her three times.

Kenny went on to say that Faber had taken the woman's car that was presently parked on Barnes Street in St. Thomas. Sergeant Black accompanied Kenny to Barnes Street where Kenny pointed out the vehicle in question. The registration of the vehicle was checked and was found to be owned by Mary Osman of 1000 Huron Street, apt. 105, London.

Sergeant David Kinnear and Sergeant Earl Smith received the information from Sergeant Black about the murder of Mary Osman. After receiving the information from the St. Thomas Police Department, they went to apt. 105 at 1000 Huron Street. They entered the residence where they discovered the body of Mary Osman lying on the floor in the only bedroom in the dwelling.

An autopsy was performed, and the examination revealed that Mary Osman had, in fact, been strangled and stabbed three times and had died from a stab wound to the heart.

Later that same day, sergeants Dave Kinnear and Earl Smith and other members of the London and St. Thomas police force attended at the 53 Gladstone apt. 1, St. Thomas, and arrested John Alexander

Faber for the murder of Mary Osman. He was transported to the City of London Police Force on Tuesday, November 12, at 8:35 a.m. At 10:05 a.m., the London officers received a written statement from John Faber where he denied any knowledge surrounding the death of Mary Osman.

As a result of the investigation into the death of Mary Osman, John Faber was charged with first-degree murder.

James Kenny said, "I have known John Faber for a good twenty years. I have known him since I was a kid. The last ten years we did a lot of drinking together, but a month or two ago, John told me he had a new girlfriend. He came to get me. He wanted me to go drinking with him. He said his girlfriend was in the car. I didn't go with them that night. I didn't meet the girlfriend.

"Sometime in October, I saw John with Mary. I was introduced but can't remember her last name. I've only seen her about four times. That would always be in a bar in St. Thomas.

"A couple times, she came back to my place with John. I have been in her car maybe three times. I can't drive it because it's a standard.

"The night John got arrested, I had to go get Mary from the hotel and pick him up because I can't drive a standard. I have never been to where she lives. I know John was staying with her somewhere in London, but I don't know where.

"All a time I was with them, they seemed okay. I know she didn't like drinking but never said much. I think she was going to school or something.

"On Monday, November 11, about 12:10 a.m., John came to my apartment. Shirley McMurphy was there. I can't remember whether she was in bed or not. John came to the door. He was drunk, and he had a bottle of whiskey under his coat. He asked me if I wanted to drink. I said no. John came in and sat in the living room. He had a drink and told me he was really in trouble. He said, 'I killed her. Everything was going so good.'

"I said to John that he was full of shit, and I didn't want to listen to his bull. That's when he told me he wasn't shitting. He said,

'I choked her until her tongue came out, then I stabbed her three times. I just left her in the bedroom. I know I killed her.'

"I told him he was drunk and told him to get out. John often mouthed off the most when he was drinking. I just figured it was bullshit. John left and took his bottle with him. I let him out. I don't remember seeing a car.

"Between 8:30 a.m. and 9:00 a.m. the next morning, John Faber returned to my apartment. He said he had been arrested overnight for being drunk. He showed me his summons. John started talking about killing Mary. I didn't believe him. That's whiskey talking from a friend. It was delivered, and John told me about killing Mary while we were drinking it. I was there along with Shirley McMurphy. As I remember it, John said, 'I killed her, everything was going so good. I really killed her.' After he said that, I believed that maybe he wasn't kidding. We kept drinking. John ordered whiskey three separate times. Each time Mrs. Money delivered it, and John paid for it. I don't know what he paid for it or even what kind it was. Anyway, after a while, John started talking about the coins he took from Mary. He also mentioned that he had stolen a radio. He said something else about there being a microwave he wanted, but he said he didn't take that. He brought the radio in a blue canvas bag into my place. I think it's still there. He said he sold the coins but couldn't remember to whom. He was mad about not being able to remember.

"When he went out to the car to get the radio, that's when he came back with a knife in his belt. He had a knife, and it was stuck inside his waistband. The only part you can see was the handle sticking out. At one point he told us that was the knife he had used to kill her. I can't remember if he actually took it out or if he just held his coat back and showed us.

"There something else. The first time he came to my house that was at midnight or so. He didn't say a lot more than what he had said so far. He came to the house and showed me some money. It was about $30 in coins and about $14 in bills. He said he wanted a bag. I gave him a plastic bag, and he put the money in it. He also threw some jewelry on the table. He flushed it down the toilet. I believe he had one ring up in his apartment that he didn't flush. The rest of it was all junk. The coins in the bag I took from John the second time he came back. Those are at his place. When the cops were there last night, he didn't mention them at the time, but they were right there, or maybe they were in the drawer. Anyways, after they left, he took the coins out, went to the bar named Gabby's. He cashed in the coins and got drunk. I guess he really shouldn't have done that, but he did. The ring and the radio he will get as soon as they are finished here. Where was I before I remembered that? Oh yeah, the knife.

"John got really drunk and fell on the floor, and the knife fell out of the holder. I didn't want him to hurt anyone, so I kicked it away from him and then picked it up and put it underneath the mattress. He later woke up and asked for the knife, but I told him that I buried it outside.

"After John passed out, I went to the police station and spoke to Sergeant Jim Brown. I told him John Faber was at my apartment, that he had told me he had killed somebody in London named Mary. I told Jim that John had her car, and it was around the corner from his house. I then told Jim about the knife and said that I believed what John was saying. I went back with Jim and showed him the car. Jim said he would check it out and get back to me. When I got back home, John was still passed out.

"Shirley and a friend of mine, Narcisse Davis, were also there. Narcisse had been there just before I left. I called Narc to come to the apartment to stay was Shirley and told her why I went to the police station. I told Narc what had happened, but he didn't believe it. He said he would wait until John told him himself.

"I then woke John up and told him we were leaving. I wanted to take the car, but Narc wouldn't go in, so we called a cab. We took a Red Line cab from my place over to Roger Baker's place. Narc, I, and John arrived, and then John passed out there. Narc and I went to the hotel, and I called Sergeant Brown and told him where we were and what was happening.

"I later went to the station. I spoke to Sergeant Black again and made arrangements to arrest John. We didn't work, but later the police came and arrested John. I spoke to Sergeant Black just prior to the arrest and told him John didn't have a weapon. He was arrested, and it was arranged that I would be arrested too. I was taken to the police station. I was placed in a cell for a short while, and then the police came back to my apartment. I remember giving them the knife and I believe the ownership of her car from under my mattress.

"I was drinking most of the day and was very upset about what had happened. I should have remembered the coins, jewelry, and radio, but I didn't. I figured once they had left, the stuff probably wasn't important. The coins I spent, but I said, the ring and the radio I will return. I did spend some of the coins at the corner store for smokes."

James Black, the police sergeant with the St. Thomas Police Department, was working Monday, November 11, at 8:30 a.m. when he released a prisoner, John Faber, from the cells. Faber had been arrested on a drunk charge.

When he was released, he was still a little under the influence of alcohol. There appeared to be little reluctance to leave. He asked the dispatcher to call a Cox cab.

At approximately 1:30 p.m. on November 11, a person he knew as James Kenny came in under an undertaking. At this time, he indicated that he would like to talk to him alone. He then related the following: "John Faber came to my house last night and told me that he had killed a woman in London."

At this time, Kenny said he did not believe him as he was in a drunken condition. Kenny asked him to leave. Kenny then went on to say that John returned in the morning and told him again that he had strangled her and stabbed her three times. Faber then said, "Give me a ride home, and I will show you her car, and you can check it out."

Kenny pointed out a car to Sergeant Black, license WXR 663, parked on Barn Street in the city. It was found to be owned by Mary Osman, York Street, London. This vehicle is parked one block north of Kenny's residence.

Sergeant Black contacted the London CID and asked them to check out the apartment of Mary Osman, 105, 1000 Huron Street, London, and see if the information is true.

Sergeant Black was advised by London that Osman was dead as Kenny has stated, and officers would soon be down to St. Thomas.

Between 2:30 p.m. and 5:30 p.m., Black had numerous conversations with Kenny, who by this time was getting drunker and paranoid. Kenny had stated that they had left his residence and work, Roger's, at 53 Gladstone Avenue.

At 5:30 p.m., Black attended at 53 Gladstone Avenue with other officers from St. Thomas and London Police Departments. The accused, Faber, was located in the rear room of the apartment. He was arrested and was taken to London by their officers. At 6:10 p.m., Sergeant Black along with Sergeant Kinear and Kenny went to 171 Wellington Street, upper, the residence of Kenny. After entering the apartment, Black asked Jim where the knife was.

Kenny replied, "I'll get it."

Black said, "No, just show us where it is. We don't want you to touch it."

Kenny replied again, "I'll get it."

Black said, "No, Jim, we have to locate it. Just show where it is."

Kenny replied, "I removed it at least three or four times."

Sergeant Kinnear said, "Jim, listen, for reasons of law, I have got to pick up the knife. I don't want you touching it, okay?"

Kenny replied, "Okay." Kenny then opened the bedroom door and moved toward the bed. He then lifted the mattress with his left hand. Sergeant Kinnear then stepped in front of him, preventing him from touching the knife. Kinnear then slid the knife along with some papers and a rag, which was wrapped around the knife, which went into a brown paper bag.

Kenny said, "That's my rag."

Sergeant Kinnear replied, "Okay, but I will have to take it as well."

Kenny replied, "Okay."

At this point, Sergeant Black checked out the rest of the bedroom, then went back to the living room.

Kenny said, "You know, Jim, he shouldn't have done it."

Black replied, "Done what, Jim?"

Kenny said, "Kill her. I am a thief, but I wouldn't kill anybody. He came here and told me. He threatened my old lady."

Sergeant Kinnear said, "What did he tell you about it, Jim?"

Kenny replied, "He told me he strangled her."

Sergeant Kinnear then said, "What else?"

Kenny said, "He stabbed her three times."

Sergeant Kinnear said, "But what else did he say?"

Kenny said, "He said he'd cash the money in, and the other stuff he just got rid of before he got here. He was also telling me about the microwave."

Kinnear said, "What about the microwave?"

Kenny replied, "I don't know. He was just talking about it."

Kinnear asked, "Did he bring anything else here?"

Kenny replied, "No."

Kinnear said, "Where do you keep the knife?"

Kenny replied, "Here." He indicated the waistband of his pants, the right side.

At 6:21 p.m., Sergeants Kinnear and Black left Kenny at his apartment at 171 Wellington Street, upper. On Tuesday, November 12, at 12:30 p.m., Sergeant Black attended at the Empire Hotel, Talbot Street, St. Thomas, and spoke to Margaret Gosse of RR 3, St. Thomas. She is the bookkeeper for the hotel and checked the day's deposits and retrieved for Black twenty-two quarters with a Mountie on horseback on them. He then took a statement from Margaret George as to her knowledge of the quarters.

The quarters were placed in a plastic bag and tagged as St. Thomas property tag #2525.

At 1:05 p.m., Black spoke with Brenda Hurl at the Empire Hotel, and she turned over to him three centennial quarters and seven centennial dimes. He took a statement from Brenda explaining her knowledge of the coins.

These coins were taken to St. Thomas and tagged #2526.

At 1:30 p.m., Black turned all the coins over to Sergeant Lucky of the London Police Department.

Sergeant David Kinnear of the Criminal Investigation Division was dispatched with Sergeant Earl Smith to 1000 Huron Street, apt. 105.

They met with the building superintendent, who unlocked the door to apartment 105.

At this time Kinnear called out, "Police, open the door!" They entered and looked into the living room. He then went down the hallway, where he looked into the bedroom where they saw a body apparently dead. He then returned to the front door where Sergeant Smith was guarding the door and informed him what he had seen in the bedroom.

He called his office and notified the staff sergeant in charge, notifying him what he had found, and requested the technical services section to attend at the scene.

At 3:45 p.m. with Sergeant Smith, they arrived at the St. Thomas Police Force and were met there by Sergeant James Black. They received information from Sergeant Black that he had received information from an informant that John Alexander Faber had killed a woman in London.

Sergeant Black stated the informant had received information that Faber had stabbed and strangled the woman and that he had the woman's car.

As a result of this information, I contact Staff Sergeant Baker, who was at the scene, and he confirmed the apparent injuries to the victim. He also confirmed that the victim's car had been taken.

Sergeant Black advised Smith and Kinnear that the accused was staying at 171 Wellington Street in St. Thomas, and as a result, Kinnear prepared a search warrant to search that residence for the knife and bloodstained clothing. He also prepared a warrant for the arrest of Faber, which he later swore to before the Justice of Peace.

That same evening, together with Sergeant Steele, Sergeant Don Millner, Constable Shipley, and Sergeant Black of the St. Thomas police, they left the St. Thomas headquarters and went to the address at 53 Gladstone Street in St. Thomas. They arrived at the premises at 5:40 p.m. where Sergeants Smith and Kinnear set up surveillance.

At 5:50 p.m., with Steele, Millner, and Shipley, they entered the apartment where the accused Faber was located in a rear room and where he was arrested. There was a brief struggle at which time Millner and Smith placed handcuffs upon Faber, and he was removed from the apartment by Millner, Smith, and Shipley. Kinnear stayed in the apartment with Sergeant Black and two St. Thomas constables. Also there was a person now known to Kinnear as James Kenny and a female and a male resident of the apartment with two uniformed officers and had to be restrained.

No other persons were in the apartment during the seizure of the knife. Kenny was drunk and would change from being cooperative to belligerent and angry.

Sergeants Kinnear and Smith went to the cells and found Faber asleep on the cot in the cell. He was asked about what happened the other night. He said he had been at Mary's, and she was drunk, and he left her there and went to Jim Kenny's place in St. Thomas. He said he was drunk and that he stopped at a bootlegger's where he said he had picked up a twenty-six-ounce bottle of whiskey at the bootlegger's on the way.

Faber was told by the officers that when he went Kenny's, he told him he had strangled Mary Osman and then stabbed her three times.

He said he couldn't do a thing like that. "I'd never hurt anybody."

They went on to talk about other items from Mary's apartment that had he taken, which included a ring that was identified as belonging to Mary.

He was later charged with the murder of Mary Osman. He appeared in court, and after hearing all the evidence from the witnesses, he was convicted and sentenced to life in prison.

Bits and Pieces 11

It was a beautiful summer day when a young lady, Doris Alderton, who was in her midtwenties, was jogging westbound on Sunningdale Road north of London approaching Adelaide Street when she was attacked by a man who had been hiding in the wooded area south of the road. She was knocked to the ground where he attempted to disrobe her. She was on her back on the shoulder of the road when she bit him in the left shoulder area. This distracted him, and he let go of her and grabbed at his shoulder. She took advantage of the surprise, got to her feet, and took off running.

She went south on Adelaide and stopped at the first house she was about to pass, where she asked to use the phone to call the police.

When the police officer arrived and found out what happened, he called the office and requested my presence at the scene.

After being advised of the circumstances, I took her into the station wagon, got out the Identi-Kit and asked her for the description of her attacker. When I had completed the picture, I showed it to her. Excited, she said, "That's him."

This photo was quickly photocopied and given to those on duty. He was located shortly thereafter walking on Fanshaw Parkway and was picked up and taken to the office, where I took photos of his bite mark on his shoulder to be used later.

The next day I picked Doris up and took her up to the dentistry building at the University of Western Ontario where I had made arrangements to meet with Dr. Stan Cogan, professor of dentistry. He was also in qualified in forensic odontology.

Forensic odontology is the study of dental applications in legal proceedings. The subject covers a wide variety of topics, including individual identification, mass identification, and bite mark analysis. The study of odontology in a legal case can be a piece of incriminating evidence. There have been many cases throughout history that have made use of bite marks as evidence. Bite marks are usually seen in cases involving sexual assault, murder, and child abuse and can be a major factor in leading to a conviction. Biting is often a sign of the perpetrator seeking to degrade the victim while also achieving complete domination.

Bite marks can be found anywhere on a body, particularly on soft, fleshy tissue such as the stomach or buttocks. In addition, bite marks can be found on objects present at the scene of a crime. Bite marks are commonly found on a suspect when a victim attempts to defend himself or herself.

I had acquired Stan's service in the past on bite marks on individuals on the bad guys and in some cases the victims. I have also had cases where the bit mark has been on a fruit such as an apple and also on a candy bar.

The culprit, Jim Turner, was charged with attempted rape and assault. Three weeks later he appeared in court, and after hearing the evidence, he was found guilty. When his criminal record was introduced, which consisted of mostly sexual offenses, he was sentenced to two years less a day.

CHAPTER THIRTY-SEVEN

Assault, Rape, and Murder

On February 16, 1978, Harry and Anna McDonald, who lived on Wonderland Road in London, went to St. Thomas and did a few personal chores. Anna went to the credit union to deposit her paycheck. She spent some time with Harvey's sister and her husband, then had lunch at Kentucky Fried Chicken and got home between 3:00 p.m. and 4:00 p.m. Shortly after 5:00 p.m., Anna went to work at the United Auto Workers Union Hall at the southeast corner area of Highway 401and no. 4 Highway.

Harry called his wife around 6:30 p.m. and talked casually for three or four minutes. He watched TV for a while, then he called her again about 8:30 p.m. He was teasing her about the movie she couldn't see. She told him that business was slow. He went to bed and fell asleep and was awakened around 1:30 a.m. when the phone rang.

It was Anna. She told him she was ready to leave and would be home soon. She normally had her coat on and had everything locked up before she would call him. She would turn the lights off and leave by the door through the alcove on the south side of the building. It usually took her fifteen to twenty minutes to get home.

After about half an hour, she hadn't shown up at home yet. Harvey was worried, so he called his son, Dave, in St. Thomas. They thought they'd wait a few more minutes before doing anything.

VICTIM

After waiting a short while, Harry called his son back. Dave said he would go out and look for her. Later, Dave called his father back from the Squires Restaurant and told him that he had checked the UAW Hall, and her car was still there. He also told him he tried the doors, and they were all locked. Harvey told his son to come and get him. About 2:30 a.m., Dave picked his father up. They went to Commissioners Road to get some gas, but the station was closed. They went to the Flying M, a gas station and restaurant south of the union hall. They checked, but she wasn't there. Harvey phoned his home, and there was no answer. They then went back to the union hall and checked her car. Harry opened the car door and got in to check for her keys. It didn't look as though she had been anywhere near the car.

They left the union hall and went to the police office. At 3:40 a.m., Harry MacDonald, accompanied by his son and his brother-in-law, John Kissinger, reported to Corporal Litski that Harvey' wife, Anna, was missing. At 3:45 a.m., Constable Peaker, who was on patrol, was advised to return to the detachment to investigate a reported missing person. At 4:05 a.m., Peaker called the key holder of the union hall, Robert J. Sutton, secretary, at the UAW Hall and requested such to meet him at the hall so he could get in and check inside for Anna.

Corporal Litsk accompanied Constable Peaker, and they arrived at the UAW Hall at 4:20 a.m. Harvey and Dave MacDonald and John Kissinger followed the police car back to the hall. On their arrival, Litski and Peaker saw Anna's blue Firenze parked outside the Union Hall. It was the only vehicle in the parking lot. They found the doors to the union hall locked, and there were no footprints around Anna's car.

At 4:35 a.m., Robert Sutton arrived at the hall and unlocked the main door. Litski and Peaker entered the hall with Sutton and found everything in the proper order. Sutton unlocked the cooler and indicated the money from the bar was all there.

Peaker checked the washrooms, and Litski checked the alcove to the exit door. On the floor in the alcove he found one large brown woman's handbag, open, one Loblaw's plastic bag containing wool and several wool skeins beside the plastic bag, one broken hair comb, one broken necklace with a medallion, one pair of eyeglasses, and car keys attached to a plastic tag. He also saw some red stains on the walls, which he believed to be blood.

The entire UAW Hall was searched, and there was no sign of Anna MacDonald. Sutton was advised to lock the hall and not to let anyone enter the building. They then checked the entire area surrounding the hall carefully, with negative results. They also checked the parking lot of a deserted motel, the service station lot across from the hall, and several other business premises in the area, but still with negative results.

Peaker was advised by Dave MacDonald that he had been at the union hall to see his mother at 1:05 a.m. When he walked into the bar, it was already closed, and his mother was getting the cash ready (ringing out the till) to store in the cooler before locking it.

When he first pulled into the parking lot, Dave parked at the northwest corner of the hall facing north. At that time he said he remembered seeing a red Dodge Valiant and also remembered a yellow pickup truck with a camper on the back parked in the lot. It looked new, a 1977 model, he thought. There was another car parked beside the garbage bin that looked like a Chrysler, but he couldn't be sure.

He said when he first walked in, he noticed everyone was sitting close to the front. He had entered the hall from the side door near his mother's car, which was parked on the south side of the building. Everyone except a couple guys were sitting near the pool table. The other two were sitting right in front of the kitchen door. He walked into the kitchen and talked to his mother. His mother gave him five dollars that she owed him. He went to the washroom, and when he came out, he waved to his mother and left. He didn't remember seeing anyone come in or leave while he was leaving the building, nor did he see anyone sitting in any cars outside in the parking lot.

George E. Kristy, a sergeant with the Royal Canadian Mounted Police stationed in London and who lived in Yarmouth Township, was driving an unmarked RCMP cruiser and was proceeding west on Brady's side road on his way to work in downtown London. He was accompanied by Special Constable Murray Simmons. At 8:05 a.m., they observed what appeared to be cloths, and there was a body they saw lying on the roadway near the clothing. At first they thought it was a kid. Constable Simmons said, "It's a naked body."

Kristy brought the car to a stop, looked back, and confirmed that it was a naked body.

Simmons stepped out of the car, and Kristy started calling their office on the radio. He managed to contact Constable Mike Flynn on the "car to car" frequency and told him to contact the police. Kristy received information that a police cruiser was close by and was on the way to their location.

After his radio transmission, he asked Murray, "Is she dead?" He walked back and carefully approached the body. He came back and said that she was cold. They had waited for five or six minutes when a police cruiser arrived with a uniformed officer. He got out of the car, surveyed the situation, and asked the RCMP officers to help him control the scene and block the traffic.

He had Constable Flynn, who was driving a secretary to work, stop eastbound vehicles on the Brady Side Road. Kristy parked his cruiser seventy-five feet west of the body on the north side of the road. When he got out of the cruiser, he observed only one other set of fresh tire tracks in the light snow on the road. He also noticed the snow tire tracks were near the body.

He stayed well away to his left on the south side of the road with his car as he drove by the body before stopping. He noticed a snow tire track as he passed, if not over, very near to the woman's right toes, which were pointing to the south side of the road. They saw a blue parka, brown suede shoes, a white sweater with bloodstains on it, and a red cloth lying above the body on the bank of snow on the north side of the road. There was some black material lying on the parka also. He couldn't tell what that was, and he did not go near the body as he didn't want to contaminate the scene or the police's investigation. The clothing appeared to have been thrown there at the same time as the body was dumped. In the immediate area there were clearly visible boot prints. Spots of blood were observed in the south snowbank where it appeared someone had endeavored to wash the blood off their hands.

At 8:45 a.m., I arrived at the scene in lot 14, concession 8, Westminster Township. Accompanying me were Identification Sergeant W. Adams, Det. Sgt. M. Parker, and Const. J. Wallace, where we met up with Sergeant Kristy and Constable Simmons waiting at the scene. Black-and-white photographs were taken of the tire tracks and footprints. Photographs were taken showing the position of the body and the area around and near the body. The body of the deceased was rigid, and there was no indication of any movement after making contact with the road surface. Injuries were noticeable to the face and neck with signs of bruising and hemorrhage about the nose and mouth and neck. Some blood was present on the right side of the chest and back, which came from the face and hands of the victim.

Photographs were taken on the south bank of the road showing the marks that appeared to have been made by hands that gathered up the snow to remove blood from the killer's hands. Someone with both hands grabbed a handful of snow, apparently to wash blood from the hands, and then shook off the snow, causing red spots, possibly blood, in the snow. This area too was photographed.

Photographs were taken of the body from different angles and facing east and west on the road from the body. Photos were taken showing the clothing on the north bank in conjunction with the body.

Detective Inspector Eldon Ball, Criminal Investigation Branch, arrived at the scene by the police helicopter with Brian Davey from Central Records and Communications Branch; the pilots were Sergeant Adams and Constable Kerry.

I went up in the helicopter and photographed the scene on the road. We then flew over and photographed the union hall and parking lot. We then returned to the crime scene. All the clothing found at the scene I collected as exhibits and bagged, as well as the red spots in the snow on the south side of the road. All the photographs would be numbered. The exhibits were numbered alphabetically.

There were no obvious signs as to the cause of death, and no weapons or foreign objects were found on or near the body. A very small portion of dirt or mineral substance adhered to the buttock area was removed for further examination.

At 12:35 p.m. Det. Insp. C. A. Carson of the Criminal Investigation Branch from police headquarters in Toronto arrived at the scene. He was to be the supervising officer of the investigation.

At approximately 12:38 p.m., the coroner, Dr. Ronin Shirk, and the pathologist, Dr. Douglas Miles, both of London arrived at the scene. It was difficult at this time to determine if the deceased was alive, dead, or perhaps unconscious when she was dumped on the side of the road. The body was identified as Anna MacDonald by Mr. R. Sutton to Dr. D. Miles, the pathologist.

Dr. Shirk ordered the body of the deceased be removed to St. Joseph's Hospital for a full postmortem examination. The body was removed by Thames Valley Ambulance by Gord Moon and Don Smith.

Further photographs were taken showing the indentation in the snow and ice after the body was removed. Exhibits, blood, and hair were removed from the indentation.

At 2:10 p.m., I arrived at the UAW hall with Inspectors Carson and Ball, Corporal Litski, Const. Pecker, Dr. Miles, and Mr. Lawrence Martin.

The alcove was examined and checked for fingerprints on the walls and door. I found one partial palm print found on the crash bar on the inside of the door leading to the outside. Bloodstains were found on each wall of the alcove. A large bloodstain was also found on the sidewalk between the outside door and the east corner on the south side of the building.

Photographs were taken in the lounge area and inside the alcove at the southeast corner of the lounge. It appeared that Anna was attacked and severely assaulted as soon as she opened the door to leave the building. Her purse and other articles she carried had fallen to the floor in the alcove. On the floor in the alcove were the articles that were knocked to the floor (brown purse, wool, Loblaw's bag and contents, glasses, brown glass case, a broken comb, and a broken chain with a medallion.) Measurements were taken showing the position of the articles.

Outside, at the base of the east wall in the snow, were two sets of footprints. A lady's boot prints were found close to the wall and a man's boot print immediately behind the lady's. A full beer bottle was propped in the snow approximately three feet southeast of the two sets of footprints.

At 5:20 p.m., I left the UAW hall and the grounds and arrived at 6:32 p.m. at St. Joseph's Hospital Morgue. Present were Dr. Miles, Const. Davis, Const. Wall, and Det. Insp. Carson. The body of Anna MacDonald was laid on the autopsy table. Photos were taken of the body and close-ups of the injuries to her head and shoulder areas.

Signs of violence were noted on the right side of the skull, with a marked degree of hemorrhage in the soft tissue and eyes. There were also signs of bruising and hemorrhage about the nose and mouth. Examination of the neck revealed marks that suggested attempted strangulation by a ligature. There was also evidence of hemorrhage about the larynx to indicate the attempt of manual strangulation. The index fingers on both hands showed some discoloration, indicating that they may have been bruised when trying to ward off her attacker.

Dr. Miles attributed the cause of death to "strangulation associated with head injuries." The pathologist also determined she had been sexually assaulted. Exhibits taken were nail scrapings from the hands, scalp hair, pubic hair, and fibers. Semen and blood samples were removed from the body and were turned over to him. It was established that during the time between midnight and 1:30 a.m., February 17, 1978, about eight men were still in the lounge. A number of the men accurately described a man, not known to them by name, as being the last one to leave. This subject was operating a half-ton Ford pickup truck, color yellow, equipped with a cap on the box.

Inquiries were made at the Talbotville Ford Plant, and the owner was identified as Christian Manley Thomson, age 25, of 201 Cascade Street, apt. 108, London. The vehicle check indicated he was the registered owner of a 1973 Ford pickup yellow, license number J13 247. Thomson's residence was immediately checked, and no one was present. Surveillance was kept on his apartment by members of the investigation team.

At approximately 2:00 a.m., February 18, the surveillance officers at 201 Cascade Street advised that a yellow half-ton pickup truck bearing license J13 247 had just arrived at the apartment building with two occupants. At 2:09 a.m. and in possession of a search warrant, they were permitted access to apt. 208 by Christian Manley Thomson. He was alone at the time. The officers assisting were Det. Insps. Carson and Ball and Consts. Wall, Wood, and Wesley. Also present were Inspector D. Anderson and Det. Larry Moss of the London Police Force. I entered shortly after. Det. Sgt. Pearce remained with the wanted truck.

Upon entry, Det. Moss had a conversation with Thomson in which he said, "The police would like to have a word with you."

"I know what it's all about, I read about it in the paper. I was home last night, it wasn't me," replied Thomson.

Thomson was requested to accompany Inspector Carson and Constable Wall to the police detachment office in London. He did not object and went with the two officers.

At 3:20 a.m., the following statement was taken:

Christopher Manley Thomson
201 Cascade Avenue, Apt. 107, London
Date of birth: 28 April 1952
Occupation: Assembly worker, Ford of Canada, Talbotville

Well, he got up at about 10:00 a.m. Thursday, February 16.

He watched television until about 2:00 p.m. in the afternoon. He went out with his truck, got two dollars' worth of gas at the corner of Clark Road and Trafalgar Sunoco station. He then went out to the Ford plant and got his pay. So he went back over to the union hall, and there was a guy he knew, so they started shooting pool. This was about 3:00 p.m. Thursday. Then another guy came in. He lost a couple games with him and then went to the bank in Lambeth and cashed his check. Then he came back down to the union hall to shoot some more pool. This was about 3:30 p.m. or 4:00 p.m. 'round there. They were playing singles for quite a while, then a couple guys came in and challenged them. They played them for most of the night. Then Anna MacDonald warned them about swearing and so on. They stayed for a little while, not too long after that. Then about midnight, around there, some men came in from the Ford plant, so they, the four of them, got into a euchre game. They played euchre until Anna said it was time to close up. Then they got up and left. He left by the side door, got into his truck, and drove home; this is about 1:30 a.m. or 1:45 a.m. Then he went home and watched some television and then went to bed. That's it.

3:41 p.m.
Signed: Chris Thomson, C. A. Carson, D/Insp. L.J. Wall, PC

When they had arrived at the apartment, Thomson was sitting on a sofa. In front of him on a footstool was a copy of the *London*

Free Press. It was open to the page where he was apparently reading the article about the murder.

Thomson's apartment was thoroughly searched, and a number of exhibits were seized. A pair of work boots with a similar tread pattern that was located at the scene and at the UAW hall were taken. Also seized were articles of clothing as described by the patrons at UAW hall on the evening in question.

The 1973 Ford pickup, yellow, license J13 247, was seized and brought to the office by myself and Sergeant Pearce.

The truck answered the description given by those at the UAW hall of the vehicle that was seen parked in the parking lot the night Anna disappeared.

When I examined the truck, I found it to contain particles of blood on the exterior of the cab near the driver's door and the passenger door. Some blood smears were evident in the cab also. The snow tire patterns were identical to the impressions found at the scene and at the hall.

Thomson was interviewed at length regarding his activities at the union hall and his involvement with Anna MacDonald. In his statement, he admitted to being at the hall in the afternoon and evening of February 16, but had left at 1:45 a.m. on the seventeenth. A very recent injury was noticeable on the right side of his face, consistent with being scratched by fingernails. He said it occurred when he was repairing a timing chain on his friend's car.

At approximately 4:00 a.m., February 18, Thomson was placed under arrest on a charge of first-degree murder involving the death of Anna MacDonald. He declined to make any further comment after the caution was given. Crown Attorney (prosecutor) M. E. Martin was advised of this charge and of the investigation that morning.

Christian Manley Thomson was born on April 28, 1952. He was married with two children, ages three and five years. He was currently employed as an assembly worker with Ford of Canada, Ltd., Talbotville. He was absent on sick leave on February 16 and 17. His ailment was described as nervous depression.

Hair and saliva samples were obtained from the accused. Injuries to his face were photographed along with identifiable tattoos. His fingerprints were taken. He was then lodged in the detachment lockup, awaiting a remand.

Further investigation revealed that on the afternoon and evening of February 16, Thomson was in the UAW lounge drinking and playing pool with other patrons. Shortly after midnight, a group of Ford workers entered the lounge after finishing their evening shift. Thomson asked if he could join them in a game of euchre. Although he was unknown by name, his fellow workers accurately described him by dress, tattoos, and knew that he worked on the Ford assembly line.

The euchre games lasted until approximately 1:30 a.m., when Anna MacDonald told the customers they must leave so she could close up. Everyone left as requested. From the statements of witnesses interviewed, Thomson was the last one out of the building.

The investigating officers believed that Anna MacDonald was leaving the building by the south exit door when she was attacked by Thomson as she opened the door. It is quite apparent she was severely assaulted in the alcove before being forcibly taken to the half-ton truck he had parked in the east parking lot. It was quite likely the victim was beaten or choked almost into a state of unconsciousness, then driven to where the body was found. Somewhere along the route, she was stripped of her clothing and was sexually assaulted by her attacker.

I was successful in raising fingerprints on the beer bottle found at the east side of the building and identified them as Thomson's. A palm print on the south exit door crash bar was also identified as Thomson's. The boot prints and tire impressions at the hall and the scene were consistent with the footwear and with the tires on his truck. Suitable charts were made to be used in court.

At 10:00 a.m. on March 3, 1978, Christian Thomson appeared in the Supreme Court of Ontario, London, before the Honorable Mr. Justice Kerber. He was represented by Mr. E. McGrath, solicitor. Crown Attorney Mr. Martin attended to present evidence at a show cause hearing with Ontario Const. Wall testifying. After hearing the testimony from Wells, His Lordship ordered the accused be held in custody pending a trial at the next court of competent jurisdiction.

Anna MacDonald had been born in Yugoslavia on October 5, 1939. She immigrated to Canada with her family at the age of twelve and later married Harvey MacDonald. They both resided in an apartment on Wonderland Road, London. She had been an employee of the UAW hall since June 1977.

Prior to the trial of Christian Thomson, the investigating team and I had a meeting with the Crown Attorney Mr. Martin. At the meeting, they discussed the case, the evidence, and the witnesses. Mr. Martin and I decided what photographs would be used at the trial. After some discussion, it was felt that the trial would last a minimum of three weeks. It was also decided by Mr. Martin that I would be the first witness called to give evidence.

On the first day of the trial, the jury selection was made with three women and nine men picked to make up the jury. The trial was then adjourned until the next morning at 10:00 a.m.

Mr. Martin gave his opening remarks to the jury, in which he gave the jury a brief description of the evidence in the case and what their duty was after hearing the evidence. They had to decide whether he was guilty as charged or innocent.

The Justice said, "Call your first witness."

Mr. Martin said, "I call Constable Ron Rupert to the stand."

I approached and entered the witness box and was sworn in by the bailiff. I was then questioned by Mr. Martin.

Q: Constable Rupert, I understand that you are a police officer and a member of the Ontario Provincial Police, sir?

A: Yes, sir.

Q: I also understand you are an identification officer, is that correct?

A: That's correct, sir.

Q: The branch that you are associated with is the Technical Identification Division of the Ontario Police, no. 2 District Headquarters London.

A: Yes, sir.

Q: How long have you been an identification officer?

A: Fourteen years.

Q: How long have you been a member of the Ontario Provincial Police?

A: Twenty-six years, sir.

Q: What are your qualifications to be an identification officer?

A: I'm a graduate of the Institute of Applied Science, Chicago, dealing mainly with fingerprinting as well as handwriting analysis, typewriting analysis, and physical comparisons. I've been to several courses dealing in fingerprinting at the Canadian Police College in Ottawa and the Ontario Police College and photography courses at Eastman Kodak in Toronto, Eastman Kodak in Rochester, New York, the Canadian Police College, Ottawa, and the Ontario Police College, Aylmer. I have also had courses in other areas, which are not related to this particular case. I'm a member of the Canadian Identification Association and a life member of the Michigan-Ontario Identification Association. I am also designated as a fingerprint examiner trained and qualified in the examination and identification of fingerprints by the solicitor general of Canada.

Q: Have you given fingerprint evidence in all levels of court, including the Supreme Court of Ontario in Middlesex, Oxford, Elgin, and Lambton counties?

A: Yes, sir.

Q: You have also on occasion provided the court with photographs of crime scenes?

A: Yes, sir.

Mr. Martin: I would like to indicate, Your Lordship, that this officer is an expert witness.

"I accept that this officer as an expert witness. I have known this witness, Your Lordship," Mr. Ted McGrath, the defense council, said.

The Justice responded, "You may proceed, Mr. Martin."

Q: Officer, were you dispatched to lot 14, Concession 8, Westminster Township on March 17, 1978?

A: Yes.

His Lordship: I wonder, perhaps a word of explanation to the jury would be helpful.

Mr. Martin: Certainly.

His Lordship: Members of the jury, you probably wonder why some witnesses are qualified as experts and others are ordinary witnesses. There is one major difference between their status, namely, when a person is qualified as an expert, he is ready to give opinion evidence. Another witness who is not qualified as an expert merely testifies as to what he or she heard or saw, whereas an expert with the special training in the field is permitted by law to give his opinion evidence based upon certain criteria material before him, and that's the real difference between the two.

Mr. Martin: Proceed.

Q: What time did you arrive at this location, lot 14, concession 8, Westminster Township?

A: I arrived at this location at 8:45 a.m. with Sergeant O'Brian, Detective Sergeant Pearce, and Constable Wall. RCMP Sergeant Kinsman and Special Constable Simmons were at the scene on our arrival. There was a naked female body facedown on the south side of the snow-covered road, and her clothing apparently had been thrown to the north side snowbank of the road.

Q: When you arrived at the scene, you took some photographs?

A: After looking over the scene, I photographed tire tracks and footprints near the body in the snow on the road. These were all taken in black-and-white with a ruler alongside the tire tracks and the footprints so that later they can be printed to the actual size of the prints. After the tire tracks and footprints were photographed, I then photographed, in color, an area on the south snowbank of the road where it appeared that a person grabbed a handful of snow and apparently washed blood off his hands and then shucked the snow and blood off into the snowbank, showing red spots in the snow.

I described several photographs, and they were introduced into evidence. The photos showed the location of the body of the woman and the clothing on the north side of the road. I also advised that the police helicopter had arrived, and further aerial photographs were also introduced into evidence showing the road with the body and also the United Auto Workers Hall and parking lot. The victim's car was the only car parked there.

I also introduced the exhibits collected at the scene:

1. Red spots in the snow on the south side of the road, which I identified as being the blood of the victim.
2. The clothing on the north side of the road, which was identified as belonging to the victim by her husband.

3. The footprints at the scene I identified as being made by the killer's footwear.
4. The tire tracks of the truck at the scene and union hall were made by the killer's truck. Charts were shown showing the comparison of the footprints and also the charts showing palm prints and the fingerprint, which showed the identical points of comparison

The defense counsel objected to some of the statements I made about the blood. The Crown countered with "These item will be proved later through other expert witnesses." The defense counsel was overruled.

Camera facing east, the body was south of the north Edge of the road, showing the tire track to the right of the body. Some of her clothing was to the left of her head.

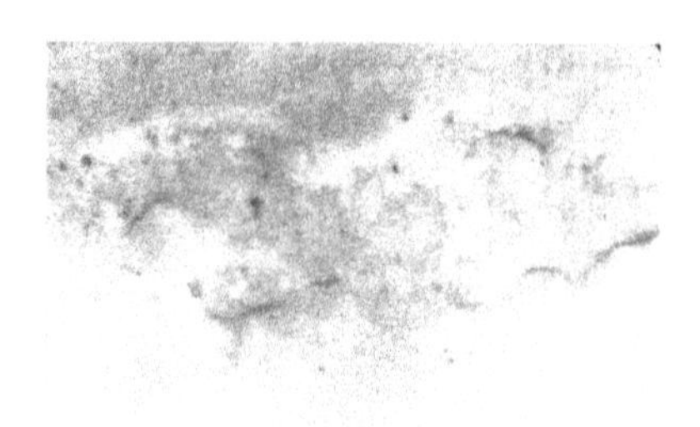

Shows where the killer walked across to the south side of the road, grabbed a hand full of snow and shook the snow and blood off his hands into the snow bank.

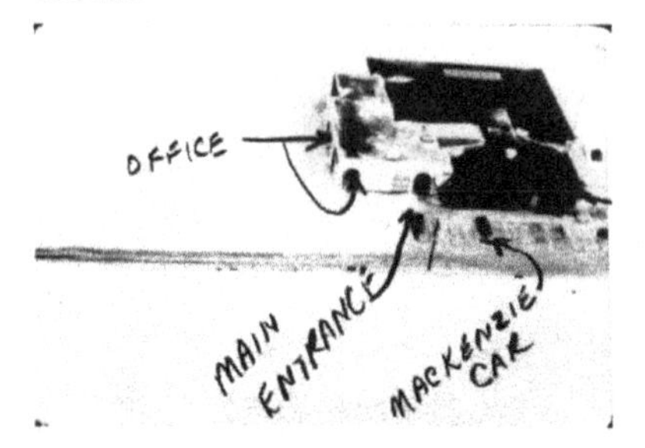

Aerial photograph showing all main entrance to the Union Hall. Her car parked on the South side of the Hall and the orange door from the alcove.

Anna's car parked on the South side of the Union Hall to the left of the orange door.

South side of union hall showing the orange door, and the rear of the building where the beer bottle was found and the foot prints of Anna, were found against the east wall with Thompson's foot print directely behind hers.

The footprints and beer bottle were found on the east side of the building. A fingerprint was found on the beer bottle, was identified as the accused person Christian Manley Thompson.

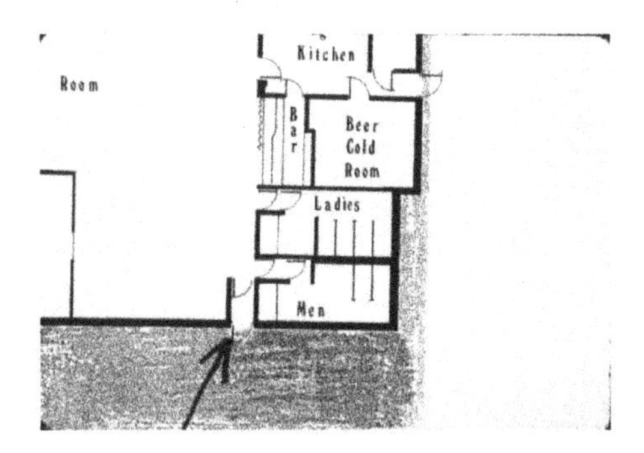

A drawing of a portion of the interior of the Southwest Inside corner of the building with an arrow pointed to the orange door in the alcove.

The alcove inside the orange door and the items she dropped when she opened the door and was attacked, and the crash bar Where the palm print was found.

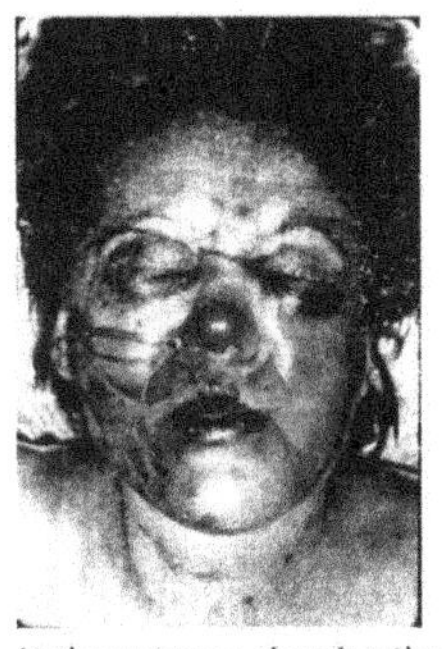

At the autopsy, showing the injuries to the victim's face.

The parka of the accused person was found on the sofa, beside him where he was sitting when we went into Thompson's apartment. Anna' s blood was found on it.

Thompson's clothing was on the floor in his bedroom; among the clothing was a pair of blue jeans, which were saturated with Anna's blood.

Photograph of Christian Manly Thompson with scratches on his right cheek.

A close up of Thompson's right cheek, showing
The scratches.

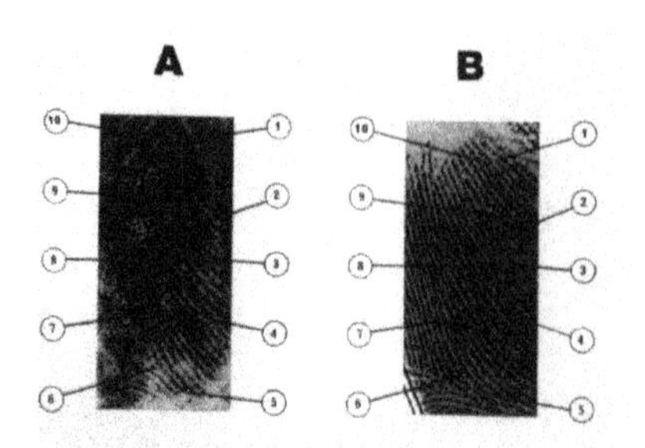

A chart of the palm print found on the crash bar
On the inside of the court orange door, identified
As Thompson's .

Thompson' s pickup truck, which he was driving
On that night, in which large amounts, of Anna's
Blood was found.

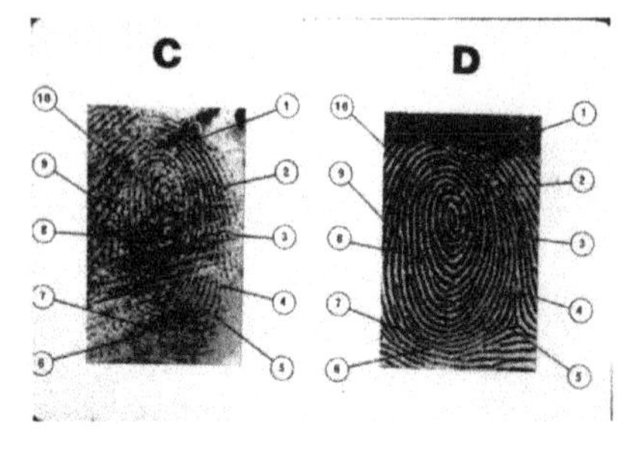

Chart showing a fingerprint found on the beer bottle
on the East side of the building, also identified as
Thompson's.

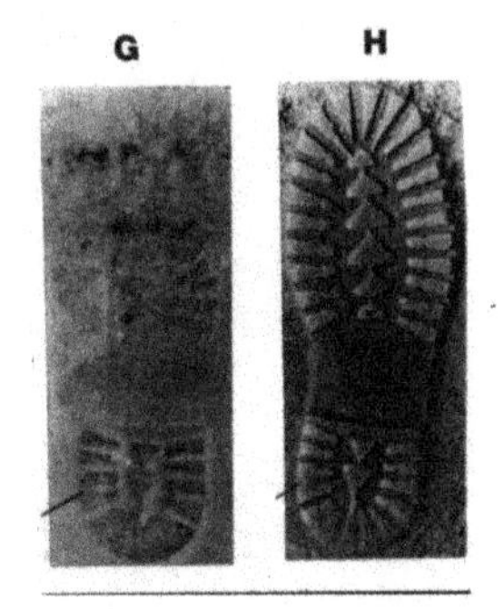

A chart showing the footprint found on the road beside the
body which identified boots of Thompson.

Q: What time did you finish and leave the scene?

A: I left the scene on the road at 1:35 p.m. I went back to the office for more film and then went to the UAW Hall, arriving there at 2:10 p.m. I was met there by Inspectors Cousens and Bell, Corporal Litski, Constable Peaker, Dr. Miles, and Mr. Marshall.

Q: Did you take more photographs at the hall?

A: Yes, sir. I went into the lounge and was shown the alcove at the southeast corner of the lounge, the main room. The inside door to the alcove was propped open, and there were the articles on the floor in the alcove, a brown purse, a Loblaw's bag, and wool, and a door with a crash bar, which was leading to the outside. I photographed the articles on the floor in the alcove. I then went out the door and photographed the car just outside to the right. It was a 1972 Firenza, license DDR 032. It was the car owned by the victim, Anna McDonald.

Photos which were taken showing the interior of the lounge were shown and described to the jury.

Q: Did you do anything with the articles on the floor you found in the alcove, and did you do anything else in the alcove?

A: Yes, sir. They were picked up, bagged, and tagged as exhibits. I then checked the crash bar and found a palm print on the bar. The print was approximately eight inches from the left side of the bar. The door is hinged on the right side. I also found bloodstains on the wall in the alcove, which were also collected as exhibits. These bloodstains were also identified as coming from the victim by a member of the Center of Forensic Science.

Q: Did you take photos of the outside of the building?

A: Yes, photos were taken from the inside, showing the exit door in the alcove. Photos were taken outside, showing the south side of the building, which showed the outside orange door from the alcove and bloodstain on the sidewalk of the building between the door and the southeast corner of the building, and a beer bottle sitting in the snow on the east side of the building. Also, photos were taken of two sets of footprints, which were 7'6" from the south side wall. The smaller pair appeared to be a lady's footprints with the toe almost touching the wall. The larger set of footprints were a man's boot print, and they were right behind the lady's, which indicated that he had her pressed against the east wall of the building.

Q: You said you found a palm print on the crash bar of the door. Did you determine who it belonged to? And did you find fingerprints on the beer bottle?

A: Yes. On March 1, I took the palm prints of the accused, Christian Manley Thomson, at the Elgin Middlesex Detention Center. The palm print I identified as being the left hand of the accused. (I produced a chart showing the palm print). On the chart I show ten points of comparison. There were actually a total of fourteen. The fingerprints of the accused were taken at the detachment office on the seventeenth of February. The beer bottle which I found was full of beer and ice. It was four feet east of the east wall of the Union Hall and 5'3" north of the elongation line of the south wall of the building. The beer bottle I checked for fingerprints at the office, and two partial prints were found. These fingerprints were thumb of Thomson. I charted ten points of comparison on the right middle finger. There were actually twenty points.

Q: The footprints you found, did you determine who they were made by?

A: The footprint I found 7'6" north of the southeast corner of the building close to the wall was compared with the footprint impression of the left shoe of Anna MacDonald. They could have been made by the same shoe, being the same size and appearance.

Photographs were taken of the footprint impressions found on the road where the body was found. Also five and a half feet south of the north edge of the road was a tire track which ran beside the body. Eight and a half feet south of the tire track, I found a footprint facing south. This was the first of a series of footprints leading to the south bank of snow and leading back to the center of the road. At the rear of the union hall, I found tire tracks with the same pattern and physical characteristics as the tire tracks found on the road by the body. This tire track was 34' from the east side of the building. Precisely one foot plus half an inch west of the tire track, I found and photographed the footprints. The position indicated that the person had just got out of the truck.

On February 18, when we entered Thomson's apartment with the search warrant, I had found a pair of boots on the floor against the west wall in the kitchen. At the office I made an impression of the right boot in plaster of Paris dry powder. Indented in the tread of this boot was a piece of foreign matter. (The boots were entered as exhibits.) My conclusion is that the footprints that led to the south side of the road and the footprints I found outside the east side of the union hall matched the impression I had made of the right boot seized from the apartment of Thomson. (A chart was shown to the jury of the boot prints.) It is my opinion that the boot prints at the scene and in the parking lot at the union hall were made by the same boots belonging to the accused.

Q: Were you present at St. Joseph's Hospital Morgue to attend the autopsy of Anna MacDonald?

A: Yes, sir, I was. I arrived at the morgue at 6:32 p.m., at which time Dr. Miles, Detective Inspector Carter, and Constables Wall and Dennis were present. I received nail scrapings, head hair, and pubic hair from Dr. Miles, which he had taken from the body. I also took the fingerprints of the body. I then took several photos (which I described to the court), close-ups of the injuries on her face and other areas on her body that she had received from Thomson. I also received other exhibits from Dr. Miles: a dirt sample from the body, three bobby pins, an elastic band, and three blood samples. At 12:40 a.m., I also received from Dr. Miles four swabs in vials from her vaginal area.

Q: Did you have further contact with the accused, Thomson?

A: Yes. At 5:20 a.m., I took several photos of Thomson (I described photos) frontal, left, and right side of the face. Also taken was a close-up photo of his right cheek, which had been very recently scratched. Photos of tattoos on areas on his body were also taken. His clothing was taken, including one pair of socks, one pair of Jockey shorts, blue jeans, a shirt, and a leather jacket.

At 11:25 a.m., Thomson's fingerprints and palm prints were taken. Also his spit was taken and air-dried and retained as an exhibit. Also a comb used by Franklin along with hair collected from his shoulder.

Q: Did you receive any further exhibits from Dr. Miles?

A: At 12:40 p.m., I received four swabs in tubes: 1 and 2, deep vaginal; 3, vaginal opening; and 4, mouth.

Q: The clothing you took from the accused, was there anything significant found in or on the clothing?

A: Yes, when I removed his clothing, which was on the floor in the bedroom of his apartment, I noticed the right side and leg area of his jeans appeared to be damp and soaked with blood. This observation was confirmed by the Center of Forensic Science. It was in fact the blood from Anna McDonald.

Q: Did you photograph Thomson's truck and examine it for blood or any indication that the deceased had been in the truck?

A: At 2:40 p.m., I received the ownership of the truck from Detective Sergeant Pearce. At the time the truck was sealed and locked in our detachment garage.

At 3:25 p.m., I entered the garage and examined the truck and then took several photos of the outside and areas inside the truck. (Photos were introduced in evidence.) Photos showed red smears on the outside doorpost near the lock plunger and also on the driver's door inside armrest. These smears were collected and were later identified as Anna McDonald's blood. I also collected debris from the floor on the passenger side in front of the seat.

Q: Is there anything else that you would like to add?

A: Sir, I mentioned earlier that a small sample of dirt was scraped from the body at the autopsy. This sample of dirt, as well as debris collected from the floor of the truck, contained numerous chips of yellow alkyd paint in the debris and a lesser number of light gray alkyd paint chips. The sample of dirt scraped from the body contained three small yellow chips of paint and one chip of gray paint. The chips I removed from the floor of the truck and the one from the body of Anna McDonald were identical and came from the same source.

Mr. Martin: I have no further questions of this witness. After the lunch break, I will call

> other expert witnesses to verify further the items this officer has mentioned.

At 12:40 a.m. on the second day of the trial, court recessed for a lunch break to resume at 2:00 p.m.

When court resumed, the defense council stood and advised the court that after hearing the evidence by the first witness, the accused wished to change his plea as charged.

The Justice said, "Will the court clerk read the charge to the accused?"

The court clerk said, "Will the accused please stand. You are charged with capital murder. How do you now plead to this charge?"

Thomson stood and replied, "Guilty."

He was remanded in custody to a later date for sentencing, at which time he was sentenced to life in prison without chance of parole for twenty-five years.

Bits and Pieces 12

In February 1971, our office was moved from the big old house on Center Street to a new two-story building at Exeter Road and the 401 Highway. This building held the staff of DHQ, which was on the second floor, and London Detachment on the first floor as well as the radio room and reception area. The identification unit where our office and the photographic darkroom were located was on the east end of the second floor. For years the completed fingerprints they took from the charged persons were filed in our office according to the Henry Classification System.

In 1859, Sir William Herschel discovered that fingerprints remained stable over time and were unique to each individual. Chief magistrate of a unique district in India in 1877 was the first to institute the use of fingerprints and handprints as a means of identification signing legal documents and authenticating legal transactions. The fingerprint records collected at this time were used for one-to-one verification only.

In 1880, Dr. Henry Faulds explained a system for classifying fingerprints to Sir Francis Galton asking for his assistance in their development. Dr. Henry Faulds and Sir Francis Galton did not engage in much correspondence, but in the following decade, they devised very similar fingerprint classification systems. It is unclear whom to credit for the classification system. However, they do know that Dr. Henry Faulds was the first European to publish the notion of scientific use of fingerprints in the identification of criminals.

In 1892, Sir Francis Galton published his highly influential book, *Finger Prints,* in which he described his classification system that include three main fingerprint patterns: loops, whorls, and arches. At the time, the alternative to fingerprints was bertillonage, also known as anthropometry. Developed by Alphonse Bertillon in 1879, bertillonage consists of a meticulous method of measuring body parts for the use of identifying criminals. In 1892, the British Indian Police Force adopted anthropometry. Two years later, Sir Edward Henry, inspector general of the Bengal Police in India, became interested in the use of fingerprints for the use of criminal identification. Influenced by Galton's *Finger Prints,* the men corresponded regularly in 1894, and in January 1896, Sir Henry ordered the Bengali police to collect prisoners' fingerprints in addition to their anthropometric measurements. Expanding on Galton's classification system, Sir Henry developed the Henry Classification System between the years 1896 and 1925.

The Henry Classification System assigns each finger a number according to the order in which it is located in the hand, beginning with the right thumb as number 1 and ending with the left pinky as number 10. The system also assigns a numerical value to fingers that contain a whorl pattern; fingers 1 and 2 each have a value of 10, fingers 3 and 4 have a value of 8, fingers 5 and 6 have a value of 4, fingers 7 and 8 have a value of 2, and the final two fingers having a value of 1. Fingers with a non-whorl pattern, such as an arch or loop pattern, have a value of zero. The sum of the even finger value is then calculated and placed in the numerator of a fraction. The sum of the odd finger values is placed in the denominator. The value of 1 is added to each sum of the whorls with the maximum obtainable on either side of the fraction being 32. Thus, the primary classification is a fraction between 1/1 to 32/32, where 1/1 would indicate no whorl patterns and 32/32 would mean that all fingers had whorl patterns.

I told Don we should put all our fingerprint files in alphabetical order as it takes less time to file that way than using the Henry system, which takes ten to fifteen minutes to classify each set of prints, where it only takes a couple minutes to file them alphabetically.

Don finally agreed, and our fingerprints were then filed alphabetically. It also makes it easier to locate a suspect's fingerprints to compare with the found prints at the crime scene.

CHAPTER THIRTY-EIGHT

One Civilian Guy Dead, Two Cops, Two Bad Guys Dead

On Saturday, October 6, 1984, on the eve of Thanksgiving at 11:50 p.m., a Montréal police cruiser pulled over in response to a young man beckoning to them.

Giovanni Delli Coles, 18, had flagged down the passing police cruiser at the quiet corner of Dagenais and Monty Streets in Montréal North. The police looked in on his roadside grievance. Delli Coles complained that the two men were carjacking his beloved ride, his Camaro.

The carjackers were Dennis Colic, 21, from Woodstock, Ontario, and Jacques Belanger, 19, from Montreal. They were maintaining their friendship, which started during their time spent in jail. They had both served time together for armed robbery and had been recently released.

The two police officers, Andre Thibodeau and Pierre Beaulieu, placed the carjacker Belanger in the front seat of their cruiser and put the victim of the attempted car theft, Delli Coles, in the back seat. Big mistake.

Delli Coles was still seriously irritated with Belanger for trying to steal his Camaro, so he leaped over the back of the front seat to beat on him. It was possible back then because there was no barrier between the front and back seats.

The scuffle distracted Officer Thibodeau, who was in the process of putting the handcuffs on Colic. In the confusion, Colic disarmed Thibodeau, and a wild gunfight ensued, with Colic shooting

Officer Beaulieu dead with two bullets into his back. One of the two bandits then shot and killed Delli Coles with four bullets as the young man was trying heroically to fight during the gun battle. Colic and Belanger took off and were speeding hard in the stolen Camaro to get out of the city.

They eventually carjacked another vehicle that belonged to a St. Leonard resident, Giles de Grandpre, 60. They had him drive them quite some distance west and into Ontario. De Grandpre had one hand on the wheel and his eyes on the gun pointed at him at all times. Colic and Belanger eventually released the old-timer in a cornfield along the way, ordering him to sing loudly as he walked away (he sang "O Canada") so they knew he was really walking away.

Colic and Belanger travelled back to Woodstock, where they told several others, including a female friend, Alydia Sinker, about their murderous misdeeds in Montréal. Sinker drove them to an abandoned house on the west side of Woodstock a short distance north of Highway 401 at 486 Norwich Avenue.

Police located the two suspects through informants and attempted to get them to surrender. They did not respond to the request.

It was decided the "takedown" of the two culprits would be carried out by the TRU Team (Tactical Rescue Unit). All other uniform officers were requested to avoid the immediate area.

Corporal Ron Franklin was on the north side of the house at 480, the house immediately north of the house where the two fugitives were. He was ready with a rifle. Belanger came across the lawn toward Franklin and fired the handgun he was using. Franklin was hit in the right hand, which was ready on the trigger to be fired, causing him to drop the rifle. He picked up the gun and, using his left hand, which he had never used to fire his gun, fired at Belanger, hitting him in his forehead, killing him.

Const. Jack Rossmoor came west from the road across the lawn at 480, an area he was cautioned not to be in. One of the TRU team members was on the north side of the house at 480; he saw a figure coming west toward him in the darkness of the night. He fired his weapon at the figure he thought was one of the bad guys, instead hitting Const. Jack Rossmoor in the chest with a fatal shot.

Jack Rossmoor was born on September 3, 1928, and was raised on a family farm in Oxford County. As a student at Woodstock Collegiate, he was interested in sports. Unfortunately, his high school education came to an end due to death of his father, requiring Jack to work on the farm.

Jack made a career choice in 1962; he sold the farm and joined the Ontario Police. Initially, Jack was posted to the Essex Detachment, but was later transferred to his home turf, Woodstock .

Colic, the only surviving bandit, eventually surrendered.

He was called, and the next morning, he arrived at St. Joseph's Hospital morgue in London at 9:33 a.m. where the autopsy was to be performed on Jack. Photographs were taken and exhibits received.

At 6:18 a.m., he arrived in Woodstock, 480 Norwich Avenue, where further photographs were taken and exhibits were received from other officers that they picked up at the scene.

Measurements and photographs were taken of the area showing the location where the weapons were left the evening before. These items were picked up along with the personal articles left from Jack Rossmoor.

In June 1985, Colic went on trial in Montreal for a number of charges, including murder.

Amazingly, in spite of the evidence given by the witnesses as well as that of Officer Thibodeau, the jury had a hard time coming to a verdict. He was eventually sentenced to life in jail for the two murders, and the other charges were not pursued.

Colic, however, would not serve much of his sentence. In June 1986, he hung himself at the Ste-Anne-des-Plaines Institution, north of Montréal, ending the ghoulish chain of events, which started by a simple roadside arrest. It is believed that he had unwanted assistance in hanging himself.

Subsequent recommendations point out that the five-death event that claimed the lives of the carjacking victim, two cops, and the two bandits would never have happened had there been a barrier in the police car between the front seat and the back seat of the cruiser.

CHAPTER THIRTY-NINE

Wife Murders Husband

At 2:05 p.m., April 28, 1980, N. Willie, the radio operator at the St. Thomas Detachment of the Ontario Police received a telephone call through an operator from a female person who, in a very hysterical voice, said, "This is Michelle Noble. Please send an officer, and please hurry!" She did not state what the problem was.

The operator dispatched Constable W. Reese, who was patrolling in the area.

After dispatching Reese, Willie placed a call to the Noble residence. A female answered the phone, and Willie, after identifying himself, informed her that a car was on the way and inquired what the problem was.

She replied, "I've just shot Gord, he tried to make me shoot myself."

At 2:19 p.m., Constable Reese arrived at the Noble residence and entered through the eastern entrance.

The woman was sitting on the floor in the foyer with a .22 caliber rifle in her hands. Reese asked her where her husband was, and she replied, "In the kitchen."

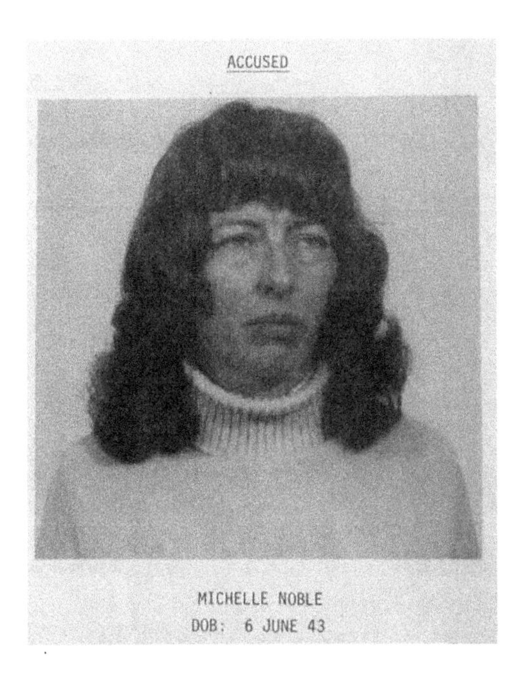

Reese removed the rifle from her and entered the kitchen area, where he found the deceased in the dining area of the kitchen in a pool of blood. Reese checked for a pulse but could not find one.

Reese returned to the foyer where the accused made an utterance to Reese. "He had the gun on me all morning. He wanted me to shoot myself. I told him I wouldn't. He was going to cut my throat with a bottle."

Corporal Dutton and Constable Manning arrived at this time, and she was removed from the house. She was cautioned on a charge of murder and placed in the police cruiser.

Investigating officer Constable G. Skelton arrived at the scene. Michelle Noble was transported by Skelton and Reese to the St. Thomas detachment.

The scene was secured by Constable Manning pending the arrival of the detective sergeant and a member of the identification unit and the coroner.

The coroner, Dr. Lester from Aylmer, had viewed the body prior to his arrival and pronounced the victim dead. He instructed that the body be removed to the Tillsonburg District Memorial Hospital for an autopsy examination.

The accused, Michelle Noble, complained of being ill and requested to see her family doctor. At 4:00 p.m., Dr. F. J. Foster of St. Thomas examined her and could not find anything medically wrong with her. Dr. Foster advised that Michelle had visited him on April 14, 1980. During this visit, she complained of having problems with her husband. She hated her husband and had a crush on her son's teacher. She felt her husband was the cause of all her problems and had considered killing him in the past, making it look like it was an accident, but felt she would get caught. She was advised to seek legal assistance.

On April 21, she had again visited the doctor for a checkup and the insertion of an intrauterine device, even though her husband had had a vasectomy. She claimed to have spent a night in London with her boyfriend. When she had told this to her husband, she did not receive much response from him. She despised her husband and had told him not to come near her physically. She appeared rational and was again advised to seek legal advice.

The Noble residence was located on the south side of County Road 52, Concession 9, Malahide Township, in the county of Elgin.

It was a one-story brick bungalow with attached double garage. The house faces in a northerly direction. It consisted of a foyer, living room, and two bedrooms along the north side. There was a utility room, kitchen, bathroom, and another bedroom along the south side. There were two entrances on the north side, one leading from the driveway into the foyer and another farther to the west, leading into the living room. The foyer and the utility room were at the extreme east end of the residence.

To the west of the foyer was a large kitchen divided into a working and dining area by a counter and cupboards. The counter ran from south to north, and the dining area was situated to the west of the counter. A center hallway led to the west from the kitchen to the two bedrooms at the west end of the house. There was an archway from the dining area to the living room and large double patio doors at the south end of the dining area.

The victim, Gordon Noble, was found with his back to the patio doors, lying on his right side with his head to the east. Near his right hand was the neck of what appeared to be a broken liquor bottle. The floor was littered with broken glass.

There was damage to the northwest corner of the counter, which appeared to have been done by the smashing of the liquor bottle. A piece of glass that could be identified as the bottom of the bottle was on the counter with brown liquid around it. They were two other gouges along the west side of the counter, which could have been done by striking the bottle against the counter.

Two spent .22 caliber casings were found on the floor. One was located in the center of the hallway leading from the dining area to the west bedrooms, the other at the edge of the north wall at the opposite end of the kitchen counter.

A bullet hole was located in the south wall of the dining area twenty-three inches from the floor and six inches from the west wall. The trajectory indicated that the projectile was fired at a downward angle from the east edge of the archway leading to the living room. The dining room table was pushed close to the counter. There were six chairs on the west wall. Several of the chairs had blood smears on the back and sides. One chair was tipped on its side.

A search of the residence revealed several boxes of .22 caliber ammunition, which were found on a shelf in the closet of the master bedroom and in a chest of drawers. A .22 caliber rifle with the only markings of "Made in USSR" was also found in a bedroom closet.

The second .22 caliber rifle, a Lakefield Mossberg model 640 KC Chuckster believed to be the murder weapon, was taken out of the hands of the accused by the first officer, Constable Reese, upon his arrival at the scene. This rifle had one live round in the chamber and two live rounds in the clip.

At 7:00 a.m. on April 29, the autopsy of the victim commenced at the Tillsonburg District Memorial Hospital by N. R. Kallie, the pathologist. Death was due to shock caused by hemorrhaging from lacerations to the aorta due to a gunshot wound.

From the examination at the scene of the shooting and interviews with numerous friends and other witnesses, the police learned that the Nobles had been married since 1965. It was the second marriage for Michelle. Michelle had been previously married at the age of twenty, but that marriage lasted for only a year and a half.

The Nobles had two children, Shawn, age 12, and Jason, age 9. They had been residing in their present home for the past year and a half.

The deceased had been employed by the Ford Motor Company, Talbotville. Michelle was employed as a part-time dogcatcher for the town of Aylmer and several surrounding townships.

It did not appear to have been an ideal marriage from the beginning. Although it appears the two did not lack material things as can be seen by their home, vehicle, and furnishings, there is evidence to indicate that both had been quarreling continually for the previous couple of years. The quarrels culminated with the deceased moving out on March 19, 1980, and residing in the town of Aylmer until April 19, at which time he returned to the residence on the advice of his lawyer. It appears that the arguments between them progressed from April 19 until the day of the shooting.

The deceased had confided to some of his neighbors that his wife wanted to have an affair with another man. They had spoken of separating and had discussed the settlement of the property. There was evidence to indicate that she was infatuated with Cyril Heath of St. Thomas, Ontario, who was a teacher of one of her children.

On April 28, Gordon did not go to work. At approximately 9:00 a.m., he phoned his father, Bernard Noble, who lived in the province of Québec, and informed him that he did not go to work as his wife would not get up and give the children their breakfast and get them ready for school. He requested his father should come and live with him and look after the children as his wife indicated she was moving out. The father, due to doctor's appointments, was unable to travel.

Lynne Wallace, sister of the accused who resided immediately to the west of the Noble residence, received a phone call requesting that she come over. Lynne walked next door with her two children as it was not unusual for the two to visit back and forth. She had been a witness to the family arguments between her sister and husband on the subject of housekeeping. While there, Lynne observed a rifle on the counter; however, it was not unusual to see a rifle in the house. The accused, in her duties as a dogcatcher, was required to use it to put down certain dogs, and she was proficient in its use. Wallace returned to her residence at 1:00 p.m. That was the last time she saw her brother-in-law alive.

At the St. Thomas Detachment on April 28, 1980, at 4:20 p.m., a statement was taken from the accused:

Michelle Noble
RR 7, Aylmer, Ont.
DOB: 06 June 1943

Q: You are charged with murder. Do you wish to say anything in answer to the charge? You are not obliged to say anything unless you wish to do so, but whatever you say may be given in evidence. Do you understand the caution that I have just read to you?

A: Yeah.

Q: If you have spoken to any police officer or to anyone with authority, or if any such person has spoken to you in connection with this case, I want it clearly understood that I do not want it to influence you in making any statement?

A: I think so.

Q: I am investigating the death of Gordon Noble on April 28, 1980. What will you tell me regarding this matter?

A: He got up with the kids and sent them off to school. I don't know if the kids were up or not, but he turned the radio up real loud. He doesn't normally put the radio on. He woke me up, and then he turned it down or off.

Then he just started being like he is. He started to call me names. I told him last night he was to get out, and he said yes. He called his lawyer today. She wasn't there. He said—he has been really getting him upset. He said he is going to beat me up. He told me he would charge him if he does. He took the bedroom door off because it had a lock, but I didn't use that room anyway. I think it was supposed to scare me.

He has been really trying to make me end up in the Ontario Mental Hospital. He said that's where he is going to put me. He is going to sign me in and not let me ever come out again. Somebody was going to come from Québec to take over—I think it was his dad. Then somebody called, and he spoke French. He said it was his lawyer. My sister was there then. She knows what was said about that. I can't remember.

I closed the door when Nickie came over. I suppose he thought Lynne was coming over too. I was really cold. I had all the heat off. The doors were closed when Lynne came over. I told Lynne I was driving the evil spirits out of him. I remember I pointed to the cross on the counter and told Lynne that the cross would burn him and drive out the evil spirits, and he doesn't go to church.

Lynne told her he shouldn't talk like that to him. He forgot what he said to Lynne. Lynne was getting upset with his talk. Just before Lynne came over, he was wiping the rifle off. He didn't want his fingerprints on the rifle. I think he wiped the clip off because he had to put it in. I think the clip was in when Lynne came.

I was worried about the gun lying on the counter. Lynne asked him what the gun was doing out there. He don't like to upset Lynne, as she was getting upset with his talk. He told Lynne to go home finally. He thought because she was over, everything was okay. Then he finally told her to go home as she was getting very shaky. He thought everything was okay. He goes funny, then he comes out of it, and things are okay.

Then he—he was supposed to wash up his dog bowls. They were in the garage. Then there was a dog that could be put down, and he was supposed go out and have an accident. He said he wasn't going to go out and put him down. He was really mad and just crazy, real crazy. I was supposed to take the rifle and shoot myself. I said I wouldn't do

it. Then he was to going to cut me up if I didn't shoot myself.
Then I picked up the gun and pointed at him and shot him. He would have killed me—he had it all worked out. Somebody was going to get it. I was supposed to go crazy and shoot myself and do him a favor. Then I called the police. I wanted to call this morning because he was really bad and help me get out of there that's all. I didn't call because he grabbed me and said he would rip out the phone if I touched it.

4:45 p.m. - Stopped for Michelle to use the washroom
5:00 p.m. - Commenced

Q: Do you recall what you said when you telephoned the police?
A: I just told the desk to send somebody, and I gave them my name.
Q: Did you dial directly, or did you go through the operator?
A: No, I don't remember—Oh, I had to call my inspector today to tell them I was quitting. I just spoke to his secretary, he wasn't in. I wanted him to get back to me. I told his secretary I would have to give back the cages and if he would please call me.
Q: Why would you feel it necessary to call your inspector today?
A: Gord said to tell—notify everybody and inspector to tell them I had to quit.
Q: Do you recall how many times a gun was fired today?
A: Once—by me.
Q: Did anyone else fire the gun?

A: No.
Q: You started to say something about a letter. What was that about?
A: I didn't type what I was supposed to. I was supposed to tell them, ah—something like my unstable mental condition, I couldn't work for them anymore. I just said don't do that.
Q: At the time of the shooting, what was Gord doing?
A: All I know is that I pointed the gun at him, and he started backing up. All I know is if I didn't...point it at him, if I didn't pull the trigger, he would get me.
Q: How would he have got you?
A: He would cut me up if I didn't shoot myself.
Q: How did the bottle come to be broken?
A: I don't know. He would have killed me if I put it down. I was scared he would have. I know he would have.
Q: When you had the gun, why didn't you leave the house?
A: I didn't think about that.
Q: Had there been problems between you and Gord for a long period of time?
A: Yeah. They were supposed to have a separation.
Q: What kind of problems?
A: He would scream and yell. He would put me down in front of the kids. He said today, if he had not gotten up to send kids off to school, where they would be. I always do it, even when I'm sick.
Q: Is there anything you wish to add or delete from this statement?

A: Yes. I went out yesterday afternoon and went over to the Trails End and locked his keys in the truck over there. Someone drove me home, and Gord really got carrying on because I locked his keys in the truck. He said he was going to drive me over to get his truck, but they close at 9:00 p.m. or 9:30 p.m. I only had—I didn't have much to drink at all, and I even left the remainder there. He saw me put it in a bag. He's got me drinking lately. I was on nerve pills with Dr. Foster. I got away on the weekend. He had moved out before the second of April. Not last weekend, about two or three weeks ago, he came in on a Saturday morning. I was alone. He was carrying on about how he was moving back in. I didn't think I could take it, so I threw some clothes in the truck and left. He went to his mother's and told Mom that he was going to take them home.

Q: Was there something you wish to add regarding the dog bowls in the garage and the dog that was supposed to be put down?

A: It seemed rather odd to me as he never gets involved with cleaning my bowls or cages. Usually after I put a dog down, it's done.

Q: Was there something you wanted to add about the phone company?

A: He told me he wanted the phone in the dog pound and downstairs taken out because he said to me that I would not need the phone as I would not be working anymore. I guess. He said that before he called them. I said, "I think I have to tell them to take it out." He called and handed the phone to me, and I told them as of the end of May, I wouldn't be in business any longer, so I didn't need the business phone. I don't know exactly what I said. She wanted a letter stating that. He didn't want a big phone bill anymore. I typed the letter to the phone company and told them that. I did state the phone to be put in his name. I remember him saying he was taking over my dog-catching job too.

Q: Was there something you wish to explain about the letters he wanted you to type and your mental stability?

A: Yeah, I was supposed to tell them I was quitting because of my—how did he say—something about I was sick in the head and not capable of doing the job. He did use the word *unstable*. I just said you don't say that in a letter. I had to make five copies for everybody. I had to make a photocopy of each.

Q: Where was the gun when you picked it up?

A: On the counter.

Q: Where was Gord when you picked up the gun?

A: Near the table.

Q: Where was he standing when he was shot?

A: He had thrown the table over or something. He was just near the table. I think in the middle of the room.

Q: Did he fall immediately when he was shot?

A: No, he staggered—he didn't go down for a minute. He scared me. I thought he was going to get me. Then he must've fallen down.

Q: How was he going to cut you?

A: He had a piece of glass. I don't remember from where.

Q: Do you want to tell about the phone?

A: When he moved out, I started to get some bad phone calls. I reported them here. I had a tracer put on, but it didn't work, so it was taken off. When he came home a couple of days later, he asked if I had gotten any more calls. Different ones thought it was him. So they stopped. I told him they had a tracer on the phone. I never got one after that. Then he told me he was stopping in here and was talking to the chief. I asked him who he was talking to, and he said it doesn't make any difference. I said, "I like to know who you are talking to." He said it was the fellow behind the desk, and he said, "I made the calls to myself."

Q: Do you wish to sign this statement?

A: Yes.

Signed: M. Noble
Finished: 6:10 p.m.
Taken by: P. C. G. K. Skelton
Witness: P. C. W. V. Reese

The trial took place in St. Thomas. After hearing the evidence from the witnesses and after hearing her lawyer giving his closing remarks, stressing self-defense, the jury came back in after deliberating with their decision—*not guilty*.

CHAPTER FORTY

Armed Bank Robbery CIBC in Arva

On Monday, February 2, 1981, at 1:00 p.m., the Canadian Imperial Bank of Commerce in the hamlet of Arva was robbed by two masked armed men of $6,576.51 in cash, British sterling, and Canadian saving bond coupons. The two robbers then escaped in a blue compact vehicle.

The hamlet of Arva is located on the no. 4 Highway in London Township, Middlesex County, about three kilometers north of the city of London. The bank is situated in a building on the east side of the highway, just a short distance north of County Road 23. The building is split into two sections, the bank at the north end of the building and a variety store on the south end of the building. The bank is operated by an officer charge, Mariam Thomas, and another female teller, Sharon Channer, who works on a five-day-a-week basis.

John Joseph Marten and Andrew Jack Spruce are accused of committing this offense. Marten owns a pig farm at lot 21-22, Concession 16, London Township. Spruce and another person, Richard William Wood, also resides at this residence. Wood, in return for his room, looks after the livestock chores on the farm.

In the early morning of February 2, Richard Webb was asleep at the residence when he was awakened by Marten and Spruce, who had just returned home. Webb was told they had been in London and had got in trouble with the police.

Marten and Spruce went to bed. They got up sometime later and left the residence sometime between 11:00 p.m. and 12:00 p.m. in Spruce's vehicle, a 1977 Plymouth Arrow, blue in color. They drove to the hamlet of Arva, driving southbound on no. 4 Highway. They backed into the parking lot behind the bank as seen by witnesses at approximately 1:00 p.m.

Spruce and Marten then put on balaclava masks and entered the bank. The tellers, Mariam and Sharon, had just finished their lunch and were sitting at their desks. Spruce was wearing a camel-colored coat and a beige balaclava. He was armed with a .22 caliber rifle. Marten was wearing a dark blue coat and a dark green balaclava. He was armed with a .22 caliber gas-operated revolver.

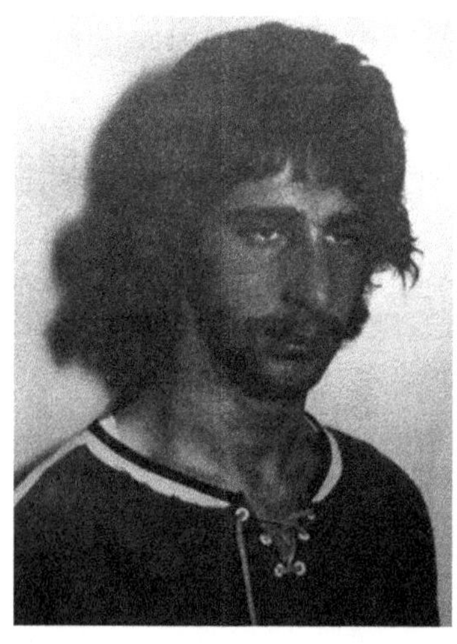

Marten jumped over the counter and into the office area. He was in control of the robbery and did all the talking. He ordered the tellers to fill a white plastic bag then pushed her out of the way and finished emptying her cash drawer. Before moving over to Sharon's cash drawer, Marten asked, "What's in the safe?"

Sharon replied, "All we have in the safe is coins."

The tellers moved over to Sharon's drawer and started emptying it. Marten moved over to the rear of the bank where the safe was located. He looked into the safe but found nothing. He returned and watched the bags being filled.

Marten then grabbed the bag of money and said, "Don't do anything for five minutes, or we'll blow your heads off." He then jumped back over the counter, and they both left the bank and ran along the alley to the parking lot at the rear of the bank to their car and made their escape.

After the robbers left the bank, Mariam activated the bank alarm and locked the front door. Mariam and Sharon then ran to the back of the bank and looked out a rear window, which gives an excellent view of the parking lot, and observed Spruce's vehicle leave the lot and head east on county road 28, where they went to Adelaide Street and turned north.

After robbing the bank, they ran around to the parking lot, jumped in their Plymouth, and sped away. Another vehicle had been parked at the front northeast corner of the entrance to the parking lot. This car was facing south. Turning left, racing out of the lot, the driver's side front fender of the Plymouth the bank robbers were in came in contact with the driver's side front bumper of the parked car.

I found small pieces of blue plastic that appeared to have come off the Plymouth fender sitting on top of the snow that covered the bumper of the parked vehicle. From these pieces of plastic, we were able to determine the color of the getaway car.

Constable Dicker, investigating officer, arrived at the bank and initiated the investigation by taking statements from the tellers of the bank. Constable Wilson recalled he received a call at 12:30 p.m. the same day. Wilson advised that Marten's former girlfriend, Linda Thomas, had called him complaining of Marten being at her residence at 10:00 p.m. on February 1 with Spruce. She told him that both Marten and Spruce had been drunk or high on drugs. She allowed Marten to stay at her apartment but made Spruce leave. After Spruce left, Marten talked to her about his financial problems, losing his farm, and about "casing a place." Marten finally went to sleep. Thomas woke around 6:00 a.m., when Spruce came back to her residence and was banging on her door. Spruce told her they were arrested by the London Police. She told them both to leave. Thomas left her residence around 7:30 a.m. She saw Marten and Spruce in a London City police cruiser.

Constable Wilson knew that Spruce was the owner of a blue compact vehicle and realized the description of the vehicle were the culprits' in the bank robbery, along with the information given by Linda Thomkins, strongly indicated they were responsible for the bank robbery.

Constable Wilson advised Corporal Wild, who had come to the bank, of the telephone conversation he had with Linda Thomkins. Corporal Wild and Wilson proceeded to Marten's residence in a plain car and observed Spruce's vehicle parked in front of the residence at 3:13 p.m. While checking the area again at 3:55 p.m., the vehicle had gone and his whereabouts were unknown.

It was later discovered that Spruce and Marten had left the residence and drove to Lucan, where they bought groceries at the IGA store and ammunition at the hardware store for a .22 caliber weapon.

Marked police cruisers had been placed in the area of Marten's residence in the event the vehicle returned. At 4:35 p.m. the vehicle returned with Spruce driving, and Marten was sitting in the passenger seat. They were arrested by Constables D. Vanier, D. Smith, S. Fielding, and Corporal D. Cain at 4:39 p.m. Marten was cautioned by Vance, and Spruce replied, "You must have a lot to do this." They were taken to Lucan Detachment, but refused to give statements about their involvement in the robbery.

At 7:30 p.m., a search warrant was executed at the Marten residence. Around $5,954 in Canadian and American currency, several weapons, and clothing used in the robbery were seized. Some of the money seized was identified as "bait money" as coming from the bank robbery. The serial numbers on these bills were kept on file at the bank, and all these bills were recovered in the currency that was recovered. The weapons used in the robbery were positively identified by both tellers, as were the balaclava masks they were wearing, the camel-colored coat worn by Spruce during the robbery, and the blue vehicle they drove off in. Other items seized at the residence was a paper money band with teller Mariam Thomas's initials. This band was around some of the $10 bills used as bait money and a pair of Adidas running shoes that were identified being worn by Marten during the robbery.

The small pieces of plastic that I found on the parked vehicle behind the bank, I positively identified those small plastic pieces to the remaining plastic around the front fender where they came from off Spruce's blue car.

They did not agree to give a statement or answer questions put to them. We had enough solid evidence with the identifying statements given by the tellers, the located money stolen as the money found in the residence, which included the bait money, which had all been divided equally between the two robbers, with the bait money also divided equally between them.

In the barn at the farm, a tri-cylinder Yamaha motorcycle that had been stolen in the city of London was also found and seized.

Charges were laid:

(1) While armed with an offensive weapon, namely a firearm, did steal from the Canadian Bank of Commerce, Arva Branch, currency in excess of two hundred dollars and thereby commit robbery.

(2) Did use a firearm to wit a .22 caliber revolver while committing an indictable offense.

(3) On or about third day of February at the Township of London in the said county, did have their possession a motorcycle the value of two hundred dollars, which had been obtained by an offense punishable on indictment.

(4) Did have in their possession firearms of a value in excess of two hundred dollars, which had been obtained by an offense punishable on indictment.

(5) Did have in their possession stereo speakers of a value in excess of two hundred dollars, which obtained by an offense punishable on indictment.

After hearing the evidence given at the trial, they were found guilty and given a lengthy sentence in jail.

CHAPTER FORTY-ONE

Drunk—Then Dead

On Sunday, May 1, 1977, at approximately 3:15 a.m., Joseph and Mary Rilett of RR 1, Newbury, Ontario, were proceeding toward their residence on no. 20 Side Road of Mosa Township near the residence of Alvin Storm. They noted a person lying on the travel portion of the roadway, which they subsequently identified as Alvin Storm. They continued the short distance to their residence where they notified the police at Chatham, who dispatched Constable D. Spicer of the Petrolia Detachment.

On his arrival, Spicer found the victim lying on his left side with his feet at the edge of the sandy surfaced road and his head toward the center. Traces of blood were detected around the nose of victim. Constable Spicer made the person as comfortable as possible without moving him and requested an ambulance be dispatched.

The location was found to be within the Glencoe Detachment area. Constables J. R. Wallace and K. C. Ward were dispatched to the location and arrived at 3:34 a.m. Constable Ward recognized the victim to be Alvin Storm, who was fully dressed in a green work shirt, green work trousers, brown nylon jacket, and a gray vest. His footwear consisted of a pair of tan-colored work boots. His trousers were wet and bore the odor of urine. It would also appear that the victim had had a bowel release.

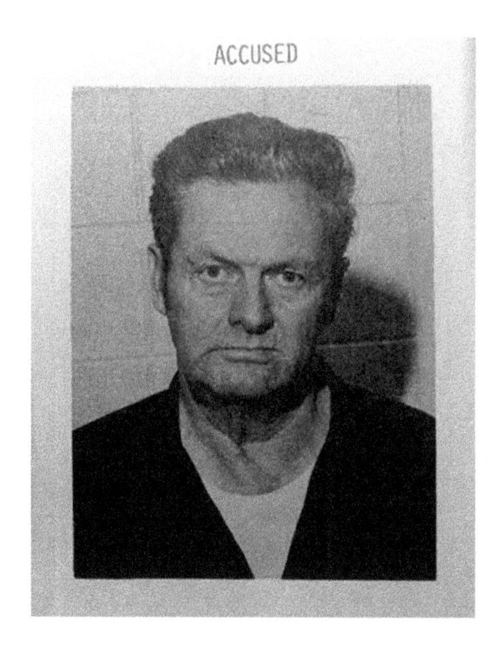

There was no evidence in the immediate area of any tire tracks that would connect to the victim and no disturbance in the soil that would indicate an altercation had taken place.

At 4:01 a.m., the victim was removed to the Four Counties Hospital by the ambulance service from Alvinston. On arrival at the hospital at 4:10 a.m., the victim was examined by the doctor on duty, who found a contusion on the victim's left eye and a large contusion on the left side of the face. From his examination, he determined from normal neurological signs that there was internal bleeding in the skull. After his examination, the doctor ordered the victim be removed to Victoria Hospital in London for further examination.

At 6:09 a.m., the victim arrived at Victoria Hospital and was placed under the direction of the chief neurosurgeon. It was determined that Storm had suffered a severe depressed fracture to the left side of his skull. An operation was performed, and a V-shaped piece of bone that was actually free had elevated. It lacerated the underlying durra, overlying the cerebral fissure and the brain itself, from which active arteriole bleeding was taking place. The piece of bone was removed at this time, and efforts were made to stop the bleeding.

Over the next twenty-four hours, Storm's condition deteriorated. It became apparent that the bleeding had not been completely arrested, and a second operation was performed. It became obvious that the patient would not survive. As a result, the Glencoe Detachment was advised, and Det. Sergeant M. Preston from the police headquarters in London was dispatched to commence an in-depth investigation.

It was determined that Alvin Storm, a bachelor, DOB February 28, 1918, resided alone in a small one-room shack near the location where he was found lying on the road. He had permitted two of his friends, Doner James Lee and Stanley McCalloy, to reside in an old-style wooden trailer on his property, about three hundred yards from his residence. These three subjects were well known in the area, which is locally called Skunks Misery, to have itinerant work habits and drink considerably.

On Friday, April 29, the three had assembled in the early evening and had spent most of the night at the residence of Storm's nephew, Lloyd Storm, drinking beer and other intoxicants. On the next morning, Saturday, Clarence Buttler, who lived a short distance away, arrived at the old trailer by prearrangement to pick up Lee and McCalloy as they agreed to assist Buttler in removing debris from his property to the local dump. Storm joined the three, and they proceeded to Buttler's farm where, except Alvin Storm, they apparently worked to some degree during the day. Storm continued drinking throughout the day and into the evening.

At 6:00 p.m., the four men drove to Bothwell and purchased a twenty-four pack of beer and some food. Then they returned to Lee's trailer. During the course of the evening, Alvin Storm became argumentative and obnoxious and, as a result, took exception to the presence of McCalloy on his property and ordered him off. Lee, who apparently owns the trailer, decided that they would remove the trailer from Storm's property. He requested Clarence Buttler's assistance, and he and Buttler proceeded the short distance to Buttler's farm where they left the car and returned with a pickup truck in order to tow the trailer to Buttler's property.

On returning in the darkness, Lee went to the back of the trailer to begin removing some wooden supports from beneath the trailer. At this time, McCalloy was inside the trailer, apparently lying down. Buttler, it would appear, was the least intoxicated and was walking from the driver's door toward the back of the truck. He said that he approached the rear corner when Alvin Storm came out of the darkness swinging his fists and was about to strike him. He reached into the box of the truck and found a piece of firewood, which he raised and swung it at Storm, striking him on the left side of the head. Stubbs fell against the rear of the truck and may have also struck the steel bumper that protruded below the tailgate. Buttler immediately checked the pulse of Storm by feeling his neck and found that he still had a heartbeat, but was unconscious. The three then continued to hook up the trailer. They said that when they drove away from the property, Storm was at the side of the road, generally in the location where he was found.

Lee's trailer was parked at Buttler's farm. No effort was made to continue the investigation through Sunday or until 1:00 p.m. on Monday.

After being made familiar with circumstances of the investigation thus far, the police officers met at the Glencoe Detachment. Present were Detective Sergeant Preston, Constables Middleton and Kendrick, and myself from the identification unit. We then proceeded to Buttler's farm, located at Part Lot 14, Con. 6, Mosa Twsp., RR 1, Newbury, where we found the three suspects present. They were separately taken to Glencoe Detachment. Buttler's truck was seized for expert examination.

At Glencoe Detachment, each of the three suspects were questioned and provided statements to the investigating officers. It became apparent from their conversations that they had been extremely intoxicated during the course of the altercation that may have taken place. Buttler, who appeared to have the least to drink, gave an initial statement, indicating that Storm had made an effort to attack him and had fallen, striking his head on the rear bumper of his truck. He would not admit making any contact whatsoever with Storm.

On Tuesday, May 3, at 3:30 p.m., the officers were advised by the coroner, Dr. R. Green, that Storm was pronounced dead as a result of the injuries to his head. Dr. Green further advised that an extreme emergency existed at University Hospital in London and that a liver transplant was required. He had contacted the supervising coroner for the province, and under the authority of the Human Tissue Gift Act, he was authorized to remove the victim's liver after having the necessary authorization from the next of kin. The victim, although officially deceased, was maintained on life support system, which would keep the organs functioning even though the brain was clinically dead.

At 5:15 p.m., the deceased was removed from Victoria Hospital to University Hospital, where preparations were made for the transplant of the liver. The investigating officer requested that chief pathologist at the University Hospital be present during the transplant operation and also the doctor who was in charge of the team that conducted the transplant operation be present at the subsequent postmortem examination, thereby providing continuity of the said organ, so that each doctor would later be able to give evidence that the transplantation of the organ had no bearing on the cause of death of Alvin Storm.

On May 4 at 7:30 a.m., the postmortem was performed at University Hospital morgue by the hospital's chief pathologist. At the conclusion of the postmortem, the cause of death was described as a severe depressed fracture of the skull. The remainder of the body was examined and found to be in good condition with no external marks of violence. However, during the course of the examination of the skull, it was determined that the fractures had continued across the skull in three separate areas, which indicated to the pathologist that the victim had experienced a severe blow to the skull.

On May 2 at 11:56 p.m. at Glencoe Detachment, Clarence Willard Buttler, DOB February 29, 1920, RR 1 Newbury, gave the following statement:

He moved to this area in 1973, and he had known Alvin Storm about two and a half or three years. He didn't normally associate with him as he was drunk most of the time.

On Saturday, about 9:00 a.m., he went to the trailer to pick up Stan McCalloy and Bucky Lee to help clean up around his place. He hadn't asked Storm, but he was there and just came along. They had been drinking before he got there. They worked all day, taking several loads to the dump in the truck. Alvin didn't do nothing but sit around and drink beer and tease the dogs. He had a beer in his hand all day, maybe drank twenty-four by himself. He got one case of twenty-four beers for dinner, and at six they went and got another. They had some when he picked them up. There was just the four of them all day.

About five o'clock, they finished up and set some stumps on fire. Near six o'clock, they went into Bothwell to get some more beer. He knew it was near 6:00 p.m. because they were just closing. They picked up some food and went back to the trailer, which was about five miles. They got in, and they cooked some wieners and ate them sitting around outside.

Before they went to Bothwell, Stan said he didn't want to go. This had upset Alvin, and he got mad 'cause he was saying Stan thought he was too good to ride with him. He told Stan then to get off his property. From then on he just picked on Stan, and he turned ugly.

After they ate and were sitting around drinking, he ordered Stan off the property, and Bucky said, "If he goes, I go." Alvin said to get the trailer off his property. Bucky asked him to get the truck and move the trailer over to the farm.

Buck and he got in the car to leave, and he thinks Bucky slammed the door on Alvin, who he guesses wanted to come. This may have made him real mad. They drove off.

When they came back with a truck, Bucky went into the trailer; he got out of the truck and was walking around the back when Alvin came out of nowhere, arms flailing and kind of running toward him, stumbling. He said, "I'll kill you, you cocksucker!" He was screaming like a madman, like out of control. As he got to him, he stepped back to the side, out of his way, and he fell into the back of the truck headlong. It made a lot of noise when he hit it. He was in a position where his head could have hit the top of the back bumper, but he couldn't really see 'cause it was dark. He seemed to have bounced back two or three feet and lay still. He was unconscious. He bent over him and felt the vein in his neck, and it was pumping. He didn't have any contact with him. All that day he drank only two beers and maybe one or two after supper at the trailer.

After he talked to Buck, they weren't sure if he was hurt or just drunk. They weren't sure so they didn't bother with him as he was ugly. They decided he was just drunk when he started to move around and mumble a bit.

He knew now it was a mistake to leave him when they drove off with the trailer. He was on the side of the road. He had been up on his haunches but was lying down when he last saw him. He was throwing up earlier.

Q: Did the truck or trailer ever come in contact with him?

A: No, we drove straight. I wouldn't hurt him deliberately or accidentally.

Q: Did he say anything to you after he was injured?

A: No, just mumbled a bit. Maybe we should have gone back. I figured if he could get up, he could get home.

Q: How far is it to his house from where he was lying?

A: About one hundred paces. Alvin was mean when he was drunk. I had nothing to do with him before. I drove him home in a hotel once. They asked me to because he was drunk.

Q: Did he have his hat on?

A: Yes, he had it on when we left.

Q: Where did you park the trailer at your farm?

A: In the barn because we had to hook it up to the hydro. Later we moved it out to the side of the barn. That was on Monday night.

Q: Did you have any fight with Alvin?
A: No. I can't be off, no OHIP, till I got to work next week. I can't afford no trouble and no fights.

Statement concluded: 1:30 a.m.
Witnesses: R. H. Kenneth, Det. Insp., CIB
Constable J. Kendrick

On May 3 at 12:22 a.m., Doner James (Buck) Lee gave the following statement.

He saw Lloyd Stubbs late Friday afternoon on April 29. He came around the corner and stopped. Ab is Alvin Storm, who owned this property where he had his trailer parked in Mosa Township. He had it there for three and a half or four weeks.

He was pumping water; Lloyd stopped and said, "I will meet you at the trailer." He said okay and took the jug water to the trailer. They drank a case of 24, of Lloyd's beer at the trailer. There was Bob Myers, Lloyd, Stan, Ab, and him. They finished the beer at the trailer. Leroy Swift might have been there. They then went to the Alvinston Hotel in Lloyd's car. They drank and then went to Bothwell. Bob Mince and he stayed in the car; they are cut off at that hotel. He drank six bottles of beer in the car. He drank the beer by the entrance to the hotel. He remembers Russey Heath being in the car.

Saturday morning he was in Lloyd Storm's trailer. He knew Stan was there. He can't remember anyone else being there. Lloyd took them home to his trailer.

Larry Buttler came over to get Stan to give him a hand to clean up around the kilns, and all three of them went—Stan, Ab, and him. They burnt some shingles and put some junk in the pickup. It seems to him they went and bought some beer someplace in Glencoe or Bothwell. After they got the beer, they went back to the trailer. They drank a twenty-four case of beer, all but two bottles. There was Stan, him, Ab, and Larry. The beer was Molson Canadian. They drank some inside and some outside. He got Larry to drive him over to

Jack Watson's at Doners. Jack wasn't home, so they came back to the trailer. Just him, Ab, and Larry went over to Watson's; Stan stayed home. They had Larry Dunn's car.

They came back to the trailer; it was getting dark. Ab called him over to his house and gave him two bottles of beer. He went back to his trailer again. Ab came with him. On the way to the trailer, there was a Coke bottle on the post near his shanty. He said he had forgotten it. There was only three inches in it of straight whiskey. Ab brought the bottle with him and drank the whiskey. Shortly after he got back to the trailer, Larry and he left. He thinks they went to Larry's place. He doesn't know if it was to feed the dogs or not. Then they came back to the trailer. Stan was standing between the road and the trailer. That is when he told him that Ab told him to leave and take the trailer with him. Stan had blood around his mouth; he said Ab shoved a jar in his mouth. Later on he told him Ab hit him.

He and Larry left to get the truck to move the trailer. He saw Ab down by his laneway. He could see by the headlights he was standing. He went down to the town line. About twenty minutes later, they came back with a truck. They went around the block by Ab's house and stopped in front of the trailer on the sand road. He got out and started to take the blocks out from under the trailer. Larry was at the truck. Stan was in the trailer putting stuff away so they wouldn't break. Ab was on the road by the truck before he got the blocks out. Ab was talking to Larry on the sand road behind the truck. The truck engine could have been running. Ab seemed to be mad about something, he was talking fairly loud. He don't know what he was saying. He could make out something like "Stay off his land."

During this time, or for that matter all evening, he didn't speak to him. He finished taking out the blocks and gathered the slab wood and piled it by the front of the trailer. He hollered at Larry to bring the truck. This time Larry was beside the truck on the driver side by the door, and Ab was ten or twenty feet behind the truck on the side of the road, about that distance. Larry and Ab were not talking. Ab was sitting on his butt on the road about ten or twenty feet behind the truck. He thought he had too much to drink. He didn't hear him say anything. Larry got into the truck and backed it in. They hooked onto the trailer, threw in the wood. Before they got in the truck to leave, he looked, and he could see Ab sitting on the sand at the side of the road, sort of hunched over. Stan or Larry did not go back to where Ab was. When they first got to the trailer, Ab was three or four feet from the rear of the truck. Larry was more at the side of the truck.

Ab didn't care too much for Stan. Ab told him this. He didn't say why. Stan had no previous disagreements with Ab, just this time when he told him to leave.

When they left with the trailer, he would say it would be 8:30 p.m. or nine o'clock. They had the lights on in the truck. The diesel fuel on the road would be from Willy Bowles; he drove for McLachlin. They just drain a gallon out of the tanks for filling the dozers for the lamp. Those tracks in front of where the trailer was were made by Lloyd's truck a week or so ago. They took the trailer to Larry's and put it in the barn.

He saw Bill Storm the next day at Larry's place. He was talking with Larry and told him Ab was in intensive care and wanted to know what happened. Larry told him Ab bumped himself two or three times against the truck falling around. When Bill first came, he said, "Did you guys gang up on him?"

Larry said, "Certainly not."

There was no talk about Ab on the way to Larry's with the trailer. Larry said on Saturday night Ab had stumbled into the back of the truck a couple of times. He never saw Ab stumble into the back of the truck; he was busy, and he wasn't watching him. There was no mention of Ab hitting his head until Larry told Bill Stubbs on Sunday. When he last saw Ab Storm just before he got into the truck to tow away the trailer, Ab was sitting hunched over on the side of the road about opposite the back of the trailer with his feet toward the center of the road. The truck was farther ahead toward the corner, about even with the front end of the trailer. The truck, he thinks, was more in the center of the road. This was before it hooked onto the trailer.

It took him fifteen minutes to take out the blocks and pile the slabwood. This was when Larry and Ab were talking on the road. Stan was in the trailer all the time.

He had never seen anybody hit Ab Storm. When they moved the trailer, he knew what he was doing. He had the same clothes on Saturday he had on now: green check shirt, black and red sweater, green work pants, calf-length engineer-type brown boots, and a brown shirt under the sweater, which he washed that night.

When they came around the block in the truck, Ab was by his gate. He saw him coming up the road. Ab was staggering some, but he does that every time he drinks anyway. He didn't see Ab lean against or stagger against the truck. He may not have seen Ab if he had done this. He was on the other side of the trailer some of the time. He didn't see Ab fall down at all. After he saw Ab down on the road, he never heard him talk anymore. When he asked Larry to bring the truck, he don't think he answered. He thinks he's got in and drove up.

Signed: W. Lee
Det. Sgt. M. I. T. Preston

On Thursday, May 5, investigation continued with a collection of exhibits and interview of potential witnesses. As a result, Constable Middleton was instructed to arrest Clarence Buttler and to further interview him in regard to the cause of Storm's injury.

At 10:20 p.m., Constable Middleton and Constable Boyko arrested Buttler near his residence and conveyed him to the Glencoe Detachment. He was duly cautioned and gave an inculpatory statement admitting that he struck Storm with a piece of firewood. He was held in custody pending formal charges.

Glencoe Detachment, 10:20 p.m.
Clarence Willard Buttler (known as Larry Buttler)
RR #1 Newbury, Ontario,
Age: 57, Married.
Occupation: Drainage Operator

Q: You may be charged with a criminal code offense in regards the death of Alvin Stubbs.

Do you wish to say anything in answer to the charge? You are not obliged to say anything unless you wish to do so, but whatever you say may be given in evidence. Do you understand the caution I have read to you?

A: Yeah.

Q: My name is Constable Harold Middleton, and this is Constable Terrence Boyko. They are assisting in the investigation regarding Alvin Storm. What can you tell us about this investigation?

A: I had no intention of hurting him whatsoever. He was coming at me like a damn wild bull, just screaming, "I going to kill you, you cocksucker." He hollered it over and over while he was coming at me. I don't really know what I did. I don't know how I got it. I got a stick out of the back of the truck. It was short, it wasn't very long. He had started to fall. I just whacked him on the head. I wasn't really afraid of him, it was just that you don't fight with Alvin Storm, especially when he has been drinking. I really don't know what happened. I only hit him once, absolutely. He did hit the truck. He was falling when I tapped him. When he fell on the ground, I checked the vein in his neck. I was stunned, and I thought he was too. His heart was pumping steady, and his breathing was regular.

We waited for a while until he started to move and got up on his haunches. They were about fifteen minutes hooking on and loading stuff in the pickup and putting chairs and stuff in the trailer. I wouldn't have left him, but he was so filthy ugly. He was mumbling away, and I thought he'd get up and go home. He only had to get up and go to the cabin. There was no malice in it. I was horrified that it happened. All the rest of this makes it doubly worse. I feel absolutely awful about it, I still can't believe it. It is something you think happens to others but never to yourself. I would never hurt anybody on purpose, let alone kill anybody.

Q: In this statement, you mentioned "they." Whom do you mean?

A: Buck Lee and Stan McCalloy.

Q: What did you do with the stick?

A: I haven't got a clue. I don't remember seeing it the next day either. I couldn't identify it if I had to. I must have got it out of the truck, but the next morning it wasn't in the back. I never saw it in the dark. It was rough in the hand and wasn't smooth, like bark rather than plain piece of wood. It might be out in the pile in the back. I helped unload the pickup behind the barn, and I didn't have a clue what it looked like.

Q: Did Buck and Stan see this happen?

A: No, Buck had gone into the trailer, and Stan was lying down in the trailer. I didn't know until Sunday that Albert had smashed Stan in the mouth. I didn't know anything about it. Stan told us the next morning. What more can I say?

Q: Did you tell Stan about that, what you had done?

A: They heard the noise, and they thought he had just fallen into the truck. He did fall into the truck. I hit him on the way down. He was there, and I just reached out and whacked him. I didn't need to, he was on his way down. I more or less hit him as he went past.

Q: Is there anything else you wish to tell us?

A: I don't know what else I could tell you. If there was something I could do to change it, I would be tickled to death to do so, anything at all. All this I am giving it to you voluntarily, just of my own free will, and no force or nothing. You don't need to hold me. I'll be around on my free will whenever you want me. I have no place to run to.

Signed: Larry Buttler

Q: Now that the statement had been read to you and you have had the opportunity to read it, are there any changes or corrections that you wish to make?

A: Just in two places. There is something left out. I had told you in your second question and answer that I hit him on the way down. As he started to fall, I was already in motion to hit him. I didn't know he was going to fall. He was already falling when I hit him. I didn't know he was going to fall. Something that is involved here is that I'm afraid to fight because I have no OHIP (Ontario Health Insurance). I'm going to have it right away. I'm started back to work today, my first day I can't get hurt. I can't go to the hospital, I couldn't let him hurt me and be out of business right there. This business of not getting hurt is always on my mind. I'm careful everywhere. I can't go to hotels so I don't get involved. The other thing you said, "Did Buck and Stan see this happen?" What I meant to say was no because it was black dark, it was impossible for anyone to see. I more or less hit at the noise if you can understand that. I more or less hit at the noise of him screaming at me. I couldn't see him clearly, it was just something coming at me in the dark. I said Buck had gone into the trailer. I am not really positive of this. I had told him this after. Stan was lying down. Stan told me this, that's all. I would have told you the other night if I knew the truth about his injuries. If he had been hit more than once, I didn't do it. I didn't hit hard. If he was hit only once, then it had to be me because I did hit him. I did not hit him on the front, I had to hit on the top or on the back of his head. I hit him downward. I didn't have it over the top of his head. I was wondering if it was my hitting him on the back of the head could have drove his head into the draw area of the bumper, that's the cut in the area of the bumper or the corner areas.

Signed: Larry Buttler

Q: Now that you have made corrections and have read them, are there any further corrections you wish to make?

A: No.

11:25 p.m.
Signed: Larry Buttler
Witness: H. F. Middleton
T. Boyko

The accused has lived in the Newbury area for about five years. He moved to this area with his wife, Carol, and four children. The children are Mickey, age 14, Jason, age 5, Tammy, age 12, and Terry, age 9. Buttler and his wife no longer lived together. She now lives at 235 Thames Street North in Ingersoll, Ontario. Buttler indicated that he does not want his wife to know what has happened to him, nor does he wish to communicate with her.

About two years ago, Buttler's house burned down. He has since lived in a small room in a tobacco pack barn. He lives alone.

Buttler started working for Richard McLaughlin in Bothwell in farm tile drainage work. He indicates that if he is released, he has this job to return to. He has been under considerable financial hardship the last few years and at the moment is very short of money.

On Friday, May 6, at 9:00 a.m., Crown Atty. M. E. Martin at London, after being made familiar with the circumstances of the case, instructed that a charge of second-degree murder be preferred against Buttler. The charge was prepared and formally sworn to by Constable Middleton before the Justice of the Peace. Clarence Willard Buttler was then brought before Ontario Court Judge Gregory, where he was arraigned on the charge and remanded in custody to May 9, 1977.

Criminal and HTA (Highway Traffic Act) Record
1950–1971 – 5 HTA speeding charges
1950 – 1 having liquor charge
1967–1971 – 4 miscellaneous HTA offenses
1972 – Possession of dangerous weapon (dismissed)

Psychiatric Evaluation

During the conversation with Buttler on May 10, he indicated that some time earlier, someone had put a curse on him. He had gone to Vera Nichol, a local clairvoyant, who told him that his wife had been the one who put the curse on him.

Vera Nichol stated that she removed the curse and informed Buttler that if the curse had not been removed, he would have died.

In view of some of the statements and demeanor of Buttler during this interview, the police believed that a psychiatric examination would be beneficial.

Conditions If Bail Allowed

Usual conditions to be applied.
Report to nearest police station weekly.
Remain away from Glencoe area.
Do not associate with relatives of the victim or the following:
(1) Stanley McCalloy
(2) Doner James (Buck) Lee

He later appeared in court. He was convicted of manslaughter and sentence to two years in jail.

CHAPTER FORTY-TWO

Attempted Murder of a Police Officer

At 10:38 p.m., July 2, 1977, a telephone call was received at the Strathroy Detachment from Philip Ast, a security guard for the St. Clair Regional Conservation Authority. He requested assistance to remove campers who had been creating a disturbance at the Coldstream Conservation Authority Park.

The Coldstream Conservation Authority Park is located off County Road no. 16 in the township of Lobo, county of Middlesex. There are sixty campsites laid out surrounding a rectangular-shaped driveway. The park is operated by the St. Clair Conservation Authority system, and admission fees are charged for camping sites.

The participants in the disturbance in the camp and subsequently in the more serious events that followed were the following:

1. Edward Green, age 18, 6'4", 210 pounds, reddish brown hair almost shoulder length, wearing a red and gray plaid shirt and long blue jeans.
2. John Green, age 21, 6'3", 225 pounds, promise scar on the left cheek, dirty blonde hair hanging over his ears, wearing dull-colored plaid shirt and cut-off blue jeans.
3. Paul Douglas Green, age 16, 5'10", 175 pounds, wearing a yellow T-shirt and blue jeans with shoelaces used as a belt.
4. William Green, age 13, 5'7", 140 pounds, wearing a blue denim jacket and pants.

The four Greens were brothers and resided in the home of their parents at 102 Foster Avenue, London, with the exception of Paul Green, who resided at 128 Forward Avenue in London.

Constables H. Finch, H. McDonald, and G. M. Best, all from the Strathroy Detachment, proceeded to the scene in one car, arriving at 10:44 p.m. On arrival they were met by Philips Abo, Kevin Michaels, and Richard Harman, all from Strathroy. The three guards were accompanied by Peter Sheppard from Canadian Forces Base, Camp Shilo, Manitoba.

The officers conferred with the security guards, and it was the decided they would observe from a short distance while security guards asked the campers to leave. The officers followed the security guard to the campsite. The guards stopped their vehicle on the road facing east, behind campsite 19. The police officers observed the guards get out of their car from the distance of about fifty yards to the west.

Paul Green came running out of the campsite and shouted, "Move that fucking car!" The guards at this time were standing at the rear of the vehicle. Paul Green ran around the front of the vehicle, which was idling. He went to the driver's side, reached in the open window, and put the transmission in gear. Harman came from the rear of the car and told Paul Green he would move the car. He pushed Green out of the way and put the vehicle transmission into park. While he was doing this, Paul Green started throwing punches at him. Harman threw punches in return.

John Green ran out of the campsite and jumped on the roof of the vehicle. He then jumped from the roof and onto the back of Richard Hardy, injuring Hardy's back. At this time, the three police officers moved into the area of the assault. There were several people involved in shouting and threatening activities. Paul Green was being restrained by various people. He was shouting, swearing, and making threatening gestures. It appeared as though he was the instigator.

Const. McDonald was acquainted with John Green and held a conversation with him. It was agreed if they left at this time, there will be no charges laid. Hardy got into the car and started backing up. The police officers were on the campsite between the campers' vehicles.

Paul Green went to the passenger's side of Harman's vehicle; he cussed and stepped around John Green, who was blocking his approach. Kevin Michaels was seated in the passenger side of the front seat and received a punch in the face from Paul Green. John Green took Paul Green back to the campsite.

William Green, who was described as being intoxicated, struck the side of Hardy's vehicle with his fists. He suffered an injury to his hand. He later told several people at the scene that he was struck by the police billy club.

Edward Green started pushing Const. McDonald with violent two-handed shoves to the chest. He tore McDonald's shirt. McDonald struck him across the shoulder with his flashlight, knocking him to the ground. McDonald was on the ground, attempting to handcuff Edward Green, when he was struck from behind on the head. He did not see who struck him.

Paul Green had been placed in the station wagon by his brother John. He got out and was warned by Constable Finch that if he did not get back in the vehicle, he will be placed under arrest. He punched Finch. He was advised that he was under arrest, and they ended up in a struggle on the ground.

The other officers and John and Edward Green all ended up in a heap on the ground. Edward Green got out of the pile and grabbed the nightstick that was held in Best's right hand. He gave two pulls, and the thong broke, releasing the stick from its grasp. Edward Green stepped back, brought the stick over his head, holding it with both hands, and shouted, "I'm going to kill you, you bastard!" He then hit Best twice on the head. Best was struggling to get out of the pile of bodies when he was struck.

Edward Green was taken to the ground by a number of bystanders. He was handcuffed by Const. McDonald. An ambulance and police reinforcements were summoned.

Const. Finch had control of Paul Green, but John Green kept interfering after being warned. He physically took Paul out of the control of the officer. John Green was pulled out of the way by Constable

McDonald and Hugh McDermot of Arva, Ontario. McDonald was bitten on the thumb by John Green.

Paul Green was placed in a cruiser driven by Const. D. R. Vince from Lucan Detachment accompanied by Cost. Campbell and Const. Finch. Paul Green was transported to London and lodged in the detachment cells. Edward Green was taken to another cruiser and, despite continual obstruction by John Green, was placed in the back seat. This vehicle was driven by Constable F. L. Adams and accompanied by Const. T. L. Dickson of the London detachment. When Edward Green was in this vehicle, he kicked Drew in the head and spit in his face.

William Green was running around the area telling people he had hit a cop. This was confirmed by Philip Abo, who observed William Green strike Const. McDonald over the head with what was believed to be a flashlight.

William Green was taken to London in the same vehicle as his brother Edward. He was taken to St. Joseph's Hospital to have his injured hand treated. He was released from custody and would be summoned to appear in juvenile court to face a charge of assaulting Const. McDonald.

On July 3, John Green went to the London police office to take some food to his brother Edward. He was questioned by Constable Finch and B. Linker of the Strathroy Detachment. He admitted biting a person's thumb, Hugh MacDermott's, who was choking him. He stated that he was the person responsible for hitting Constable Best on the head. Cary James McGall, age 19, of London accompanied John Green to the police office. He told a story that corroborated Green's.

Greenwell and McGall stated that the officer came running up with a riot stick. He made a motion to hit Paul Green in the stomach. John Green spun the officer around, took the riot stick out of his hands, and hit the officer twice on the head. The statements of John Green and McGall are contrary to the statements of the bystanders.

Kevin Michaels, the security guard, describes the officers being on the ground with a man in a yellow T-shirt, Paul, and two big men, Edward and John. The man with the basically gray shirt, Edward, got out of the pile. He grabbed the nightstick from Best after jerking it twice. He stepped back a bit, raised the stick over his head with both hands, and said, "I'm going to kill you, you bastard." He then swung the stick and hit Best twice on his head. He was standing four feet away when the officer was struck the second time. A number of spectators put them on the ground and held him. He later saw this man being forced into a police cruiser by officers while kicking at the officer in the front seat.

Edward White corroborates the statement of Michaels. He saw a large person strike Best with the nightstick. He later saw the same person taken into custody and kicking at the cruiser door.

Sandra Caro Manning of London heard a disturbance. She saw the people on the ground and identified two of them as policemen by their uniforms. She observed the head sticking out of the pile with the other bodies on top. A large man wearing a plaid shirt appeared with a policeman's nightstick, which he raised above his head, and beat the head sticking out of the pile at least twice. She observed the other big man, John Green, and the man with the yellow T-shirt, Paul Green, on the ground.

Manning later observed the person who swung the stick being arrested and put in the police car and observed him kicking the officer in the front seat. During this time, the person in the other plaid shirt, John Green, was interfering and had to be physically removed. Other campers in the park corroborated the statements of Manning in whole or in part.

The area where the assault took place is poorly lit, and most of the witnesses would probably be unable to identify the person responsible by his facial features. However, the person who struck Best was immediately wrestled to the ground by the spectators, handcuffed by Const. McDonald, and wrestled into the police car with difficulty. This person was Edward Green. John Green was not taken into custody at that time. Constable Finch and McDonald did not witness the assault on Const. Best. Best cannot recall the assault due to his injuries. John Green was charged with assaulting Richard Hardy, causing bodily harm; common assault on Kevin Mitchell; assault on police officer Constable Fix; obstruct police officer Constable Fix; and assault causing bodily harm to McDonald.

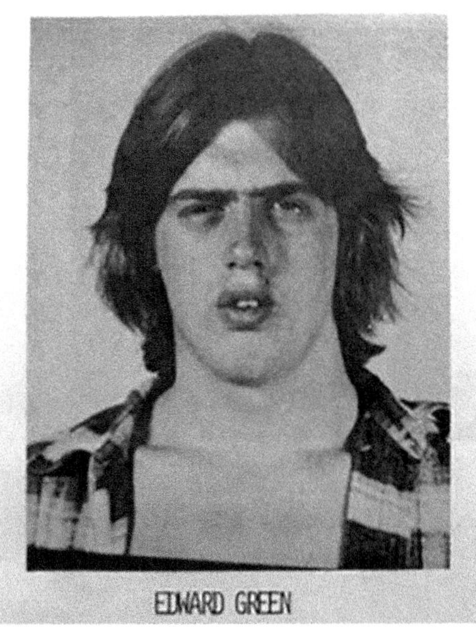

On Sunday, July 3, at 10:22 a.m., the following statement was taken from Edward Green of 28 Macy Crt., Pickering, Ontario.

"You are charged with assault of a police officer."

The caution was read to Green.

Q: Do you understand the offense and the caution?

A: Yup.

Q: Okay, we are investigating the disturbance at the Coldstream Conservation Area camping grounds, which happened last night at about 11:00 p.m. What were you doing there?

A: Camping.

Q: Who was with you?

A: A lot of people—my brothers, all three of them, my sister, her boyfriend, my brother's girlfriend, and a couple other people.

Q: What happened there?

A: Well, we were just about to leave. Some car pulled in behind us and wouldn't let us out. One of them grabbed my brother Paul, so I jumped on top of the guy and told him to let go of my brother Paul. After that, some of the other people came. I don't know who they were. They started pulling us around, so we started pulling them around. The next thing I knew, there was a cop on top of me bleeding, so I pushed him off and got up on his feet. There was about ten people that jumped me, and the one policeman put the cuffs on me, and they all sat on top of me. I was yelling at them to get the fuck off me, but they wouldn't. They got me up and brought me over to the cruiser and tried to put me in the back seat. I would not go in the car, so one of them started hitting me on the back and shoulder with a stick. I finally fell in the back seat, and they closed the door. They just drove me down here and then put me in the cell.

Q: When you say that you "jumped on top of the guy," do you know who he was or what he was trying to do?

A: No, but he just pulled out in front of us when I was backing up my station wagon out to leave—this big car blocked the road. I and my brother jumped out, and I jumped on his trunk, and Paul walked around and tried to get in the driver's seat to move it after asking the driver to move it. Paul tried to move it, and I guess he tried to pull Paul out, and then I jumped him.

Q: Had you been drinking alcohol last night?

A: Yup, and I stopped an hour before I was leaving.

Q: Anyone else in your campsite drinking then?

A: I think so.

Q: Anyone there using drugs?

A: No.

Q: What condition would you say you're in when you were leaving?

A: I wasn't really drunk, but I wasn't really sober—just in between.

Q: You mentioned that you were just about to leave. Why were you leaving?

A: My brother Paul and my sister Kathy were having a bit of a problem, a family dispute, and it had been going on for a while in the park, and the superintendent had told us to leave earlier on, but someone talked him out of it as long as we cut the noise down. So they started to fight again, so I said, "Fuck it, let's go," and I started putting the stuff into the station wagon. I got into it, and then the car pulled in behind us.

Q: When did you first see the police?

A: When that one was on top of me bleeding.

Q: When you are pulling people around, did you hit anyone or were you injured?

A: I didn't hit anyone, no—my injuries, I guess I got these injuries on right-hand knuckles when I fell. I'm not sure where I got these.

Q: After you were arrested, there was a vial of what appears to be hashish found. Was that yours or Paul's?

A: We didn't have any.

Q: Is or anything else you want to tell us about what all happened last night?
A: I think that's about it.
Q: After having read this statement, is there anything you want to add or change in it?
A: Not right now.
Q: Were you forced into making this statement, or were you given any promises of advantage made to you?
A: No.

Signed: Ed Green
Completed: 11:29 a.m.
State and taken by: Constable B. Linker
Witnessed by: A. R. Ferrell

Constables G. A. Best and Constable H. McDonald were taken from the scene to the Strathroy Middlesex General Hospital by Denning's ambulance of Strathroy. Constable McDonald received a laceration on top of his head that required three stitches. He also had abrasions to the shoulder and back.

Constable Best received a fractured skull and a concussion. He was admitted to the hospital and released on July 8. It is estimated that he will be off for at least a month.

Constable Finch received bite marks and abrasions on both hands and wrists. He was given tetanus shots. He was not admitted to hospital.

Hugh MacDonald was given tetanus shots for the bite he received on his hand.

The nightstick involved was thirty-six inches long. It is manufactured Mananda and is constructed of lynxite. During the assault, it broke into two pieces at the handle. One piece was recovered at the scene by the officers. The other piece was recovered by Brenda Mae Ridley of London. She found it at the park at her campsite.

Paul Green was charged with assault on Constable Finch and two charges of common assault on Richard Harman and Kevin Michaels.

Edward Green was charged with assaulting Best and Constable McDonald. When being searched, a substance believed to be hashish oil was found in his possession. A further charge was laid under the Narcotic Control Act.

John Green, Edward Green, and Paul Green all appeared before the JP on July 3 and were released on an undertaking.

Crown Atty. M. Martin, QC, was consulted by Detective Sergeant Preston and Constable Finch. He suggested that Edward Green be charged with attempted murder. The charge was laid, and he was arrested at his residence on July 7 by Preston and Finch.

GARY BEST

Edward Green appeared before Ontario Court judge on July 8 in London. The Crown was represented by Jerry Buchanan, assistant Crown attorney. Green was represented by E. McGrath and was remanded until July 11 for bail hearing. At the bail hearing, he was ordered released on bail of $5,000. No surety deposit was required. It was signed by his mother, Catherine Green.

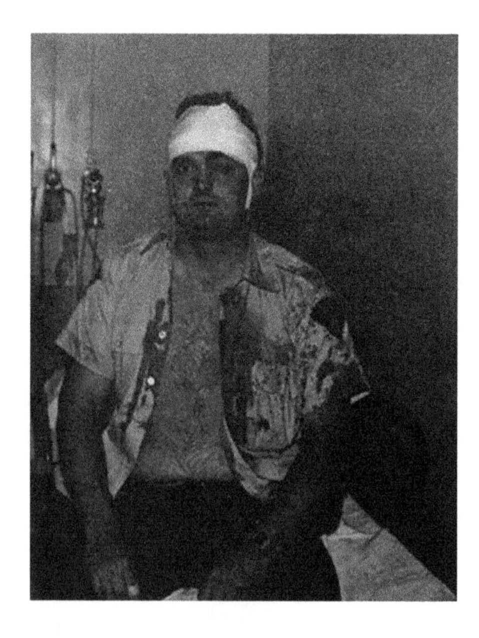

On July 11, Constable J. McGoogan, London Detachment, interviewed Janice Diane Chapters of London, who gave the following statement:

She arrived at the Coldstream Park with her husband Donald and two friends, Catherine and Casey Hooper, also of London, at 7:00 p.m. on Thursday, June 30. They camped at lot number 3, and the Hoopers were on lot number 4.

There were about ten or more young people in the lot behind them and down a way. Nothing unusual occurred until about 8:00 p.m. on Friday, July 1, when she saw the older park attendant go over to these young people, and then the young people turned down the stereo, which had been playing loudly on top of their truck. Things were reasonably quiet for the rest of the night. Three of these young people were walking on the road near our campsite. They were drinking beer and seemed to be staggering quite a bit. She could hear them telling the park attendant who would walk by that they were not there at the park to cause trouble. He talked to them for a while. She could hear him telling them that if there was any more trouble, he would have to put them out of the park.

About half an hour after this, these three young people had gone back to their own campsite. They then heard some yelling from that campsite.

Me and my husband and the Hoopers sat on our picnic table and watched what was going on. She heard one of the young men who had been previously talking with the camper attendant shout a remark to the effect, "She's nothing but a hose bag." This fellow was average size and had shoulder-length brown hair. Another fellow said, "She is not." This man was smaller and thinner. She heard a man shout, "She sleeps with me and dreams of you." She doesn't know which one of the group, of which there were three girls and seven or eight men, said this.

At this point, several men began pushing and shoving each other, and some of the men were trying to stop them. They all appeared to be under the influence of drink or something at this point. One of the males in this group appeared to be only about thirteen or fourteen years old and was staggering and screaming and was very upset. One of the girls, who it appeared had been what the fighting was all about, left the group and came and stood by our car. She was tying up her shoelace; she then went up and sat by the graveyard for about a half hour.

At this point, one of the security guards arrived and quieted things down. Shortly after the security guard left, the girl who had been sitting near the cemetery came back to their campsite, changed her clothing, then walked out to the highway.

A second girl went after her and began to talk to her out on the highway. The young boy, he also went out to the highway, and he was staggering and falling. He began to scream at the first girl, words to the effect that she could not pay any attention to them, and if they "bugged" her, to tell them to "fuck off." He seemed hysterical and was screaming at the top of his lungs. Then the three of them came back to their campsite.

About an hour later, between 6:00 p.m. and 7:00 p.m., two security guards, the older one and another young one, went to the campsite and spoke to them. Then they saw the young people start to tidy up their campsite as if leaving. However, this leaving process appeared to drag out for quite a while, and the stereo came back on until it became apparent they were not leaving.

Nothing else happened that she noticed until about 9:30 p.m., when the police car arrived. There were three police officers. It was quiet for a little while, and some shouting started. You couldn't mistake the young kid's voice. He was screaming in the high-pitched voice. They seem to be saying, "Okay, they are leaving!" Articles were being thrown into their trunk.

They decided to go down to an empty campsite near where the trouble was and watch. There was some scuffling and pushing going on between the young people and the police. Somehow two of the policemen were being pushed to the ground. One of them tried to get up, but one of the youths on the ground pulled him backward on top of the other officer. At this point, a man who appeared to be the biggest of the entire group involved in the fight bent down and took up one of the officer's sticks. She saw him take one end of the stick in both hands and reach back over his head and brought the stick down with a great force on the officer's head. He did this three times. The first one of these blows, she heard a crack and thought it was the officer's head that made this sound.

There were three of the youths involved in this fight with the police. The first was the biggest. He was about 6'4" tall and weighed about 200 pounds, almost shoulder-length brown hair, and was wearing a gray-checkered shirt and blue jeans. This was a man who hit the officer with a stick three times.

The second man was close to six-foot, about 5'11", weighed about 150 to 175 pounds, with sandy brown hair, not dark brown, but sort of light brown hair about ear length, not as long as the bigger man's, wearing a yellow sweatshirt and a blue bathing suit. This man was one of the three who had been talking to the older park attendant about one o'clock in the afternoon the same day. She did not see him do anything in particular during the fight with a policeman.

The third was the young boy who seemed to have been hysterical all day. He was about 5'3" with shoulder-length blond hair. He had a blue jean jacket on and a light or white T-shirt and blue jeans. During the fight, he said that the police had broken this thumb with the billy, but she didn't see this happen as she didn't even see a stick or billy until she saw the biggest man hit the policeman with one.

When she saw the big man hit the policeman with the stick, she along with Kathy Hooper told her husband's to go and help the police, which they did. All the men standing watching this fight then went and grabbed the big man, and five of the men wrestled him down and held him down on the ground. Then one of the officers put his handcuffs on him. The men held this big man down until more policemen arrived about fifteen or twenty minutes later.

It was just after the policeman had been struck on the head when Casey Hooper and she went to the police car that was unoccupied, and Casey got the police radio and said, "This is the car at Coldstream, they need help right away, three officers are down and badly hurt. Send an ambulance too." The girl dispatcher came on and asked him to repeat his message, which he did.

It was about five or ten minutes before the police arrived in a second car. She didn't even recall this car arriving, just suddenly she noticed it there parked beside the first one, when a friend of the man in a yellow T-shirt was persuaded him to get the police car. There was a policeman there too, but he was letting the yellow T-shirt's friend do the talking. Yellow T-shirt told the policeman if he'd locked him up, he would go crazy as he suffered from claustrophobia, but he got in the cruiser, and his friend sat and talked to him and kept him calm for a long time. Meanwhile the young kid was running around and screaming like crazy. No one is paying any attention to him.

The big man, who hit the policeman, was still being held by the five spectators. An ambulance from Strathroy arrived, and they put Constable Best into it. He had told them his name as they had covered him with a blanket, and they wanted to keep him conscious as they were afraid if he passed out, he would stay that way. The other officer who had been hit was bleeding from the head and had gone to try the radio, but they told him they had already called. He must've been hit by the big man as well as Best as he had been lying beside Best as the big man had been swinging the stick.

The young kid had taken off somewhere, but one of the young people went and found him, and the police put them in the cruiser.

The big man was lifted off the ground by the police assisted by the Caribbeans, and he was fighting furiously all the time. They got him to the police car, but he wouldn't get in. A policeman asked him to get in, but he just kept fighting and would not get into the car, and finally an officer had hit him with a stick on the back. He was then put in the car. He started screaming and fighting inside the car very shortly after he had been put in. This was the same car the young boy was put in as a young boy jumped out again, as if he was afraid he was going to get kicked by the big man.

Anyway, the young kid was put back in the cruiser, and they all left.

Signed: Janice Diane Chapters
Taken by: J. McGoogan

Green appeared in court and was sentenced to four months in jail.

Bits and Pieces 13

In the early seventies, I attended a meeting of our no. 2 District Police Association. During the meeting, it was decided that they required a social committee, and as a result, they asked for someone to volunteer to chair a committee. No one volunteered to chair a social committee. When no one came forward to chair a committee, I took on the job. It ended up that I became the whole committee.

My job was to arrange all social functions, dinner dances, picnics, and any other social function they wanted.

For the dinner dances, I had to arrange the location, the meal, the music (whether it was a live group or a DJ). At a few dances I acted as the DJ with my many cassettes of good dance music, which I used periodically for friends' events.

On one weekend I had off, I DJ'd a dance at a club I belonged to. While setting up my equipment for the dance, one of the members of the club came over and said I was wanted on the phone.

I went to the phone and found that it was the dispatcher, Jim Branchflower, from headquarters, requesting my presence at a murder in Lambeth. I asked Jim where Ray was as he was on duty at the time. I was told that he was at an arson and murder in Port Stanley. I found out later that David Rossmore had murdered Michael Watson as a result of arson.

I then asked about Charlie and what was he doing. I was told that he was in Port Stanley where a nun's body was washed up on the beach in her full habit. They didn't know at this time if it was accidental, a suicide, or a murder, so they had to assume the worst.

"What about Don, what is he doing?" I was told he was somewhere between the two locations at the moment.

I went back up on the stage with my wife Linda and one of the other members of the club and gave them instructions on how operate my music system with all the music pieces numbered. I then left the hall and went to the office to get a vehicle and equipment and headed out to Lambeth.

When I arrived at the murder scene, it was the residence of an older couple. The woman was very active with her lady friends going to several different functions together. Her husband was not very active as he had difficulty moving about because of health issues.

I was told that a male person had entered the house through the front door, which was not locked, and went up the stairs, which is right inside the front door. I looked in the bedroom to the left at the top of the stairs where the woman was in the bed. I turned around and saw that the husband was in the bathroom across the hall from the bedroom.

The male went into the bathroom where he shot the husband, killing him, then went into the bedroom and shot a hole in the floor next to the bed. He then ran down the stairs and took off.

The woman was interviewed as to what happened, and she related the facts to the investigating officer.

The wife, I thought, because of her attitude and her apparent lack of concern for her husband, I felt that she had arranged for the death of her husband. I relayed my thoughts to the investigating officers. They felt the same way but couldn't prove it as she stuck to story.

The culprit could not be found or identified, and no charges were laid.

The wife carried on with her social life.

CHAPTER FORTY-THREE

Eighty-Eight-Year-Old Woman Murdered

Const. Ray Pat Parsons came into the ident. unit a few years after I arrived. He was stationed at the Grand Bend Detachment when I met him about five years after I started in the unit. He told me that prior to being hired by the police, he was in the RCAF (Royal Canadian Air Force). He also told me he had been a photographer in the air force and would like to get into the ident. unit. I told him that I would see what, if anything, I could do to help get him into the unit. Two or three months later, he was transferred from Grand Bend to the ident. unit.

The following is one of his cases.

Jean Gunn McGanes, age 88, was born in Scotland. She married Everett McGanes in Scotland while he was serving as a soldier in the Canadian Forces during World War II.

Approximately ten years ago, Everett passed away. Since that time, Mrs. McGanes lived in Woodstock. They had no children, and her closest relative was the niece, Patricia Lindsay. She lived in Hamilton, Ontario.

Jean was hard of hearing and was recently having difficulty walking; however, she was in reasonably good health. Mr. Frederick Barnes, born in 1914, lived across the street and did odd jobs for her.

On April 13, Barnes spoke to Mrs. McGanes about 2:30 p.m., inquiring as to whether she needed groceries from the supermarket. She requested he get her some ginger ale. Shortly after 3:00 p.m., Barnes returned to his home with his groceries, and a short time later went to Jean's residence with the five cans of ginger ale. He gave her the ginger ale and left. At this time, Barnes entered and left through the southeast front door, which was unlocked.

Shortly after 7:00 p.m., Barnes returned to the McGanes residence to obtain a newspaper. He knocked on the southeast front door and walked in. He found Mrs. McGanes lying in a pool of blood on the floor of the den near the door leading to the back porch.

Her house was situated on the north side of Park Row west of Mill Street. The property backs up to the CNR (Canadian National Railway) right of way for the mainline. The area is residential and, for the most part, are single-family dwellings.

The house is a one-floor cottage with a living room and bedroom at the front. From this area, there are five steps down to the dining room. West of the dining room there is a bathroom and a small galley-type kitchen. To the east of the dining room is an entrance door from the south and also a garage to the east. Directly north of the dining room was a kitchen, and to the west of the kitchen is a den where the body was located. North of the den is a small enclosed porch with access to the outside of the house.

GRAPH NO. 6 - SHOWS EAST END OF SITTING ROOM BODY AND FURNISHINGS.

After finding the body, Barnes went home and returned with two people who board at his residence. They called the police.

Sgt. H. Moore and Constable Larry Carson of the Woodstock Police Force arrived at the scene at about 7:16 p.m. They called for assistance, and shortly thereafter, Deputy Chief Joseph Moss and Det. Dave Mason arrived. The coroner, Dr. J. Blackwood of Woodstock, attended the scene at 7:20 p.m. He ordered a postmortem to be done at the Center of Forensic Sciences Morgue in Toronto.

The officers found the body lying in a prone position with the head toward the rear door in a pool of blood. There were obvious injuries to the head. The body was dressed in a blue and white dress, nylon stockings, slippers, and a gray sweater. To the east of the body was a gray shawl.

A toaster was lying near the body, smashed into several pieces. Between the legs was found a kitchen knife with a blade approximately eight inches long. The blade was bent to about a ninety-degree angle. A hammer was under a chesterfield to the south of the body. There were pieces of what appeared to be mica scattered from the area of the sofa and chair situated west of the body. Beside the chair was a purse. It was open, and the contents, including $50, did not appear to have been disturbed. A flowerpot on a ledge was turned on its side.

The door beside the body showed signs of having been forced. Two butterfly-type latches situated on the inside of the door at the top and bottom were bent inward. This would allow the door to open. On the outside of the door, there was paint knocked off, which was lying on the floor of the porch. A door leading from this porch to the outside also showed signs of forced entry. A window had been forced inward, thus allowing a person to reach in and open the door.

There were drops of blood found on the floor in several rooms in the house and the galley kitchen drawers. In the bathroom it appeared as though blood had been washed off in the sink. On a nearby towel rack, a bloodstained towel was found.

In the living room was a piece of cellophane that appeared to be from a cigarette package. It was on the floor near the door to the living room. In an ashtray in the dining room were two Players and one Export cigarette butts.

Both front doors to the house were unlocked, and several lights in the house were on. Mr. Barnes later commented on this being unusual as Mrs. McGanes did not leave many lights on.

Constable R. Pat Parsons arrived at the scene at 10:38 p.m. He was assisted by Const. P. Cutler as he started photographing the scene and then checked for fingerprints and collected exhibits.

On April 14, assistance was requested from the Biology Section at the Center of Forensic Sciences and the Forensic Fingerprint Unit at General Headquarters, Toronto. Keith Kelder, Biology Section at the center, William McAlindon, and Rossmore McCracken were flown to the scene in the police helicopter. Kelder examined the bloodstains, and McAlindon and McCracken attempt to locate fingerprints on the body using the iodine silver plate transfer method.

The autopsy examination was performed on April 14 at the Toronto morgue by John Deck, MD, Department of Pathology at Toronto Western Hospital. In his opinion, the cause of death was multiple wounds of the face and scalp, more on the right than on the left side, depressed fracture of the skull, laceration of the brain, and exsanguinations. Other abnormal findings were multiple irregular lacerations and abrasions to the face and scalp associated with the depressed fractures in the right temporal area and a broken right mandible.

At the time of the autopsy, there was a large open wound of the right side of the head through which portions of lacerated and disrupted brain material had fallen. The hole was a shape of the head of a hammer. There was also a vertical wound approximately two centimeters in length over the sixth rib. This was on the right side of the back and appeared consistent with a knife wound. The clothing covering this wound was punctured.

The examination by Kelder revealed the blood of the victim was type B, and the blood on the tile and on the floor was type O.

Examination of the scene by Constables Pat Parsons and Cutler produced several latent fingerprints. One of these prints found in blood and was found above the body behind the curtain on the window frame. A search outside the premises did not reveal anything to assist in the investigation. Neighbors and friends were contacted with negative results. A door-to-door survey for several blocks produced negative results.

A search of the residence revealed $220 in cash hidden in a pair of oven mitts in a buffet located in the dining room. Located in the same buffet was $694 in uncashed checks.

During the summer of 1977, Mr. Barnes's nephew, Larry Grissom, and three other men had painted Mrs. McGanes's house. Grissom was contacted by Det. Mason and Insp. O'Rourke.

Larry Grissom, born in 1949, had a criminal record and lived on Main Street in Beachville. In his interview, he stated that during the summer of 1977, he repaired the McGanes house and painted it. He advised he was assisted by Edward Scott and two other men. They were all from Windsor. He knew the other two men as Randy and Terry. He also advised that Mrs. McGanes gave him a $100 bill to purchase the painting supplies and then paid them off with another $100 bill.

On April 19, a special meeting of the Board of Police Commissioners for the city of Woodstock was called. A reward in the amount of $10,000 was offered for information leading to the arrest and conviction of the persons responsible for the murder of Jean McGanes. The reward was to expire December 31, 1978.

On April 20, Larry Grissom contacted Det. Mason and advised him that on April 14, Terry Kelly of Windsor had called his wife while he was out. He remembered that he was one of the people who had helped paint he house.

Nancy Lee Brody, born 1964, from Beachville, is the common-law wife of Grissom. She was interviewed and stated that Terry Kelly had called her home at 8:30 p.m. on April 13, stating he was in town and they were staying at the Oxford Hotel. He wanted to speak to Larry, who was not home. She assumed the way he was talking that he would drop out that night or in the next few days, but she did see or hear from again.

On April 24, Constable G. Daily of the Essex Detachment, who had been assigned to conduct interviews in the Windsor area, had contacted Edward Scott. However, he had not been able to contact the other two persons who were now known to be Terry Kelly and Randy Quellette.

On April 21, information was received that Clause Lempke, born 1952, of Melbourne Street, Woodstock, had seen Kelly in Woodstock. He was subsequently interviewed and advised that on April 14, at about 1:30 a.m., he had seen Kelly and his girlfriend, Eve, in the Double Luck Restaurant in Woodstock. He borrowed three dollars from Kelly. At this time, Kelly mentioned going out for a few drinks on Saturday afternoon, but he did not see him again.

On April 26 at 7:30 p.m., Terry Kelly was located at his residence. He accompanied Det. Mason and Insp. Orton to the Windsor City Police Headquarters. He willingly gave his fingerprints for elimination purposes, hair samples, and a blood sample, which was taken by Dr. L. M. Brown, Grace Hospital and Windsor.

Kelly stated that he helped paint the house that previous summer. He had gone to Woodstock by train on April 13 to visit his girlfriend, Eve, who is an exotic dancer. He arrived in town with $11 in his pocket. He visited Eve at the Southside Hotel, and they went to visit Mrs. McGanes shortly after 3:00 p.m. He left there about 4:30 p.m. or 4:45 p.m. He took a cab both to and from the house. He could not remember what the cabdrivers looked like or the cars they were driving.

Kelly stated the while at the McGanes house, he fried himself and Mrs. McGanes some eggs and made some toast. He describes the toaster he used as similar to the toaster that was used as a weapon. (The knife beside the body had a wooden handle, and there were no eggshells found at the scene.)

He describes his exact movements in the house and stated he was near the back door. He describes Mrs. McGanes as being in good condition when he left. He then returned to the Southside Hotel by taxi.

Later that evening, he and Eve rented a room at the Oxford Hotel, Woodstock. They later went out for a Chinese dinner at a local restaurant. After eating, he and Eve stayed together at the hotel. He left Woodstock for Windsor on the first train in the morning.

During the questioning, it was noted that he had a small cut on the top of his right ring finger and another small cut on the inside of his right thumb. Photographs were taken by a Windsor police officer that were examined by Dr. L. M. Brown. Kelly said that he cut his hands on glass in the backyard of his sister's house.

Brenda Kelly appeared at the Windsor Police Station while her brother was being questioned. She stated that he cut his hands on glass in her backyard.

Kelly, who had no previous police record, was released, and search warrants were executed at his sister's home on Bridge Street, Windsor, and at his apartment on University Avenue, where he had lived and just recently moved. Articles of clothing were also seized for examination.

Further investigation revealed that Laurie Anne Miller and Hazel Pachelo Demelo, both born 1956, both went to the Double Luck Restaurant with Kelly and his girlfriend, Eve. They all ate. The bill came to $17, and Kelly insisted on paying. They noticed that his hands had cuts. When asked about this, he stated that he was in a fight on the way down to the train.

Investigation at the Oxford Hotel revealed that Kelly did stay there in room no. 7. The registration card was seized.

Evangeline (Eve) Lee Albaladejo, born 1949, is Kelly's girlfriend. She was located working at the Pine Hotel in Thorold. She is a stripper on the circuit. During the week of April 3, she was employed at the Southside Hotel in Woodstock. She has a poor memory and is not sure of anything. She attributes this to the use of marijuana.

Above the body was a bloodstained curtain. Behind this on the window frame and door molding was a palm print, two fingerprints. The prints were all identified as Kelly's with more than 10 points of comparison in each.

Just above the door handle on the outside of the back door in the porch, a fingerprint was located. This print was also identified as Kelly's right thumbprint. The blood on the curtain near the fingerprints was consistent with Kelly's. The blood where the fingerprint was located could only be identified as human blood. All latent fingerprints were identified with the exception of the one on the back door near where Kelly's thumbprint was found.

All taxi drivers had been interviewed as well as the employees at the Southside Hotel. A cab cannot be found that went to or from the McGanes residence. Nothing of value was ascertained at the Southside Hotel.

On April 30, a charge of first-degree murder was laid against Kelly. On May 1, his sister, Brenda Kelly, was contacted and advised she had not seen him since he went to see Michael Stoyka, a lawyer, in Windsor during the morning of April 27.

On May 19 at 6:05 p.m., Terry Nelson Kelly was arrested at the home of Linda Perch, 23, located in Bruce Street in Windsor. On information received by members of the Windsor Police Force, they located and arrested the suspect at this residence.

Linda Perch stated that on Sunday, May 24, Terry Kelly came to her back door and asked if he could stay with her for a few days. He told her to introduce him as Jack whenever she asked him about anything. He told her it was none of her business. He never went outside, except on the day of his arrest. He then went into the backyard.

Ellen Goetschel, 50, went to see her neighbor, Linda Perch, on May 17. She was introduced to "Jack" (Kelly) by Perch. On May 19, she again went to Perch's. When a police car came down the alley, "Jack" got up and started walking up the back steps. The police came out of the house and arrested "Jack" on the back porch.

Terry Kelly was returned to Woodstock May 20. He was remanded by the Justice of the Peace to the Middlesex-Oxford Detention Center in London. He appeared in Woodstock Court for prosecution. Legal aid duty counsel appeared for the accused.

The trial was held in Woodstock, and after hearing the evidence that was presented during the trial, the jury, after deliberating for an hour and a half, returned with their verdict: "Guilty as charged."

Kelly was sentenced to life in prison.

CHAPTER FORTY-FOUR

Arson Murder

On Thursday, February 15, 1979, David Rossmore and Michael Watson had been drinking at two bars in the city of St. Thomas, the Wheat Sheaves and the Schooner Inn.

At approximately 1:00 a.m. of a Friday, February 16, they returned to the Rossmore residence at 422 Edith Cavell Boulevard, Port Stanley, via Cox Taxi out of St. Thomas. Watson would be described as being "intoxicated" and Rossmore as being "talkative" but not intoxicated. The Rossmore residence is located on the south side of Edith Cavell Boulevard at 422 and consists of five bedrooms, two bathrooms, one laundry room, one storeroom, one kitchen, one kitchen/eating area, one dining room, sitting area, and one living room, which is located in the extreme south side or back of the house and faces the lake and the beach. The residence is quite cut up, having been added to on several occasions, with the latest addition being completed in 1978. The entire house and attached carport is of frame construction covered with a white vinyl siding. There are three entrances to this house: one at the front, one at the back, and one from the east side leading in from the carport.

David Rossmore Jr. lived at this home with his parents and sisters who were all at home in bed at the time of this fire. They are his father, David Rossmore Sr., mother Ellen Rossmore, sisters Cheryl, age 16, Donna, age 13, and Mary Katherine, age 11.

Shortly after arriving at the residence, David Junior and Watson proceeded to the living room located at the back of this residence to watch television and drink beer. Watson, who was quite intoxicated, fell asleep in an upright position while sitting on the chesterfield.

At sometime after 1:00 a.m., Cheryl Rossmore awakened and discovered that the dining room drapes were on fire. She immediately ran to her parents' bedroom to arouse them and inform them of the fire.

The parents immediately aroused the other children in the house, and while Mrs. Rossmore led the girls from the residence, Mr. Rossmore proceeded to David Junior's room to awaken him. He found David lying on his bed with his trousers on and in an apparent deep sleep. After rousing David, his father returned to his own bedroom for his boots but suddenly realized the fire had accelerated to an inferno, and he rushed from the house through the door leading into the carport.

The parents did not know how David Jr. escaped from the house, but a short time later, he was observed emerging from the smoke along the east side of the house and stated that he jumped through the east window of his bedroom. It was at this time they discovered that Michael Watson was still in the house as Mr. Rossmore was not aware that Watson had come home with David Jr. By this time, the fire department was on the scene, and the house was a raging inferno, and it was for anyone to enter the building.

At the time the parents were awakened by their children, they observed a small fire at the curtains in the dining room near the west window. At this time the fire was quite small, and it was believed that there would be time to extinguish it once the children were out of the house, but the fires spread too rapidly.

A neighbor, Harold Jacobs, noticed the fire and phoned in the alarm at approximately 2:00 a.m. The fire call was received at 2:08 a.m., and the first fireman at the scene was Fire Chief John Vary, who observed flames showing from two different buildings: one at 414 Edith Cavell and the other fire at 412.

Once the fire was extinguished, the body of Michael Watson was located on the floor of the living room, lying face up approximate three feet east of the chesterfield with his head in the northeast direction and partially covered by insulation and debris, which had fallen from the ceiling.

At 2:45 a.m., Constable Gary Sheddon from the St. Thomas Detachment proceeded to Port Stanley regarding a house fire. Accompanied by Staff Sergeant Money, they arrived at 3:30 a.m., at which time they were met by Fire Chief Jack Vary of the Port Stanley Fire Department and Constable Mike Rowe Reid of the St. Thomas Detachment.

They proceeded to the rear portion of the residence where they were further met by Const. Gerry Beech. They entered the rear door of this residence and living room at the back of it. They were shown the body of a male person lying on the floor at the doorway between this room and the adjoining room. They had been advised prior to entering this room that all members of family living at this residence had escaped; however, there was a male in the house at the time of the fire identified as Michael Watson. This person was known to the police from prior occurrences.

They viewed the body that was lying on his back. Part of the facial features were covered by what appeared to be ceiling plaster. The person was tentatively identified as Michael Watson of 331 Edith Cavell Boulevard, Port Stanley.

Sheddon returned to his department car and notified St. Thomas detachment to call the coroner and to also notify the fire marshal's office and then proceeded with Fire Chief Vary to 412 and 414 Edith Cavell Boulevard, where they viewed two other cottages that had received fire damage. The cottage at 414 had received extensive damage to the rear and to the inside. The cottage at 412 had a plastic covering the windows and a window had been broken, allowing access to the inside of the cottage where a mattress had been set on fire.

The coroner, Dr. F. J. Foster, attended at the scene at 4:30 a.m., viewed the body, and pronounced the victim dead.

D. Campbell, the fire investigator from the Ontario fire marshal's office, Toronto, arrived at 10:00 a.m. to commence his investigation and gather several exhibits that were pertinent to the fire investigation.

At 11:07 a.m., the body of Michael Watson was removed from the residence and positively identified by his father, Milton Watson, of 331 Edith Cavell Boulevard. The body was then conveyed to the morgue at St. Joseph's Hospital, London, by the St. Thomas removal service for postmortem examination.

Throughout this entire investigation, the scene and the body was secured by police personnel.

At 2:20 p.m., Dr. Katherine Turner, pathologist, of St. Joseph's Hospital conducted a postmortem examination of the body of Michael Watson. The cause of death was established as smoke inhalation and carbon monoxide poisoning. There were no internal or external signs of violence on the body apart from burning.

All exhibits of this postmortem examination were taken in the care of Constable Pat Parsons, the identification officer who was assigned to the investigation. All the exhibits were removed from the scene with the exception of the exhibits removed by D. Campbell, the fire investigator.

Subsequent investigation indicates that the Rossmore fire originated inside of the residence in the dining room area at the curtains near the west window. All possibility of electrical or accidental ignition has been eliminated.

At the time of the Rossmore fire, two other fires were discovered at vacant cottages approximately one hundred feet east of the Lacroix residence, which were next door to the Rossmore residence. These two cottages located at 412 and 414 Edith Cavell are owned by Robert G. Richards of Westland, Michigan, USA.

The cottage at 412 received minor damage with only a mattress being destroyed. Evidence at this location indicated that an attempt had been made to ignite the plastic protective covers over the back door and the west bedroom window. In addition, one pane of glass in the west bedroom window was broken, and the mattress at this point was ignited but only smoldered and was removed by the firemen at the scene with a minimum of damage to this cottage.

Further information revealed that David Rossmore Jr. was a prime suspect in two previous fires on Cavell Boulevard, which occurred on January 13 and February 2.

As a result of our suspicions and information received during this investigation, Cheryl Lacroix, age 16, the sister of David Rossmore Jr., was reinterviewed with regard to discovery of the fire at the Lacroix residence in the early morning of February 16. She stated that at 1:14 a.m., she heard her brother, David Jr., and Watson go into the living room, and the TV was turned on.

Sometime later, David entered Cheryl's room and was rummaging through her dresser, looking for matches. She directed him to some matches on the top of the dresser. A short time later, Cheryl got out of bed and went for a drink of water and saw David putting on a blue bomber jacket. Watson was asleep on the chesterfield. David appeared to be startled to see Cheryl and immediately sat down with his jacket on. Cheryl returned to bed, and a few minutes later, she heard a door slam and a bit later heard David talking to the family dog, Bingo.

After hearing what sounded like matches being struck lit, Cheryl looked out through her bedroom doorway toward the dining room and saw David running away from in front of the curtain at the west window of the dining room. At this time she could see that the curtains were on fire. Once David reached his bedroom at the back of the house, Cheryl went to her parents' bedroom and told them about the fire.

Cheryl gave a statement. "*Starsky and Hutch* was on the TV, I was alone, it was twelve midnight. I went to bed 12:15 a.m. At that time my brother David was not at home. The last time I looked at my clock, it was 1:14 a.m., and the TV was on. I thought David was home. I saw Dave go into the bathroom, Mike went into the kitchen. Both went into the TV room. I don't know what time it was, but Dave came into my bedroom looking for matches, a cigarette in his hand. I told him there was some on the dresser. I don't know if he got any or not. Paper matches I just picked them up from anywhere. Mum works at St. Thomas Court House. Dave went back to the TV, I guess.

"I lay in bed a few minutes and was going to get a glass of water. I went to the TV room first. Mike was on the couch sleeping. Dave was on the other couch. I don't know if he was sleeping or not, his back was to me. The TV was on. I returned to my bedroom. I don't recall falling to sleep. Maybe I was dozing. I smelt smoke, got up, and went into the living room entrance. Saw the fire, got my parents up. Returned to my bedroom, got my shoes, boots, jewelry box, and my coat. I waited for Donna and Mary, and we all ran out together. Out on the road I saw Baird Reeves and Wayne Majors coming from Mike Wilson's place. Dave was out on the road screaming. Wayne ran up and put a coat on Dave. I think they went to check the other cottages. Mom was at Nash's. Mom returned and got into a cab to keep warm. I looked for Mary and Donna at the Jacobs house. My dad said go to the Emmett house, and we did, Donna, Mary, Mom, and me.

"Around 3:00 a.m. the night of the Stork Club fire, Dave came home and said something about the Stork Club being on fire. I thought he was fooling around. He took his coat off sat down, and I made him a toasted sandwich. On Thursday, February 15, I came home about 10:20 p.m. Dave, Mike, Donna, Mary, and Mom were in the TV room. A pizza arrived shortly after from Dr. Pizza. After the pizza was eaten, Dave and Mike left in a cab. Dave was wearing blue jeans, white pullover sweater, and a blue bomber jacket. Mike's clothing, I don't know, blue jeans, vest.

"Before the smoke, I heard a noise from the back of the house. It sounded like Dave's bed."

On February 18, 2:20 p.m., a second statement was taken from Cheryl Rossmore.

"I woke up and wanted a drink for a sore throat. A short time after Dave got the matches, I went out to the doorway between the living room and the family room. The floor lamp was on beside Dave at the end of the couch, the TV was on. Dave was bending over the black stool in front of the coach. It had an ashtray on it, but I did not see cigarettes. Dave looked up and said, 'What are you doing?' and I said, 'Nothing.' I did not answer, and I asked him, 'What are you doing?' and he said, 'Watching TV.' I don't know why he was bending over the table, but he laid down right after he told me he was watching TV. I then looked in at Mike. He was sitting up on the end of the couch, but it looked as though he was asleep. I then went back to bed and closed my eyes, and next thing I remember was Bingo, Donna's dog, barking, and then I felt him jump up on my bed. Then I opened his eyes and petted him and said, 'What's wrong?' Then I laid there and smelled smoke and thought something was on fire and got up to see. I went out of my room, and I saw the curtain in the dining room was a fire on the bottom and little on the side. It looked like it just started. I did not see anything on the wall. There was a bit of smoke where the fire was. There was no lights on other than the light from the flames, and I don't think the TV was on, otherwise I would've seen the light from it.

"I ran to my mom's room and turned on the light and told her the house was on fire. She yelled for Dad, and I went back to my room and grabbed my boots, coat, mitts, and jewelry box and went out of the house by the front door into the carport. The door was not locked. Dave doesn't usually lock it. After I left my room with my things, I looked at the fire, and it spread out toward the middle of the room, and I left.

"When I looked behind, Mary and Donna were running out of the house, and we went out to the road. Then my mom came out. Then she was going to go back in for Dad, and then he came out. I don't remember whether Dave came out or my mom went to Nash's first, but Dave come out and fell on the road coughing. He was not wearing a shirt, he had blue jeans and his blue shoes on, but when I saw him in Nemmetts after, I don't think he had socks on. I saw Wayne running down the road, and he took off his coat and gave it to Dave. Dave said, 'Where's Whizz?' and 'Did he get out, did anybody see him?' After he got up from the road, then he ran back to the front door of the house and was kicking it, and he never went in, I think David got him. I then went to Nemmetts where I stayed there for a while. I went out later and talked to Dave because the Nemmetts people were there. He was lying in the snow, and he got up, and he said, 'Whizz is still in there.' Then he went into Nemmetts a little later and said to me, 'There goes his euchre buddy,' then I left.

"Before I smelled the smoke, I heard a noise, sounded like the door of the family room. I wondered about it because the door is usually locked. I thought Dave may have gone out."

The damage to the Rossmore residence, which is completely gutted by fire, is estimated at $30,800 by the Western General Insurance Co., who holds the policy on this residence.

The damage to the Robert Richardson cottage, located at 414 Edith Cavell, was extensive and has an approximate value of $10,000. The damage to the cottage at 412, also owned by Robert Richardson, received minimal damages. Only one window was broken and one mattress destroyed.

The funeral of Michael Edward Watson was held on February 19 at 3:30 p.m. in the chapel of Williams Funeral Home, St. Thomas, with interment at Union Cemetery. The Rev. Karl Sievert of the United Church Port Stanley officiated.

On Friday, February 16, the investigation was discussed with John Buchanan, the Crown attorney at St. Thomas, at which time he was apprised of the details of the investigation.

On February 16, 1979, at 7:40 a.m. David Joseph Rossmore Jr., DOB 26 March 1958, 422 Edith Cavell Boulevard, Port Stanley, Ontario, unemployed, was interviewed regarding the fire at his residence, 422 Edith Cavell Boulevard.

Q: Where were you last evening, February 15?
A: I and Mike were at the Wheat Sheaves in the Schooner Inn.
Q: What time did you leave St. Thomas?
A: I don't know. We got a taxi. It was late.
Q: Did you know the cab driver?
A: No.
Q: Where did you go from St. Thomas?
A: To my place.
Q: Did Mike Watson go with you?
A: Yes.
Q: Do you remember what time you got home?
A: Nope.
Q: What did you do when you got home?
A: Went to bed.
Q: Where did you sleep?

A: In my bedroom.
Q: Where did Watson sleep?
A: On the couch.
Q: Which couch?
A: The biggest one.
Q: Where in the room would that be?
A: Next to the partition facing the lake.
Q: What do remember about the fire?
A: Nothing.
Q: Were you drinking last night?
A: Yeah.
Q: How much did you have to drink?
A: Quite a bit, a fair amount.
Q: How did you get out of the house?
A: Through the window.
Q: Which window?
A: The one facing not the beach but the other way.
Q: How did you know the house was on fire?
A: I didn't even know.
Q: If you didn't know, why would you go out the window?
A: I don't even remember.
Q: Were you in a fight last night?
A: I don't know.
Q: When you went out the window, did you see anyone outside?
A: I don't even know nothing.
Q: Do you remember talking to your sister when you came home?
A: I think I got a cigarette. I don't know if we ordered a pizza or not.
Q: Where was Mike when you got the cigarette?
A: I don't know.
Q: Was he sleeping?

A: I don't know. I smoked my cigarette, and we were drunk, and we just crashed.

Q: Did you go out the back door for any reason when you came home?

A: No.

Q: Were you drinking when you came home?

A: We had a beer in the cab. We took one from the Schooner.

Q: Who did you talk to at the Schooner?

A: I think we were just by ourselves. Yeah, we were, and we sat next to the bar.

Q: Where did you go after you came out of the window of your house?

A: Out to the street. Wayne Majors gave me his coat.

Q: How long after you came home did you go to bed?

A: I don't know.

Q: Who was drinking Labatt's Blue in the TV room at your house?

A: We had one in the cab, and I imagine that we brought it into the house.

Q: Did you watch any TV when you came home?

A: Yeah, I guess when I had my cigarette. We played chess or checkers sometimes, that's how drunk we get.

Q: How long after you came home did you borrow a cigarette from your sister?

A: I don't know, maybe right away.

Q: Do you remember what woke you up?

A: Nope, I just couldn't breathe.

Q: You know anyone by the name of McCormick?

A: Billy, yeah.

Q: How old is he, nineteen, twenty? Did you see anyone else in the street when you get there from your house?

A: Nope, nope.

Q: Do you recall your father trying to wake you?

A: Nope.

Q: Did your sister try to wake you?

A: I don't know. All I remember is trying to get out the window.

Q: I don't understand why you wanted to go out the window if you didn't know there was a fire or something wrong?

A: I don't know.

Q: Do you remember going to bed?

A: I remember going to bed.

Q: Do you remember waking up?

A: Nope.

Q: How did you get out the window?

A: I think I just jumped through it. I don't think I could see it. I think I hit the wall.

Q: You don't remember opening the window?

A: I don't think I opened the window.

Q: Do you remember getting from the bed to the wall?

A: No, I don't even remember waking up.

Q: Do you feel that someone purposely set fire to your house?

A: I don't know, I would say so.

Q: Why would you say that?

A: In my opinion, yes, just like the rest.

Q: What you mean the rest?

A: Whizzs, the Stork Club, Jim's, whatever.

Q: On the night that Mike Watson's cottage was burned, you took a cab to Port Stanley. Is that correct?

A: Yeah.

Q: Where did you go between the time you came out the cab to let you off and Mike's cottage burned?

A: At home.

Q: Where did the cabdriver let you out the night of Mike's cottage fire?

A: At home in front of my cottage.

Q: How did you get burnt tonight?

A: I don't know.

Q: Tell me again what took place from the time you got out of the cab until you were back on the street and your father's home was on fire?

A: Mike and I went into the house. We went in through the door at the carport. I went to Cheryl's room and got a cigarette and smoked it and went to bed.

Q: What happened then?

A: I don't know.

Q: Was there any flames in your room?

A: I don't know.

Q: Can you see the TV room for your bedroom?

A: Yeah.

Q: Did you look into the room before you went out the window?

A: I don't know.

Q: Do you have any idea who may be setting the fires in Port Stanley?

A: If I did, I'd tell you. I was just bluffing the last time. What about the guy who said he did it?

Q: I want to put your thinking cap on and tell me why you woke up and why you went out the window?

A: I don't know.

Q: The door that goes out to the beach, is it used as much?
A: To let the dog out. Just take him out and tie him to the step post. My sister might use it. It's used all the time.
Q: Do you think it strange that in almost every case of fire in Port Stanley, you are either around or at the fire?
A: I don't know.
Q: Do you know what you're doing when you get drunk?
A: Oh yeah.
Q: Are you using any drugs?
A: Yeah.
Q: What are you using?
A: I'm not going to talk about it.
Q: On the night of second of February, when Michael Watson's cottage burned, where were you?
A: I was uptown drinking at the Sheraton, Killarney, and the Schooner. I got a taxi home.
Q: Where did you get the taxi?
A: From Cox Cab.
Q: Where did you go in Port Stanley in the cab?
A: Home.
Q: Did you go directly in the house from the cab?
A: Yup.
Q: What house are you talking about?
A: 422 Edith Cavell Boulevard.
Q: What time was it when you arrived home?
A: I have no idea.
Q: Did you see that Mike Watson's cottage was on fire?

A: No. I heard the alarms. My brother saw that I was sleeping on the couch.
A: What did Cheryl say?
A: Yup.
Q: How do you know?
A: I looked out the door.
Q: Do remember coming from St. Thomas to Port Stanley?
A: Yes.
Q: Were you drunk at the time?
A: I was not drunk. The officer just arrested me to question me. I was drunk but not drunk.
Q: Do you remember the taxi driver turning around crossing the Stork Club and letting you out on the south side of street at the west end of the Stork Club?
A: He missed my laneway, so I told him go on around the turn around and come back.
Q: Why would a cab driver state that he let you out at the Stork Club?
A: I never do that.
Q: Isn't it true that you stay in Watson's cottage when you get drunk or high on drugs?
A: I am not going to answer.

Statement: "I tried to get back in the army as a firefighter, but there were no openings."

On February 17 at 10:15 a.m., David Rossmore was interviewed again.

Q: You are charged with murder. Do you wish to say anything in answer to the charge? You are not obliged to say anything unless you wish to do so, but whatever you say may be given in evidence. Do you understand the caution that I just read to you?

A: Yup.

Secondary Warning

Q: If you have spoken to any other police officer or to anyone in authority, or if such person has spoken to you in connection to this case, I want it understood that I do not want it to influence you in making a statement. Do you understand this caution just read to you?
A: I want a lawyer.
Q: I am investigating the death of Michael Watson in a fire at 422 Edith Cavell Boulevard, Port Stanley. What can you tell me regarding this death?
A: (No answer given).
He phoned his lawyer.

On Saturday, February 17, David Rossmore Jr. had been at the St. Thomas Detachment for questioning, was arrested, and charged with second-degree murder of Michael Watson.

The trial was held in Ontario Supreme Court in St. Thomas, and after hearing the evidence of the witnesses, the jury came back into the courtroom with the verdict "guilty as charged." He was sentenced to a life sentence in jail.

Bits and Pieces 14

On a farm down near the community of Bothwell, an eleven-year-old boy came up missing. A large search for the boy took place throughout the county, with negative results. Posters describing the boy complete with a picture (the boy with the white shirt) were distributed and posted in and around the community with negative results.

It was two or three months later, and as the result of a long period of very little rain, there was a water shortage in the area and on the farm where the boy had disappeared from. As a result, it was realized the well on the farm where the boy disappeared had pretty much dried up with very little drinking water available.

The pump on the well was removed, and the farmer looked into the well in an attempt to determine how much water was left in the well they could use. Very little water remained in the well. In the remaining water, and partially submerged, they found the skeletal remains of a small person in the water, which was a few inches deep, left in the well.

The skeleton remains were removed from the well. The task at hand was to identify the skeletal remains. This was then put in the hands of medical assistance.

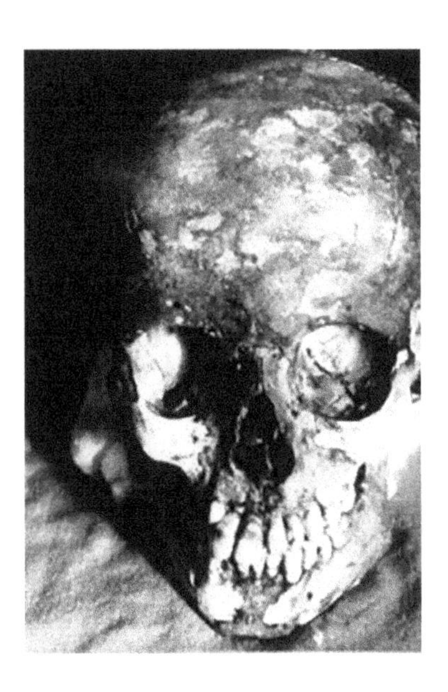

A picture of the boy was obtained from the parents, which was to be used by the person responsible for the identification to be made so that persons would be able to match and to try to match the picture to the skeleton in an attempt to identify that this was the missing boy. Contrary to that old saying that a picture being worth a thousand words, images do not speak for themselves; they require interpretation. The doctor we got applied several methods of photo-anthropometry, morphological analysis to the images, including the overlaying of two similar-sized images, known photographs superimposition, the rapid transition between two images. By this method, the skeleton remains was identified as the missing boy.

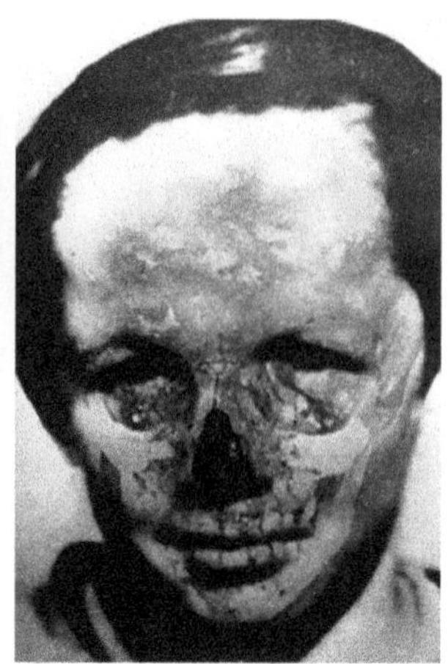

CHAPTER FORTY-FIVE

Skeletal Remains Found—Murdered

On Sunday, May 18, the skeletal remains of a body were discovered near Catfish Creek approximately four miles south of St. Thomas.

The remains of a male person were lying on top of the north bank of Catfish Creek, well above the high water mark. The body had not been exposed to water and was pretty well obscured by trees and brush. The remains were approximately one hundred yards north of number 3 Highway near an old road running parallel to the highway.

The body was nude and appeared to be totally unmolested. No clothing, rings, watches were evident on the body or in the adjacent area. There was some evidence of burning under the body in the center, which appeared to be between the thigh bones. Burning was noticeable on trees along the side of the body and dried overhanging vines from last season's growth. No metal objects such as belt buckles, buttons, or zippers were found.

Robert Bruce Jensen, age 18, of St. Thomas located the remains while on a hiking trip in the area. It was this young man who called the St. Thomas police detachment, advising them of his find. Officers from the detachment responded immediately.

Corporal Johns and Constable Peters were at the scene when Constable Pat Parsons from the identification unit, no. 2 DHQ, London, arrived to photograph the scene.

Due to darkness having set in, the body was not moved on May 18, 1975. An overnight security detail was set up, and the investigation would resume early the following day. On May 19, five police officers from St. Thomas and four auxiliary officers from the London and Tillsonburg units assisted in the methodical search of the area for evidence. The entire surroundings were raked, and the shoulders on each side of number 3 Highway were checked for the articles of clothing or identification. Earth directly under the body was sifted then bagged for further examination. Control samples of the earth were taken from the perimeter. A metal detector was employed to scour the riverbed. The searches were unsuccessful in locating any evidence of value.

At 9:12 a.m., May 19, the remains were removed from the scene and were transported by Constable Pat Parsons to the morgue at 86 Lombard Street in Toronto.

The following list of the exhibits were also delivered by Constable Pat Parsons to the Center of Forensic Science for examination:

1. Charred wood from the area where body was found.
2. Pieces of fabric material found in the area between legs and body.
3. Substance from area around crotch of body.
4. Charred wood pieces found on a slope west of body.
5. Base of small tree (cut down) bound to the left hip of the body.
6. Siftings of earth under the body.
7. Sifted area around the body.

On May 22, a postmortem examination was conducted by Dr. J. Hilldon-Smith.

Race:male occasion
Age: between 18 and 20
Weight: 125 lbs (approx.)
Build: slim, small feet and hands, long fingernails
Hair: light brown, 5" long
Teeth: Lower – natural with no noticeable dental work have been done
Upper – full upper denture; third molars present, covered partially by tissue

It is the opinion of Dr. Smith that the death occurred sometime in the late summer of 1974. Cause of death could not be established.

The body did not show any particular signs of violence or having been burnt.

The jaws were removed and handed to Dr. J. D. Purvis, forensic odontology, 170 George Street, Toronto. Fingers and thumbs on both hands were removed and an effort will be made to raise identifiable fingerprints. A small sample of hair was taken for examination at the Center of Forensic Science.

The area where the body was found is farmland owned by Mr. Louis Stafford, age 71 years. Mr. Safford and many of his neighbors were interviewed but did not possess any knowledge of this matter.

Ontario hospitals, youth centers, and all correctional institutions in the St. Thomas, Woodstock, London, and Palmerston areas were checked for missing persons and elopes. An Ontario Alert was sent out on May 22 and outlined the details of this occurrence and description of the unidentified body. Little response was received from the message from the police Central Records Branch, and "offline" search was made on all missing or wanted persons across Canada fitting the description provided. Around 445 subjects were presently being checked out for elimination. Our intelligence at Niagara Falls and Essex are assisting of missing persons from United States border towns.

On May 26, Dr. Purves provided a dental chart recording his examination of the teeth. His inspections revealed the following:

Specimen:	Upper and lower jaw skeletonised.
Observations:	Retain upper third molars covered partially by tissue. These heavily decayed. All lower teeth present except for a left lower third molar and no fillings present.

Conclusions:	A young male in midtwenties. Only premortem dental service involves removal of all of the teeth except the molar. Upper denture has no labial flange, which suggests an immediate denture following extraction of teeth. Central incisors, 8.5 mm wide and 10.0 mm long.

Dr. Purves would not enter this chart in the monthly dental journal as the dental work fails to provide a sufficient detail for identification. The police bulletin, "For Identification," has been published and disseminated to all police forces throughout Canada. It includes a full description of subject with pictures and charts of the teeth.

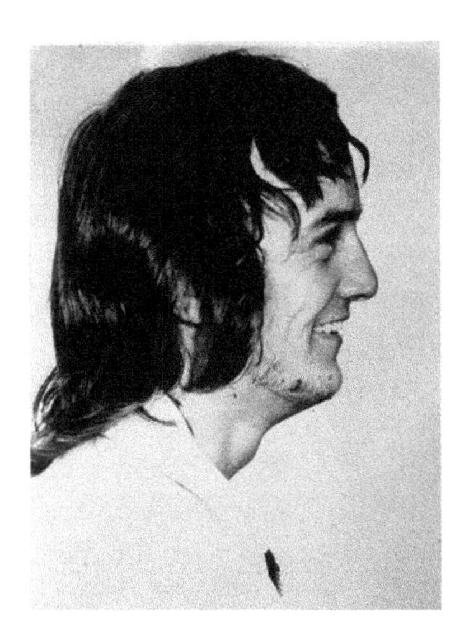

As mentioned earlier, the fingers and some were removed from this unidentified body for the purpose of raising identifiable prints. These exhibits were placed in a formaldehyde solution for approximately eight weeks before any effort was made to take impressions. With great care and expertise, Constable Pat Parsons was successful in obtaining impressions from four fingers on the left hand and the ring and little finger on the right hand. The prints were then forwarded to J. F. Hines, supervisor, Forensic Analyst Section, Police Identification Services.

On July 8, Mr. Hines advised of a positive identification had made to the criminal fingerprint file:

Jacques Paquet	
DOB:	December 5, 1954
Born:	Gaspe, Quebec
Parents:	Mr. and Mrs. Louis Philip Paquet
	St. Ann Desmonts, Gaspe, Quebec

With assistance of officers from the Québec Police Force, a follow-up investigation was made on the teeth of Jacques Paquet. The records kept by a family dentist in St. Desmonts were obtained and supported the observation and conclusions of James D. Purves, DDS.

The parents of the deceased were officially notified of the death of their son by an officer of the Québec Police Force on July 10. Mrs. Paquet reported that she had not seen her son since the spring of 1974. She further stated she had not reported her son as a missing person.

Investigating sessions were conducted in the Hamilton, Delhi, and Alymer areas. It was learned that Jacques Paquet first arrived at Hamilton in January 1974. While there, he resided in various rooming houses and the YMCA. He was unemployed most of the time. He began an intimate friendship with Dr. Herbert J. Carleton on Proctor Street in Hamilton. Dr. Carleton was employed as a veterinarian with Essex Packers in Hamilton.

Dr. Carleton was interviewed, and a lengthy statement was recorded. It was learned from this that Dr. Carleton rented two cars for Paquet's use. Paquet did not have the essential credentials or money to rent a car himself. The second vehicle was rented from Action Daily Rentals in West Hamilton on August 1, 1974. This vehicle was seized by the RCMP in Swift Current, Saskatchewan, on August 20, 1974.

Further investigation revealed that it had been driven to that area by the following subjects:

1. Richard Joseph Denommee
DOB: January 19, 1952
20 Newstead Crescent
Brampton, Ontario

2. Catharine Smith
Alias: Catharine Baker, Heather Northmore, Catharine Benson
DOB: April 15, 1955
247 St. George Street
Sudbury, Ontario

3. Alan Charles Parker
DOB: March 10, 1955
233 Cecil Street
Pembroke, Ontario

Denommee, Parker, and Smith were arrested by the Medicine Hat Police Department on August 22 and charged with the murder of Peter Van Eerde, age 17. Van Eerde was an attendant at the service station at 15 Bennett Court in Medicine Hat. The trio entered this station, and when attempting a robbery, Van Eerde was beaten over the head several times with a blunt instrument. He died as a result of his injuries.

At the time Parker was arrested, he was in possession of identification in the name of Jacques Paquet and travelling under that alias. He also possessed a driver's license, Social Insurance Card, Ontario Health Insurance Card, Ontario learners permit, and an Auto League card. These were all contained in a brown leather wallet, and each item was in the name of Jacques Paquet. Parker, Denommee, and Smith were also in possession of a gasoline credit card in the name of

H. J. Carleton. The credit card was used for the purchase of gasoline on the trip from Ontario to Alberta.

Each accused had separate trials. Denommee was convicted and is serving a life sentence in the Prince Alberta Penitentiary. Parker was incarcerated in Calgary to await his trial. Smith was released and the charge against her was withdrawn. She went to Vancouver to live. Her current address is on file with the Vancouver Police Department.

As a result of the many inquires that were made, it would appear that Jacques Paquet was last seen alive in Hamilton by a girlfriend, Gloria Manns. This was on August 12, 1974. Paquet was known to have associated with Denommee and Parker, having met them in the summer of 1974 during tobacco harvest in the Delhi-Simcoe area. Parker and Denommee also worked part-time that summer for Bernard Amusements of Richmond Hill.

On August 16, 1974, a service station in the city of St. Thomas was robbed of $300. During the robbery, the attendant, a young eighteen-year-old man, was beaten on the head in the same fashion as the victim in the Medicine Hat occurrence. This occurrence by the St. Thomas Police is still unsolved. The victim in this robbery is a permanent patient in a mental hospital.

It was the opinion of the investigating team, or at least possesses direct knowledge of the circumstances regarding Paquet's death, tt would appear that Paquet died on or about August 15, 1974. The fact that Denommee, Parker, and Smith were in possession of Paquet's rented car and all his personal identification material leaves many questions unanswered. It is also believed that the three were responsible for the robbery at the St. Thomas service station. There is a noted resemblance in the method of operation.

Efforts were made to locate Katherine Smith, alias Baker. This woman should possess a great deal of information in regard to the case, and it is imperative that they should interview her.

On contacting Vancouver Police Department, the investigating team was advised Katherine Smith lived in Vancouver and that she could be picked up at any time upon request. When attempting to set up an interview with Smith, her whereabouts was unknown. The Vancouver Police Department held a Canada-wide warrant for her arrest on a charge of soliciting. The follow-up investigation in Vancouver was purposely delayed, waiting for the testimony of this witness.

On November 3, Detective Inspector Cousens with Constable Petz travelled to Calgary and Medicine Hat, Alberta.

Alan Parker was interviewed on November 5 at the psychiatric hospital near Edmonton, Alberta. They spent most of the day with Parker discussing Paquet's death and the robbery of the service station in St. Thomas. He seemed reluctant in making a statement at that time. Parker was advised should he consider discussing the matter, he could contact Detective Orr of the Medicine Hat Police Department.

Richard Denommee was interviewed at the Prince Albert penitentiary in Saskatchewan. He would not comment on any events involving Paquet's death or the service station robbery.

On returning back to St. Thomas, Crown attorney Wallace was consulted in regard to total charges against Denommee and Parker for the murder of Paquet. After this discussion, the charges were laid against them.

On November 15, a call was received from a detective from the Medicine Hat Police Department, advising that Parker had given him a statement telling how he and Denommee had killed Paquet.

Parker related how he and Denommee were hitchhiking on a no. 401 Highway when Paquet picked them up in his rented car. This was either the thirteenth or fourteenth of August 1974. According to Parker, the three drove around in the St. Thomas area until about midnight. Denommee was riding in the rear seat when he ordered to back up and pull to the side of the road. Then Denommee put his belt around Paquet's neck. He told Parker to grab the other side, which he did; both pulled tightly, causing Paquet to asphyxiate.

Parker and Denommee completely stripped Paquet's body then dumped it on the side of the highway. They then poured gasoline over the corpse in an attempt to dispose of it. In the next two days, Denommee and Parker used Paquet's car and drove around the area of Aylmer where they worked at a carnival. On August 16, the two decided to go west. Prior to leaving, they committed the assault and robbery at Loveday's Service Station in the city of St. Thomas. Parker did not recall if Katherine Smith was with them or not when they robbed the service station. Evidently, she did not witness the murder.

At the time Detective Orr took the statement, he did not advise Parker that he was or may be charged with murder. When taking the statement, it was not witnessed by another officer. In view of this, it was decided that a second statement would be taken with a proper warning and charge read to him.

On December 2, 1975, Peters and Carson returned to Calgary and reinterviewed Parker at the Calgary remand center. The purpose of this return trip was twofold. One was the taking of a second statement; secondly, it was now believed that Denommee may have in his possession some of the deceased's clothing. It was their intention to seize any items that could be identified.

When interviewed, Parker wrote out a six-page statement involving himself and Denommee in Paquet's death. He further wrote in a statement, admitting that he and Denommee were responsible for the St. Thomas service station occurrence.

Denommee was reinterviewed at the Prince Albert Penitentiary the following day. He was shown a copy of Parker's statements, but would not comment. A number of articles of clothing held by the penitentiary in Denommee's name were seized under the authority of a search warrant.

On November 14, 1975, Alan Charles Parker gave the following statement after being cautioned. The statement was witnessed by Detective Orr, signed by Parker.

He met Rick Denommee in Pembroke, Ontario. He was working for a fair. He asked him if he would like to be his partner, so he thought it would be nice to see some new towns and faces. So the next day he started because it was pretty late at night when he first met Rick. So he was high on dope all that night until they left Pembroke. They then left for Arnprior. It was a warm day. He was feeling really good while he was still high on speed and acid. So he started work. Rick was a hustler. He'd make money for himself and for his boss. But he would go really big, keeping a lot of it. He tried to but put it back because he didn't feel like losing one of his first jobs, and besides, they gave him his free meals and money at night when they would close down.

When they were finished there, he wasn't sure, but he thinks Ed, their boss, left them off in Toronto so they could spend a few dollars. They went down to the mall. They met some people he knew. They sat down and had a few beers. Then they met Kathy and a few other women. They left for something to eat. Then he told Rick they should get back and wait for Ed, but he said they'd have lots of time. So he just let it ride. So then they went down to Young Street where he was to meet an old-time friend who gave him a free bag of speed. So they ended up partying. He remembered the place Eddy had left them. So he got a taxi up there. When he found no one but a trailer that belonged to the carnival, he thought they would be back soon. Then he fell asleep on the grass because he was feeling a beer and the speed that he had taken.

He doesn't know what came next until Rick came and found him on the grass. He was with a carload of people all stoned and drunk. Then they said goodbye to them all, and he and Rick went to sleep in the trailer. The next morning they were looking for a ride to meet the rest at the grounds. He didn't even know where they were headed.

They started hitchhiking, and they got a ride from an older couple. They left them off on the 401, then a got a ride by Jacques Paquet in a Grande Torino. It was white in color. They were driving for a while, and Rick was talking French to him. About five minutes later, they picked up two girls. Jacques said something to Rick in French, and then Rick got out and got over to the driver's seat. Jacques was hustling a broad, and he guess the broad didn't really like it, so Rick said something to Jacques. They drove the girls to a town. They left him off at a café, and they drove around town a bit. It was getting pretty late, so he went to a hotel. They stayed there about an hour and left. They were driving down the highway.

Rick said something to Jacques in French to pull over. Rick's voice seemed to get louder, and Jacques pulled over to the side. Rick put his belt around Jacques neck. The first words that he heard Jacques speak in English were "Please don't hurt me. You can have this car." Rick said, "Fuck you." Then he told Parker to grab the other side of the belt. He told him that he didn't want to, but he said, "Come on, are you fucking crazy."

By this time he was really scared because he'd never been in violence before, and he was still pretty high. So he told him again to grab it, and he did. He only had it for a few seconds and then let go. Then Ricky was squeezing tighter, and stuff started to come out of the guy's nose, and he was breathing funny, and he sort of went limp. Then Rick told him to drive down the road, and they turned down a dirt road where Rick dumped him off. Then Rick said, "Drive to a gas station," and he drove there. Rick went into the gas station, and when he came out, he had a red gas can in his hand, and the guy filled it up.

Then Rick drove to where they left the guy off; they dragged him into the bush, then took the guy's clothing off, poured the gas on him, and set it on fire. Then Rick drove them back to the fair again. They kept Jacques's car. It was pretty late when they got there. Then they went into a small town, and Ricky met a few of the carnival workers standing in front of the hotel, and they went in and had a few beers. After the hotel closed, Rick and he drove up the motorway. Ricky made a U-turn. The guys said Ricky had a stolen car. Ricky said, "Fuck you," backed up, and drove off.

They were driving down the highway. They stopped and saw a girl. She worked for the carnival, so Rick asked her where she was going. She said, "To a motel." Rick asked her if she wanted to go for a drive. She said, "Okay." They stopped at a motel. They all went into the motel, and she woke up another guy who was only about sixteen. She got about one ounce of hash and brought it along with her. They were driving down the road, all smoking dope except for Ricky, and they ended up going back to the carnival.

They stayed at the carnival a few more days then left, still driving Jacques car. They went back to Toronto. There they met Kathy Smith, who they had met before. Then Ricky asked Kathy where she likes to go, out east or out west. Kathy said west. Cook she's been out east.

He picked up some dope around Toronto, then Kathy Smith, Rick, and he started heading west, still in Jacques car.

They drove through so many fucking towns. Rick and Kathy were in the front, and he was in the back sleeping. They came to a town pretty late at night and drove around the side of the gas station. He's not sure if it was a white or gray building. He was still pretty sleepy.

Rick got out and said he'd be right back. He told him to stand in front of the gas station while he went in, then he asked the guy about some tires or something. The guy went and checked and didn't have the kind, so the guy got on the phone and phoned some other garage. He got off the phone and told Rick that he did not have the tires that Ricky wanted. Then the guy went into a small room, and Ricky hit the guy over the head with a pipe. At this time he was in the gas station with him.

The guy went against a wall, and Ricky took out a knife. The guy grabbed the knife from Ricky and was yelling, "Please don't hurt me, I'm only sixteen!" The guy tried to get away, and Ricky told him to close the door. The guy started swinging the knife, and he cut his arm. Ricky hit him with he don't know what it was, but the guy went down. Ricky grabbed the knife and stabbed him in the stomach a few times. Ricky wiped his fingerprints off the pipe.

Then they went into the office of the station. Ricky opened the till, took the money, and he took a couple cartons of cigarettes. Then they left. He thinks this happened in Ontario. Then they came out in the west and were stopped in Swift Current by the Royal Canadian Mounted Police. They still had Jacques's car.

He read all of the statement that he had given. He'd been given the chance to correct any mistakes, but it is correct.

Witnessed: Det. Orr

Signed: A. Parker

At a later date, Richard Joseph Denommee appeared in Ontario Supreme Court in St. Thomas, and after a brief trial, the jury returned with a verdict of guilty. He was also sentenced to life in the Jacques Joseph Paquet murder.

The trial of Allen Charles Parker was also heard in St. Thomas, at which time he was also convicted.

Newspaper story after trial:

CONVICTED MAN THANKS JURORS FOR HEARING CASE

St. Thomas (CP) – Ontario Supreme Court jurors who convicted Allen Charles Parker of Pembroke of murder were thanked Wednesday by the accused, through his lawyer, for hearing his case.
The jury found Parker, 21, guilty of murder upon his life imprisonment in the death of Jacques Joseph Paquet, 20, of Ste. Anne Des Monts, Que., on Aug. 14, 1.
The charge was laid in November, 1975, before Criminal Code changes were approved by Parliament. Under the amendments, Parker would have been charged with second-degree murder.
The conviction carries a life sentence, but Mr. Justice D. H. W. Henry whether he will accept a parole recommendation. Parker said he helped a friend strangle Paquet with the belt after they had been picked up by Paquet while hitchhiking. He said he acted under threats of violence from his friend and was under the influence of drugs.
The body was found burned in a wooden area.
Parker's companion is still awaiting trial.

CHAPTER FORTY-SIX

Girl Missing, Raped, and Murdered

Georgia Jacobs was a twenty-year-old girl. She was an active member in the local Jehovah's Witnesses community and the local Kingdom Hall. She worked part-time at the Aylmer Dairy Bar where they served milkshakes and short-order items at the snack bar. The dairy bar was located just north of the main street on John Street North (Highway 73). She lived at home on Pine Street with her family, a short distance from the Aylmer Arena where most of the Aylmer residents would be found on any given night during the winter months.

She worked part-time at the Aylmer Dairy Bar in the town of Aylmer, where she was regarded by customers and coworkers as a quiet, unassuming girl. She left work at the dairy bar on February 18, 1966, shortly after 6:00 p.m., intending to go back to work the next afternoon. She was not seen again. Salesgirl Linda Holmes may have been the last person to see Georgia when she purchased shampoo from her between 6:30 p.m. and 7:30 p.m.

Georgia's parents began to worry when Georgia still hadn't arrived home for dinner after 7:00 p.m. It was not normal for Georgia to be late coming home for dinner with the family. Her brother and sister at the request of her mother went out as a pair to look for her on the route she would normally take to go home. On the way back to their residence, Georgia's brother and sister went into the arena and asked some of their friends and others if they had seen Georgia. They returned home shortly after 8:00 p.m. and advised their parents that they did not find Georgia, and they all realized that something had gone wrong.

They called the Aylmer Police, who were apparently not at all concerned, suggesting to Georgia's father George that his daughter must have run away, that foul play at this time could be ruled out. Her parents were assured that foul play didn't exist in this neck of the woods. A basic report was taken by the police with the Jacobses being told to call if and when she returned home.

About forty-eight hours later, the phone rang at the Jacobs home. Georgia's mother picked up the receiver and heard nothing on the other end of the line other than some background noise. She got the impression that the caller was outside at a pay phone beside a roadway with the door to the booth open. She repeatedly said hello, only to get no answer. She thought it was a wrong number. Before she could hang up, a muffled and muted voice chimed in on the other end, which sounded like someone, a man trying to disguise his voice, pretending to be her daughter. "I'm downtown, and some men have me." Then the line went dead.

Georgia's mother thought the voice was maybe that of her daughter, although she couldn't be sure. She thought it was Georgia being forced to make the call in an attempt to throw off the authorities with "some men" and "downtown." Or perhaps it could've been a cruel crank call, or perhaps it was from her abductor or killer, disguising his voice of some sadistic game he was playing to buy time and to throw police false hope before the investigation even got started. Or perhaps it was a killer hoping that investigating finally would get started, and the investigators would find the series of taunting clues that they left for them.

The police slowly started the investigation, and Ontario Police were called in to assist in the investigation. Georgia's family was sick with worry after the following months. The Jehovah's Witnesses community and local residents got together to search in and around Aylmer. What they thought was that they would find the body of Georgia. The scarf that Georgia was wearing the night of her disappearance was discovered along 73 Highway (Elgin Road), apparently thrown out of a moving car. Georgia's winter coat, covered in blood, was found behind a tree in a field of the lower concession road, known as Glencolin Line. Because of the Jehovah's Witnesses practices, Georgia's blood type had never been taken, making it impossible to determine the blood found in the cold was hers. Things were beginning to look bad.

A reward was created for anyone who located her, dead or alive, in the hope that it would come from people with useful information if they came forward. It would also entice some other people with information to come forward. Several calls were received, but to no avail. It was believed that Georgia would not get into any car with a person she did not know or trust.

A month after Georgia disappeared after last being seen leaving the Aylmer Dairy Bar and a few days after the reward was announced by the police, on March 16, 1966, a local farmer located the girl's body and would receive the $500 reward. The body was found in a secluded bush lot of Springfield Road between the Glencolin Line and Dingle Line, a short distance from where her coat was found. It was assumed by the investigators that the killer was familiar with this area. She was found lying on her back. Her left ear was missing, apparently chewed off by animals. Also her left arm was bare to the bone, apparently also eaten away by animals. She also had a severe open wound to the head, which was surely not made by animals.

A very active investigation was continued on for several months after her body was found. Many persons were interviewed and vehicles checked with negative results.

It was a young seventeen-year-old who took a lie detector test just prior to an inquest that was held in the fall of 1966. He did not seem to have a vehicle, and he passed the test.

During the inquest, the police made much less of this lead, but they were under fire for saying she had just run off and would like to be back someday. The one thing the police kept repeating and they had that was right was that they felt Georgia was taken and murdered by someone she knew and trusted.

The Jehovah Witness people are the ones who broke this out into the open six years later. They somehow uncovered this and brought the murderer to the police six years later. It was a fellow church member.

Some woman from above Springfield had been calling the Aylmer Police about this David Button being involved with this murder, but they never paid her any attention. He was a real sadist; he had planted her shoes and some undergarments in several remote places to tease the police until her clothes were found along the road.

A three-page typed confession of rape and murder signed by David Button, 27, of Kitchener was read to an Ontario Supreme Court jury at the trial.

St. Thomas lawyer Dave Little, who defended Button against the charge of noncapital murder, raised doubts as to whether the confession was true.

Button was arrested and charged in January 1972 with the sex slaying of Georgia Jane Jacobs, 20, of Aylmer in February of 1966.

The trial opened on a Monday before Mr. Justice Campbell Grace. The all-male twelve-man jury had been excluded from the hearing since 4:00 p.m. on the Tuesday while the lawyers argued over the admissibility of certain evidence.

DAVID BUTTON

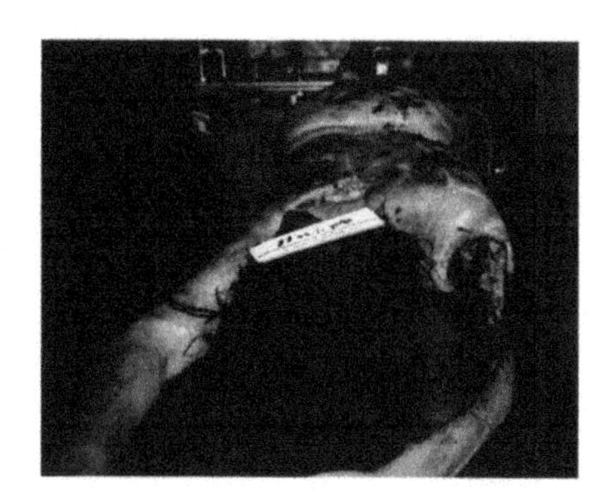
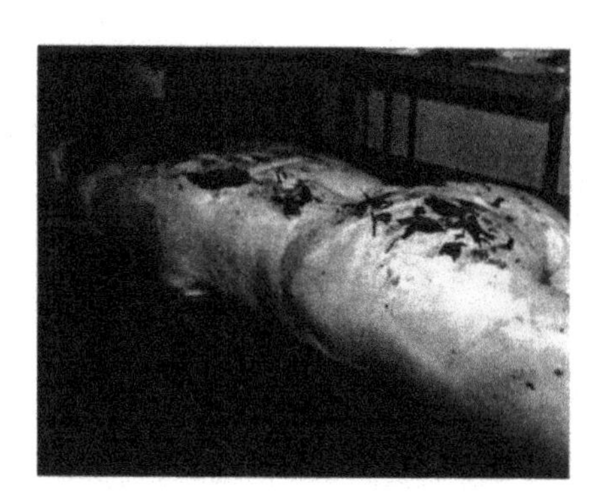

Georgia worked and went missing from the Dairy Bar, shown on the left side of the picture at the top of the page. Her body was found about 50 feet south of the road in the wooded area. Her bra was found 25 feet north of where her body was found in the next picture. The 2 bottom photos were taken at the morgue. The one on the left shows where animals chewed part of her left arm.

Mr. Justice Grant ruled earlier Thursday afternoon that two statements allegedly made by the accused on January 24, 1972, were admissible as evidence in a trial, and the jury was recalled at 4:00 p.m.

Arthur Powers, a district supervisor or "overseer" of the Jehovah Witness sect, was one of four senior members of the sect in Button's Kitchener home when Button made the alleged confession. Mr. Powers admitted under cross-examination by Mr. Little that he had wondered many times whether Button, also a Jehovah Witness, was telling the truth in confessing to the murder. "A person who commits such a major sin must repent and make it known to God's servants," Mr. Powers had said. "And David Button had made the first step that is necessary to get back in God's favor by confessing to this crime."

"Even if the confession isn't true?" asked Mr. Little.

"It has occurred to me that perhaps a confession isn't true," replied Mr. Powers.

Mr. Little then suggested that Mr. Powers's doubts about confession were so strong that he had visited Button in his jail cell to reassure himself.

Mr. Powers, visibly disturbed by this remark, replied that he paid the visit to convince this man who has suicidal tendencies not to commit another grave sin.

That statement, in turn, aroused Mr. Justice Grant, who scolded defense counsel for directing the question to the witness and warned Mr. Lindsay, "We don't want anything to happen here that might require a new trial."

Mr. Little replied, "I think it's very crucial point for the man to whom the confession was made doesn't believe it himself."

According to the confession read in court on Thursday, Button picked up the Jacobs girl about 6:30 p.m. on the night of February 18, and after driving around the town for a short time, he parked on a side street. He put his arm around the girl, and she resisted his advances. When she continued to struggle and started to scream, he struck her on the head twice with a soft drink bottle to knock her out. He then drove to a side road south of the town and parked again just as she started to come to, and she began screaming again.

Button says in the confession that he placed his hand over her mouth and nose in hopes that she would faint and stop screaming. While his hand was over her face, he raped her.

When he removed his hand from her face, he realized she was dead and became frightened. He then drove to another area east of Alymer and dragged the body into a wooded area some distance from the road.

He returned to his car and realized her coat was still there, and he drove to another area before stopping and putting in the coat behind a tree.

Button then returned to Alymer and went to help his father-in-law, Albert Crockett, who was working as a night janitor in a bank. He arrived there at about 7:30 p.m.

Later that night, he returned to his rented home in Avon, a village north of Alymer, where he took his bloodstained coat and gloves Ms. Jacobs was wearing from his car and stuffed them in a hole in the house's foundation. He then wiped the blood off the seat of his car using snow and a rag on the floor behind the passenger seat.

The next day, he continued his confession that he joined the search for Ms. Jacobs. Her coat was recovered nine days later. Another nine days went by before her scarf was found. Finally, twenty-six day later, on March 18, 1966, her body was found where Button in his confession said he left it.

Mr. Powers explained how he obtained the confession; he said he was in Alymer early in January on congregational business when he heard rumors that some member of the Alymer congregation was responsible for the Jacobs girl's disappearance and death. Both Button and Mr. Jacobs remembers the rumor in the congregation of the Jehovah Witness.

This statement was read back to Button, who then signed it. His signature was witnessed by the other four men.

Button was arrested by police and charged with non-capital murder later the same day, about three weeks after Mr. Powers had commenced his inquiry.

Under cross-examination by defense counsel, Mr. Powers said that he had told Button during the visit in the previous Friday, "If there is a person in our midst who has done this thing, he should come forward because if he doesn't…he will be caught sooner or later anyway because the angels ferreted him out. God executes his judgment on the wicked."

He said that he used that phrase or other scriptural references like it throughout his inquiry to exhort members of the congregation to divulge information that they might have had held back previously.

Button said Mr. Powers then asked if such a person who rules life at God's hands confession were not made to members of the sect. Mr. Powers replied, "That's right."

Mr. Powers testified that members of the Jehovah Witness sect believe in a new heaven and a new earth with a removal of disease, pain, and even death. They believe that the New World will come to the one as it presently exists if it is destroyed in the near future.

They believe they were approaching the end of the system that if a person has done something condemned in God's will and it is still secret, God executes his judgment, then that person will be ferreted out and die. Others in harmony with God "will live through to the day of judgment," he said.

Mr. Powers testified that in the interest of those under suspicion and the general welfare of the congregation, it was decided to get to the root of this talk that had been going around.

Consequently, Mr. Powers, assisted by a circuit overseer from Toronto, Charles Rossmore, began interviewing all of those persons who would have been members of the Alymer congregation in 1966 to see what each recalled about the evening of February 18 when Ms. Jacobs disappeared.

Button, one of several members who had moved from the area, was interviewed in his home on Friday, January 21. Mr. Powers said that Button was not suspected at that time of having any direct involvement of the girl's disappearance, but there were some inconsistencies in reports of Button's whereabouts that night.

Mr. Powers said that he and Mr. Moss were satisfied with Button's answers to their questions and left it to continue the investigation elsewhere. However, Mr. Powers was contacted about 1:00

a.m. on Monday, January 24, that Delbert Crookett told him that Button wanted to talk with him as soon as possible. A meeting was arranged for later that morning at the Button home.

When Mr. Powers, Mr. Rossmore, and Mr. Crooker, arrived about 10:30 a.m., they found Button sitting at a small table in the kitchen with his head cupped in his hands and sobbing.

When he regained his composure, Mr. Powers said that he offered a prayer that "the Creator help David to bare his heart and tell us what was troubling him."

Button, according to Mr. Powers, then hesitantly launched his confession of raping and murdering the Jacobs girl. The three other men each took notes of what Button said and then called Herbert Katzmier, Button's congressional overseer in Kitchener, to come to the house and type the confession.

On February 1972, it was read to the Ontario Supreme Court jury on Friday morning.

The statement read on that morning was made to Detective Sergeant Dennis Allsop at the London headquarters of the Ontario Police on January 24 after he had been charged with a girl's murder.

Police had escorted Button to the headquarters after learning he made a confession early in the same date to the members of the Jehovah Witness sect of which he was a member.

The second of two confessions signed by David Button that he raped and smothered Georgia Jacobs in February 1972 was read to the Ontario Supreme Court jury on Friday morning.

In a confession to the police, Button said that when he first picked the Jacobs girl up near Spicer's Bakery in Aylmer about 6:30 p.m. on Friday the eighteenth, 1966, his intention was to drive her home. "I didn't have any thoughts of killing or doing anything else to her," he states in the confession.

When he parked on an Alymer side street later, he said, "I don't know what got into my mind to do this, to put my arm around her. I hit her two or three times with a pop bottle when she struggled." Button later in the confession said, "I don't remember some things that went on that night."

After hearing all the evidence and the summation by the defense council and the Crown attorney, the jury exited the courtroom for their deliberation. After some time passed, the jury brought in a verdict of guilty.

He was sentenced to life in prison.

CHAPTER FORTY-SEVEN

Rape and Attempted Murder

On May 22, 1979, I was dispatched to the Woodstock Detachment office, where I was informed that Mark Edward George Wells was arrested for the rape and attempted murder of Irene Parker. I was told that Mark Wells had been driving east on County Road 28, a road southwest of the town of Tavistock, when he went into the ditch on the south side of the road about midnight. He walked across the road and through a field to the farmhouse where Irene Parker lived. He found the back door to the residence was unlocked. He entered the house and found himself in the kitchen, which was in the northwest corner of the house. To his right was an archway, the entrance to the dining room. In the center of the south wall of the dining room, he found a stairway leading to the second floor. At the top of the stairs he turned down the hall to the left, and on his left he found the bedroom where Irene was sleeping.

He entered the room and raped her. He attempted to kill her after raping her. He used a metal coat hanger, which he pressed hard to her neck. She tried to fight him off, which left cuts and bruises to her hands and arms and her throat where he applied pressure with the coat hanger. She also left deep scratches on him. She passed out, and he thought she had died.

He left the house and walked over to 59 Highway a mile away to the east, where he hitchhiked. An hour or so later, he was picked up and dropped off in Woodstock.

Shortly after Wells left the farmhouse, Irene regained consciousness, got up, and left the bed. She went to the phone where she phoned the police in Woodstock. She described her assailant as best she could. She stressed the fact that he had red hair and described as the best she could a description of his clothing.

About 3:30 a.m., Mark Wells was found walking the street in the west end of Woodstock. He was picked up and taken to the Woodstock detachment office.

I took photographs of Wells, front and back and both sides, back of head behind his left ear showing bloodstains, and the back of his hands also showing bloodstains. His clothing was bagged and taken for examination. I took saliva sample and scrapings from both hands. His fingerprints were also taken.

At 11:08 a.m., I arrived at the residence of Irene Parker with Constables Vance, Adams, and Corporal Willson. We walked through the house and discussed the occurrence. We left the house at 11:45 a.m. and proceeded to the Stratford General Hospital.

At 12:15 p.m., we arrived at the Stratford General Hospital and to the room of Irene Barker. Photographs were taken of the injuries to the right and left sides of Irene's head and the injuries to the neck and her hands. We then left the hospital and arrived at Irene's house at 2:00 p.m.

Photographs were taken facing east and west on County Road 28 showing the location of the 1971 Chevy Impala, license AFY 050, in the ditch on the south side of the road. Photographs were taken in the kitchen and dining room area and in Irene's bedroom where the attack took place, as well as the entrance to the stairs leading to the second floor. Photographs were also taken in Irene's bedroom, the items in the bedroom, and with the quilt removed from the bed showing the bent-out-of-shape pink hanger that was used as a weapon on Irene's neck.

A fingerprint examination was conducted throughout the house. I found a thumbprint that was found on the west side of the door casing between the kitchen and living room. Four prints were found on the right side of the wall of the stairway to the second floor. Prints were found on the kitchen side of the door leading to the stairway.

All fingerprints were identified as being left there by the hands of Mark Wells.

At 8:30 p.m. in the Woodstock Detachment, I received from Constable Roy Vance a sealed envelope containing three vials of the vagina swabs, a vial of blood, combed pubic hair, pulled pubic hair, and scrapings from left index and little fingers. These were taken by the staff at the hospital from the victim, Irene Parker.

A few days after, I took aerial of the farmhouse and the general area around the farm house from the police helicopter.

Mark Wells was charged with rape and the attempted murder of Irene Parker. At the trial and after hearing the evidence, the jury brought in a verdict of guilty on both counts. He was sentenced to eight years in jail.

CHAPTER FORTY-EIGHT

Murder of Two Women and Two Young Boys

It was Friday, June 15, 1990, when I came to work at the Woodstock Police Department and found out I had a murder to go to three doors west of the police station in an apartment building.

On that morning, Robert Channer found the semi-clad body of his thirty-year-old sister, Christine, lying on the floor in the small kitchen of her apartment, a bent fork in her hand. She had been strangled and beaten. Robert had warned his sister about Mark Wells, whom he had seen in Christine's apartment a few weeks before he found her murdered. Wells was "bad news," he had told her.

I spent the day in the apartment photographing the body with bruise marks around her neck and a bent fork clutched in her hand. A search for fingerprints was conducted, but none were found. It was decided the body would be removed and taken to Toronto for the autopsy where I'll be taking further photographs and exhibits.

When I arrived at the office on the Saturday morning to prepare for my trip to Toronto, I was met at the back door by Detective Ron Freeman, who advised me at that time to get my gear together to go to more murders.

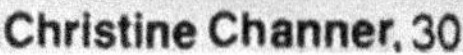
Christine Channer, 30

Annette Norton, 28:

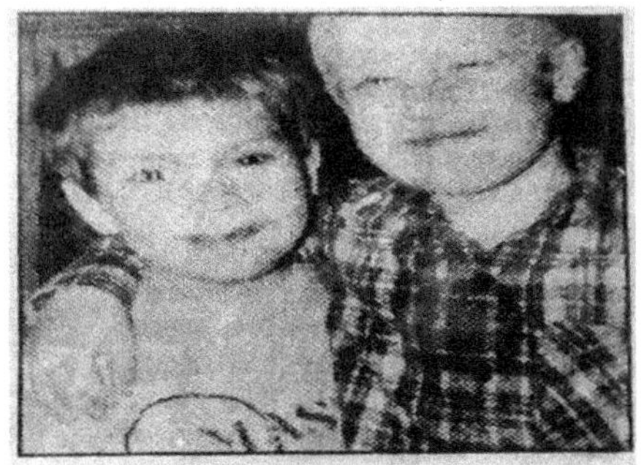
Richard Norton, 8:
Christopher Norton, 7:

He took me to a small house on Simcoe Street in the West End of Woodstock. A boarder at the house discovered the bodies of Annette Norton, 28, and her two sons Richard, 8, and Christopher, age 7. The boys' throats had been slashed. Their bodies had been stabbed many times. Annette's hands were tied behind her back with a cord from a television converter. She had been stabbed several times. There were large bruises on her body, and she had two black eyes. The pathologist concluded all four victims had been badly beaten before they were killed.

It was readily believed on Saturday night that Mark Wells was a suspect in these killings. He was no stranger to violence. He had just been released from jail for a short period of time after spending eight years in custody for the attempted murder and rape of Irene Parker, age 44, southwest of Tavistock. He was convicted on November 29, 1979, on those charges when he was eighteen years of age. Wells had entered the woman's home through an unlocked back door going in the ditch and walking across the field to the house. He picked up a nine-and-a-half-inch knife, went upstairs to the bedroom where she was sleeping, and attacked her. Wells strangled her with a coat hanger until she was unconscious. Thinking she was dead, he left the bedroom and the house. She had a three-inch gash across the forehead. Wells pleaded guilty to a charge of attempted murder. The charges of rape and robbery were withdrawn.

The judge noted Wells already had three convictions for robbery, armed robbery, and assault. This attack took place a few days after Wells was released from a correctional center in Guelph after serving a twenty-month sentence for armed robbery and assault after spending an eight-year sentence for rape and attempted murder. A psychiatrist's assessment of Wells at that time said he suffered from a deep ingrain personal identity disorder. Psychiatrist urged long-term therapy to tame his demands.

After years behind bars, Wells found it difficult to adjust. He was nervous and worried that he wouldn't fit in or that people wouldn't hire him. He said he'd been locked up for so long, he couldn't deal with it, he had told her sister.

After spending so much time in jail, he had a hard time adjusting being out of jail. He had a hard time getting steady work, and he was short of cash. The relationship with his girlfriend, Brenda Mitchell, was on the rocks. Wells lived with Mitchell at her Woodstock townhouse for a couple of months before she kicked him out in early June, about a week before the murders. She paid for groceries and rent while Wells was often drunk. She called the police after the quarrel and said she didn't want Wells on her property.

On the morning before the killing, Wells was having a coffee with a friend. He told a friend, "I feel like killing somebody." The friend says, "No, you don't, Mark."

On June 15, I spent the day photographing the bodies and the interior of the residence, checked for fingerprints, and searched for other items to be used on the case.

After the death of Channer, detectives on the case worked trying to piece the circumstances of the death that morning.

Wells spent the day screaming to obtain cash. He finally borrowed money from friends. He stopped at the Ontario Services Office and asked about his welfare check. He saw his caseworker, who told him his welfare had been cut off because he hadn't appeared for an interview in May. He stopped at a residence in Woodstock demanding money for work he had done on a Simcoe Street home a short distance from Annette Norton's, the victim's home. About 7:00 p.m. on the Friday, Wells purchased a bus ticket for Toronto. The next morning, the bodies of Annette Norton and her sons were discovered in Norton's Simcoe Street home.

On June 17, the redheaded Wells was standing on the steps of a church in downtown Toronto sharing a hash joint with two prostitutes when he heard the sounds of sirens. He was a mess, unshaven and bare-chested under a jean jacket. The two women noticed he was slobbering and spreading saliva when he spoke. Something about the sound of sirens screaming across the city set him off.

Mark Wells—"Red" to his Toronto friends—decided it was fire trucks and not really police cars. He thought they were coming for him. He was about to make his first confession.

He told the prostitutes he was wanted for murder in Woodstock. He said, "I killed two women because they were stupid bitches." He said he cut her children's throats because they were witnesses, and he could go to jail for a long time.

One of the women laughed it off. Wells got madder and madder as the sirens closed in. Another woman left in disgust. Later that month, she had sat in a Woodstock courtroom at Wells's preliminary hearing and told the judge, "When someone says to me they killed kids, I don't want to hear it. A couple days earlier, back in Woodstock, I was told two women and two children were dead."

A phone call was received from a prostitute in Toronto advising the Woodstock Police that Wells had purchased a bus ticket to head west toward British Columbia. The Police departments in the main cities between Ontario and BC were notified of this information and requested a check be made on any buses heading west from Toronto.

Checking the bus that arrived in the Calgary bus terminal, the Calgary police arrested Mark Wells. Our office in Woodstock was advised, and Detectives Ron Freeman and Jeff Lake flew out to Calgary. An arrest warrant was issued, and Wells was returned to Woodstock with Freeman and Lake, where he was charged with four counts of murder.

Mark Wells was found guilty on all four counts of murder. He automatically received a life sentence without eligibility for parole for twenty-five years.

Wells was born in Toronto, the fifth of seven children, four girls and three boys. The family soon moved to Woodstock so they would be closer to Wells's parental grandparents. Even at a young age, people said he looked like the "oddball" in the family. With his red hair—the rest of the children were blonde or brunette—he stood out.

The family moved often, and money was usually short.

One sister remembers the seven children fighting to shine their father's boots for a nickel. The father, Ed Wells, was a machinist and later managed to sing in country and western bands, sometimes inviting the kids to sing along at Christmas parties.

Mark's upbringing rested largely with his older sisters. "We took care of him a lot, that was our responsibility—he was a good little boy, he really was."

Although three sisters were reluctant to discuss details, there is no doubt booze contributed to the turbulent, even violent, tenor of the Wells household.

Wells's mother, Ruth, refused to comment, and Ed Wells could not be reached. But the sisters felt the story should be told.

"We all had a hard life, all of us did, and all of us are still recovering from it," says a sister.

As a teenager, Mark told friends he'd try to break up fights between his parents, and he'd get beaten by his father for coming to his mother's defense. He would show up with broken glasses and lash out at anyone who asked about them.

One sister was afraid of what would happen when their parents arrived home from a night out. "We never liked the alcohol bit. It wasn't a very good thing to know that perhaps when someone came home that evening, there could be problems." The sister said she was the age of fourteen when she went to a foster home.

Leaving was "the right decision. [Years in a foster home] were the best years of my childhood," she says.

When Wells was twelve, he went to live with a sister who had just married. He was later placed in a foster home and remained there about two years.

Wells tried to appear tough, but it didn't make him many friends. "He thought he'd look tough to everybody, in that way he'd have pals."

One acquaintance remembers giving Wells a lift in his car and Wells yelling obscenities out the window at a woman. "He didn't care really what he said to them. They were kind of below him."

A woman whose family grew up near Wells found him creepy. "He was just really scary. I didn't want to ever be alone with him."

The woman says Wells tried to rape her when she was sleeping in her sister's home. "I was sleeping, I woke up, and he was on top of me. He was wasted, he couldn't even walk."

When Wells was about fifteen, his friend Jake remembered him being reluctant to go home, always asking to be dropped off downtown instead. Wells finally admitted he had been living in a horse barn at the Woodstock Fairgrounds about a week. Jake's parents took Wells in for several days.

It was about that time that Wells's parents separated, and Wells took it hard. He went to live with his father in Stratford because his mother couldn't deal with him, a neighbor recalls.

When Wells was sixteen, he was convicted of armed robbery and assault and an instance in Stratford involving a woman. He was released in May 1979 after serving twenty months in juvenile detention.

Three days later, he was arrested and charged with attempted murder of a forty-four-year-old woman (Irene Barker). He pleaded guilty and was sentenced to eight years in prison.

The judge said Wells was "prone to violence," and a psychiatric assessment said Wells had deep family-rated problems and needed long-term therapy.

While in custody, Wells corresponded with his sister in Woodstock. "He was lonely, he was scared, and he did miss the family a lot."

Later, Wells told Jake that life in jail was "worse than any movie I'd seen." He told Jake he was beaten and raped in prison.

In the spring of 1987, Wells was released and returned to Woodstock to live for a short time with a sister.

Wells would make dinner and babysit her two children while she was at work and even went to church with her and another sister on occasion.

Friends and family—all but one sister and Wells's father still live in Woodstock—do hope from the changes to Wells. He was clean, his hair was cut, and he wore new jeans. His foul mouth was subdued, and his manners had improved.

It could have been a new beginning for Wells.

It wasn't.

"We [sisters] really try to help Mark, but he couldn't deal with society. He couldn't live on the outside because he was so used to being on the inside for so long."

The sister felt Wells needed to be placed where he'd have constant support.

It was about that time that Wells was told by his mother that he had a different life than the rest of the children, says another sister.

"He came to my house, and he was crying. He was really upset about it."

The sister told Wells that wasn't true. "I was just afraid. I didn't know how he would react to it."

Wells never mentioned it again.

The sisters tried to support Wells, but all had families and jobs.

"He depended on us too much."

Wells had a hard time getting a full-time job. He felt discriminated against because of his criminal record and was once evicted from an apartment because of it.

"Family was really important to him, but I think what happened is he slowly started to deteriorate. I don't know what length of time, but you can see how he started to deteriorate and become involved with people who just weren't encouraging to him."

In June 1990, Wells erupted in an orgy of violence.

His sister could not predict the tragic deaths of four people, but she knew her brother's life was on a downward spiral. "It's like somebody who has cancer," she says. "They're okay, and then it eats away at them, and I really think that's kind of what happened. You could see it, and we really had no control over it."

CHAPTER FORTY-NINE

Two Police Officers Slain

When I was stationed in Milton in the late '50s and early '60s, a friend, Constable Jim Smith, was stationed at number 3 District Headquarters in Burlington. We would get together every month or so, have a dinner and an evening of euchre, and maybe a couple beers.

Jim was promoted to corporal and was transferred to the headquarters in Peterborough.

The first report of trouble from the picturesque lake country, six miles east of Mindon, was a minor domestic trouble called in about 4:00 p.m. A woman called the police to say she and her son had received a threatening call.

Investigating officers drove to a cottage and found themselves faced with a distraught man who waved a .44 rifle out the doorway.

By 9:00 p.m., more than a dozen officers from the Minden Detachment were outside the house. Detective Sergeant Lorne Chapitis and Corporal Smith, the Peterborough training officer and a teargas expert, had arrived and were ready to lope gas into the home.

Then the armed man said he would speak to the four officers. Chapitis and Smith followed by Constables Barry Connolly and Mike Maher walked toward him as he stood in the doorway.

Two rifle shots rang out when they were eight feet away. Connolley and Maher jumped to either side, grabbed the man, and wrestled him to the ground.

Their two companions, Chapitis and Smith, lay dead in the snow.

Later, a staff officer referring to the calibre of rifle, said, "You don't live long when you're shot by something that big."

Here's the timetable of the shooting:

About 9:00 a.m., the parents and two younger brothers of the man left him alone in the family's seven-room lakeside home.

About 10:00 a.m., a woman called. "Please help," saying she had been threatened.

From 11:00 a.m. to 3:00 p.m., police checked relatives and with others in town looking for the man.

Just after 4:00 p.m., they found him at the cottage.

At 5:30 p.m., five members of the Minden Police Detachment called for teargas to be brought from Peterborough.

At 9:00 p.m., the police radio called for two ambulances and broadcast a message to our office that two officers had been shot. Police Commissioner Erik Silk went to Peterborough less than two hours later to tell the wives of the two dead officers they had the sympathy of the entire police force.

Sergeant Chapitis recently passed his examination for promotion to inspector.

The funeral service for Jim Smith was held in Hamilton. It was the largest funeral procession I've ever been to or seen. There were marked police cars from police departments from towns and cities throughout Ontario. There were also police cars there from Quebec, the state of New York, and the state of Michigan. There were also police officers there from other towns and cities throughout North America.

CHAPTER FIFTY

Husband Kills Wife

Martha and Harold Cambell were married in 1930. This union produced only one child, a son, David, born on February 20, 1943.

Harold had been employed at the Strathroy Flour Mill until his compulsory retirement at age seventy. He had worked at this company in excess of thirty years.

The Cambells rented an apartment that occupied the entire top floor of a two-story commercial building, facing the main street of Strathroy. This building was immediately adjacent to the Strathroy Police Department. They had resided in the same building for thirty-five years. During 1977, efforts had been made by the owners to have them evicted as it was their intention to demolish this very old structure. Finally, arrangements were made to move the couple to another house by December 4, 1977, but due to a snowstorm, this was not accomplished.

Both Martha and Harold, generally speaking, appeared to enjoy moderately good health. They tend to stay pretty much to themselves, and, while there are suggestions that domestic difficulties were experienced in the past, there is no record at the Strathroy Police Force concerning any violent acts or domestic quarrel in the past ten years. The Cambells live alone and seldom entertain any guests.

The Cambell apartment could be described as running from west to east. There was one entrance only, and that was at the west side of the building. This entranceway led into a utility room at the southwest corner of the dwelling. Directly east of this room was the kitchen, and across from the kitchen, on the north side, was the bathroom.

Continuing east from the kitchen could be found a guest bedroom, the master bedroom, then the dining room, and finally, in the east side of the bedroom, the living room. The hallway ran from the bathroom and the full length of the apartment, along the north wall.

There were two oil-forced space heaters. One was placed near the bathroom and the other in the dining room.

At 7:45 a.m. on December 12, 1977, Catherine Dundas, a dispatcher at the police office, smelled smoke. She went out onto the street and could see a fire was in progress next door. She returned to her office and contacted the fire department, who arrived in record time.

Const. Willson of the Strathroy Police Department went immediately to the apartment and found it impossible to see inside due to the smoke. However, he did enter and reached as far as the kitchen, and lying on the floor, he found Harold Cambell in a semiconscious condition. Willson managed to drag the man to the entrance, and once there, he was assisted by other officers and placed in a police car. He was immediately transported to the Strathroy Hospital a short distance away.

The fire department was totally committed by 7:57 a.m., but because of the intensity of the heat due to the fire and smoke, they were unable to see the second story of the building, including the roof.

At approximately 9:22 a.m., fireman William Brooks discovered a badly charred human body lying upon a bed in the master bedroom. The identification of the body of this time was not possible.

Smith then telephoned the hospital and asked Mary H. Boske, RN, to inquire of Mr. Cambell as to who else may have been present in the apartment with him. The nurse put this question to the patient, and he replied, "Yes, my wife. I killed her."

He was then asked, "What do you mean?"

To which he said, "I hit her over the head."

Once this information was received by Sergeant Smith, it was then relayed to the chief of police. The assistance of the Criminal Investigation Branch of the Ontario Police was requested.

A police guard was immediately placed upon the scene and at the hospital on the instructions of Inspector T. Hall. The coroner, Dr. W. Butler, viewed the remains in the apartment at 9:55 a.m. and ordered an autopsy performed at an appropriate time.

After receiving permission from the attending physician, Dr. N. Buma, Sergeant Smith and Constable Hornby interviewed Harold Cambell.

Cambell was informed that he was under arrest and will be charged with second-degree murder. He was then read the police caution and subsequently provided an inculpatory statement concerning his wife's death.

"You are charged with the murder of your wife, Martha."

The police caution was given.

Q: Did you understand the caution?
A: Yes, I killed her, but that's all there is to it.
Q: Why did you hit your wife?
A: I just went crazy this morning. I've been bugging it up all this week, always awake. She was asleep.
Q: What did you hit her with?
A: Piece of pipe, 2.5"×6".
Q: Where did you get the pipe?
A: Around the house, I don't know where I got it.
Q: Where is it now, the piece of pipe?
A: Around the house somewhere.
Q: Where did you hit her?
A: On the head.
Q: How many times?
A: Six or seven times, I don't know for sure.
Q: And about what time did you hit your wife?

A: Seven o'clock or a little after. I'm not sure, the clocks don't work too well.

Q: How do you set the fire?

A: With a match and piece of paper, pushing the fuel oil on it.

Q: Had you been drinking last night?

A: No, sir, I haven't had a drink for a month.

Q: Had your wife been drinking?

A: No.

Q: What time did you set the fire?

A: A little after seven o'clock. I don't know, I was nuts.

Q: What caused you to get upset?

A: Because we had to get out of the apartment, and my wife had been hassling me all week, whatever I said the right. We couldn't find another place to live. The snowstorm got me down.

The Cambell's apartment, was on the second floor of

of the building, next to the police station on the right.

The burnt out bedroom, of the Cambells.

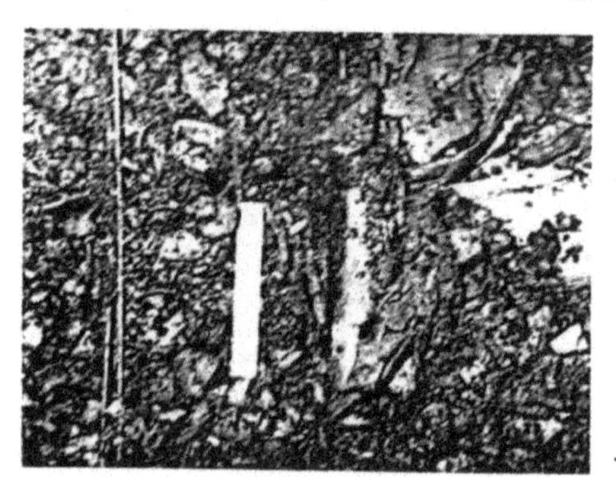

The piece of pipe that was used to do the damage

to her head.

Mrs Cambell on the autopsy table

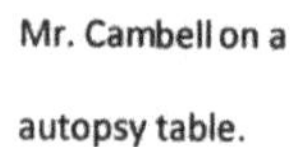

Mr. Cambell on a

autopsy table.

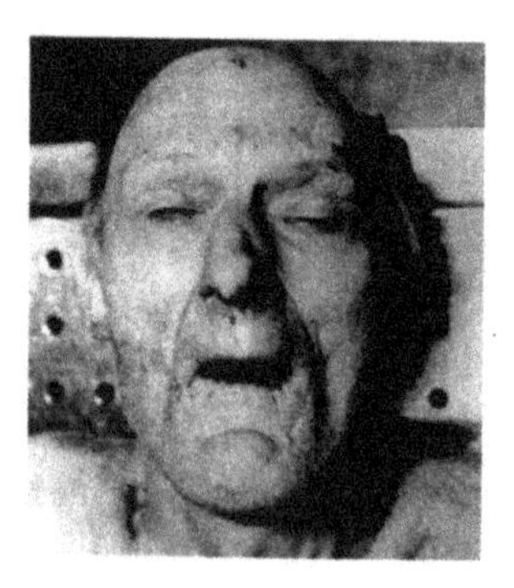

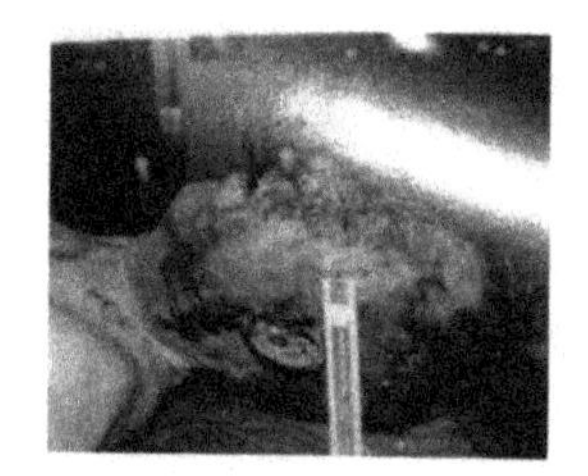

Fire damage to the side of his head

Q: Why did you set the fire?
A: I don't know why I did, maybe I just set the fire and was going to stay there until I was all burned up.
Q: Where is your son, Bruce?
A: RR 4, Parkhill.
Q: Has he got a telephone number?
A: No.
Q: Did you know if your wife was dead before you set the fire?
A: I think she was, I'm not sure.
Q: Did you mean to kill her?
A: I don't know what I meant to do, or just nuts.
Q: What made you feel that way?
A: I don't know. I felt like hitting and knocking her down two or three times this week. I tried to drown myself twice at a lake a couple days ago, but only went partway to the lake.
Q: Which lake?
A: The lake by the Head Street Bridge where it is good and deep, but I couldn't see any water, only the snow.

Statement was not signed.

At 11:55 a.m., this statement was read to Mr. Cambell by Sergeant Smith, and he was asked if he wanted to make any changes or additions to the statement, and he replied, "No."

Mr. Cambell was asked if he wanted to read the statement himself and replied, "No, I don't have my glasses, and they are probably burned up in the house."

Clothing belonging to Harold was later seized. It consisted of a set of pajamas and a pair of socks. All items smelled strongly of stove oil. The socks in particular were almost saturated with the fluid.

Shortly after the arrival of Detective Inspector Hall, he called an investigator, D. Reads, from the Ontario fire marshal's office. Reads along with a local fire department personnel commenced removing extraneous material from the bedroom prior to the police examination of the scene.

While this was being done, Det. Hall interviewed the Cambell's only son, David, who had been given permission to speak to his father at the hospital. David at first was reluctant to discuss their conversation but eventually gave Inspector Hall a signed statement in which his father admitted to him that he had struck his mother on the head and set fire to the apartment.

The remains of Martha were lying face up on the bed at the southeast corner of the room. There was a strong smell of fuel oil present. Samples from the bed and surrounding area as well as from the victim were taken for expert examination.

A piece of steel pipe threaded on both ends was discovered resting against the victim's right hip. This pipe was covered in a film of fuel oil.

The body was removed, under police guard, by Denning's Funeral Home to the St. Joseph's Hospital morgue at 5:00 p.m. for the autopsy.

Once the body had been removed and the remains of the bed and mattress raised up, a large burn hole was found directly under.

On Tuesday, December 13, an autopsy was performed on the remains at 9:00 a.m. X-rays of body were taken by the technician under the direction of Dr. Davies and radiologist Dr. Linsdell. Identification at this time proved a difficult problem because of extensive burning of the face. However, the doctors later compared the x-rays taken of Mrs. Cambell in 1973 to those taken at the autopsy. Both doctors were satisfied beyond reasonable doubt that the x-rays taken were of the same person.

Dr. Davies was able to identify seven separate distinct wounds to the right side of the skull and right side of the face. In addition, there were two large areas of recent bruising. When the skull was open, Dr. Davies found a massive fracture on the right side of the head. This fracture was so severe that it ran completely across the front of the base of the skull and the left side of the skull.

The hyoid bone was intact, and the windpipe contained a very small amount of ash.

Cause of death was comminuted fractures of the skull with lacerations of the meninges and recent extradural and subdural hemorrhage.

It was Dr. Davies's opinion that these wounds were consistent with the victim being struck about the head and face by the piece of steel pipe.

Later that same day, Sergeant Smith and Detective Inspector Hall presented their findings to the Crown attorney Mike Martin, QC, in London. Mr. Martin agreed with the ample evidence that existed to charge Cambell with murder. Harold Cambell was charged with second-degree murder of his wife, Martha.

On Wednesday, December 14, at 3:47 a.m., Hill was informed by Constable Smith that Harold Cambell had died. Inspector Hill proceeded directly to the hospital where he was met by the coroner, Dr. Butler.

Cambell, who had been in the intensive care unit of the hospital since his admission, expired at 3:34 a.m. and was pronounced dead by Dr. Butler at 4:13 a.m. Butler ordered an autopsy and authorized transportation of the body to St. Joseph's Hospital, London. Inspector Hill was given a written order, signed by Dr. Butler, to obtain copies of all hospital records, including nurse's notes, pertaining to the treatment of Harold Cambell. All such records were in his possession by 8:45 a.m.

On Wednesday, December 14, an autopsy was performed on the deceased at St. Joseph's Hospital, London. The autopsy was performed by the regional pathologist Dr. E. M. Davies. The body bore two small lacerations. One was on the scalp center to the nose, and the other was just above the left eye. There was a heavy blackening of the windpipe evidence of a chronic lung disease.

Cause of death was pulmonary edema associated with smoke inhalation superimposed on a chronic obstructive lung disease.

William Stewart, inspector with Ontario Hydro, found no liquid damage of any kind to the fuse panel. Not even a fuse was blown.

Harold Smith, Energy and Safety Branch, Ministry of Consumer and Commercial Relations, examined two space heaters. The heater located at the west hallway was manufactured by Coleman. The stove was undamaged except for the carburetor, which had been melted by heat exposure. There was no excessive heat evident inside the stove. All damage was to the exterior. The pipes were in good condition. The heater situated at the east side of the apartment was manufactured by Enterprise. This unit was not damaged except for a minor heat exposure to the exterior. No excessive heat was evident inside the stove. The pipes were in good condition.

Fire Investigator Reads, after thoroughly examining the premises, expressed the opinion that the fire was incendiary in nature and would have been spread about the master bedroom and in several places in the hallway and the rest of the apartment.

Martha Violet and Harold Barron Cambell were buried together at the Strathroy Cemetery on Friday, December 16.

Bits and Pieces 15

At and Indian Reservation near Moosonee, Ontario, just south of James Bay in the far north, two Indian men were arguing. The husband was upset that the guy he was arguing with was trying to make time with his wife. The husband at that time was carrying a .22 rifle. The argument got quite heated, and the husband shot the other guy.

The injured Indian was taken to the Moosonee Hospital, and the man was airlifted to University Hospital in London where he would get the help that he required. He got the treatment, but he died a few days later.

The Indian who shot him was charged with manslaughter.

I was dispatched to the hospital morgue to attend at the autopsy, where I photographed the body and received the exhibits from the pathologist. The exhibits were taken to the Center of Forensic Science in Toronto for examination.

About three or four months later, I received a summons to appear in court in Kapuskasing where the shooter was to stand trial.

I flew up to Timmins where an identification officer of the D.H.Q in Timmins picked me up at the airport and drove me up to the courthouse in Kapuskasing where I went into the Crown attorney's office and where I met the CIB inspector. He asked me what I was doing here. He said that all the witnesses in Toronto were canceled. I told him I was from London, not Toronto, and I was responding to the summons I received. He just shook his head and walked away.

CHAPTER FIFTY-ONE

Escapee Rapes Two Girls

A young couple, Bob and Sally Fielding, were driving along Highway 2, west of the city of London, when they saw a girl standing on the north side of the road near the tree line. She was standing there completely naked. Sally got out of the car and went over to see why she was naked and if she needed help.

She said that she and her friend, Betty Richman, were raped, and she wanted to go to the police. They headed straight to the police office on Exeter Road to report this. Bob had some old clothes in the back seat and told her to get some something and get dressed. She said her name was Nancy Sealey.

Nancy then said that she and her friend were walking along the street in St. Thomas when a car pulled to the crib a short distant in front of them. The driver got out, opened the passenger door, and grabbed them roughly and forced them into the back seat of the car. He then drove the girls up here and took them into the woods, ripped off their clothes on this poor excuse for a road.

He had her friend sitting on the front fender and was licking and playing with her vagina. While he was doing that, Nancy sneaked away and ran hard to the side of the road. She ran through the bushes and got a few scratches on her and cuts to her bare feet.

They drove her to the police office and went inside with her to report the crime.

The officer, Joe Wall, took a statement from the girl with a description of the vehicle the suspect he was driving. She told him how she and her friend were picked up in St. Thomas. She also described the car as a blue two-door, what she thought was a Ford. She also said she remembers the first two numbers of the license plate, 68. She also gave, as best she could, a description of the man. She also said he was wearing silver-rimmed glasses.

The officer went into the radio room and had the dispatcher dispatch a car to the area that was described to him by Bob Fielding where they picked up Nancy Sealey and brought her to the office. When Patrol Officer Bill Grimes got to the area and walked into the woods to try and locate Betty Richman and her abductor, he eventually found her naked. He took her back to the road and left her in the wooded area while he went back to the police car to get his raincoat for her to put on. She was the taken to the police office.

When Joe got back to Nancy, the dispatcher came into the office and told Joe that St. Thomas just reported that a patient from the St. Thomas Psychiatric Hospital had escaped. The escapee was described as a convicted sex offender who been brought to the St. Thomas hospital from a jail in Nova Scotia for treatment. He was apparently doing well with the treatment and was granted to leave the facility in the afternoon period. This had been going on for a week with no problems until this time.

Tom Granger was dispatched to the area from Lambeth. He was proceeding west on no. 2 Highway when he passed an eastbound car. It was a blue Ford, and the first two numbers on the plate were 68. He made a U-turn and went after the Ford. He called Tim Thomas, who was farther west of his location, and requested his presence east of where he was.

He got the car stopped a short distance west of Lambeth. He asked the driver for his driver's license. He told the driver to step out of his car and get in the cruiser, at which time Tim Thomas arrived.

He had Tim call for a tow truck to have the Ford towed to the office garage and had him stay at the car until it was parked in the garage.

He was called and requested to check the car for prints or anything else that may have come from one of the girls.

On the hood of the car and the top of the area over the right front tire, he found the image of a bum. To the right of the bum, he found a left handprint, and on the left he found a right handprint. At the top of the fender he found a larger right handprint on the right side of the bum print, and on the left side of the bum he found a left handprint.

Back in the office, I took the fingerprints of both Nancy and Betty and their palm prints as well.

Joe Wells had taken the driver of the car into an interview room to question him. All the man would say was that he wanted a lawyer. I took him downstairs where I fingerprinted and took his palm prints.

While a lawyer was being called, we decided to have a lineup so the girls could identify their attacker. I called the city police to get the use of their lineup room. This is a room that is divided into two sections. The one end of the room has a raised floor area about two feet higher than the lager area of the main room. It is about five feet wide and about ten feet long. It has a thick glass wall separating the two rooms. This room has a separate entrance door through which the prisoner enters with eleven other persons. The prisoner has the option of standing anywhere in the line of men he chooses. The lights are turned on and are focused on the lineup. With the lights on, the prisoner would not be able to see the witness.

I had phoned an optician, a friend of mine, requesting the use of twelve pairs of silver-framed glasses for an hour or so to be worn by the eleven men and the prisoner.

The lawyer for the prisoner was shown the line with his client in place with all these men wearing silver-framed glasses.

The witnesses are brought in one at a time after being told to look at all the men in the lineup before pointing to the prisoner. Nancy was the first one to be brought in. She started at one end of the lineup and stood in front of each of the men before moving on. After looking at them all, she went and stood in front of the prisoner and said, "That's him."

When Betty came in, she went to one end of the line and then moved to her left and looked at the men until she got in front of the prisoner where she said, "That's him."

The girls were driven back to our office while the prisoner was handcuffed and taken back to our office.

When we were back at the office, he was taken into an interview room with his lawyer present; he was cautioned and asked if he wanted to make a statement.

He admitted that he was convicted in Halifax, Nova Scotia, for sexual assaults where he was convicted and given a lengthy sentence. After several years, he said he was brought to St. Thomas about six months ago for treatment. He said that after months he started getting day passes to leave the facility and was permitted to leave the hospital for four hours in the afternoons.

On this afternoon, he said he was extremely horny and needed some sex, which he did what he did, steal a car, and drove around until he saw the two girls whom he picked up.

He was charged with escaping custody, theft of a vehicle, and assault and rape. He was convicted and sentenced to a further lengthy time in jail.

CHAPTER FIFTY-TWO

Wife Killed by Estranged Husband

Paul McFee walked into the Oxford County Police Station after 11:00 p.m., February 7, 1998. His left hand was bleeding and stuffed in a plastic bag. He had a deep cut, which went right through his left thumb. He told the Const. McEdwards that he had been in a fight with his wife, Brenda Marie Swartz, at her Senior Pavey Street apartment. He also told McEdwards that he wanted to talk to a lawyer. He told McEdwards that he stopped taking his medication for depression the previous week and blacked out.

McEdwards asked McFee how he hurt his hand. McEdwards did not get a response to the question. All he would say was something happened to his wife, but would not explain as to what happened. He was taken to the Woodstock Hospital, where the entrance and exit wounds were stitched and closed. He said that he had been to the hospital a few days earlier because of a suicide attempt.

McEdwards asked him, "What happened to your wife?" Something happened to his wife, but he did not elaborate as to what happened.

They went to the apartment where they found Brenda lying on the floor beside her bed in a pool of blood. Her vital signs were checked; there was no pulse. There were pieces of rope around her wrists and what appeared to be a bathrobe belt tied around her neck. She was fully clothed, wearing a sweater and a pair of jeans.

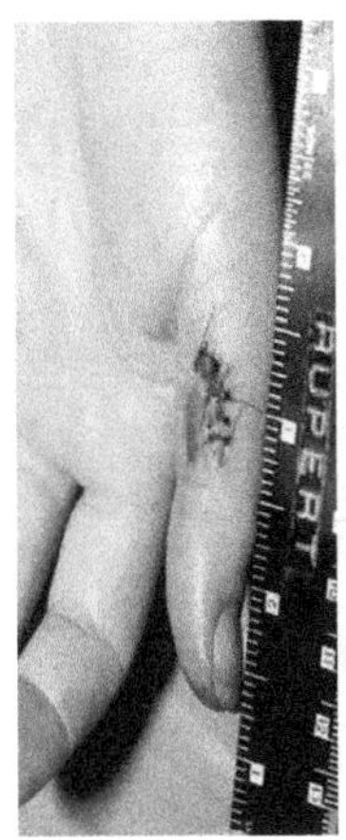

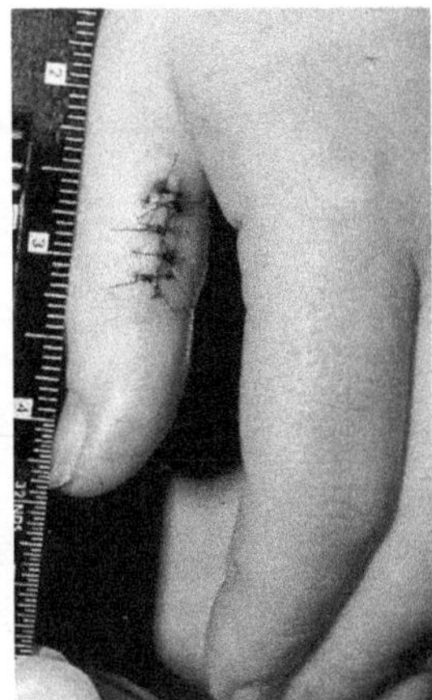

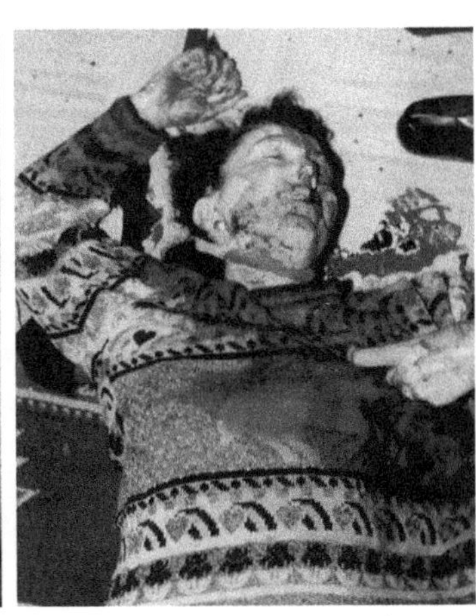

On the left side of the bed and the covers, there was a large quantity of blood. It was on the bed that her injuries occurred before falling to the floor beside the bed.

There was a trail of blood on the bedroom floor and on the wall to the right of the door leading to the hall and the front door and in the kitchen on the left of the hall. Just inside the door to the right was a closet. In the closet he found a few more pieces of rope, the same that was used on the wrists of the victim. The trail of blood led to the door and also into the kitchen area. The back door of the apartment building led into the parking lot. There was a trail of blood leading across the lot to Paul's 1987 Dodge Charger and blood inside the car. There was a large quantity of blood on the steering wheel and the upholstery in the vehicle, which was registered to Kenneth.

Blood was found in the bathtub, floor, and counter in the kitchen, in the hallway, on light switch plates, and sheets and pillows in Brenda's apartment.

They then went to Paul's room on Graham Street above the Studio 9 Strip Bar. A bloodstained rope and blood-soaked plastic bag was also found in Ken's room. The rope was consistent with the rope used on her wrists.

After the body was found, McFee was arrested and was returned to the police station.

An autopsy was conducted at the Woodstock Hospital on the body of Brenda McFee. When the clothing was removed from the body, they found that she had seventeen stab wounds to her chest. One of the stab wounds was in her heart and another damaging stab wound in her neck. On both wrists there was bruising where the rope had slipknots that had been pulled and tightened to keep her under control.

The knife cut to the thumb from both sides. The body was found on the floor after being stabbed on the bed and fell to the floor. There was also a bloodstained door handle to the apartment. The trail of blood leading to the husband's car is indicated by the tags placed on the blood.

There was blood around the kitchen taps and the counter. Beside the counter, there were two coffee mugs. The mugs were checked for prints. On one of the mugs, thirty-three of the husband's prints were found, and the victim's prints were found on the other mug. They apparently conversed together while drinking their coffee.

It appeared that Brenda got annoyed with the conversation and went into the bedroom and lay on the bed, where he entered and killed her, and she fell off the bed where they found her.

McFee admitted in his statement that she had made coffee, which they drank while they chatted. The conversation between them, which turned nasty and not to her liking, upset her. She got up and went into her bedroom and lay on her bed.

He went into the kitchen, and from one of the kitchen drawers he found a knife, went into bedroom, and started stabbing her as she lay face up on the bed.

She rolled off the bed and onto the floor where her body was found.

Paul McFee was charged with first-degree murder. He pleaded not guilty, and after all the evidence was heard, the jury returned with a verdict of guilty.

He was sentenced to life in prison.

CHAPTER FIFTY-THREE

Other Cases

Over the years in the time I spent doing crime scene investigations, I had over sixty-five murders. I went to many suicides, accidental deaths, fatal car crashes, some plane crashes, and some arson cases. A very small number of the cases that I was involved in were not solved.

On one occasion, in March 1968, I was dispatched to a shallow area on the west side of the Thames River about a mile north of the highway that leads to Thorndale, where the body of a nine-year-old boy was found facedown in the river water. His back was burned by the sun to a dark brown. The boy, Frankie Jenkins, went missing a month earlier in February.

The body was taken to St. Joseph's Hospital where an autopsy was performed. The normal exhibits were taken by the pathologist. His mouth was stuffed with paper, cutting off his attempt at breathing.

Many weeks were spent trying to locate his abductor who killed him. All we could determine was that it may have been a person who travelled in the south and east of London.

On another time, in March 1972, I was dispatched to the St. Thomas Detachment where I met Constable Jim Kent. I was told that two guys in a canoe on a bright sunny day were travelling north about a mile north of Port Stanley on Kettle Creek. They came across an arm caught up in some weeds on the west side of the creek.

Jim and I walked across a freshly plowed field to the creek where we found the arm that had been reported to us. I photographed the location where the arm was found and the general area. The arm was then bagged, and the next day I took it to the Center of Forensic Science in Toronto. The arm was examined by the pathologist, and it was determined the arm was cut from the body using a crosscut saw. The arm was retained at the center by the doctor.

I fingerprinted the hand, and I took the prints to our fingerprint section at general headquarters, where they were identified as belonging to Priscilla Merle, 21, who had one conviction on record for shoplifting.

We advised London City Police of finding the arm and identifying the arm with the fingerprints. They were told that Priscilla had been in the Ride Out Tavern on the night she disappeared. She apparently left the Ride Out and staggered home where she was living with her sister. She was last seen that night getting into a vehicle sometime after midnight by her sister.

Three weeks later at the north end of Port Stanley, the upper torso was found in the creek. I was again dispatched where I took photos of the upper torso and the area. The next day I took it to Toronto, to the Center of Forensic Science, at which time it was compared to the cut on the arm. It matched the cut on the upper torso to the fingerprinted hand of the arm found three weeks earlier.

The Police dive team arrived at the scene where the arm was found and searched the creek bottom with negative results. Three weeks later the lower torso was found, which was also taken to the lab in Toronto and matched up to the other parts. They never did get any of the other parts of the body.

After weeks of investigation, they had one suspect. They executed search warrants at his residence and vehicle on Gray Street. We found nothing pointing to this occurrence for us to arrest him. The only item we took out of the residence was a box about fourteen inches square, two to three feet long. It was closed and sealed with a padlock. It was taken to the lab in Toronto where it was forced open. The terrible smell coming from the box spread through three floors of the building. He had been putting shit in it from time to time for the last two or three years.

About a hundred yards north of where we found the arm, we found an old dark-colored quilt. We found out our suspect had lived in Brownsville, a small community west of Tillsonburg, with a woman. They found out she had moved sometime ago to Timmins.

After arranging a meeting with her by phone, I flew up to Timmins, taking the quilt with me. I was met by a member of the local detachment, who took me to her residence. I showed her the quilt to see if she could identify it as belonging to our suspect. She thought it looked familiar, but she couldn't say for sure.

I took a statement from her regarding her relationship with the suspect. It was the worst worded statement I had ever taken. The things he did to her and a few others were disgusting. On one or two occasions, he shit on the bed, picked it up in his hand, and spread it over her naked body. When they went for a drive, he would sit in the passenger seat, play with himself, and masturbate.

When I got back to the office, I took the statement up to the stenos to have it typed out for me. Someone brought it back and gave it to me. She was almost sick to her stomach typing it. She said, "Don't ever bring anything that filthy up here again."

We found out sometime later that the suspect had moved down east and sometime later had been charged in that area with a serious crime.

On the eighth of October 1969, I was working the day shift, 8:30 a.m. to 4:30 p.m. Charlie was working the four to midnight shift and asked me if I would change shifts with him as he had an important meeting he had to go to. I agreed to make the switch to the afternoon time.

At about 9:00 a.m. the next morning, and because Charlie had been called to occurrences west of the city, I got a call to go to a break and enter at a large factory on the east side of the Crumlin Road, which was at that time just outside the city of London, so I got back in uniform and headed to the break-in.

I spent most of the rest of the day at the factory checking for fingerprints in the large main office, which had been badly ransacked, as well as other areas in the working area of the factory.

I left the BE and theft about 4:00 p.m. and headed to Mr. Donut on Dundas Street East where I had a coffee. As I was leaving the coffee shop, I met a friend from the city police, Detective Bob Young. I asked him how things were going in the city. He told me that he was extremely busy with the disappearance of Jackie English five days ago. We discussed this occurrence for minutes, and then I left and went home for supper and got back to work for the afternoon shift.

While eating, the phone rang, which I answered, knowing it would most likely be the office calling. It was. I was told that the body of the girl Bob had told me about earlier was found face up and nude in Otter Creek south of the village of Otterville.

I attended at the scene and photographed the body in the water and also after it had been removed. The area around the creek was also photographed. She had an injury to her head. I headed home and got some sleep about 3:00 a.m. I was back up at 8:00 a.m. and headed to Tillsonburg Hospital where the autopsy would be performed. I photographed the body, including the injury to her head. Also found in her hair was a small piece of metal, which was retained. I received the exhibits from the pathologist as well as the piece of metal. I then left the hospital about 2:00 p.m. and headed to the Center of Forensic Science in Toronto with the exhibits.

The biology section and I determined that the piece of metal found in her hair broke off the zipper of the body bag. The other exhibits would be examined by the biology section.

I left the center and returned to London and the office. The investigators were waiting for me when I arrived back at the office after 10:00 p.m. There was a vehicle in the garage at the office that had been partially burned. I examined the car, fingerprinted where I could, photographed it, and finished up after 2:30 a.m. The exhibits weren't very much, and I was on the road to Toronto again, arriving at the lab just after 8:30 a.m.

When I got back to the office, they had a vehicle they checked at the Ontario Police College just outside of Aylmer, which they heard that it had what looked like fresh blood on the floor behind the from passenger seat, which I collected and headed back to the lab in Toronto. It was examined, and it was found to be blood from a bird the owner of the car hunted and shot.

We spent a lot of time checking other areas with negative results.

One woman came forward and accused an individual. On checking this person out, as well as interviewing him, we determined he was not involved in her murder.

A previous boyfriend of hers was subjected to questioning with negative results.

It is still to this day a cold case still on file.

We went to a lot of suicides from time to time. We went to several where the persons committed suicide by hanging themselves.

Ray went to one where a man had climbed a very high tree and hung himself near the top of it. He was not discovered in the tree for three or four weeks. When he was found, his body was stretched out to about seven or eight feet, and it was full of maggots. I had to fingerprint the body to be identified.

I got called to Park Hill on one occasion where we thought we had a murder. With my help, it was determined that this man took a stepladder into the two-car garage. He placed the ladder in the center of the garage. He then put a rope over a beam and tied it around his neck. After that, he shot himself with a .22 rifle. After the shooting, the ladder fell behind him, and he was left hanging from the beam. The rifle flew out of his hands toward the garage door.

I also had a few people gassing themselves in their cars with exhaust fumes, drove into bridge abutments, some jumped off tall buildings, and some drowned themselves in rivers, creeks, and lakes, and some deliberately overdosed on drugs or took a poison substance.

CHAPTER FIFTY-FOUR

My Last Day

From the Woodstock newspaper:

HE'S MURDER ON CROOKS

Officer retiring today after half century of policing

WOODSTOCK – If there's one thing area criminals have feared over the years, has to be the skills of Ron Rupert.

The city police special constable and expert identification officer can often look at a fingerprint and instantly give you a name.

Such talent has stood him in good stead at police detachments across Ontario for the past 47 years, and when he steps into retirement today, it will be over 60 homicide investigations and thousands of other criminal cases under his belt.

"I guess I'm going to have something else to do," said Rupert, still photographing prints from broken glass yesterday morning. "It's going to be tough to leave."

Classified as a fingerprint examiner by the Solicitor General of Canada, Rupert came out of retirement from the Ontario Police 1987 to join the Woodstock force as an identification court officer. However, it was 36 years before that when he left his job at the Welland A&P to attend the Police College in Toronto, and launched into a policing career that almost stretched to his 70th birthday next week.

Initially working under-cover with the police in Toronto, he joined the force's headquarters and a Parliament building patrol at Queen's Park. Moving to Dundas, Milton and Acton detachments over the years, he eventually joined the Police Identification branch in November 1964. He joined the Woodstock force part time in 1987. He has continued to commute from London where he lives with his wife Linda, and in 1990 he was asked to come on full time.

"I started studying fingerprints about 10 years before I got into identification," said James. "I found it very interesting and had been doing it ever since."

He takes pride in the investigations he had done over the years. In a case in 1969, a murder suspect pleaded guilty after hearing only James's testimony on the stand.

"It was probablyone of the most rewarding cases," said James. "A woman had been murdered at the union Hall on the old Highway 4 (in Middlesex County) and her body had been found on the road in Glenworth".

"I had had enough points of identification on the case for three murders. I was the first witness and after a day and a half of testimony, the accused just pleaded guilty." Police Chief Oscar cited such police skills as James will be greatly missed with the new Oxford community police.

"Ron's hard work and expertise throughout the years have added greatly to the success and the fine reputation of the Woodstock Police Department," said Oscar.

> *Initially hoping to continue working one or two days a week, James said some unfortunate personal circumstances are forcing him to full retirement. However, he said he is looking forward to associate with identification officers, and will now find more time to spend on woodworking projects and take pictures of more than just crime scenes.*

Joe Oscar, the chief of police, made arrangements through the newspaper that a luncheon will be held at the police office on my last day at the Woodstock Police Department. The fellows I worked with in London and other friends in London arrived for the luncheon. Social workers whom I did work for from family services and other friends in the city of Woodstock also attended. It was a good social luncheon.